# CROSSFIRE

## BY NANCY KRESS

NOVELS

*Prince of Morning Bells*
*The White Pipes*
*The Golden Grove*
*An Alien Light*
*Brainrose*
*Beggars in Spain*
*Beggars and Choosers*
*Oaths and Miracles*
*Beggars Ride*
*Maximum Light*
*Stinger*
*Yanked!*
*Probability Moon*
*Probability Sun*
*Probability Space*
*Crossfire*
*Crucible**

SHORT COLLECTIONS

*Trinity and Other Stories*
*The Aliens of Earth*
*Beaker's Dozen*

**forthcoming*

# CROSSFIRE

## NANCY KRESS

A TOM DOHERTY ASSOCIATES BOOK
NEW YORK

This is a work of fiction. All the characters and events portrayed in this novel are either fictitious or are used fictitiously.

CROSSFIRE



This book is printed on acid-free paper.

Book design by Michael Collica

Edited by James Minz

A Tor Book
Published by Tom Doherty Associates, LLC
175 Fifth Avenue
New York, NY 10010

www.tor.com

Tor® is a registered trademark of Tom Doherty Associates, LLC.

Library of Congress Cataloging-in-Publication Data

Kress, Nancy.
Crossfire / Nancy Kress.—1st ed.
p. cm.
"A Tor book"—T.p. verso.
ISBN 0-765-30467-8
1. Life on other planets—Fiction. 2. Space colonies—Fiction. 3. Space warfare—Fiction. I. Title.

PS3561.R46 C7 2003
813'.54—dc21

2002036671

First Edition: February 2003

Printed in the United States of America

0 9 8 7 6 5 4 3 2 1

# ACKNOWLEDGMENTS

This book owes a large debt to my husband, Charles Sheffield, who graciously loaned me the McAndrew Drive, originally created by his character Arthur Morton McAndrew, with the proviso that when I was done with the drive, I return it cleaned and in good condition. Thank you, Charles and Arthur.

I would also like to thank my editor, Jim Minz, for his many valuable suggestions for revision.

In wartime, the truth is so precious that
it must be protected by a bodyguard of lies.
—Winston Churchill

They change their clime, but not their
minds . . . who rush across the sea.
—Horace

# CROSSFIRE

# PROLOGUE

*My God,* thought Jake Holman, *I did it.*

He looked up at the faces watching him from the natural amphitheater of the California hillside. Six thousand faces, white and black and brown and golden, large and small, bare and garishly painted, plain and ugly and genemod beautiful, rapt and wary, with and without headgear. Six thousand people ready to go to the stars. And every single one of them crazy.

"No one thought we could possibly do this," Jake said into the microphone. "No one believed that a small, privately held corporation could actually mount this expedition to Greentrees. No one believed we could raise the money, could build the ship, could equip and staff her. No one believed any of it would happen."

*Because no one believed rich people would leave Earth forever to go God-knows-where.* The enormous fare, the critics said, was the stumbler. Historically new worlds were explored and claimed by governments and then colonized by the poor and wretched of society: starving Irish potato farmers, persecuted Puritans and Jews, deported convicts. People with nothing to lose. Of course, half of those historical emigrants died aboard ship, and half of the survivors died in the first year from disease and hostile natives. Greentrees was already ahead of the curve—the ship was safe and Greentrees had no sentients, hostile or otherwise. Still, the unknown was always dangerous. So why, asked the critics, would anyone with enough money to buy passage on a starship use the money to leave Earth in favor of a nonexistent colony on an unclaimed, unexplored planet sixty-nine light-years away?

It had turned out that there were as many reasons for the rich to emigrate from Earth as there were emigrants. The critics had meant logical reasons; the colonists had reasons of the heart.

"We are a diverse and miraculous group," Jake continued, and from her seat in the front row his business partner frowned. *Not too flowery,* Gail mouthed at him. Jake ignored her. "And we have chosen this path for diverse and miraculous reasons."

Now some of the New Quakers were frowning at him as well. Quakers, Jake had learned, didn't believe in miracles. Well, too bad for them. This was the last Jake would see of any of them, except William Shipley, for over six years. Only the Governing Board would be awake for the journey out, and only as many of them for as long as they could stand it.

"But all of us will have one thing in common: our new home. Greentrees. Mira Corporation salutes your choice of that home and wishes you joy of it. To the ship that carries us there: Godspeed."

Jake strode away from the microphone. Applause started, tentative at first, then stronger as the translators put his little speech into Arabic, Chinese, and Spanish. Gail smiled, no doubt relieved that Jake had been brief. A coordinator took the mike and began directing the first group aboard the *Ariel.*

Jake watched the various groups, as separate here as most of them wished to be on Greentrees, rise from the sere grass and cling to each other before their long cold sleep. The Quakers, almost two thousand of them. The deposed Arabic royal family with its enormous retinue, the women veiled and sitting separately from the men. The Chinese, meekest of the contingents, obeying their leaders without question. Larry Smith's dubious tribe of "Cheyenne," a thousand strong and possibly the craziest of all. Gail's huge extended family, convinced that Earth had only one more century as a life-sustaining biosphere. Plus the scientists, adventurers, star-lottery winners, and miscellaneous millionaire eccentrics.

And Jake Holman, uncaught criminal.

*My God, I did it.*

"Ready, Jake?" Gail said. Her brown eyes shone—unusual for the efficient and pragmatic Gail. Jake looked at her sun-scarred, middle-aged face (no genemods for beauty here), at the triumphant stance of her strong body. Feet apart, torso tilted forward, chin lifted. Like a boxer just before a match.

He smiled at her. “More than ready, Gail. For a long, long time.”

# 1

Gail Cutler loved the *Ariel.* That astonished her, because after Lahiri's death she had not expected to genuinely love anyone or anything again.

As Gail walked the narrow passageway that led past the tiny sleeping chambers to the wardroom, she shot out one hand and stroked the gray metal bulkhead. It was a quick, tentative stroke; she didn't want anyone else to know how she felt about the ship. For one thing, it was damn silly, this affection for a huge hunk of metal. For another, the *Ariel* would be disassembled and converted once they reached Greentrees. Who could love, say, a sewage-purification vat?

"You seem to be in a cheerful mood, Gail," Faisal bin Saud said as she entered the wardroom. The others were already seated at the lunch table, except for Captain Scherer and his officers. "Good news from Earth?"

"No news," Gail said briefly. After two entire years, she still wasn't sure she liked Saud. He was too polished, too artificial. He seemed to embody too many contradictions: a Muslim who prayed several times a day facing Sol, a Martian-educated connoisseur of Terran Elizabethan folios. His women lived the segregated lives of the *andarun,* yet he dealt with Gail as a financial and political equal. Also, he was unfailingly tactful and accommodating, surprising in one who had been a prince.

"There must be *some* news," Ingrid Johnson said belligerently. "They don't waste quee link on nothing, Gail."

Gail gazed calmly at the geneticist. There was no ambiguity about her reaction to Ingrid: Gail detested her. It was a point of pride, however, to keep this contempt well hidden. *In the closed, confined environment of a long-duration space voyage,* she and Jake had written in the guidelines for the Board of Governors, *courtesy and tolerance will become as important as keeping productively occupied.*

"Yes, of course, you're right," Gail said to Ingrid, "there was some news. The United Atlantic Federation passed stiffer penalties for illegal genemods. The war in West Africa is worse. The rebellion in China has escalated. Another earthquake along the Pacific Rim. Coffee crop failure in Colombia. The Genetic Modification Institute has announced another drug to combat melanomas. You can get all the details printed on a flimsy right after lunch."

"I will do that, also," Faisal said in his impeccable, sexily accented English. Gail, of course, was immune to the accent, but she suspected Ingrid wasn't.

Transmissions came twice a month from Earth by quee, Quantum Entanglement Energy link. By now the *Ariel,* moving at 1.25 gees, had reached some sizable percentage of c—Gail was no scientist. Quee was instantaneous, if costly. It was the *Ariel*'s only tie to home; every week left farther behind not only in space but, thanks to the relativistic speeds the ship would attain before it began deceleration, in time as well. When the colonists disembarked on Greentrees, they would have spent six years and seven months aboard ship. On Earth, nearly seventy years would have passed. Earth would be an unimaginably different place, and most loved ones long since become dust. Which was, of course, why most colonists brought their loved ones with them, traveling in groups. Gail's entire extended family, 203 people, lay asleep belowdecks.

"Well," Ingrid said peevishly, "I wish you'd paid for weekly news instead of just twice monthly. It couldn't have cost that much more—we're already paying for that second quee link, anyway. What's for lunch? Not fish again?"

"I believe it has a different sauce today," William Shipley said. "Doesn't it smell good!"

Shipley's cheerful tact irritated Gail almost as much as Ingrid's pettishness. *Slow down,* Gail told herself. *Keep control. We expected this.*

Two years gone, four plus to go. Already everyone who had paid to stay awake was tired of the food, tired of the available entertainments, tired of the exercise room, tired of each other. Three of the twenty had already elected to be put into cold sleep for the rest of the voyage: Gail and Jake had a bet on how much longer the rest would last. Cold-sleep boxes awaited each of them. Only Captain Scherer and his crew of six were really necessary before the interstellar voyage ended, and the captain, unlike the civilians, had the military appreciation for keeping his sailors fully occupied as a defense against boredom, depression, and hostility.

"Where's Jake?" Shipley asked, helping himself to fish and rice that until ten minutes ago had been frozen solid. "He wasn't at breakfast, either."

"He's with the other meal shift," Gail said. The wardroom could seat only ten when the table was lowered from the wall; meals had been planned in two shifts. She and Jake ate with each shift, sometimes separately, sometimes together to compare notes. It was important to track everyone's mental stability. The only significant selection procedure for these colonists had been their money. "What did everyone do this morning?"

Todd Johnson, Ingrid's mild and dominated husband, said pleasantly, "We analyzed once again the bacteria genomes from Greentrees' soil samples."

"Not that we haven't been over them twenty times already," Ingrid said.

"We'll have new data soon, honey, from Greentrees."

"Oh, is another quee transmission due from the planetary probe?" William Shipley asked with interest. "May I see the data?"

"Certainly," Todd said, while Ingrid pursed her lips in professional territoriality.

Shipley, the New Quaker representative ("We have no leaders"), was interested in everything. Gail could not have defined her exact expectations of a New Quaker, but Shipley wasn't it. The New Quakers were supposed to be a return to austere First Principles, a rejection of the "worldliness" that had crept into the religion since its plain and humble beginnings in the seventeenth century. Shipley, like his 1902 sleeping fellows, dressed in unadorned gray coverall with no jewelry or implants. One look at him was enough to show he had no genemods: gray where he wasn't bald, wrinkled seventy-year-old skin, fifty pounds overweight. He liked to eat . . . how was *that* austere? How austere was his keen interest in Earth events, in classical music, in genetics, in the ship's drive . . . in everything. And he was a medical doctor, which was certainly material rather than spiritual.

On the other hand, Shipley never cursed, never watched vids, never used VR, never took fizzies or drank what passed aboard ship for wine. Every Sunday he invited his awake shipmates to "meeting." Gail wasn't sure if anyone had ever gone; she hadn't.

Captain Scherer strode into the wardroom and slid into his seat, followed by Lieutenant Gretchen Wortz.

"Good afternoon, Commander," Faisal said in his impeccable English.

"Hello, all. Ah, fish. Good." He helped himself liberally.

The ship's crew, like everyone else, was never returning to Earth. They had all served in the tiny Swiss space fleet and had applied to Mira Corp together. Efficient, stable, interested in the biggest ship and longest voyage that would ever be available to them, they nonetheless remained enigmas to Gail and Jake. Military men served in military organizations; on Greentrees these seven people would be the only military that existed. For a while, anyway. Jake had contracted with them to form the police force of Mira City, the central city-state of the complex set of fiefdoms that Greentrees was slated to become.

Rudolf Scherer had agreed readily. He and his crew, he told Jake with calm assurance, would make an excellent law enforcement team. This was probably true; Jake had them subjected to background checks that would have turned up a failing mark in grade-school spelling. All seven Swiss were as clean as snow had once been. They were also polite, efficient, and genemod attractive, all seven of them.

So why did they make Gail slightly uneasy?

"Where is Lieutenant Halberg?" Gail asked Scherer. Three crew were scheduled for this meal shift, four for the other.

"He finds a routine machine error." Scherer's English comprehension was excellent, and Gail suspected that he could speak in more than present tense if he wished to.

"Rad error?" Todd asked. Cosmic bombardment regularly created bugs in the ship's computerized equipment.

"I am sure." Scherer began to eat with good appetite. The sailors all kept to stringent exercise schedules, as well as structured work, leisure, sleep, and meal times. For all Gail knew, Scherer may have devised bathroom routines for his crew. Maybe all that structure was what had kept them noticeably more cheerful than the civilians.

*Depression, tension, anxiety, and hostility can result from long-term close confinement,* Jake had written. *It is important that all awake colonists realize how trivial difficulties on ship may loom unreasonably large.*

"If the equipment had been better shielded," Ingrid said acidly, "there might not be so much computer error."

Scherer said between bites of breakfast, "The shields are standard."

Ingrid's face grew red. "What do you mean, 'standard,' Captain? How can there be tested standards when we're only the fifth interstellar colony ship and the other four—all military!—had much shorter trips to much nearer planets?"

"Ingrid," her husband said gently.

"The shields are standard, Dr. Johnson," Scherer said mildly. He drained his hot coffee with no wasted motion.

"Don't just brush my question aside!" Ingrid said.

"Honey, he's not doing that," Todd said carefully. Gail had often wondered why such a quiet, bland man had married a harridan like Ingrid. But, then, why did anybody marry anyone? And Ingrid was beautiful, with delicate blond genemod looks and eyes like sapphires. Gail suspected that one reason Ingrid was so brash was that her astonishing beauty had been a professional liability in being taken seriously. Parents could be such fools. Not to mention men in lust.

Ingrid said to Todd, "Don't tell me what the captain said! I can hear as well as you!"

"But not as quietly," Gail said, mustering her authority. This had gone far enough. "Ingrid, may I see you in the office, please?"

It was not a request, and Ingrid knew it. Her face grew even redder, mottling the pale rose skin. But she stood and followed Gail.

The Mira Corp office was a small room set aside for backup

documentation on nonelectronic media in case of catastrophic computer failure on Greentrees. Colonist records and contracts were stored here, along with written procedures for doing everything from ocean navigation by the stars to sawing down a tree. Gail and Jake used the room for private conversation in an environment where privacy was scarce. She motioned Ingrid to Jake's chair. The two seated women occupied most of the tiny space.

"Ingrid, I don't need to tell you what stress we're all under at this point in the voyage, or all the reasons why."

"That's still no reason for that sanctimonious—"

"I don't need to tell you what stress we're all under at this point in the voyage, or all the reasons why," Gail repeated. Ingrid got the point. Gail was going to go on saying the same thing until Ingrid responded. It was a technique Gail had learned from Jake, not easily.

"All right," Ingrid said sulkily.

"And I know you've been making a major effort to control your emotions for all our sakes." God, the lies a leader had to tell. Why wasn't Jake doing this? "But I'm afraid I'm going to have to ask you to increase that effort."

"But Scherer—"

"I'm afraid I'm going to have to ask you to increase that effort."

"Gail, please don't talk to me as if I were a child!"

"You're not that. But, Ingrid, I have a clear obligation to this expedition, and I can't let you endanger it. I won't."

That was enough. Ingrid had signed the Mira Corporation contract; she was aware of Gail's power to enforce cold sleep if Gail deemed it necessary for the good of the expedition. Jake, the former lawyer, had drawn up the contract. Rudy Scherer would enforce it without question. William Shipley would sedate Ingrid so quickly she wouldn't even realize it had happened until she woke up on Greentrees.

Gail watched Ingrid struggle with her temper, her outrage, her totally understandable, space-induced paranoia. They all felt it. Ingrid had given in, but only in a minor way. The geneticist was volatile by nature but not disconnected from realities. Gail had counted on that. She hadn't even armed herself.

"All right, Gail," Ingrid muttered. "I'm sorry. I'll try to keep myself in control."

"I never doubted it," Gail said with totally false warmth, and waited. One, two, three . . . yes, Ingrid slammed the door as she went out.

This pathetic show of defiance depressed Gail more than the entire rest of the incident. What would all the awakes, including her, be like when they finally reached Greentrees? The people still out of cold sleep were all intelligent and accomplished. There were the members of the Governing Board who had elected awake: Faisal bin Saud, William Shipley, Liu Fengmo, and Scherer's military, who were the most disciplined bunch Gail had ever seen. The scientists were usually focused and resourceful: Ingrid and Todd; the quiet, mousy paleontologist, Lucy Lasky; Maggie Striker, the ecologist; Robert Takai, energy engineer; and the rest. Competent and seemingly stable, all of them.

But everyone who colonized outside the solar system was, by definition, anomalous. They had overwhelming dreams, or fears, or—like Gail—beliefs. Of course, she thought wryly, *her* beliefs reflected reality more than the others aboard. Well, egotism aside, they *did.* She was leading her large, intelligent, wealthy family to an unknown planet because the planet they had occupied had no more than another few generations left.

Gail's people had always anticipated, and profited from, global economic changes and global social changes and, now, global ecological change. "The Canny Cutlers," the press called them. Canny and clannish and calculating. Led intellectually by Uncle Harry and legally by Gail, they were clear-eyed about the coming ruin of Earth's precious biosphere. And they were getting out.

Jake's fledgling corporation had come along at just the right time. The family hadn't wanted to move to Mars, or Luna, or Europa. Hostile environments, all of them. But the four planets already claimed by different Earth governments were not yet open to colonization. The fifth, a newly discovered and viable biosphere, was empty. The landing probe said so. It had been sent out decades ago, when the United Atlantic Federation had still had tax money to do such things. The probe had been in transit for over a Terran century; its detailed information had come back instantly by quee. Soil composition, atmospheric content, genetic analysis of the life within its limited range. DNA-based, of course. All five planets were. The scientists argued . . . no, Gail wasn't going to rehash that old argument in this fugitive moment of quiet.

She rubbed her eyes and leaned forward, elbows on Jake's console. God, another day of noise, boredom, captivity. That's what it was, for all of them: captivity, despite all the careful provisions made for recreation, work, exercise, all of it. But nothing ever *happened.* Every day the same. Gail had always prided herself on being self-sufficient and adaptable, but *this*! She hadn't, couldn't have, imagined the ennui and irritability and distortion of all normal interactions. Of course, it would be different when they reached Greentrees, but—

"Gail?" Jake stuck his head into the office.

"Jake, what kind of stupid name for a planet is 'Greentrees'? Who picked it?"

"You did. You wanted something inoffensive in any language, and it's certainly better than that UAF designation: '64a pending.' Gail, we have a problem."

She looked up. "A problem? What sort of problem? Lieutenant Wortz's computer error?"

"No. A human problem. Lucy Lasky."

"What about her?" The paleontologist had been the least trouble of anyone on ship, spending more and more time in her tiny sleep chamber. Studying, Gail had assumed. Lucy was inexperienced in comparison to the other, older scientists. Mira Corp hadn't needed to recruit a top talent. Nobody thought their survival depended on paleontology. "Isn't she in your meal group?"

"She didn't come to breakfast," Jake said.

"Well, where is she?"

"She's locked in the hold. She unpacked a laser rock cutter and she's threatening to carve the ship into tiny pieces."

# 2

This is my fault," Jake said as they hurried along the corridor to the hold hatch.

"Of course it is," Gail snapped. "Mountains fall and it's your fault; stars go nova and it's your fault. We haven't got time for any existential guilt now, Jake."

Which just showed, Jake thought, how much Gail could misunderstand human motivation. This wasn't abstract guilt. Lucy Lasky was holed up crazy and dangerous in the hold because Jake hadn't spent enough time observing and reporting on her increasing withdrawal. He knew why he had failed in that duty. Not that Gail, that forthright lesbian, was going to understand it.

Gail said to the screen on the outside of the hatch, "Activate."

"Retina scan, please," the screen said. Gail leaned forward and positioned her eye over the scanner and Jake looked away.

Even after all this time, even in these circumstances, he still flinched at any retina scan.

"Abigail Sandra Cutler, Mira Corp, vice president," the scanner said. "Authorization alpha."

"Open the hatch," Gail said.

Jake said impatiently, "Don't you think I tried that?"

"Opening," the screen said. And then, "Equipment failure. Opening mechanism destroyed on the opposite side."

"Method of destruction?"

"Laser cutter."

"Play surveillance vid."

The screen replayed the recording Jake had already seen. Lucy, suited and helmeted for the airless hold, entered it through this same hatch. Her movements looked unhurried and deliberate. She keyed in the correct manual code (and how had she gotten it?) to open the crate holding the heavy-duty laser cutter designed to slice through the hardest of igneous rocks. Carefully she released the mechanism that held its rollers immobile. Jake felt the same disbelief as his first viewing. Lucy Lasky, with her slight, almost boyish figure, her wisps of fine light brown hair, her wide eyes under slightly too-high eyebrows, so that she always looked surprised. Lucy Lasky, silent and pleasant and practically invisible, rolling out the laser cutter against the 1.25 gravity and positioning it precisely to point at the outer hull. Her thin fingers keyed in the code to turn it on.

"Jesus," Gail said.

Lucy gave the laser cutter a brief proprietary pat. Then she unpacked a small cutter, the type that would eventually be used for cutting up subsections of the ship, and methodically destroyed the computerized hatch mechanism. Now the hatch could only be opened manually.

Gail demanded, "Why the hell didn't alarms sound?"

"They did," Jake said. "That's why I came. You didn't hear them?"

"No!"

"Well, I did. She must have disabled some but not known how to get them all. But she got Scherer's."

Gail swung around to face Jake. "You didn't *call* him?"

"Not yet. Gail, think. If we can talk her out of there, we can put her in cold sleep before anybody else finds out this even happened. Everybody's jumpy enough without—"

"You put way too much faith in talk, Jake! Jesus, lawyers. While you're reasoning with a lunatic, she could breach the hull." Gail raised her wrist to turn on her phone.

"No, wait—" Jake began, and another voice behind him said, "Yes, Gail, wait. *Please.*"

Jake whirled around in the narrow corridor. William Shipley stood there, his rotund body squeezed between the gray bulkheads, his face urgent.

Gail said harshly, "This is an unauthorized location for you, Dr. Shipley. Return to the wardroom immediately."

"Let me just talk to her, Gail. Please. I wouldn't ask if I didn't think I could do some good."

"Yeah, well," Gail said, "*I* think Captain Scherer can do some good. Bridge . . . Captain, we have a situation at the cargo hold hatch. Code One. Lucy Lasky has locked herself in and—"

Jake stopped listening. Something in Shipley's eyes held him. The man was a religious crazy, but more than once Jake had seen him talking to Lucy, engaging her in low, intense-looking conversation. That was more than anyone else had done. Gail squeezed around Shipley, still talking into her phone, and ran back along the corridor. Probably going to meet Scherer halfway.

"*Please,* Jake," Shipley said.

Jake said to the still-activated screen, "Two-way communication."

"Retina scan, please."

He made himself lean into the scanner, fought the nausea that rose into his throat. God, after all this time . . .

"Jacob Sean Holman, president, Mira Corporation."

"Two-way communication, damn it!"

Shipley stepped forward, nudging Jake aside. "Lucy? It's Dr. Shipley." His voice had lost its urgency; it was quiet and warm.

The image of Lucy on the screen froze. Then she moved quickly to the large cutter and said, "Go away, Doctor. Please. I don't want them to hurt you, too."

"Who, Lucy? Who's going to hurt me?"

"Them," she said desperately. "The others. You know who I mean."

"No, I don't, Lucy. Can you tell me?"

"Them!" she said, and even through the tension Jake could marvel that her voice stayed low. He had never heard Lucy raise her voice.

Maybe that was part of her trouble.

"Lucy—" Shipley said.

"Please let me concentrate, Doctor. Very soon now I must fire."

Jake's chest turned cold. Gail's voice on his wrist phone said,

"Jake—" and he clamped his other hand over it. Lucy could hear whatever Gail said.

Gail's voice came through his fingers, muffled and urgent. "Jake, Rudy's going to do an EVA. Crawl along the hull and enter from the outside. He and Gretchen are suiting up now."

Something was wrong with time. Jake could hear Gail's voice, could hear Shipley talking softly to Lucy, but he could also visualize Rudy Scherer and Gretchen Wortz crawling along the hull, hurtling along with it at nearly c. Then entering the hold from the outside hatch, suited and armed. It hadn't happened yet, but to Jake it was just as real as Shipley's bulk a foot away. Rudy raised his own laser gun and took aim, and the little figure of Lucy crumpled beside the laser cutter even as Shipley said, "Lucy, do you know what your name means?"

Something in Shipley's voice had caught her attention. "My name?"

"You said the enemy ship coming toward us learned your name, remember? And that's why you must fire on them, to save us all. But do you know what your name means? It's very important."

Beside the laser cutter, its activation light glowing, Lucy turned her small, thin face toward the hatch. "My *name*?"

"Your name. 'Luxina.' It means 'little light.' And so you are, Lucy. But if you fire that laser, you will breach the bulkhead and be sucked out into space, and that would deprive us of your light."

"I have no light anyone would want!"

"Oh, you are so wrong, my dear. Every soul carries light within. And you, especially, because you understand the meaning of silence. We New Quakers believe that wisdom begins in silence, you know. You must not deprive us of your light."

"I have no light," Lucy said flatly. "And you don't understand. Aliens are out there. They're going to destroy us unless I fire!"

Jake sucked in his breath. This wasn't working. Shipley was a fool to think it would. A moldy, archaic religion—

"If you fire, you will also be depriving us of the aliens' light," Shipley said.

Lucy said nothing. She turned back toward the laser cutter, which Jake now saw as a cannon. He took a step forward, helpless.

Once before he had confronted terrible violence, and had known how to profit from it. But not this . . .

"The aliens have their light, too," Shipley continued, just as if Lucy's imaginary aliens actually existed. "Death is not an evil, my dear, but the taking of lives *is*, because it deprives the world of others' light. Who knows what we might learn from these creatures?"

"But they want to kill us!" Lucy cried. She looked much more agitated. Was that good or bad? Jake wondered. Did Shipley really know what he was doing? And why had Jake, supposedly the smooth-talking universal negotiator, let him do it?

Because Jake himself had had no idea what to do.

Shipley said, "You think you're protecting us, doing the right thing." His voice never wavered from calm warmth. "But just consider this, Lucy. When we do the right thing, we have a sense of inner peace, no matter how much outer turmoil we create. Do you have that sense of inner peace and resignation, my dear? Do you feel guided by the Light?"

"I—"

"Because if you do not, then this is not the right action for you to take. If you feel inner conflict, anger that seems to be tearing you apart inside, then this is not the moral course of action. Look inside, Lucy. What do you feel?"

"Doctor," Lucy said intensely, "I never feel inner peace and resignation."

*Nor do I,* Jake thought, and looked at the image of Lucy on the screen. He had never suspected they were so much alike. Or maybe he had, and that was another reason he had avoided her.

"Inner peace and right action are too much responsibility for one person to bear," Shipley said. "That's why we Quakers seek the guidance of the Light in the meeting consensus. Everyone's Light has something to contribute, Lucy, and the best way to deal with others is to address the Light in them."

"These aliens have no Light in them!"

"Can you say that with complete responsibility?" Now Shipley's tone had grown in intensity. "Do you have that much knowledge and insight? Can you really have that high an opinion of yourself?"

My God, Shipley was appealing straight to Lucy's weakness: her low opinion of herself. Was *that* a moral action?

"I don't think you are that egotistical, Lucy. Please come out and let us experience your Light, and you experience ours. Help us reach a good decision on this."

An appeal to Lucy's desire to be of use, as well as her self-doubt. Jake looked at Shipley with profound distrust. He had had no idea the Quaker doctor was capable of this much subtlety, this much manipulation.

And Lucy Lasky turned her face back to the laser cutter, hesitated, and deactivated it. She walked to the hatch and manually opened it, straining with the effort. As soon as it opened, Shipley reached for Lucy and drew her to him. She put her head on his shoulder. Jake saw she was trembling.

"Jake, get my bag from my bunk. Phone Gail, and Rudy if you can. Lucy and I will wait here." Gently he kicked the hatch closed.

Dazed, Jake did as he was told. On the hatch screen he saw Scherer and Wortz, suited, come around the edge of a huge tethered crate with their weapons drawn. A second later Gail's voice leaped from his wrist phone, and the two menacing figures on the screen halted, suddenly as still as if time itself had stopped.

"Her levels of cortisol, catecholamine, and arzendrol were about as high as a body that size could stand," Shipley said. "It's a wonder she held together as long as she did. A young woman of great soul."

"Oh, right," Gail said. "Such great soul she almost killed us all."

Lucy had been sedated, sampled, and put into cold sleep for the rest of the voyage. Jake, Gail, and Shipley sat in the "library," the most popular room on the ship, which they had just ordered vacated. In addition to the wardroom and the gym, the library was the only other general gathering place. It held a VR console, bins of vids and music for viewing on individual cubes, and computer access to ship's library. It also had a window, which alone would have attracted everybody. Usually the library held as many off-duty people as would fit. But the Mira office and the equipment-jammed two-person gym were both too small for Shipley to join Gail and Jake, and so Jake had cleared out the library, to much grumbling.

He said, "What are those blood chemicals you named?"

Shipley leaned back into the molded red chair. Bright colors, Jake's research had said, are important on long, confined voyages. Not that red chairs had done Lucy Lasky a whole lot of good.

Shipley said, "Catecholamine is an enzyme produced by the body under time urgency. Cortisol is a generalized response to stress. Arzendrol is produced under conditions of psychotic delusion."

Gail said, "So Lucy is psychotic? That mousy little thing always so eager to please?"

"Being eager to please is part of it," Shipley said patiently. "What happens is . . . let me start at the beginning. Usually when the body responds to stress, after the stress is over, the nervous system returns to equilibrium, where all its chemicals are in balance. But if the tension is constant, it can never recover equilibrium, so you get a chronic nervous disequilibrium that over time can—"

"What stress was Lucy under that the rest of us aren't?" Gail demanded. "She's a paleontologist! We have no dinosaur bones on ship—nobody asked her to do anything at all!"

Shipley folded his hands on his ample belly. "That was part of the stress, Gail. A person like Lucy needs to feel she's accomplishing something. She also finds constant interaction with people stressful, even under conditions of noncrowding. Some people do. And there isn't much way to avoid interaction on the *Ariel.*"

"She spent most of her time alone in her bunk," Gail argued.

"Which made her feel even less useful. Lucy needs a great deal of time alone, but alone in an environment that lets her work at her own pace. She didn't become a paleontologist by chance, you know. Once we reach Greentrees, she'll be fine."

Jake wasn't so sure of that. Lucy might feel so ashamed of her breakdown that shame itself stressed her. Jake knew something about that himself.

Gail turned unwelcome attention to him, damn her. "Jake, when I first told you about Lucy, you said, 'This is my fault.' Why?"

Shipley was watching him closely, reason enough to not reveal much. Jake said, "Oh, I just meant that I'm supposed to be on the alert for this kind of thing in all personnel. As president of Mira Corp."

"No more than I am," Gail said.

"True," Jake said lightly.

*No, it was my fault because I deliberately avoided Lucy. Because I found her very attractive, that sweetness and intensity combined, and any relationship with a woman like that always means more than physical intimacy. They want genuine intimacy, to know you, to learn for real who you are. And I cannot allow that. Ever. So I pushed Lucy away, and she felt it, and retreated farther into isolation and rejection.*

"Well, the problem is solved now," Gail said.

"Yes," Jake agreed. "Dr. Shipley, thank you again. I have to admit that I wasn't pleased that you chose to stay awake. But we've all benefited from your unique point of view."

*"Lawyer talk,"* Gail called this, all smooth misdirection. Jake was good at it. It was not a point of pride.

Gail stood and stretched, her raw-boned figure extending itself luxuriously in the rarely empty room. Who filled Gail's sexual thoughts? The libido suppressors only worked to a limited degree. As far as Jake knew, all the other awakes were straight. But Gail had never really gotten over Lahiri's terrible death. Maybe she never would. Just as he had been inalterably changed by Mrs. Dalton's death.

Shipley left first. Gail took advantage of the privacy before anyone else returned to the library to say quietly to Jake, "I still don't like him."

"Why not?" He was meanly pleased.

"He's a manipulator. Using his religion to defuse poor Lucy."

Jake struggled briefly with his thoughts; honesty won. "Gail, I don't think it was manipulation. He genuinely believes all that stuff."

"Well, then that's worse," she said illogically. "The last thing I want around is some sort of hovering saintly Buddha, judging us all on our souls and blood enzymes."

This seemed to Jake a complete misreading of Shipley, but he said nothing. Gail, like Lucy, wasn't immune to the stresses of a long voyage in constant contact with uncongenial people.

Nor, Jake knew, was he.

But it wasn't any internal stressor that made her knock on his bunk door later that night. "Come in," he called, surprised. Sleeping bunks, each seven feet by five feet by four feet high, were sacred. You never bothered anyone with his door rolled down over the only actual privacy any of them had. You even averted your eyes if you passed a rolled-up door, careful not to notice the occupant's choice of decor, usually personal pictures and mementos, unless invited.

Gail ignored all that. She ducked her head and sat on the edge of Jake's mattress, rolling down the door behind her. Her legs squeezed sideways into the one foot of space between the bunk and door.

"Jake, I just talked to Rudy. Erik Halberg found his computer error."

Jake sat up, careful not to bump his head on the shelves installed on the bulkhead. "Where was it?"

"In the astronomical data. The program had flagged a fast-moving object where no path had been projected, and Erik had at first assumed it was a bug due to cosmic bombardment. But he ran it and checked it and compensated for it every way possible, and he insists it wasn't an error."

"Uncharted comet," Jake said. "Run-away planetoid, accelerating rock from a gravity swing-by . . . God, Gail, it could be anything."

"Erik says he checked everything. It wasn't."

Jake thought, *You can't ever assume comprehensive exclusion. Fallacious reasoning.* He did not say this aloud. Gail hated lawyer talk. "So what does Erik think it was?"

"He doesn't know. But he says it was moving at ninety-eight percent of c. Nothing large except us should be moving at that speed in this section of space. He says it's a fabricated object. Such as, for instance, another ship."

"From Earth, you mean."

"No. If anything else had launched from Earth, we'd have learned about it by quee. You know that."

Jake stared at her. Four colonized planets outside the solar system, and no advanced civilizations discovered. Hell, not even any sentient life forms. The best that had been managed by evolution anywhere other than Earth was a warm-blooded, armored, turtle-like predator with the intelligence of a pigeon. Greentrees had not of course been explored, only sampled by the quee probe, but nothing in the atmospheric composition had indicated any industrial emissions of any kind.

"Gail, could Lucy have—"

"No, of course not. She didn't know what Erik had decided about his computer error. Hell, he hadn't even decided it when Lucy cracked. That part's coincidence. But if that thing *was* a ship—"

"It wasn't," Jake said. "If—"

"Don't tell me," Gail said crossly, "tell Halberg. And everybody else. They're in the wardroom, and they want you."

Jake found Halberg, Scherer, Shipley, Liu Fengmo, Faisal bin Saud, and the energy engineer Robert Takai squeezed into the wardroom. They had all evidently been arguing with Halberg. The lieutenant looked as upset as Jake imagined he ever got: agate eyes and a jawline like an erection.

"There was not a computer error! *Nein!*"

"Friend Erik," Shipley began, but it was Faisal whose smooth voice cut through the close air.

"Lieutenant, what you saw could not have been a ship of any kind. Look at the evidence. Look at the scale. In cosmic terms, we humans have only stepped a few feet outside our own back door. A little territory and we've been probing it robotically for a century and a half. If there were star-faring aliens zipping around, if civilizations existed here with that advanced a technology, we'd have found some indicators by now."

"More than that," Robert Takai said, "*they'd* have found *us.* That 'object' in your data passed within ten thousand kilometers of us. If it were any kind of ship, she must have picked up the electromagnetic or thermal signals from the *Ariel.* No way could she miss us. And there's been no attempt at contact, hostile or otherwise. So it wasn't a ship."

"But—"

"It wasn't a ship, Friend," Shipley said gently.

One by one, the others nodded in agreement. Jake felt something loosen in his chest. Faisal was right; a ship only ten thousand kilometers away would inevitably have detected the *Ariel.* So it wasn't a ship. Halberg's computer error had been a comet or a gravity-boosted planetoid or even just that: an error.

There was nothing there.

# 3

*There is everything here,* William Shipley thought. *Everything anyone could ever need.*

His legs still hadn't fully accepted Greentrees' lighter gravity. After nearly seven years of the *Ariel*'s 1.25 gees, the planet's 0.9 gee made him feel springy and light, but of course his body wasn't light (and probably never would be again). Either he used too much force per step, sending him into a little off-balance bounce, or he used too little and stumbled instead of walking. The younger people, he noted, were doing much better.

And a good thing, too, since they were doing most of the manual labor, bringing materials from the *Ariel* to the 'bot builders and diggers and welders. Objects were strewn everywhere, metal and rocks and foamcast, broken apart and rejoined and unfinished and discarded. What would one day be Mira City looked at this moment like a junkyard.

But none of that mattered next to the sheer, unearthly beauty of Greentrees.

Shipley had seen pictures, of course, sent by quee from the probe. Endless pictures. But the colors had been off, somehow—a different spectrum of sunlight? Shipley was no physicist. Whatever the cause, the effect was of light cooler than Earth's, bathing the strange delicate plants and high narrow trees in a tranquil glow. The temperature hadn't yet gone below jacket weather. The ubiquitous groundcover, a purplish broad-leaved plant, grew thicker than grass. Most flowers seemed to be purples or blues, adding to the feeling of sweet repose.

Shipley bent to pick a wildflower that had somehow escaped being trampled in the building frenzy. The flower was a pale blue with four long, slim, petallike things folded back over some delicate alien structures of deep purple. Not stamen or pistil or anything else Terran . . . *alien.* Just thinking the word left Shipley breathless. He, William Shipley, stood on ground that had not been born with Sol, that had never known Sol's cheerful yellow glow. Did that awe-ful fact dazzle the others as it did him?

" 'This other Eden, demi-paradise,' " he said aloud. " 'This fortress built by Nature for herself—' "

"What?" Maggie Striker called, rushing past.

"Nothing," Shipley said, but she was already gone.

Not that Greentrees was Eden. The planet held predators, some of them large and dangerous, although Shipley hadn't yet seen any. Maybe they feared the human camp, or maybe the ecologist, Maggie Striker, had already taken steps to keep them away. There were probably also dangerous insect-analogues, but those, Shipley knew, had been eliminated in the small circle of camp activity. Beyond that circle, nature undoubtedly carried on just as violently as she had when Earth had belonged to primitive mammals.

Nor did anything in the camp match Shipley's sense of planetary repose. People worked like 'bots, tireless and efficient. They were so glad to have something to do again! Planetfall had energized the twelve who had stayed awake for the entire voyage. Petty differences had disappeared, and Shipley watched Jake Holman, assisted by geneticist Ingrid Johnson and deposed Arab prince Faisal bin Saud, as they set a girder in place on the community hall for 'bot welding. The combination of personalities tickled him.

Gail Cutler raced by, carrying a tray of something. Samples for Todd McCallum, probably. The scientists were rabid to analyze everything, but they had agreed to spend a certain number of hours per "day" in erecting habitats, and they were keeping their bargain. Nobody was sleeping much, nobody had really adjusted to the twenty-two-hour-and-sixteen-minute day, and nobody cared. It was a giant, frenetic, productive party.

"Dr. Shipley," Gail called, "Lieutenant Wortz wants you."

"Where?"

"Shuttle." She raced out of sight.

Shipley's joyous mood evaporated. He could guess what Lieutenant Wortz wanted.

Captain Scherer's crew had stayed awake for the entire voyage, seven of the twelve people who had managed to do so. Shipley found this intensely interesting. Scherer's military schedules and employments undoubtedly accounted for some of the crew's stalwart endurance, but not all of it. There was more going on here. The sailors all kept a certain formal distance from everybody else, despite the crowded conditions . . . look how everyone else still referred to most of the sailors by title. "Lieutenant Wortz," not "Gretchen." She would be in charge of the gradual ferrying down of newly awakened colonists, the order of awakening having been set by a combination of needed skill and passenger lottery.

"Dr. Shipley," Gretchen Wortz said pleasantly, "we seem to be ahead of the building schedule. Jake Holman would like us to begin awakenings a day earlier than planned. Can you be ready to leave in an hour?"

"Yes, of course." A day earlier. Shipley made himself nod and smile. The first load of colonists, then, would be landing on Greentrees tomorrow. Among them were four New Quakers, which should be a cause of rejoicing. And *was,* he told himself fiercely. The lack was in himself, and nowhere else. This time he would strive to do better, to give himself up to the guidance of the light instead of trying to impose his own will on the situation. This time would be a new beginning, on this new planet.

This time he would seek peace with Naomi, instead of their everlasting, heartbreaking war.

"How does it look down there?" Tariji Brown asked wistfully.

"Wonderful," Shipley said. "You'll be there soon, my dear."

Tariji snorted. "Not while they need me up here. I was a damn fool to tell them I'm a medic. Should've said I was a plumber. Plumbers they need. Let's get at 'em, Doctor. None of them are getting any younger."

Shipley smiled at Tariji. Just looking at her made him feel good. A tall, strongly built black woman with hair trimmed close to her shapely head, she radiated cheerful, wry capability. Tariji could deal with anything that might go wrong, up here or down there. On Earth, she had helped him organize the more fearful New Quakers who wanted to colonize Greentrees but didn't want to face anything unfamiliar. "Now, you can't swim without getting wet," Tariji had said. "You diving in or staying on shore?" Her deep laugh had taken any pushiness out of the demand, and most of the New Quakers in the United Atlantic Federation had ended up coming.

"I got the list here," Tariji said. "Twelve people. You ready, Doctor? The first one is Goldman, Benjamin Aaron, engineer."

"Three of the twelve are engineers," said Shipley, who knew the list by heart. Unlike Tariji, who'd spent the voyage in cold sleep, he'd had nearly seven years to memorize it.

The procedure was simple. Shipley keyed in the right coffin—terrible word, someone should have known better—and the conveyor delivered it to what had been the library. Next he keyed in the "awake" codes, and the coffin did all the rest, draining out the fluids, warming the body, administering the right drugs in the right order.

"Here he comes," Tariji said. "Welcome to Greentrees, Mr. Goldman."

Benjamin Goldman, naked, struggled to sit up. He fell back on muscles stiff from years of disuse. He looked so comically surprised that Tariji laughed her rich, reassuring rumble. "Take it slow, Ben. You're going to be wobbly, then nauseated, then hungry, but it's got to happen in order. Just take it slow, take it easy, take my hand."

"Are we . . . there?" Goldman gasped. Tariji helped him sit. The coffin had been placed to face the window, and the planet happened to be in view, a blue-and-white globe looking so much like Earth that it was a long moment before the grateful eye registered the strange configuration of continents, the three moons.

"Aaahhhhhhhh," Goldman said in deep satisfaction, and threw up into his coffin.

After Shipley and Tariji got him stabilized, dressed, and sitting up in a chair in the wardroom, they started on Barrington, Thekla Belia, agriculturist, who immediately demanded to know what plants down there had proved edible.

"None so far," Tariji said, "because nobody tried to eat anything.

Think they'd start the feast without you? They're living on *Ariel* rations, Doctor, and eating their heads off with work and joy."

"I want to go down!"

"Soon. You gotta vomit your guts out first, and we gotta wake up ten more people . . . there you go, that's good, get it all out."

By the time they'd woken up the ninth colonist, the first two were ravenous. Shipley moved them to the tiny galley, out of sight of those awakes who were still queasy, and showed them how to order from the synthesizer and use the instabake. He returned to the library.

"Frayne, Naomi Susan," Tariji said, and Shipley felt himself stiffen.

Naomi's coffin slid into place. The machinery hummed softly; the lid slid back. Naomi—Nan, she wanted to be called, he had to remember that—fought to sit up, her body so thin that her clavicle jutted like coat hangers. Her shaved head with its tattoos and artificial skin crest looked faintly blue. The inlaid metallics on her small breasts glittered.

"Lord, you don't have any body fat at all," Tariji said. "What do you plan on using to keep yourself warm?"

Naomi tried to speak, but no words came out. Just as well, Shipley thought. She would have scorched Tariji for her presumptuous concern.

Tariji said, "Welcome to Greentrees, Ms. Frayne."

Naomi glanced at the window. No planet this time, just stars. The corners of her mouth turned down.

"Just sit still a minute, you're going to be sick," Tariji said cheerfully. Naomi glared at her, then at Shipley.

"You . . . here. Already."

"Yes, Naomi. I'm here."

"Should have . . . known. No . . . escape."

Tariji looked puzzled. Shipley said, "Tariji Brown, this is my daughter," just as Naomi leaned deliberately over the edge of her coffin and threw up on her father's shoes.

*What does one do when a child goes wrong?*

For years, Shipley had sought for reasons, as if a cause would provide a cure. Through the childhood defiance and stealing that had become the adolescent drugs and running away. Through the destruction that the adult Naomi had brought to everything she touched. Through the horrific self-scarring and more horrific suicide attempt. Through the robbery conviction and jail sentence, which at least had kept her safely locked up for five years.

Perhaps, Shipley thought despairingly, it had been her mother's death when Naomi was only six. But the defiance and pointless anger had begun before Catherine died, and their other children had not reacted like that, Seely and John and Terry, all still in cold sleep with their families.

Perhaps it had been genetic. Shipley was a third-generation Quaker doctor. He had combed Naomi's genescan, looking for known genetic abnormalities . . . but so little was certifiably normal. The deeper that humanity had gone into its own genome, the greater the diversity had become. At the cellular level, people were amazingly different—not in their DNA, much of which man shared with apes, mice, fruit flies, and peach trees. No, the differences lay in how the genes generated proteins, in how those proteins folded, in how their various combinations affected cellular machinery. There was so much genetics hadn't known. And as the state of Earth worsened globally, scientific funding dried up, and less was learned each decade.

But the real problem with blaming Naomi's genes, Shipley knew, was that it was an evasion. People were more than their chemistry. People bore the responsibility for their decisions and choices.

So perhaps it was Shipley's own choices that had shaped Naomi. Silence, simplicity, truth . . . he had tried his entire life to be guided by the principles of the Light. But silence, the profound quietude that let one hear the inner light, also meant that others were not spoken to, not sufficiently guided. Simplicity . . . he had been so fearful of imposing his will on his children, of making them his own instruments instead of their own. Had he erred too far in that direction, so that Naomi felt his reticence as indifference? And as for truth . . . well, Shipley had not needed a medical practice to understand that there were people who could not bear much truth.

And maybe, for a child, that truth *had* been unbearable. Seely had said once to Shipley, "Naomi thinks you love God better than you love us." *I do,* Shipley thought, but Seely had not been the child who'd insisted on facing that.

Now Shipley lay, exhausted, in his bunk on the *Ariel,* staring into the darkness. He and Tariji had awakened thirty-six people, of the six thousand in cold sleep. Twenty-four had already gone down to Greentrees, including Naomi. The other twelve would go down tomorrow morning, when Shipley would begin reviving another thirty-six. After that, the awakenings would pause until the people on the ground had built enough facilities to temporarily house the next groups of arrivees. It had all been planned carefully, taking advantage of the quee-described experiences of military settlers on the other four Earth-like planets, and of Jake and Gail's meticulous, intelligent research.

Meticulous. Intelligent. Planned. Such good qualities, and not one had helped Shipley with his daughter. Just as nothing helped now.

Why had Naomi even chosen to come to Greentrees? It had been decades since she'd attended a meeting for worship. Shipley had been astonished by her decision to join the rest of the family in emigration. Astonished, then elated. Maybe, he had thought then, Naomi's own inner light could still be found, still be heeded. Maybe she had begun to heed it. Greentrees could be a new beginning for her, just as it was going to be for the New Quakers who desired to pursue their faith away from the corrupting, deadening, blaring materialism of Earthly global culture.

Now Shipley was not so sure. Lying in the darkness, he chastised himself for his doubts. Naomi had chosen to come here, to leave her former life. He, her father, must have faith in her. Act in accordance with trust in the Light, and the rest would follow. "Let your life speak," George Fox had told the first Quakers nearly six hundred years ago. Shipley must do that, and then trust that his life, and the shared life of the Meeting, spoke to Naomi.

His eyes burned. He wished he could still love her. That was the worst, the struggle to love his own daughter. It horrified him that he wished Tariji Brown were his child instead of Naomi. Or the brisk, pragmatic Gail Cutler. Or even Lucy Lasky, whose psychotic episode on the *Ariel* had actually shown to Shipley the humility and pliancy of the girl's essential nature.

He lay there sleepless above the beautiful planet, trying not to hate himself, trying to love his terrifying daughter.

# 4

Gail stood beside Jake Holman at the edge of the "city," its work-in-progress clutter behind her and the rolling Greentrees plain before her, saying good-bye to 967 Cheyenne Native Americans. Nothing, she thought, about this new planet was as amazing as these demented romantics and their demented plans.

"We are leaving now," Larry Smith said formally. He was a short, stocky man with brown hair and intelligent light gray eyes, dressed in a brown coverall of practically indestructible Threadmore. On Earth, he had been a cattle breeder. Now he was a Cheyenne chief.

Beyond him, on the plain covered with dense purple ground-cover, men and women began to pull travois made of newly felled trees reinforced with rods of diamond fiber. Heaped on the clumsy hybrid contraptions were packs covered with Threadmore tarps. Among the travois moved solar-powered rovers, looking as if they'd strayed in from a different millennium. As, of course, they had.

"You can comlink with either us or the ship whenever you choose," Gail said to Larry, because she had to say something and what could possibly be appropriate? There were no precedents.

"We won't choose to," he said. "Not unless you break the contract."

And what could one say to that? *We promise to keep our treaty with your people?* There was a rich history of how well *that* had worked out.

"Well, good-bye," Gail said awkwardly.

"Good-bye, Gail Cutler. May the spirit be with you."

"And you," Gail said.

Larry Smith turned to his waiting tribe. They had all been awakened over the last weeks and transported downstairs by shuttle, where they had immediately erected temporary teepees beyond the perimeter of Mira City.

When Smith was out of earshot, Gail said accusingly to Jake, "You might have helped me out there, instead of just standing there grinning."

"I wasn't grinning."

"You were grinning inside. Oh, Lord, how weird people are! They really think they can duplicate a tribal, hunter-gatherer civilization that's mostly a romanticized figment of the imagination anyway."

"That's too harsh," Jake said, watching the Cheyenne pull away. "They're making modern adaptations, planetary adaptations."

"They certainly *are*," Gail said. "Look over there. That's a fully equipped genetics lab in that huge rover."

"It's only until they determine what's edible and what's not," Jake said.

Gail snorted. The Cheyenne rovers, genetics lab, and gear had taken up a surprising amount of room on the *Ariel*, for which the Cheyenne had paid well. Smith's "tribe" was a splinter group, made up of individuals and families burning with idealism for this new life, which was being financed with the genemod clinic earnings of several generations. Their contract with Mira Corp detailed just what services the corporation would provide until and through awakenings, and then specified that there would be no formal ties at all after that, and no "intrusion" on the large subcontinent they were claiming as their own.

"Do you think they'll make it?" Gail asked Jake. She watched a woman struggle to pull a travois a respectful distance around a patch of red creeper.

"Of course they'll make it. They know as much about the planet as we do."

"Which is to say, effectively nothing."

"Gail, have you ever been on a Native American reservation?"

"No. Have you?"

"Yes," he said, surprising her. "And I've read about them. Once they were terrible places, the dregs of the arable land, full of poverty and alcoholism. Since the natives figured out that as a separate nation they could legally offer services that places part of the United States could not, they flourished. First gambling, then genemod and pet-cloning clinics, and—"

"I'm aware that reservations are great scientific centers," Gail said dryly. "And greenly rich. That's why I don't understand why this lot wants to dump it all and go back to living as if the last two or three centuries hadn't ever happened. But with genetic labs in tow, of course."

"Ah, you're a socialized creature," Jake said. "Planted in the middle of your huge family."

"Hardly. Only six of them are awake yet. My family's at the end of the list."

"A quibble. You're a social person, and you never seem to realize that many, many people want desperately to escape society and never look back."

Gail looked curiously at Jake. He still watched the retreating Cheyenne, growing smaller as they trekked across the grassy plain toward the distant mountains. Jake seldom spoke about his past. She wasn't sure he was doing so now.

"Jake—"

"Do you know that Larry Smith is changing his name? All of them are. But they'll wait to choose new names until some incident happens to them or the tribe sees some personal characteristic emerge. Apparently that's how it was done once."

"So the next time we see Larry Smith, he'll be Man Who Owns Genetic Lab?"

"You think it's funny," Jake said. "Do you think Shipley's funny, too, escaping to a new life with his New Quakers?"

She had to be honest. "No, or anyway not as funny. At least he's prepared to live with a star-faring civilization. But I can't even figure out what his group believes or doesn't believe. Can you?"

"I don't try," Jake said dismissively. After seven mortally long years, Gail knew well that Shipley made Jake uneasy. The New Quakers were being steadily awakened and transported downstairs—how was Jake going to react when he lived surrounded by two thousand of them?

She said, "Tell me—did you include the Quakers in the voyage only because without their third share, you wouldn't have been able to raise enough money?"

"Of course. That's why we included everybody, including your family and Larry Smith's Cheyenne. You know that."

"But I don't know why you couldn't have waited a few more years to see if anyone more congenial to you turned up. What difference did a few years make when you were leaving Earth forever?" She had wanted to ask him this for a long time.

"No difference," Jake said lightly. "Anyway, I worry more about the Arabs than the New Quakers. Shipley's lunatics are at least democratic. I know Faisal explained to us how his family has always been political and religious moderates and that's why he had to leave his country when a new militant regime took over so they wanted a new start in a fresh place. But nonetheless . . ."

Gail stared at Jake. They'd been over all this many times before; Jake sounded as if he were offering the rehash mostly to distract her. From what?

Abruptly he said, "Come on, we'll be late for the Board meeting," and strode back toward camp.

She should be used to his evasions by now. After ten years as partners, nearly seven of them confined to the *Ariel,* Gail knew everything about Jake: what he liked to eat, how often he burped, what jokes he thought funny, what gifts he'd received on his sixth birthday, his grades at law school. Yet she sometimes felt she didn't know him at all, that he understood her far better than the reverse.

Or maybe she just wasn't that hard to understand.

At eight years old, Gail had been taken by Aunt Tamara, now in cold sleep on the *Ariel,* to a religious meeting in a huge, gleaming sports arena in Portland, Oregon. Preachers had thundered about the death and destruction coming to adulterers, geneticists, thieves, and the nonbelieving nonrighteous. They would all perish in rivers of fire and ravishments of the Earth. The next day, a quake in the fault under Portland had killed seven thousand people.

The effect on Gail had been the opposite of the preachers' intentions. She watched the newsvids, and even at eight she could see that both the righteous and the nonrighteous, believers and non-, had all died the same way. She'd been impressed by the impersonal, immense power of nature, that same power she thrilled to in thunderstorms, and had decided then and there to become a scientist.

Gail's mother, an evolutionary biologist, had been furious when she found out that Aunt Tamara had taken Gail to the revival. Emily Cutler was an evolutionary biologist of strong but eccentric views. She believed that men and women could never live happily together. "It's the only reasonable conclusion," she'd said patiently, "for anybody who will *consider* reason. Male and female humans evolved to fill different niches: hunter-competitor and gatherer-nurturer. Eight thousand years of so-called civilization can't undo five million years of evolution. Men and women aren't different species, but they are variants of the same species, and to expect them to enjoy living together is like expecting wolves and poodles to share a lair. They should live separately and visit."

A decade later, when Gail announced to her family that she was gay, Aunt Tamara blamed her sister Emily's teachings. Everyone else nodded and smiled and asked why Gail was failing both chemistry and physics.

Science bored her. But money did not, and at nineteen she had a degree in business. At twenty-five she was managing more of the familial investments than anyone else in her sprawling, ecologically-obsessed family. By then she'd met Lahiri and life was full and complete, sweet with the buttery-rich taste of happiness.

Then Lahiri had died, slowly and horribly, of a genetically altered virus released by a terrorist trying to hold Minneapolis hostage to some cracked political demand. Lahiri shouldn't even have been in Minneapolis; it was an unplanned business trip. The UV and $CO_2$ levels of Earth had risen in twenty years to heights that hadn't been supposed to occur, according to scientific predictions, for another century. The rich grew richer, and as the poor grew poorer in a federation of North Atlantic nations not used to patience, domestic violence and domestic terrorism increased. International terrorism had become a given. Genetic fixes to crops began to lose the race against resistant blights and increased population.

Gail's family voted to get out. Gail had come to Jake, and from the first he had seemed to understand that after Lahiri, there would never be anyone else for Gail. No one else understood that. Jake and Gail had become working partners and squabbling friends, and never once had she felt he'd let her see who he really was.

"There goes Faisal, elegant as usual," Jake said as they approached the ugly inflatable structure serving as a general gathering hall. "All the royal family seems to be adjusting well."

"The male half, anyway," Gail said acidly. "How would we know about the women? They hardly ever leave that compound or whatever it is, and then they're veiled."

"You know that when we talked to them before we left Earth," Jake said mildly. "All of them agreed that this was how they wanted to live. Even with voice-stress analysis."

And what a battle *that* had been, to get the Arabs to agree to voice analyses of their women. Gail suspected that Faisal, cosmopolitan and practical, had used leverage Gail didn't want to know about. But Jake was right: even under VSA, which had shown no deception, the Arab women, royals and servants alike, had avowed that this was the way they wanted to live. Behind walls, in Mira City but not really of it.

So now the northern section of the city east of the river was surrounded by a ten-foot wall of foamcast. Within the medina, Gail knew but had not personally seen, were more walls segregating the women's quarters, the *andarun*. She imagined courtyards out of old Persian woodcuts, with fountains and flower beds and veiled dark-eyed women, childlike and protected. But she didn't really know. When he was outside its walls, Faisal spoke very little of his private kingdom. His lieutenants—all male, of course, many of whom seemed to be his sons—followed his example. Except for ceremonial occasions, Faisal wore the same brown Threadmore coverall as Jake, as Gail herself.

She knew he had three wives, Jabbareh and Homy and Khanom, but he never mentioned them. All that Mira City was allowed to glimpse of life in the medina was the minaret rising tall above the walls, the cry calling the faithful to prayer, the occasionally interrupted meeting while Faisal knelt, without prayer rug or apology, toward Sol to pray.

"We wish to restore the true Islamic ways," he had told Gail and Jake when first he'd come to them with his proposition to join the Greentrees colony. "The warm, joyful heart of Islam, grounded in family. Not the fanatic warmongering it has become."

"But your women—" Gail had begun, Faisal cut her off.

"Our women themselves will assure you that they wish to live by the old precepts."

And so they had, even through the VSAs Gail had insisted on. She didn't like it, this perpetuation of a patriarchy on a new planet, but as Jake had acidly pointed out, she didn't have to like it. As long as the Arabs would live and let live, which they had done, their gods did not have to be her gods.

"I think they only have one," she'd said through gritted teeth.

"Whatever," Jake had shrugged.

And, really, was it any stranger than Larry Smith and his Cheyenne going off to resurrect the dead gods of Nature?

"Hello," Faisal said, pausing at the door of the tent. Today, for whatever reason, he'd put off the coverall. His white robes actually looked comfortable and attractive against Greentrees' cool blues and purples.

"Hello, Faisal," Gail said. Did his retinue call him "Your Highness"? Only the Chinese contingent and Gail's own family, it seemed to her, had come with their faces turned toward the future and not the past.

Jake said, "Are they all in there? And will we be able to get any of them to speak English?"

Faisal laughed. The Board of Governors met twice every month. A "month" had been defined as the transit of the largest of the three moons, Gamma. (And how much imagination did it show to name them Alpha, Beta, Gamma? Never mind, there was enough else to imagine.) One monthly meeting was to assess and plan progress on Mira City and to cope with any problems, which so far had been astonishingly few. The second meeting, held today, was to hear reports from the scientists who provided the raw data for assessing, planning, and coping. It was the scientists, with their specialized jargon, who didn't speak English.

They were a varied lot. Nine scientists in various disciplines, and only Robert Takai, engineer, had paid his own way. The others were all funded by the Wellcome Trust, a British foundation with a centuries-old tradition of taking risks on scientific endeavors without any payback except information of benefit to humanity. Gail wasn't sure that the information from Greentrees, faithfully sent back by quee, was of any use to the Wellcome Trust, or to anybody else on Earth. Strange to think that all the trustees who had funded these scientists were dead and buried. Seventy years had passed on Earth.

And everything was as bad, or worse, than when the *Ariel* had left. Water, hunger, terrorism, despair, air quality, politics, greed. $CO_2$ levels up, food production down, global weather so extreme that much of the planet was in either flood or drought.

"I've identified and analyzed three more geological strata," said Roy Callipare, the geologist, and Gail stopped listening. These reports were necessary but boring. Although not to the scientists, who heeded, argued, laughed with, and attacked each other as if the presence or absence of beryl was a matter of life and death.

Gail gazed furtively around, trying not to be obvious about her inattention. Fengmo, the Chinese member of the Board, was absent today, busy with something else. The others, except for Faisal in his white robes, blended with the inflatable: brown or green coveralls against the dull green walls and gray foamcast furniture. Well, eventually Mira City would become more colorful. The inflatables were only temporary, and so were the coveralls, although new clothing was far down everyone's list of priorities. Still, someone could have at least brought in a vase of Greentrees flowers.

Lucy Lasky gave a brief report as colorless as the surroundings. The paleontologist had kept to herself since her awakening, going out every day with the geologist in one of the two-person rovers. They'd sampled more than a dozen sites and then settled on one about seven miles away that, as Gail understood it, had both a lot of rocks and a lot of fossils. Gail put herself on automatic throughout Lucy's presentation.

She did the same with Maggie Striker, ecologist; Benjamin Goldman, building-materials engineer; and George Fox, biologist. Gail considered it hilarious that George, a smiling exuberant man with a taste for fizzies, had the same name as the man who had founded the original Quakers in the seventeenth century. William Shipley merely said that many people bore such a common name. Jake had just nodded abstractly, and so Gail had to savor the joke alone.

She tuned in to Robert Takai, energy engineer, long enough to learn the state of his solar-, wind-, and geothermal-driven energy projects. All were on or ahead of schedule. The geneticists, Todd

McCallum and the tiresome Ingrid Johnson, reported on more flora and fauna, stating that every single one so far was DNA-based. Well, big deal. Every life form on every settled planet was DNA-based. Panspermia was the general scientific consensus, a cloud of spores that had drifted through the galaxy billions of years ago, leaving behind it the genetic code for life.

And a good thing, too, or Thekla Belia Barrington, the British agriculturist, would not be reporting such sunny prospects for growing and eating, after a few judicious genetic alterations, so many of the local plants. Maybe as many as fifteen percent, she said happily. "Better than anyone expected. Bloody *wonderful,* in fact. The first experimental beds are already planted."

Even William Shipley was smiling.

Then Nan Shipley strolled in and shattered everything.

Attendance at Board meetings was supposed to be limited to Board members, which meant leaders of those groups that had purchased stock in Mira: New Quakers, Cheyenne, Gail's family, Liu's Chinese, Saud's Arabs, plus Jake and, as a representative of the Wellcome Trust, George Fox, senior scientist. Nan Shipley sauntered in as if she belonged there. Although probably near thirty, she was dressed in a loose tunic sewn with tiny mirrors and cut out in many tiny holes, through which could be seen shifting glimpses of blue-painted skin. The latest teenage fashion of seventy years ago, Gail thought meanly. Among the utilitarian coveralls everybody else wore, Nan looked as exotic and useless as a peacock's tail.

"Naomi, this is a private meeting," Shipley said stiffly to his daughter. "I think you should—"

"There's a comlink message from the *Ariel,* priority one," Nan said casually. Clearly she was enjoying herself. "It came into Mira Corporation planetary headquarters, and I happened to be in there. Rudy didn't want to put it on the general frequency so he asked me to tell you all what it is and then get Jake or Gail."

"What were you doing in Mira Corp headquarters?" her father asked. Gail saw his embarrassment and irritation. Nan had irritated Gail, too, on several counts: by being in the Mira Corp inflatable, by snidely referring to it as "planetary headquarters," by sauntering in here as if a priority one were beneath her notice, by calling

Captain Scherer by his first name. And why had Scherer entrusted her with the content of a priority one? Didn't make sense.

Jake said sharply, "Well, what *is* the message?"

Nan paused a moment, then smiled. "The message is that the *Ariel* scout was doing a low flyover, for mapping and such, and Lieutenant Wortz found a village. Two villages, actually. With thatched huts and outdoor hearths and cultivated fields.

"We're not alone on Greentrees."

# 5

*Not possible,* was Jake's first thought. His second was, *Of course it is.*

The galaxy, or rather this tiny section of it, had proved empty of intelligence but loaded with life, all of it DNA-based and remarkably similar in cell construction. Wherever the panspermic drift of spores had fallen onto a viable planet—and there were a lot more of them than originally thought—they had deposited starter genes that gave rise to life. Life had then taken diverse evolutionary paths. Only Earth's had had the lucky conditions, or the time, or the something, to get as far as sentience. Colchis hadn't even gotten as far as flowering plants. That was the theory, anyway.

There was no reason part, or all, of the theory couldn't be wrong.

When Jake came out of his stunned shock, biologist George Fox was already sputtering. ". . . out of range of our explorations so far! If they came from star systems we haven't reached yet, they could—"

Ingrid Johnson said acidly, "Star-faring? With outdoor hearths and thatched huts?"

George said, "Maybe Captain Scherer was wrong about those. Or a star-faring civilization might establish primitive-type vacation camps . . ." He trailed off, knowing how weak this sounded.

Jake forced himself to calm. "We can't conclude anything without more evidence. We need information."

"An expedition," George said eagerly. "To introduce ourselves!"

Gail made a face. Her green eyes still looked appalled. "An expedition could be dangerous, if they're unfriendly and Captain Scherer has mistaken their level of technology. Or even if he hasn't. Spears can kill, you know." She paused. "Spears or whatever they . . . use."

"You don't know that they 'use' anything," Ingrid said.

George said, "The chance to learn—"

"The probes never reported—"

"—always knew probes could only sample a small area, plus whatever was visible from space. Small huts—"

"—gains for extraterrestrial biology—"

"There are legal issues here," Jake said loudly. The others looked at him in surprise, but he suddenly felt on more solid ground. Lawyer talk.

"I mean it, there are legal issues. The Planetary Federation issued guidelines a century ago"—now almost two centuries—"covering contact with any sentient species that humanity might encounter interstellar. There are issues of eminent domain, peaceful assumption, good faith in—"

"Enforceable by *whom*?" Ingrid said scathingly.

"Doesn't matter, does it, then?" Thekla Barrington said. "We have a moral obligation to respect this people's first claim . . . God, what am I saying? We don't even know if they're really sentient!"

"But we'll find out!" George Fox said, and the babble started again. Jake tried to gather his thoughts, to reason clearly. If these were sentients, how many were there? Did they inhabit every continent? If so, did they have their own customary—

"There are no sentients on Greentrees! None!"

Lucy Lasky, rising to her feet and shouting, such a surprising sight that everyone else instantly fell silent.

The paleontologist's face mottled maroon. Jake, who was always uncomfortably aware of Lucy's presence anyway, watched her closely. He had sensed her hesitant, continuing shame over her breakdown on the *Ariel* and over the enforced cold sleep that had followed it, and he'd pitied her. Or was it more like identification?

But Lucy didn't look shamed or hesitant now. When her color faded, she stood straight, a thin small figure, and spoke with a force Jake had never expected from her. "Listen to me, all of you. I've spent three months sampling the fossil record on Greentrees, at more than a dozen different sites. There is no indication anywhere of anything made by sentience."

Gail said, "So you haven't sampled the right site yet."

Lucy had calmed herself. "You don't understand. The evolutionary path is *long* to sentience, let alone to thatched roofs and cooking pots. There would be relics everywhere, if only stone axes or flaked knives. No relics, no sentience. That's true on Earth, on Colchis, on all five planets humans have settled on. I'm positive about my findings. No sentience evolved on Greentrees."

"Are you saying these . . . beings came from somewhere else?" Thekla Barrington said skeptically. "And then their civilization degraded?"

Todd McCallum said, "That would leave stuff behind, too, wouldn't it? A degraded culture built on a more advanced one has layers of debris. Like Carthage, or Kinshasa."

Jake said, "Lucy? What about that?"

"Yes. No," Lucy said. She seemed to realize she was still standing, reddened again, and sat down. "I only know what I've found. Or haven't found. There are no signs of evolved sentience or devolved cultures."

Ingrid said, "Lucy, let's be frank here. First you see aliens that aren't there, on the *Ariel,* and now you refuse to see aliens that are there. Could the problem be you?"

"Shut up, Ingrid," Jake said, surprising himself. "Personal attacks don't help anything."

"It wasn't a personal attack! It was—"

Gail spoke louder than Ingrid, drowning her out. "Jake's right. The thing to concentrate on is what we do next. This is probably a matter for the Board of Governors, since Jake has brought up legality and our contracts with each of your populaces is pretty specific. But Jake and I have no intention of shutting out you scientists."

She looked at Jake for confirmation. "No, certainly not," he said, wishing he hadn't defended Lucy so harshly, or so publicly. Or was he just focusing on that to avoid thinking about what was really at stake here?

"The first thing—" Gail said.

"The first thing is to answer Rudy," Nan Shipley said, looking amused. "He's still waiting."

They had all forgotten she was there. In fact, they'd all forgotten Scherer. Jake said, "I'll go. Gail, get things organized." He stood and strode toward the door, grabbing Nan firmly by the elbow as he went by. God, he disliked her.

"All right, I'm removed," she said outside. "You can let go of me now."

"Nan, I don't have to tell you that you shouldn't talk about this to anyone. Don't spread unnecessary alarm. In fact . . . why did Captain Scherer even tell you about the villages in the first place?"

She smiled. "Can't you guess?"

Scherer and Nan. After a moment, Jake shook his head. "No. Not Scherer. No matter what his taste in women. He's too good a soldier."

"You're right, Jake. I didn't think you were that perceptive." She strolled off, allowing him glimpses of her blue flesh through the undulating holes in her tunic. She hadn't answered his question.

No time for that now. Jake hurried to the Mira Corp inflatable and took Scherer's call from orbit.

Everybody wanted to go, except Gail. "You can tell me about it," she told Jake. "There's a lot of things to sort out here. People are still being awakened. The pipe-installing 'bot program has a bug the techs can't find. Thekla's getting the greenhouse up next week. And Liu's people have some sort of dispute over city boundaries. Also, the more I think about it, Jake, the more I think that Scherer's reports don't show anything that we should worry about. So you go and establish diplomatic relations."

"Nothing to worry about? *Aliens?*"

"No. Not unless they attack."

"The air-surveillance reports say that's not likely," Jake said. Actually, the air-surveillance reports were puzzling. Low flight had identified only four villages, with no other settlements within hundreds of miles. Very low flight had brought the skimmers right above the huts at a height of three hundred feet. Lieutenant Wortz reported villagers raising their heads to look up at the aircraft. Yet there had been no running, gathering, pointing, or attacking. The creatures had simply raised their heads, stared, and resumed doing whatever they had been doing, neither scared nor interested.

How could they be neither frightened nor interested? And if that were true, how could they be sentient? But, given the detail Wortz had recorded, cooking pots and woven thatch, how could they not?

The recording had been viewed eagerly by the nine scientists and five Board members, over and over. The aliens were bipedal and bisymmetrical, about four feet tall, covered in thick reddish-brown hair that had immediately earned them the name "Furs." They had long snouts, crests of darker fur high on their backs, squat powerful-looking bodies, and thick tails.

"Balancing tails," George said, "like kangaroos. They can probably jump." He frowned.

"What is it, George?" Jake asked.

"I can't say for sure, of course . . . but Greentrees is a warm planet, warmer than Earth, without much seasonal change because of the very minor axial tilt. And it doesn't have much predatory activity, at least not compared to Earth at the same stage of evolution. But the fur on those aliens, the powerful balancing tail—those usually evolve on a colder, higher-gravity planet. And look at those eyes: two in front *and* one near the top of the head. That evolved on a dangerous world full of flying and walking predators. Greentrees isn't."

"It isn't dangerous now," Ingrid said, "but maybe it was in the past. Maybe they killed all their predators. We did on Earth."

"We don't have eyes on the top of our head, either," Todd said. "Didn't kangaroos have tails like that, before they went extinct? *They* evolved on Earth."

"True," George said, leaning closer to study the images on the screen.

Jake said, "We'll just have to wait until we get there and see in person," which instantly raised the group tension. Who should go? Everyone had an argument for being included.

Finally Jake and Gail decided. "I know you don't like it," Jake told the scientists, "but we made our choices based on who would be useful there and who can't be spared here. Do you know that out of five thousand people we don't have a single real linguist?

We decided English-Chinese translators, say, won't be helpful. Also, we don't want to overwhelm the aliens with too many people. So it's me, George, Ingrid, and Lieutenant Halberg, in the shuttle. Lieutenant Wortz will pilot and stay inside the craft."

To Jake's surprise, William Shipley said, "I think I should go, too."

"You?"

"I'm a doctor. You've included a biologist and a geneticist, but Ingrid works at the DNA level and George isn't trained in pathologies. I think I should go."

Ingrid said, "How the hell would you recognize a pathology on an alien?"

"I can assess the general health of the aliens by comparing them to each other in details you wouldn't notice."

Jake said, it having just occurred to him that Shipley shouldn't be downstairs at all, "Why aren't you doing awakenings aboard ship?"

"I turned it over to Tariji Brown. She's as capable as I am at this point, and she's got an assistant. Besides, Jake, Mira City has plenty of doctors, if no linguists. I'm not vital here."

George said awkwardly, "Will, I'm not sure you're needed there, either." Jake noted yet again that George was comfortable calling the Quaker "Will," one of the few who was. George seemed to have no feelings at all about Shipley's religion.

"Yes, I am needed," Shipley said. "I know that Lieutenant Halberg will have all sorts of weapons to protect you, but it's possible one of you might get hurt anyway in some way the lieutenant can't anticipate."

That made sense. Jake said, "Just one more thing, Doctor. You mentioned weapons. Lieutenant Halberg will be fully armed, everything from tanglefoam to icers, and he'll be supplying the rest of us with small arms. I know you New Quakers don't approve of violence ever, under any circumstances."

"That's right," Shipley said pleasantly, "and I won't personally carry any arms. But your decision is yours, according to your own consciences."

That held a whiff of sanctimony that Jake didn't like. But Shipley's point about having a doctor present was good, and the small skimmer held six. Also, Shipley was a major stockholder, with whom it would be good to cooperate. They might someday want a favor from him. Jake looked at Gail, who shrugged and nodded.

"All right," Jake said, "you're in, Dr. Shipley. We leave as soon as the small skimmer returns from mapping."

It took longer than that. Halberg insisted on each person demonstrating proficiency with the weapons he issued them. This exercise took place well away from the camp, on the open plain from which Larry Smith's Cheyenne had departed. Jake seldom left the disinfected, mostly defoliated, electronically protected confines of Mira City. It felt odd to be so out in the open, standing on untrimmed purple groundcover. What, if anything, might be crawling through it? Some large creatures flew overhead, crying raucously, and he felt again that sense of alienness that often deserted him on his daily Greentrees. What did those flying things eat? How aggressive were they about getting it?

Halberg put them through formation drills for approaching the village, covering each other with weapons, carrying wounded, and retreating to the shuttle. Shipley participated in three of these, portly and puffing. Halberg watched the Quaker doctor expressionlessly. The lieutenant was genemod handsome, like all Scherer's team, and he shared Scherer's uncommunicative stolidity. Finally he was satisfied with everyone's performance.

Gail comlinked Jake as the exercises were concluding. "I've been thinking. Maybe you should take the villagers some presents. Tokens of goodwill."

"Like South Sea islanders? What presents do you choose for an unknown alien, for God's sake?"

"Ask Shipley," Gail said.

Jake didn't see why, but he did as she asked, and to his surprise Shipley had a ready answer.

"I've been thinking along the same lines as Gail. We could bring slightly improved versions of articles they already have and will recognize. Some alloy cooking pots, or hearth grates. They're going to find us eventually and realize we have more advanced things than they do. Pots and a grate would begin to establish that without frightening them."

Jake said, "Where do we get a hearth grate?"

"Gail will find something."

She did, a lattice work of carbon fiber freshly assembled by a die 'bot. She brought it in a Mira Corp rover, roaring over the horizon to their makeshift training ground like cavalry reinforcement. "United Shopping and Parcel, that'll be three million dollars, sir."

"Ha ha," Jake said humorlessly. "How's everything at Mira?"

"Falling apart without you, you vain creature. No, everything's normal. One of Fengmo's people has filed a formal complaint that the city park boundary is off by six inches. I'm beginning to think the Chinese are just as crazy as everybody else, they're just quieter about it."

Six inches. Sentient aliens on Greentrees and six-inch boundary deviations. Jake just shook his head.

Finally, they lifted off and started to the village.

Jake hadn't seen Greentrees from low flight before now; he'd been too busy to leave camp. The twenty-two-hour-sixteen-minute day was nearly done. Long cool shadows slanted across the bluish-purple groundcover. An analog of bacteriorhodopsin, George Fox had told him, closer to a class of Earthly bacteria that converted sunlight to energy than to chloroplasts. The Greentrees plants all used it, which gave them their tranquil purplish hues.

From the groundcover the tall, narrow trees rose like graceful spires. The blue river wound its slow, broad way between low hills, through groves and meadows. A herd of something large and gray lumbered toward a lake. "We're calling them 'teelies,' " George said into Jake's ear. "Warm-blooded herbivores, brains the size of walnuts. Move very slowly."

"Why don't they get eaten?"

"They do. But not easily—that's a thick carapace you're seeing on the adults. Also, there's speculation that their flesh tastes bad to the dominant predators."

"God bless evolution," Jake said.

The landscape didn't change as they covered hundreds of miles. Restful, beautiful, monotonous. This part of Greentrees lacked mountains, although they rose elsewhere, sharp and high. It was a young planet compared to Earth.

"Approaching the village," Lieutenant Wortz said in her guttural accent. "Landing imminent."

Jake wondered briefly if he'd ever heard any of Scherer's crew talk without stiff military lingo. Halberg, maybe, but not Wortz, whose English was limited.

Jake's brief glimpse of the village from the air looked exactly the same as the recordings. Thatch-roofed huts, outdoor stone hearths, small fields beyond. A few Furs walked between the huts; when the humans emerged from the lander, they stopped and watched.

Watched—but nothing else. The three adults and one child didn't flee, or approach, or as far as Jake could see, change expression. He took a deep breath. "Let's go, people."

Halberg left the skimmer first, ready to cover the others if necessary. Then Jake, followed by the scientists, with Shipley bringing up the rear. Jake had learned long ago how detached and artificial could seem the most important moments of one's life, as if you watched yourself from the outside. *I'm walking toward humanity's first contact with aliens,* Jake thought, and although his chest tightened, he still felt like an actor playing a faintly ludicrous part.

The four Furs had not moved. Weren't they going to do *something*? Apparently not. Jake stopped, Halberg to his right, a few yards from the closest one and smiled. No response.

"Hello," Jake said carefully.

Nothing.

"Humans," he said, pointing to himself and then Halberg.

Nothing.

Behind him, Shipley said, "Give him the gifts."

Jake half turned and Shipley was right there, ready with the cooking pot, which Jake had forgotten about. Ingrid and George were undoubtedly recording. Jake took the pot and offered it to the Fur. The other three Furs had not moved, even the child.

The Fur looked at the shiny pot but made no move to take it. Jake held it out for ten seconds, twenty, thirty. Finally he put it on the ground at the Fur's feet and, smiling, pointed from it to the alien.

"Back away from the gift," Shipley suggested, "so he realizes we're leaving the pot for them."

Jake did. The Fur watched impassively. A full minute went by. Then the Fur walked away, leaving the pot on the ground. Halberg tensed. The Fur went to the edge of the closest field, picked up what seemed to be a primitive hoe, and began digging up plants. The other Furs started to move about what was presumably their normal business.

George said, "I think we've been rejected."

Jake said, "More like they barely registered us. Just a momentary interruption, then routine as usual."

Ingrid said, "What now? Can we go into the village?"

Halberg said, "Counterindicated."

"Oh, for God's sake, Lieutenant," she snapped, "they're obviously not belligerent. And what's the point of coming at all if we don't make some sort of connection?"

George said, "Jake?"

"Might as well." He felt helpless. What did you do when aliens considered you irrelevant?

They walked forward as a group. The adult with the child had moved to a cookfire and was stirring something in a large pot. It smelled vile. As the humans approached, the Fur looked up but didn't stop stirring. The child stood as impassive as the adult.

Children, if they weren't shy, were usually curious. Slowly Jake reached inside the pocket of his coverall and pulled out a small flashlight. It was bright orange, with a blue button. Jake pressed the button and a beam of light shone onto the stones of the hearth. Jake released the button and held the flashlight out to the child. He heard someone draw in a quick breath. Images of animals savagely defending their young flashed across Jake's brain, but he went on holding out the flashlight.

The child didn't take it.

Jake laid it on the edge of the hearth and moved back a step. The child didn't pick up the flashlight. The adult Fur went on stirring the pot.

"Jesus Christ," Ingrid said. "They're either stupid or blind."

George said, "If they're not going to notice anything we do, then I want to take some samples."

"Counterindicated!" Halberg said. George ignored the soldier and stepped up to the child. He put his hand on the child's furry head, and Jake tensed for attack. The child looked up briefly at George and then returned to watching the pot. Deftly George snipped a handful of fur with the cutter concealed in his palm. Neither Fur reacted.

In the field, the other adult hoed. The fourth Fur had gone inside a hut.

Now, perversely, Jake *wanted* some reaction from the aliens. Attack, fury, anything but this stolid pretense that the humans barely existed, were somehow as insubstantial as ghosts. He said, "We're moving toward that hut."

Halberg didn't even say, "Counterindicated." Maybe even he was frustrated by this nonbehavior. The five humans moved to the open door of the nearest hut. No one tried to stop them. Jake peered inside, George eagerly beside him, Ingrid and Shipley crowding behind.

The inside of the hut held a pallet of tree branches, a cooking pot full of the same smelly stuff as the first Fur's culinary efforts, and an adult Fur nursing an infant. She lay on the ground on her side, the baby lying beside her with its mouth fastened on the teat exposed from underneath the thick reddish fur. She stared at them without reacting.

Jake felt an odd reluctance to remain. "We've gone far enough into these . . . people's privacy as it is. Back to the skimmer."

The group moved out of the hut and walked back to the skimmer. Not one Fur looked up or ceased work as they boarded and lifted off.

"Something," George Fox said, "is very wrong with this picture."

# 6

William Shipley sat in meeting and knew he was making a mess of it.

Meeting for Worship was usually the best time of Shipley's week. He emptied his mind and waited, in blessed silence, for the inner light. If it did not come to him, it might come to another, who would be moved to rise and offer vocal ministry. From these voices, over time, came the harmony and simplicity of truth, and Shipley left the meetinghouse feeling at peace with himself. This was true even if the entire hour passed with no one saying anything. In the shared silence was a shared spirituality, sweeter than words.

But not this week. Shipley looked at the Friends seated on the simple foamcast benches of the new meetinghouse. It, too, was foamcast, a plain windowless room without distracting adornment. New Quakers, like the old, had no icons, liturgy, priests, or theology.

They had been meeting outdoors, but it had rained hard three Sundays in a row, and so each meeting had taken the time and allocated the resources to erect a meetinghouse. Nineteen of them dotted Mira City, which otherwise consisted still of inflatables with the occasional converted section of the *Ariel* a gleaming hard anomaly. In the medina, Faisal said, the Arabs had begun constructing a wooden mansion with wood from the newly formed, ecologically safe Mira Logging Company. So far the mansion was merely a frame. Mira City was green inflatable buildings and gray foamcast meetinghouses.

Nearly a hundred Friends sat in silence, eyes cast down or closed, for half an hour. A few were missing. Alia Benton had fallen and fractured her femur; Shipley had her in a monitor cast that delivered genemod meds to help the bone mend faster. Paul Dubrowski had developed an allergy to something on Greentrees, which was interesting because it meant the human immune system was adjusting to new irritants. Marlie and Harrel Forrester had been moved to attend a different meeting this week, as had young Guy Lowell, whom Shipley suspected of interest in a young woman there. And, of course, Naomi was missing.

But his daughter was not what was distracting Shipley from worship.

Cameron Farley rose. She said, "I wrestled with myself this week. A coworker at the greenhouse, not a Friend, wore a necklace of beautiful pink stones. I wanted it. I asked her if she would sell it for Mira script, and she said she would. I have the script. But I know that the necklace is pulling me away from simplicity. I feel it. I would not own the necklace, it would own me. I haven't bought it . . . but I still want to." She sat down, a beautiful young woman troubled in her mind by a string of pink stones.

No, by a struggle with materialistic desires. A person preoccupied with things is ill-suited to sit in silence and listen for the still small voice of God.

Nor, Shipley thought, is a person preoccupied with genetic information.

George Fox, Ingrid Johnson, and Todd McCallum were holding a meeting—so different from *this* meeting—later today to discuss the results of their genetic analysis of the hair taken from the child Fur. The biologist and two geneticists had been working furiously for a week. In that time Jake had led expeditions to two of the other three villages, and he, too, was going to report the outcomes. A small group had been dropped off just this morning outside the first village, to camp there and see if prolonged contact made any difference to the Furs' impassivity. And none of this should have been cluttering up Shipley's mind during Meeting for Worship.

Old David Ornish rose. "New Quakers don't need or want a lot of things in their lives. That's why we came here. So our children can be freed from the relentless pressure of owning things and find the Light." He creaked down again.

Ten more minutes passed. Then Olivia Armstead rose and Shipley suppressed an uncharitable groan. Olivia was an intelligent, educated woman with no STOP code. More than once someone had risen after twenty or thirty minutes to tell Olivia, "Friend, bring your message to a conclusion."

"These aliens on this planet," she began with no preamble. By now everyone knew about the aliens, most people watching the recordings whenever they had pauses in the endless work of setting up a pioneering society. "Historically there are five states in which diplomatic relationships can exist between peoples."

And they were going to hear all five, Shipley knew. He made himself listen. If Olivia was moved to share this, then it was part of her Light and a contribution to the truth that emerged only as the Light brought out the best in each worshipper.

Olivia said, "First, there is complete detachment, no relationship at all, as when countries refuse to recognize or trade with each other.

"Second, there is healthy negotiation from a basically allied position, with mutual-aid pacts, trade agreements, arbitration, open borders. This is the relationship that we New Quakers have with the other contractees of Mira Corp on Greentrees.

"Third, there is covert struggle, with no open hostility but no negotiation, either, and with subversive actions to undermine each other.

"Fourth, there is a dominant/dependent relationship. It may be benevolent or tyrannical. This is what imperial powers have had with their colonies throughout Earth's history.

"Fifth, there is war.

"We must not engage in war with the Furs. Nor in dictatorship, nor in covert struggle, nor in pretending these people do not exist. We must treat them as allies." She sat down.

Shipley was impressed. Olivia had been not only intelligent but relatively brief. But how did you treat as "allies," with mutual aid and trade pacts and contractual agreements, people who were treating you with "complete detachment"?

No one else spoke. When the hour was over, David Ornish reached for the hand of the person sitting next to him. Everyone raised their heads and then clasped hands. The shift from inner faith to outer activism was complete, and the Meeting for Worship was over.

Outside, people mingled and chatted. This meeting was a sociable lot. Many Friends looked refreshed and cleansed. Shipley thought that he himself might as well have spent the time growing med cultures. He had been incapable of receiving the Light.

He hurried along the unpaved "streets." These were lately clean of garbage or debris, and around a few of the inflatables bloomed beds of those transplanted native flowers approved by Maggie Striker, the ecologist. Before the Furs had been discovered, George Fox had been creating a taxonomy and genetic history for Greentrees flora. Now that he was working day and night on the alien samples, people had started to invent their own names for the prettiest flowers. Shipley had heard the same delicate mauve blossom referred to as "moonweed," "Greentrees lace," and "sweet Leela."

When he reached the inflatable, Ingrid Johnson had already begun talking. The scientists and Board of Governors listened with all the rapt focus Shipley had not been able to summon in meeting.

"Todd and I finished the genome analysis. In the short version: the Furs' genome is DNA-based, like everything else we've encountered in space, which only strengthens the panspermia theory. They're pretty much like Earth mammals: warm-blooded, probably viviparous. The crest of darker fur on their backs seem to occur only in males. The genes that correspond to a neural system in the other Greentrees mammals, however, are not very numerous. They're an old species—there is a lot of incorporated fossilized genetic material, from analogues to viruses. We've started matching protein expression to genetic sequence, but of course without tissue samples from the Furs we're just guessing. The basis for our guesses is the data we have from other Greentrees' mammals, which may or may not be analogous."

Todd said, with his quiet smile that Shipley always found so much more appealing than his wife's assertiveness, "In other words, we don't know anything."

"Not true, Todd," Ingrid said, contradictory even with her spouse. "We have some information."

"Okay," Gail said. She seemed to be chairing the meeting. "We can hear the long form later. Will we nongeneticists understand it?"

"No," Ingrid said.

"Yes," Todd said, "if we explain well enough."

Gail smiled. "Who's next? Jake?"

"We visited the other three villages in the cluster, if that's what it is. The reaction was exactly the same: total indifference. We might as well not have existed. We left some more gifts, and when we went back the Furs were using the cooking pots and hearth grates, but they gave no sign the things were in any way connected to us.

"One village is the same size as the first one. The other two are much smaller. In fact, one has only sixteen Furs in it and seven empty huts."

Shipley said, despite his vow to simply listen, "They're dying out?"

Jake made an odd gesture with his left hand, swiping it sideways through the air. "It would seem so. We actually looked for some sort of graveyard, but we didn't find any markers for it. Maybe they don't have any death rites."

George Fox said, "I'm a biologist, not an anthropologist, but there's no human civilization at that level that didn't have *some* death rites."

"Well, then, maybe they do," Jake said. Shipley saw that the subject made him uncomfortable. "We didn't see it."

Gail said, "Could there have been a plague or something? And these are the only survivors?"

"No," Lucy Lasky said. "That's not possible."

Shipley studied her. Lucy spoke firmly but met no one's eyes. Color mottled her cheeks. Clearly she was still deeply ashamed of her breakdown on the ship and thought that because of it, no one would take her seriously. Equally clearly, she was certain of what she was saying.

It was always the conscientious, hardworking ones, Shipley thought, who were the most vulnerable. The people who cared. Those who didn't care, who just wanted to get through the job or the day or the hour and to hell with everyone who didn't like it—those people were protected from shame by their own indifference.

Like Naomi.

Lucy forced herself to continue. "I know I've said this before. But there is no fossil record of the Furs. They weren't a numerous species wiped out by plague. They didn't even evolve here. I've been to the village with Jake and took subterranean soundings. There's some archaeological debris there, which there isn't here by Mira City. The Furs might have been there as long as a thousand years. But no longer. There just isn't any paleontological evidence."

Todd said, "But, Lucy, if they'd been here even a thousand years, there would be more of them. The gene pool is really small."

"*Yes,*" Lucy said. "That's what I'm saying. The evidence doesn't add up. The Furs didn't evolve here. They were brought here, no more than, say, twelve hundred E-years ago. They were *brought.*"

"By whom, Lucy?" George said gently. "We've never found any evidence of sentient life anywhere outside the solar system. Let alone a star-faring civilization. Surely we'd have detected them—or, more likely, they'd have contacted us. We're not all that far from home, remember, in interstellar terms."

"I know all that," Lucy said, not without dignity.

Shipley thought suddenly of that object streaming past the *Ariel* at ninety-eight percent of c, back when the ship had still been light-years from Greentrees. Everyone had finally decided it had been either a computer error or a natural object, convinced by the fact that the "object" didn't seem able to detect the *Ariel.* Only Erik Halberg had maintained otherwise.

Lucy continued, "But the evidence on Greentrees still says that the Furs were brought here."

"You mean, absence of evidence," Ingrid said. "You've only offered what isn't here. As far as we know yet."

Gail said, "Captain Scherer?"

Scherer said in his German accent, "The satellite data fail to show some additional settlements of Furs on Greentrees. But I caution. We have a good resolution, to a quarter meter, but the computer still orthorectifies all data, it does not finish yet. And the planet is big. If some settlements are small and put themselves under many trees, we maybe not find them. Not yet, anyway. We look, still.

Nothing we discover presents a security risk to humans."

Ingrid said acidly, "You don't know if there's a biological risk. Contamination by parasite, for instance. That's why Todd and I need to—"

George Fox cut her off. "There can't be just this one group of Fur villages, Captain Scherer. That really would be anomalous."

Scherer said stiffly, "We find only one group."

Lucy looked close to tears. Jake said tactfully, "Let's consider for a moment that they might be an exiled group, dropped out here by their own species as . . . oh, a penal colony or political exiles or medical quarantine."

Shipley said, startled, "Medical quarantine?"

George's eyes lit up. "Maybe that explains their zombielike behavior."

"If that's true," Gail said, "could their disease be dangerous to us? Doctor?"

"It's rare for diseases to jump Terran species, let alone species with entirely different evolutionary paths. And any microbe would need time to adapt to us. No, I don't think we're in danger." Gail looked relieved.

Ingrid said impatiently, "An entire other planet as a quarantine area or penal colony seems a bit extreme, if you ask me. Besides, I'm still not convinced the furry beasts just don't belong here."

Shipley said mildly, "They're not beasts."

Gail broke in. "Well, wherever they came from, for whatever reason, the Furs are here. Looking at it scientifically is interesting, but from a practical standpoint, I can't see that it's going to make much difference to Mira City. There are only a handful of Furs, they're over a hundred miles away, they aren't bothering us. If they indicate they don't want us camped beside their village, we'll stop bothering them. But our plans for Mira City aren't going to be affected at all, as far as I can see. Anybody disagree?"

Everyone stared at her. Staggered, Shipley said, "Gail . . . you're just going to ignore them? The only contact humanity has had with sentient aliens?"

Faisal bin Saud, silent until now, said, "They do not sound very sentient to me. I agree with Gail. These Furs are negligible to our plans."

Gail said, "What do you want us to do, Doctor? We sent a report to Earth by quee . . . haven't we?"

"Um, not yet," George said. "Since we're so limited in our quee transmissions, we wanted to gather more definitive information first. Besides, we've all been so busy studying the Furs that—"

"Well, that's the real problem, as I see it," Gail said, with sudden heat. "Half our scientists are either at the Fur village or working day and night on Fur data in the lab, and work is getting neglected here. Dr. Shipley, I appreciate that you at least have stuck around in case some human actually needs medical help. But Ingrid, Todd, George—Thekla is complaining that your input into the agricultural effort has come to a complete halt. George, we don't have any kind of index of possibly poisonous plants or creatures. Jake, administrative problems are—"

"All right, all right," Jake said testily, surprising Shipley. Jake usually had an outer shell of forced calm. "We see your point, Gail."

"Good. Who's out at the village now for this extended campout? And who thinks they're leaving for the village this afternoon?"

"I am," Lucy said. No one contradicted her. Mira City didn't have urgent need of an evolutionary paleontologist.

"I am," Ingrid said. "Tissue samples—"

"Tissue samples can wait," Gail said.

"Issues of possible biological contamination—"

Jake broke in. "We'll just have to take our chances. But I'll tell you what, Ingrid—you write the report to Earth."

Ingrid smiled, pleased as a stroked cat. Whoever broke the news to Earth would have an instant place in history, Shipley knew. Jake knew his people. Ingrid would stop clamoring to go to the village. And since quee link could only take so much data for the stored energy they had, the report would be short enough to not consume too much of Ingrid's time.

Captain Scherer said with his precise diction, "Five people stay now by the alien village. Private Mueller, for security. Two scientists—"

"From our genetics staff," Todd said with strained cordiality. "They were supposed to fill in only while Ingrid and I analyzed the alien hair samples. This afternoon—"

"No, you two are staying here," Gail said. "One of your staff can stay; you pick. Get the other back here when the skimmer takes Lucy. This is a colonization effort, remember, not a scientific expedition."

*And you people signed contracts,* she didn't say. Shipley knew everyone heard the words anyway. Jake would have been more subtle. But Jake had lapsed into pensiveness, seeming not to listen.

Captain Scherer continued, "One of Prince Faisal's group—"

"My fifth son," Faisal said. Evidently this was news to Gail, if not to Jake. "We are interested in the natives. Salah investigates for us."

"Interested how?" Gail said, frowning.

Faisal smiled his charming, impenetrable smile. "Purely intellectually, Gail."

"Good. And the fifth person—"

"—is Miss Frayne," Captain Scherer said.

Shipley's heart jolted. Naomi? What was she doing there? She hadn't told him.

"What is she doing there?" Gail said. "She's not a scientist."

Scherer said, "She asks to go."

Gail said, "Half the city wants to go, to at least have a look at the aliens! Captain, who authorized this?"

"I did," Scherer said.

The table fell silent. Scherer stared straight ahead, but the flesh above his tight collar throbbed. Shipley watched it, dazed. Naomi at the Fur village . . .

Gail said levelly, "Why, Captain? You have the right to do so, of course, but why did you give Nan Frayne permission and passage to the village?"

"I see no reason to say no to Miss Frayne," Scherer said, which was no reason at all. Shipley's chest turned over. What was going on between Naomi and this man? Not the obvious, Shipley suspected. Scherer was too controlled, too militarily correct, for sexual bribery, and anyway Naomi hardly seemed someone who would appeal to him. So what?

Jake moved the meeting past the awkward moment. "All right, then, we've finished with the Fur village. Ingrid, pick one of your staff to stay there and comlink the other to be ready for pickup when Captain Scherer takes Lucy. Lucy, do you need an assistant?"

Faisal said, "My son Salah would be honored to assist you, Dr. Lasky. He is untrained in paleontology, of course, but then so is nearly everyone else on Greentrees except yourself. And Salah can provide you with anything in our compound's power, anything at all."

Lucy knew a good thing when she saw it. She said, "Thank you, Mr. Saud. I'm sure Salah will be very useful." Jake Holman scowled.

"Then let's move on to legitimate colony business," Gail said. "Jake, about the solar panels—"

Shipley stopped listening. He slipped out of the room, avoiding everyone's eyes. Outside, he walked in a straight line to the edge of the human activity, nodding brusquely when anyone spoke to him but not slowing down. By the time he cleared the last inflatable, he was puffing.

Beyond the embryonic city, the wide river flowed between low grassy banks dotted with wildflowers. These flowers were beautiful; perhaps all flowers were beautiful. Ancient Egyptians had included flowers among the treasures sealed into tombs with the dead. However, since George Fox was still testing native flora for substances toxic to humans, and since nonedible flowers were not high on the biologist's list, no one knew yet how many of these blossoms might be poisonous.

So far the humans had been remarkably lucky. They were, according to George Fox, in the best possible position. Because life on Greentrees was DNA-based, it was possible to alter the genome of many plants to make them digestible to the Earthly interlopers. The altered seeds would be cultivated as soon as the geneticists and the agriculturists were done tinkering with them. On the other hand, Earth's and Greentrees' evolutionary paths had been different enough that the local parasites hadn't evolved to colonize human guts, eyes, or brains. The same might be true of plant toxins as well; they had evolved to affect other life, not humans. Only the predatory vine nicknamed "red creeper" had proved dangerous. It tangled small mammals in remarkably fast-moving, ground-level tendrils and dissolved them. All red creeper had been eradicated inside the city perimeter.

This section of riverbank, however, with its lush wild growth, was still outside the perimeter and off-limits, even though the river was the reason humans had settled at this site. Testing the river water had been the biologist's first job. George had determined that filters were needed, due to high traces of minerals Shipley couldn't remember, plus unidentified microorganisms that might—

What did any of that matter now! Shipley pulled out his comlink.

In their desire for simplicity, New Quakers didn't usually carry comlinks. But Quakerism had always been a more flexible religion than outsiders imagined. Individual conscience counted more than rules, and Shipley was one of a few dozen physicians for five thousand people. He carried a comlink so patients could contact him quickly, just as he used a computer to aid in diagnosis. The point was not to turn one's back on technology, as Larry Smith's Cheyenne were attempting to do, but to subordinate it to the living souls of men and women. This was the first time Shipley had ever used his comlink for a personal reason.

He didn't know Naomi's private code, if she had one. Of course she did. But he knew the code for Private Mueller, a young man even more silent than most of the Swiss security people. Shipley keyed in the code. Mueller answered instantly.

"*Ja.* Private Mueller."

"This is William Shipley. May I speak to Naomi Frayne?"

"I key you." Another shrill.

"Yes?"

"Naomi? This is your father."

"Ah, Daddy. Just noticed your derelict daughter is gone?"

Shipley said, "Why didn't you tell me you were going to camp by the alien village?"

"Why don't you tell me that you care one way or the other? I won't believe you, of course, but you can tell me anyway."

He contained his despair. "Naomi, what are you doing there? Ingrid Johnson says there could be a chance of contracting parasites or microorganisms from—"

"Tell you what, Daddy, if I get alien fleas I promise not to bring them around to you."

He said nothing, the familiar hurt and frustration and guilt swamping him. Oh, Naomi—

Her voice unexpectedly softened. "You won't believe this, but I'm actually working. How about that, Dad?"

"Working?"

"Observing. Making notes on the Furs. Seeing if we can find their communication mode with each other and maybe decode it."

"Naomi, you don't know anything about—" He stopped. Wrong, wrong.

"Anything about anything, is that what you were going to say, Daddy? Poor untrained useless Nan. But this work consists mostly of sitting still, watching carefully, and running recording equipment. Startling as it is, I can actually do that as well as a trained baboon."

He said humbly, "I'm sorry. Are you . . . is the work interesting?"

Again her voice warmed unexpectedly. "It *is* interesting, in a hopeless sort of way. Your worthless daughter might even end up making a minor scientific contribution."

"That's wonderful, honey." He wanted to ask her about Scherer, about why the captain had brought her there, but he was suddenly afraid of jeopardizing this temporary, unhoped-for rapport. "Take care of yourself."

"You, too, Dad. Bye."

She cut the link. Shipley stood staring at the comlink in his pudgy hand, then out at the curve of the river through the tranquil purple land. He saw neither. Was it possible that Naomi . . . if she actually found something constructive to do . . . might she also find her inner light?

Joy filled him. Shipley closed his eyes. Even though he knew it was premature, was unearned, was in fact ridiculous, he gave himself to the sweetness of grace and relief.

"Doctor?"

Jake must have followed him from the meeting. Shipley opened his eyes and smiled.

"Doctor, you're out beyond the perimeter. This area hasn't been disinfected."

Shipley said, "Jake, have you ever thought a situation was hopeless and then suddenly some completely unforeseen door opened out of it? A door you had mistakenly thought led only to more disaster?"

To Shipley's surprise, Jake turned his back and walked abruptly away.

# 7

He shouldn't have done that. He hadn't ever done anything that revealing before.

It was this planet, Jake thought. He tried to walk casually back into the meeting, as if he'd merely gone to use the toilet. Which must be what everyone assumed because Gail kept on talking without even glancing at him. Did she think Shipley, too, had had a sudden bladder emergency, as if the two of them were some sort of urinary clones? Who knew what Gail thought. Who cared.

Jake cared. He made himself sit down, look interested, get himself in control. Usually that was easy. It wasn't the planet that was fucking with him. It was Shipley.

Gail tended to dismiss Shipley as a rich, harmless religious nut, the nuttiness inexplicably coupled with unusual skill as a physician. Jake had tried to view Shipley the same way. But something about the man disturbed him. Some quality of perception, of penetration.

*"Have you ever thought a situation was hopeless and then suddenly some completely unforeseen door opened out of it? A door you had mistakenly thought led only to more disaster?"*

Jesus Christ, Shipley hadn't been talking about Jake! He knew that. But he had stalked off stiffly anyway. There was no better method of suggesting guilt. He, Jake, was a platinum fool.

Gail said, "Jake? What do you think?"

He said, not missing a beat, "I think we need to consider all the implications before we make a decision on this."

Gail nodded, just as if he'd actually said something. Faisal bin

Saud said, "Yes, that is what I have said all along. If we—" Jake tuned out again.

He looked across the room at Lucy Lasky. In profile, her small face looked even more serious. Her thin arms, bare to the elbows, stirred him. She leaned forward a moment and her fine brown hair, cut to the angle of her delicate jaw, swung over her face and then back. She nodded at something Gail was arguing forcefully.

*Lucy,* Jake imagined himself saying, *there's something I need to tell someone. I've kept it secret for fifteen years, and it's the entire reason any of us are on Greentrees in the first place. But now that we're here—that I'm here—the momentum is gone. I've lost the inertia that kept me moving forward, and the secret is going to crush me.*

"—sixteen percent of energy from water power by—"

"—down to one millionth per part and then—"

"—geothermal energy tapped into successfully so we can—"

*You must know what it's like to teeter on the rim of fear. I suspect you live there all the time, Lucy. Why is that?*

"—jurisdiction should fall to—"

"—agreement we made prior to the vote held for—"

"—greenhouse space allotments according to—"

*Lucy, I did something genuinely heinous. And got away with it. Should that matter now, after so long, so far away from Earth? Everyone involved is long dead. Why does it still matter to me?*

He would never say it. Not Jake Holman, Jake the successful, Jake the smooth talker.

"Jake, do you agree with Faisal?" Gail asked.

"I think he's raised a really interesting issue," Jake said, "but I'd like to hear a bit more about that last aspect before making up my mind."

"Good point," Todd said. "You always cut to the heart of things, Jake."

Three days later in the late afternoon, Jake sat at his computer, accessing data in the ship's library. Very little of the *Ariel* was left in orbit, or left as a ship. After everyone had been awakened and transported downstairs, and all the gear shipped down as well, cannibalization had begun. Everything went as planned, in itself remarkable. Whole sections of the *Ariel* had been brought down, controlled by thrusters and parachutes. Those sections were now functioning hydroponic vats, genetics lab, infirmary, water filtration equipment, and half a dozen other structures.

One chunk of the vast ship, however, remained in orbit. It included orbital defenses, sensors, and the main library. With the comlink satellites in place, the library could be accessed, copied, added to from any terminal on Greentrees. What it could not be was physically destroyed by activity on the planet, natural or human.

Jake said, "Quee-link data. Non-solar system. Most recent."

"Accessing," the terminal said. "Spoken, on-screen, or printout?"

"On-screen. Translate all to standard English."

Quee-link messages were short; they required considerable energy. Someday the *Ariel* would stop transmitting. Of the ships in orbit around other colony worlds, one, the *Phoenix,* had already ceased. Whatever had happened to the quee, neither Earth nor the other three worlds would ever know about it. A settled colony might have the energy to run a quee, but hardly the elaborate manufacturies to build a new one.

Quee reports appeared on-screen from the UAF vessel, the *Winston Churchill,* and from the Chinese ship, the *Good Fortune.* Jake scanned them, slowed by the computer's strange translations of Chinese, a cross-cultural software problem never really solved in a hundred fifty years: *Population now sixteen thousand of souls in successful spirit . . . Heaven makes water system crisis not chronological . . .*

He was looking for what was not there. No sentient life had been discovered on either Avalon or New Hope. Nor did either contain any new information about developments on Earth.

Ingrid had composed her momentous quee message to Earth about the Greentrees Furs. The message, a model of compressed data, had been sent two days ago, after approval by the Board of Governors meeting in special session. Quee still had the power to awe Jake. Instantaneous transmission, thanks to the quantum entanglement he didn't understand at all, across sixty-nine light-years of space . . . to be received by whom? What was Earth like now, seventy years after the *Ariel* had left her?

The message had been addressed, like all their quee messages, to the World Governance Alliance based in Geneva, a body of useful figurehead value and no actual power. The answer had come back an hour later, in English:

**WGA disbanded. Geneva under siege. Cannot help with alien invasion. Proceed at discretion.**

"What the bloody hell?" Thekla had said. " 'Alien invasion'?"

George exploded, "Doesn't it even register that we've discovered the first aliens in the *universe*?"

Liu Fengmo's quiet voice somehow rose above the indignant babble. "This is a military person who speaks by quee. His interest is limited to his own desperate situation in Geneva."

*Desperate situation.* Jake looked closely at Liu Fengmo. The Chinese, small and neat and self-contained as a biochip, rarely spoke of anything but pragmatic matters. Jake had never heard Liu speculate before . . . although Liu's words didn't carry the tentative ring of speculation. Liu, Jake suddenly recalled, had been a soldier in General Chu's disastrous war against India. *"His interest is limited to his own desperate situation."* Jake felt sudden coldness at his spine.

Todd McCallum had spoken for all of them. "What could be going on back on Earth?"

No one knew. No other quee message had come since.

Now a diffident voice interrupted him. "Jake? Are you busy?"

"No, come in," Jake said automatically, blanking the screen.

Frank Byfield stood in the Mira office doorway. He was the head of one of Mira City's political and judicial subdivisions, Section Six. "Do you have that decision for me? On the supplies dispute?"

Jake had completely forgotten to bring it up at the Board of Governors' meeting.

"Frank, they're still considering all the factors involved. I know you're eager to get this settled, and you're absolutely right. I'll see what I can do to hurry them along."

Byfield said unhappily, "Thanks. We really need to know before we can move forward at all."

"I know you do," Jake said warmly. "I'll talk to Gail myself this afternoon."

"I appreciate it." Byfield left.

God, the administrative details in running a colony! Why hadn't he understood that back on Earth? He *had* understood it; he'd been a lawyer, after all. Not a great lawyer, but adequate. And now, with six thousand people (minus a thousand Cheyenne) in his care, he wasn't even adequate.

At least he could take care of Byfield's problem right now.

He comlinked Gail, who said, "Jake? Why are you bringing this up *now*? It should have been thrashed out at the meeting."

"Yes, but Frank Byfield hadn't yet given me all the information. Now he has. The situation is that—"

"For God's sake, I can't listen to it now, I'm about to descend fifty feet underground into the new iron mine. The 'bots are finished with the preliminary excavation. You knew that."

"Yes, you're absolutely right, but—"

"Find me later." She broke the link.

Jake stood, took several deep breaths. He went to find Lieutenant Wortz.

She had returned with the skimmer. Jake caught her heading through the warm dusk for the women's baths, still in the uniform Scherer required of his people, with a towel slung around her neck. Jake wondered briefly what she'd look like naked. Too fleshy, he decided. He'd better resume the libido suppressors.

He was lying to himself. He wasn't going to resume them.

"Lieutenant Wortz. Can you take me to the Fur village? I know you're off-duty, but no one else is available."

She didn't react to the lie. Maybe it wasn't a lie; Jake hadn't checked. Gretchen Wortz said in her careful English, "To the Fur village? Now? I return just from there."

"I know. I'm sorry. Something's come up."

She didn't ask what; Scherer had his soldiers trained to military acceptance of authority, and on Greentrees authority was Jake. Usually this irritated him, but now he was grateful for it. Twenty minutes to walk to the skimmer, parked out beyond the electronic perimeter that kept away Greentrees' predators, and they were in the air. Two of the three small moons were up, the close one moving visibly across the darkening sky. Sunset happened fast here; Mira City sat not far from the equator.

Lieutenant Wortz surprised him by offering actual conversation. "Look down, Mr. Holman. The rhinos."

Below them moved a herd of warm-blooded, turtlelike predators. George Fox had named them something, Jake couldn't remember what, but not "rhinos." He grinned. People were using their familiar names for the unfamiliar, even though the creatures below looked nothing like rhinoceroses.

He said, "They're so slow."

"*Ja.* But I see the fast eaters. The lions. They live in the trees."

Jake tried to imagine tree-living lions, but gave up. Lieutenant Wortz said nothing else.

Expertly she set the skimmer down in the "meadow" beside the alien village. Purplish groundcover made a lush carpet. A few Furs were working fields. They didn't look up as Jake walked, watching carefully for red creeper, toward the cluster of huts set between the meadow and a wood of tall bluish trees. The human camp had been pitched on the east side of the village. Lucy Lasky was alone in the largest inflatable, working at a terminal.

"Hello, Lucy."

"Jake? What is it?"

She stood, looking alarmed. Of course an unannounced visit by the Mira Corp president would make her think something was wrong. Jake said quickly, "Nothing's wrong. I'm just making a routine visit to see how the work is going."

Now alarm was replaced by wariness. She thought he was checking up on her: her diligence or her relevance or her sanity. The incident on the *Ariel* still haunted Lucy. She said stiffly, "The work is going fine."

"Actually, Lucy, Dr. Shipley wanted me to look in quickly on his daughter. He's . . . concerned. Although I'd prefer you didn't mention that to Nan Frayne."

He watched her relax. "No, of course. But Nan's doing fine, too. In fact, better than fine. She got a Fur to talk to her."

"She did!" His surprise was genuine.

Lucy smiled, a rare event, and he saw how it lit up her whole face. "She did it by pure nerve. She stood in front of a Fur on its way to a field and wouldn't get out of its face. Every time the Fur moved, Nan did, too. Lieutenant Halberg had a fit."

"I'll bet he did. She was risking her life."

"She didn't think so, because they're so passive. Anyway, the Fur tried to get around her for twenty minutes. Can you believe it? Finally the Fur just gave up and sat down on the ground. Nan sat, too, still crowding the Fur face-to-face, and started to talk. Just her own name, pointing to herself, over and over. And the Fur eventually answered!"

"What did it say?" His heart had begun to thud slowly. *Alien communication.*

"Nan doesn't know. It was just one sound, sort of like 'eeeeeerat.' It might be a name, or not. It took her five hours to get that much."

"Five hours of saying 'Nan'?"

"Yes!" Lucy laughed. Jake realized he'd never heard her laugh before. "And Nan's still there. This only happened today, which is why you don't have a report on it. Do you want to see?"

"In a minute. Is Halberg still standing by, covering Nan with some weapon or other?"

"Yes!" She laughed again. "They resemble one of those unmoving medieval tableaux."

"And your work? Any breakthroughs?"

Her mirth vanished. "No. Just confirmation of what I already told you all."

"That the Furs didn't evolve here. That's what I want to hear more about. Can we walk and talk? I've been sitting in the skimmer."

"Okay."

Outside, the air smelled sweetly tangy. They set out across the meadow, parallel to the edge of the wood. The tall narrow trees cast long shadows blurred by the purple groundcover. Jake drew Lucy out about her work, using every conversational skill he had, and after a while she began to talk freely, without her usual muted despair. He listened without interruption, letting her say everything she wanted to get out, sometimes nodding respectfully. The lobes of her small ears were delicate and pink as shells.

Slowly Jake felt himself unknotting.

"Do you believe me, Jake?"

"Yes. I do. I don't see how the Furs could be native to Greentrees. Not with all the facts you've uncovered."

She let out a deep breath, somewhere between a sob and a sigh.

"Lucy . . . do you like it here?"

She answered more quickly than he expected, as if she'd already given the question considerable thought. "Yes. I do, even with everything that . . . happened. Greentrees is beautiful, and I can do work here that nobody ever would have let me anywhere near on Earth."

"Is that why you came? For the work?"

"No." After a moment she added, "I volunteered to the Wellcome Trust because I couldn't stand to be on Earth any longer. Or even anywhere in the solar system. It won't make sense to you, maybe, but there was . . . my husband left me for somebody else. He didn't even wait for our marriage contract to run out."

She said it starkly, without emotion, but Jake heard the emotion anyway. Yes, a person like Lucy would love with her whole heart, her whole universe, and if she were betrayed she might well flee an entire star system. That ought to have made her ridiculous. But, walking beside him with quiet dignity, taking the risk of telling him this, she seemed to Jake something rare and precious: a person capable of unswerving commitment.

He said, "You didn't have any children? Or other family ties to keep you on Earth?"

She shrugged. "A sister. Some cousins. No one I genuinely cared for. I'm afraid I don't love very easily. I'm cold."

"That's not coldness. That's depth."

She laughed. "Pretty to think so, anyway. Did you leave anyone important on Earth?"

"I had a brother once, but he died."

She nodded, watching the treeline, and Jake went icy all over.

He had never mentioned Donnie, not to anyone, not in fifteen years. Jake's personal records listed no brother. The news clippings in the library archives had documented him extensively—SUDDEN BILLIONAIRE TO LAUNCH FIRST EVER PRIVATE STARSHIP!—without finding any brother. What the hell had made him mention Donnie now?

"Lucy," he said, and she must have heard some terrible note in his voice, for she turned to him wide-eyed, "I never mention my brother. Please . . . don't."

"Of course not. I never mention my husband, either, Jake. That's why I wanted to tell you."

He almost said, *I did something horrible that I never mention, either,* but he didn't say it. Instead he leaned forward slowly, took her in his arms, and kissed her.

She came more eagerly than he'd expected. Her lips were soft, her thin body light in his arms. Instantly Jake had a huge erection. He pulled her closer, letting himself drown in her scent, letting the moment obliterate everything else.

Something screamed.

It was a high shriek that pierced the soft dusk like a missile. Jake and Lucy tore apart and looked around wildly.

"It's coming from the village!" Lucy cried. She took off running.

Jake raced after her. At the edge of the village they met Lieutenant Halberg and Nan Frayne. Halberg had a drawn gun in one hand and a tanglefoam wand in the other. Nan Frayne yelled, "There!"

Beside a hut on the edge of the village, a creature dragged a Fur child. Instantly Jake saw what Gretchen Wortz had meant about "a lion that lives in the trees." The animal had the long sleek body of a cat but with tentacled forelegs and tail that probably wrapped around branches. Its tentacles held the child as long, wicked teeth tore at the furred flesh. It balanced on powerful hind legs, backing away with its prey.

"Fucking hell, shoot it!" Nan cried. Halberg, after a quick look around to ascertain the safety of every human, moved to get a clear shot and fired.

The animal dropped to the ground, a laser hole in its head. Before Halberg could grab Nan, she had darted to the child. It had stopped screaming and even from thirty yards away Jake could see that it was dead. One furry arm hung only by a few shreds of muscle. He looked away.

Two adult Furs stood off to the left. They watched Nan, Halberg, the dead predator, and the child. Their faces didn't change. Then they both continued, hoes still in hand, toward a smoldering cookfire and peered into the pot. One dipped in a hand and began to eat.

Lucy drew a sharp breath.

Halberg said to Nan, "Get away from the carcass, Miss Frayne."

She actually complied. Nan stalked over to the adult eating his dinner and peered into his face. Then she did the same to the second adult. She walked over to Jake.

Lucy said unsteadily, "They don't care that one of their young was just killed."

"No," Nan said furiously, "and they *can't* care. But they aren't like that naturally. No species is, or at least not any species that can build huts and hoe fields. *Fuck.* What the shit is going on here?"

Lucy said, "They're sick. All of them. That's why my findings show that the species is dying out. They've got some mental defect that makes them stupider and more indifferent with every generation. They won't last two generations more."

Nan stared at her. Slowly she nodded. Jake was startled to see grief on that usually sullen face. "Yes. Yes, Lucy, you're right. They're sick with something we don't understand. A virus?"

Lucy raised one hand, let it drop helplessly. "How would we know? The physiology is completely alien."

"Then let's make it less alien!"

Nan started back toward the double carcass. Halberg put a hand on her arm to stop her, and she threw it off contemptuously. Pulling a tiny laser gun from her pocket, she sliced off the head of the Fur child. Blood, or some substance like blood, spurted out in a brownish fountain.

"Hey!" Jake called, meaning, *Guns are forbidden except to Mira City security!*

Nan ignored him. She picked up the small severed head and wrapped it in her jacket. "Jake, how did you get here? Skimmer? Take me back to the labs now."

Jake said quietly, "Don't give me orders, Miss Frayne."

His tone reached her, as he'd intended it should. But instead of a scornful insult, she said sadly, "Okay. Just get me back, please. We need answers before the Furs are gone completely."

Halberg said stiffly, "The others here—"

"Can stay, and you, too," Jake said. "Lieutenant Wortz is with the skimmer. Come on, Nan. Lucy?"

"I . . . will come, too."

The severed head had bled through Nan's jacket. She held it on her lap anyway, climbing into the second row of seats in the skimmer, Lucy beside her. Jake sat in front. "Back to the city, Lieutenant Wortz."

"One moment, Mr. Holman. Please to hear this. It comes since two minutes ago. Computer, repeat the last message."

"Jake," Gail's voice said, "where are you? We need you. We have a situation here."

*A situation.* Various disasters tumbled through Jake's mind: an outbreak of some native plague, a horrendous construction accident, a skimmer crash, a colonist gone berserk and shooting . . .

"It's Larry Smith. He just comlinked," Gail said, which was the last thing Jake had expected. The Cheyenne had been very clear about severing all ties with Mira City. "The tribe came across a bunch of aliens living in a village. The aliens attacked instantly with spears and clubs, trying to kill everybody they could, for no reason at all. The Cheyenne have got four dead and ten injured.

"Larry said the aliens are tall and covered with reddish-brown hair, with big sharp teeth. They sure sound like Furs to me."

# 8

It was one thing when a bunch of primitive aliens stayed in a few distant villages and refused to interact. That was no threat at all, thought Gail. It was quite another when aliens started throwing spears and swinging clubs at humans, even if those humans were not under Mira Corp's jurisdiction. The second situation required a personal evaluation.

Scherer had not wanted her to go: "Mr. Holman is already at the site. It is the unacceptable security risk for both leaders of this colony to go."

"Why—do you think your soldiers can't protect us? If your laser cannons and what-all can't beat off a bunch of spear-chuckers, then we're all in more trouble than just losing Jake or me."

"I think it is not advisable," Scherer said stiffly.

Gail ignored him and climbed into the second skimmer with George Fox and Dr. Shipley. Shipley had crammed as much of his infirmary as possible into the empty seats.

Shipley said, "Gail, will the Cheyenne let me treat them? They're supposed to have left behind all vestiges of modern civilization."

"Then what was Larry Smith doing with a comlink? Come on, Private Mueller, let's go." She hoped Mueller could fly the skimmer. Scherer insisted on staying to "protect" Mira City, and both Wortz and Halberg were at the camp beside the first Fur village.

Of course Mueller could fly a skimmer; Scherer had trained all his people to do everything. She wasn't thinking clearly.

The first thing Gail saw when she got out of the skimmer was a group of Cheyenne braves making spears. No more than sixteen or seventeen years old, the young men squatted in a circle and sharpened stones with Y-powered diamond cutters. A pile of fresh wooden lances sat beside them, ready to be tipped with stone. One of the boys glanced up at the group from the skimmer and then back to his work, flicking back long light brown hair circled with a headband. Gail saw his eyes, glowing with excitement.

"The eagerness of youth for war," she said to Shipley.

Shipley shook his head. "I think there's more than that here, Gail."

"Oh, sure. Mysticism. Nostalgia. Deep psychological weirdness."

"More than that."

"I thought you New Quakers were opposed to this sort of violence."

"Completely opposed," Shipley said. "But remember, the Cheyenne didn't ask for this. They had something else in mind."

Whatever it was, Gail wasn't impressed by it. Conical tents dotted the plain, which bore the ubiquitous purple groundcover. She saw open cooking hearths, a few animal skins stretched taut between poles. The huge rovers weren't immediately visible. In fact, the place didn't look all that different from a Fur village. Why would a people want to go backward?

Shipley said, "Is that *Naomi*?"

Gail squinted into the dusk. Yes, Nan Frayne walked quickly toward them. She carried something, and Shipley gasped at the same moment that Gail realized Nan's tunic was covered with blood.

"No, it's not me," Nan said irritably. And the "blood" was the wrong color, Gail now saw. Too brown.

Shipley said, with a forced calm that Gail gave him much credit for, "What happened, Naomi? Were you here when the aliens attacked, instead of at the Fur village with Lucy?"

"No. I was there. This is—fuck it, where's the lab these morons are supposed to have in the middle of their primitive insanity? Did you see Jake or Lucy pass by?"

Jake was here. Good. Although why was Lucy Lasky with him? If there was one thing this situation didn't seem to need, it was a paleontologist.

George said, "The rover is behind those trees. See?"

They hurried toward the dim metal bulk. It was nearly full dark now. Mira City was of course illuminated; night on this plain, lit only by open fires, suddenly seemed very alien to Gail. Did she really belong now to this strange planet, with its cool, fertile beauty and murderous predators? Overhead, strange configurations of stars appeared, along with a pair of too-small moons.

Inside the lab rover, however, modern Earth abruptly reasserted itself. A Cheyenne tech (and wasn't *that* contrary to Larry Smith's grand vision?) worked at sophisticated biomed equipment. Seven people lay jammed together over most of the available floor space. All were quiet, probably sedated. Shipley ran an expert eye over them and knelt by a woman with blood-soaked bandages on her exposed belly. Her eyes were closed.

"What have you given them?" he asked the tech, and Gail wondered if she'd hear of some exotic Earthly herb carried seventy light-years across the void.

"Assiterline," the tech said and Shipley nodded, apparently satisfied.

George Fox said, "The report said ten injuries. Are the others able to talk to me?"

"Yes. Only superficial wounds. Ask at the teepee of Blue Waters."

"Who's Blue Waters?" George said.

"The former Larry Smith."

Blue Waters. Gail stopped herself from rolling her eyes. Yet Shipley had said "*something else in mind*" in a respectful tone. What in this soft-headed experiment did he see that Gail was missing?

George said, barely able to restrain his eagerness, "Do you have anything that humans used to strike back with? Anything that might have alien hair or blood or tissue on it?"

The tech looked at the biologist. She was a short, dumpy woman with startlingly beautiful green eyes. She said quietly, "Better than that. We have an alien corpse. We killed one of them. Out back."

George was gone instantly. Nan Frayne, who'd been talking to someone outside, pushed her way past Gail. She said to the tech, "Now you have two alien corpses. Or at least the head of one. I want to do some sort of brain scan on this. To see if there are parasites or viruses or something. It's important."

"No," the tech said. "It's not."

"Don't you try to tell me—"

"We don't do brain scans here. This lab is a temporary necessity, to identify those foods and animals we can safely eat, and to treat our people medically while we're adjusting to Greentrees. We have no advanced equipment for meddling with the brain. Eventually we'll destroy this entire rover, and the other two as well. We need nothing from the Volcano Man."

Nan said, "You're crazy. All of you. You deserve nothing but contempt."

The tech turned her back on them.

Gail took Nan by the arm and pulled her out of the rover. "Nan, stop that talk. Now. We are guests here, this subcontinent is Cheyenne land, and we will behave with courtesy and respect. You do that for the Furs, why not for your own species?"

"If you don't know the answer to that already, you're incapable of understanding my explanation."

Gail laughed. "You think that sort of sophistry impresses me? Or hurts me, the way you're hurting your poor father? Someone else you don't treat with respect because you, Naomi Shipley Frayne, disapprove of his beliefs. What do you think you are, the standard for the universe? Does the word 'hubris' mean anything to you?"

"Isn't that what Lahiri always used to accuse *you* of?" Nan said and stalked off, leaving Gail feeling as if she'd been punched in the stomach. How had that little bitch known . . . what had she accessed and where . . .

Gail stood still, pulling herself together. It took longer than it should have. Then she turned on her flashlight and set out to look for "the teepee of Blue Waters."

It sat in the center of the nomad encampment, with two animal skins stretched on poles outside it. This time Gail looked closely at the skins. One was light tan, almost hairless. The other, much smaller, was a gray-purple pelt, also hairless. She remembered George saying that the Furs could not have evolved on Greentrees; their heavy fur belonged to a much colder world.

How long would it be before the Cheyenne stretched Fur pelts outside their teepees?

Seeing no way to knock or ring, she lifted the tent flap and waited to be recognized. Larry Smith sat on synthetic rugs in his plastic teepee with five other men and women. They all wore a bizarre combination of Threadmore coveralls, work boots, belts made of some native fiber, and colorful headbands sewn with small glittering nuts, stones, and feathers. The air was blue with a thick, sweet smoke.

"Come in, Gail."

"Larry, I—"

"Not 'Larry,' " he said. "Blue Waters."

"Okay. Blue Waters, I'd like to talk to you and your . . . your tribal council about this attack."

"We welcome you, our guests," a woman said. Her hair, long and lustrous, was braided with purple feathers. Her eyes were obviously genemod for augmented vision.

"Thank you," Gail said. She felt an insane sense of disorientation.

"Please sit," Larry—Blue Waters—said. "You want to know how the Cheyenne will meet our new enemy."

"Yes. They . . . they were here first, you know. I'm sure that a Cheyenne tribe can recognize that sort of claim." Damn, where was Jake? This was his sort of negotiation.

Blue Waters said calmly, "They were not here first. Your own scientists say they are no more native to this planet than we are."

"That is still a disputed point even among our own scientists," Gail said.

"Listen, Gail. We understand that the aliens have a claim. But so do we, by contract with Mira Corp. Yes, it stipulates that any sentient native life on this subcontinent supersedes our claim, but these are not natives. Still, they *are* here, and we're prepared to live with them in peace. Their numbers are small, and so are ours. They aren't polluting or desecrating the land. There's game and room enough for all. But if they go to war, we have no choice but to respond."

"Larry, the foundation of life on Greentrees was supposed to be no violence between any groups. Live and let live. That's written into every contract, every land charter—"

The woman with braids said angrily, "So do you want us to

simply let them slaughter our people? Or should we bomb them out of existence? Maybe you think a laser sweep from orbit would solve your problem."

"No," said Gail evenly, "that would only compound the problem. But you could negotiate."

"We intend to," Smith said. "But what we've seen so far isn't encouraging. If they will not negotiate, we will protect ourselves."

"With spears? I saw some young men actually chipping spears!"

"With what we can fashion from the land. We will not let ourselves be decimated again. The Cheyenne are a proud people."

*Oh, for God's sake,* Gail didn't say aloud. She'd read the personnel records. Larry Smith was one thirty-secondth Cheyenne. The "tribe" included Irish, German, Spanish, Swedish, and French blood, and it was in the majority. One brave was three-quarters Chinese, with features that no seventeenth-century Native American had so much as ever set eyes on.

She said only, "Nobody wants violence, Lar . . . Blue Waters. Yes, this is your land, and Mira Corp won't interfere with you. But the aliens, native or not, have precedence according to our charter."

He said, "Does that mean you will protect them? By violence against us?"

It was the real question, of course. Gail didn't have the answer. She said honestly but pointlessly, "We don't want violence."

Blue Waters said, "When you have an answer to my question, come back. Otherwise, please leave our lands."

"We're here at your request! For Dr. Shipley to help your wounded!"

"I know that," he said. "And we thank you. It is a temporary situation; we are still learning how to adapt our own healing methods."

Gail stood to leave. She had accomplished nothing. The woman with braids said scornfully, "Volcano Man."

"At least keep your comlink for now," Gail told Larry Smith. Communication was better than nothing.

Maybe.

The skimmers took off together, in a confusion of people and objects milling around in the dark. George carried a Fur corpse wrapped in plastic, aided by an unwilling Lieutenant Halberg. Gail saw Jake gingerly holding a plastic bag. Lucy carried three recorders—to whom did the others belong?

"Jake, where the hell were you? I talked to Larry, and he said the tribe will retaliate against these Furs if there's another attack. He asked what we will do. What will we do?"

"We need to talk about it."

"We certainly do. Where were you? And what's in that bag?"

"The head of a Fur child," he said.

*"What?"*

"The child was killed by one of those predators sort of like lions. George is going to run a brain scan, or something."

"Killed? You mean, here?"

"No. At the first alien village. Gail, we'll talk back at Mira City. I'm riding in the other skimmer." He hurried off, setting down his plastic bag to help Lucy load what looked like several buckets of dirt into the larger skimmer.

Gail climbed wearily into the smaller skimmer. Lieutenant Wortz, an oasis of stolid calm, sat at the pilot console.

"Lieutenant, the other skimmer is taking off now. We're waiting for Dr. Shipley to finish his doctoring. Two Cheyenne will escort him here."

"Yes," Wortz said neutrally.

Gail put her head back on the seat and closed her eyes. She was glad not to be riding in the other skimmer, with an alien corpse and an alien severed head, plus several spears tipped with Fur tissue samples. And dirt. What did Lucy want with all that soil? Probably checking it for evolutionary artifacts, after which she would again insist that the Furs came from somewhere else.

From where? And how? They hadn't ridden here on brooms like some folkloric witches. Lucy must be wrong. It was another unstable delusion, like the one Lucy had had on the *Ariel,* when she'd tried to annihilate a nonexistent alien ship.

Something tugged at the back of Gail's mind, something connected with Lucy's breakdown . . . she had it. Lieutenant Halberg had reported on a computer glitch, an object in the astronomical data supposedly moving at ninety-eight percent of c. Nothing like that had ever been detected again, and eventually everyone except

Lieutenant Halberg accepted that it was a bug in the program due to cosmic bombardment.

"Lieutenant Wortz—" Gail began. And then, "Never mind." Gretchen Wortz probably wouldn't know any more than Gail about astronomical data. And if she did, the aloof soldier wouldn't tell her anyway.

Despite herself, Gail slept. When she woke, they were already in the air. Shipley sat beside her.

"Doctor, what's 'Volcano Man'?"

It seemed to take him a long time to focus. He must be exhausted. "What's what?"

" 'Volcano Man.' Two different Cheyenne referred to that, or called me that. What is it, do you know?"

"It's an old American Indian legend, I think. The Volcano Man came sputtering up from underground and started despoiling everything, digging mines and shitting in lakes and killing bison and destroying forests. It came to be associated with Western civilization wrecking the wilderness the Native Americans depended on to survive. But it also meant a total disregard for the spirits of the land, the life force that flows through all things and makes them valuable as more than themselves. The life force that sees the world as sacred and precious."

Gail was silent.

"Not a bad viewpoint," Shipley said, and now Gail heard the quaver in his voice. More than just exhaustion.

"Doctor, where's Nan?"

He didn't answer.

"She went in the other skimmer, right? It was very confusing there at the loading . . ."

"She didn't go in the other skimmer. She stayed behind. To learn what she can, she said."

"From the *Cheyenne*?"

"No," he said, pain etching his tired face. "From the Furs trying to kill them."

# 9

It was nothing short of amazing, Jake thought, how individuals persisted in elevating the events of their personal lives over the world-altering events of history. People could ache with despair through peace, prosperity, progress. They could find happiness in the middle of war, chaos, uncertainty.

Jake was happy.

Lying in bed beside a sleeping Lucy, her thin leg flung over his and her face burrowed childishly in the pillow, he reflected on this astonishing happiness. Certainly it didn't come from any inner calm or sustained idealism. He didn't have, for example, Shipley's largeness of vision, which was funny when you considered that it was Jake's vision that had gotten the entire Mira expedition to Greentrees. But that was because, at that time in his life, his own circumscribed vision happen to focus on founding an interstellar colony. And that focus came from one choice made fifteen years earlier.

An entire life, he reflected, lying on his back and gazing up at the green ceiling of his inflatable, could be shaped by a single choice. But even if his life hadn't been, even if that night in Mrs. Dalton's library had happened differently, Jake would still differ profoundly from Shipley. They simply began from different assumptions. Shipley believed in group decision, graced and guided by the Light. He believed that consensus of many humble minds, no matter how long it took to achieve, would always lead to the best course of action.

Jake's assumption was different. If you wanted something to happen, you had to make it happen. You alone, because no one else was ever going to do it for you. All you had was yourself.

Jake had made happen this sweetness with Lucy. She had been fearful and anxious. But he had brought to bear every persuasive technique he'd ever learned, glad that this time he could use them not out of manipulation but desire. And belief that this would be good for both of them.

And it was.

However, Jake thought, lying with his hands locked behind his head and the sweet morning air drifting into the inflatable, the sweet things in life were sweet only if you haven't had to pay too dearly for them. Jake was not going to pay too much for this idyll with Lucy. He was not going to tell her, ever, about Mrs. Dalton. Lucy was not, he'd come to realize, the sort of woman who would accept evil. If she were, he wouldn't have wanted her. She wouldn't be the idealistic person she was.

His wrister vibrated. Gently he shook Lucy's shoulder. "Time to get up, Lucy. Breakfast meeting in half an hour."

She made an inarticulate noise and burrowed deeper into the pillow.

"Reports from the bio groups today."

Instantly she sat up, blinking. "Oh! Yes!"

He grinned. She looked delectable, sitting on her knees with her light, fair hair tumbling around her head, her pink nipples staring at him like blind, knowing eyes. He reached for her.

"Jake, no, we don't have time!"

"We do if we skip bathing. Which would you rather do—sit at the meeting clean or sit at the meeting satisfied?"

She laughed, and her eyes darkened in the way, he had come to know, that meant desire. She laughed again, a lower pitch, throaty and inviting.

The second Jake and Lucy walked into the inflatable, Jake knew this was not going to be just another routine meeting. In addition to the Board, the full contingent of senior scientists was present: Maggie Striker, Roy Callipare, Robert Takai, Ingrid and Todd, Thekla Barrington.

Gail whispered, "What kept you?" Jake didn't answer.

George Fox looked somewhere between exhausted and elated. "I did as complete a tissue analysis as I had time for. You can all access my report, if you want to, but I warn you that it's pretty technical. Here are the highlights."

The biologist paused. At another time the pause would have seemed just George's natural theatrical exuberance, but not this time. George Fox, it seemed to Jake, was genuinely dazed by whatever he'd found. Around the foamcast table everyone tensed.

"First," George said, "the Furs' biological systems are identical. Both groups, the stupid passive ones and the aggressive ones, have exactly the same systems chemistry. They're the same species."

Ingrid said, "We can confirm that at the DNA level. But there has been some minor genetic drift, which suggests that the two groups have had no contact with each other for maybe a thousand years. Given their distance apart and level of technology, that fits."

George nodded. "Second, the bodily systems, respiratory and circulatory and muscular—hell, people, you must keep in mind that I don't really know how all those systems work. This is DNA-based and warm-blooded, but it's the result of a totally different evolutionary path from warm-blooded life on Earth. I'm making educated guesses here."

"We understand that," Gail said. As the person least interested in the aliens, she had the most patience with qualifiers.

George ran a hand through his thinning and uncombed hair. "Anyway, the bodily systems are not only radically different from ours, they're radically different from any other mammal-like creature I've seen on Greentrees. Lucy was right. The Furs, all of them, are as alien to this planet as we are."

Ingrid said, "Again, the genetics agree. There are the similarities we've learned to expect anywhere in the galaxy, given that panspermia seeded DNA everywhere. But there aren't enough genetic similarities between Furs and anything else to suggest co-evolution."

"Third," George said, and from his tone Jake knew that this was the big one, "I ran MOSS scans on the brain of the dead child from the passive Furs, and on the brain of the Fur killed by the Cheyenne. The—"

Jake said, "What's a MOSS scan, again?"

"Multi-layer Organ Structure Scan. It maps organs right down at the cellular level. The two Fur brains are identical, within the parameters you'd expect for individual differences. With one exception. A small section of the passive Furs' brain is inert. Covered with scarring. My guess is that it doesn't function."

"A tumor?" Jake asked.

"No," George said. "Tumors are out-of-control growths. This was very precise, affecting what seems to be a carefully delineated area of the brain. Also, since all the Furs in the four eastern villages act exactly the same way, indifferent and passive, I'm guessing that all their brains would have this same blanked-out area. Tumors don't do that; every growth is out of control in its own way. A better guess is some sort of virus, or virus-analogue, that destroyed this section of the brain and only this section and then self-destructed."

Shipley said quietly, "Microorganisms aren't usually that specific."

"No," Ingrid said. "Not unless they've been very skillfully engineered."

*Engineered.* The word shimmered in the air like a cloud of deadly gas.

Maggie Striker, the ecologist, frowned. "Let me test my understanding here, George. You think a virus infected the four villages of the passive Furs, making them passive, but never reached the Furs in Cheyenne territory. And you think the virus was deliberately created to do exactly what it did, to only that particular group."

George flung his hands wide. "How would I know for sure? I'm only offering one hypothesis that fits the facts. If anyone has a better hypothesis, I'm eager to hear it."

Silence. Apparently no one had a better hypothesis. Finally Lucy said timidly, "Couldn't the virus have evolved by itself to attack that section of the brain? Without somebody's engineering it?"

"Again, how do I know?" George said.

Ingrid added, "It doesn't seem likely."

Jake didn't see why not, but this wasn't his field. He struggled to assimilate everything. "So you're saying some advanced civilization brought the Furs here from somewhere else, and then maybe infected just one group of them?"

Thekla, the agriculturist, had been listening avidly. Now she said, "Before anyone answers that, there's something I want you all to see. A recording. Two recordings, actually. Gail?"

"Go ahead," Gail said. She did not look happy.

Thekla said, "This first recording came from Captain Scherer. He's still section-mapping Greentrees from space, of course, and when his satellites picked up this, he did a low flyover himself. He gave this to Gail last night. Computer, on. Show file 4593."

The wallscreen brightened. Jake saw a space recording, already translated from the digital, of piles of . . . something. Small dots sat motionless between them. Abruptly the recording changed to highest resolution at low altitude. The "somethings" were thatched huts, and the motionless dots were Furs, somewhere in a mountainous setting.

A third group of aliens on Greentrees.

Each Fur sat on the ground beside dead cookfires. These Furs were very thin, and their hair had fallen out in scruffy patches. But what surprised Jake the most was their faces. Even through the reddish-brown fur and alien features, one could see that these Furs were expressing some other emotion than had the Furs in the passive villages. Eyes and mouths were both wide open, exposing the impressive teeth. And the eyes . . . they reminded Jake of something, but he couldn't quite say what. As he watched, one Fur rose, staggered in irregular circles, and fell down again.

"Are they sick?" Todd asked.

Thekla said, "I don't know for sure, but I don't think so. Now, this second recording was made by one of my techs in the ag lab. They've all been working hard, and they're young, and . . . well, you'll see."

The screen brightened to show a young woman with glossy black hair, sitting cross-legged on the lab floor and staring at a shoe. She raised her head and looked at the camera. Her pupils were highly dilated, and on her face shone a look of such awe, such innocent miraculous wonderment, that Jake knew instantly what he was seeing.

Thekla said dryly, "There has never been an Earthly human culture, except the Eskimos, that didn't eventually discover at least one psychotropic plant and make use of it. This one is a genemod version of some wildflower the kids are calling 'highgreen.' They tested it first on poor Fluffers, but she doesn't seem to mind."

The camera angle broadened. Now the screen included a cat, one of the several dozen domestic animals brought from Earth. Most were still in cold sleep, but Jake knew the ag and genetics labs had awakened some, cats and dogs and goats to use as test subjects in developing feed that would flourish on Greentrees. The cat staggered in circles and then fell down. A close-up of its face showed a feline version of the same ecstasy that lit up the girl's.

Thekla said, "The recording was made by her lab mate, as a joke. I came across it in the computer and gave them hell. It's too dangerous at this stage of our work to be trying substances on humans, and we can't recklessly risk our limited number of test animals, either. But neither Fluffers nor Kendra suffered any damage, so my guess is that we won't be able to suppress highgreen even if we tried."

George said, "Now that the cat is out of the bag," and despite himself, Jake laughed. Lucy looked at him fondly. Jake suddenly wondered what Shipley made of all this. New Quakers didn't use fizzies or even caffeine. Did Shipley realize that most of the religions since the beginning of time, from the Rig Veda through Islam and the Great Spirit, had used chemical enhancements to reach mysticism? Of course he did.

Maggie said, "So the third group of Furs are using some sort of psychotropic drug. What does that tell us?"

"If that's what they're actually doing, nothing," Thekla said. "But in light of what George found, I'm wondering if there isn't something going on in these creatures' brains that's producing the same effect, continuously. Look at them—they're not just having a good time and then going back to their lives. They're not eating. Their bodies are neglected. The thatch is falling off their roofs. The cookfires are all out. Maybe something has lodged in their brains to cause altered consciousness all the time, so that each generation gets worse and slips farther backward in technology and civilization."

Lucy said slowly, "Something created, you mean. Genemod. Like the virus making the other Furs passive."

George said, "We need one of those brains!"

"Well, we haven't got one," Gail said acidly, "and nobody's going to start another war to get one."

Nods around the table. Larry Smith—"Blue Waters"—had not comlinked about his "war" with the Furs. Scherer's satellite surveillance had not caught any bellicose activity, either. No one knew what was happening on the Cheyenne subcontinent, if anything, unless Nan Frayne had comlinked to her father. If so, Jake hadn't been told about it.

Maggie said thoughtfully, "Posit for a minute that the sky-high Furs *are* victims of another genemod virus-analog. What do we have? Some unknown entity brought three groups of Furs here and set them down about a thousand years ago in widely separated areas. Then, maybe at some later time, that entity, or maybe a different one, released different 'viruses' in each group to affect their brains, making one passive and one aggressive and one permanently high—" Her eyes widened.

"You're describing an experiment," Ingrid said flatly. "With the entire planet as a Petri dish."

"My God," George said. "If—" He didn't finish.

Jake sat back, staggered. A planet-wide biological experiment stretched over a thousand years. More . . . you'd need ship time to get to Greentrees from wherever the Furs had come. What sort of beings . . .

"I don't like this," Maggie said. After a moment she added, "And I don't believe it."

"Why not?" Ingrid demanded.

"Occam's razor," Maggie said. "The simplest explanation that fits the facts is that the Furs evolved here in some weird evolutionary path."

Lucy said, her small fists clenched, "They did *not* evolve here!"

"Maybe not on this continent," Maggie said, "but on Greentrees. That would make sense; we haven't examined the other continents closely. Then these Furs came here and contracted some sort of virus they weren't immune to—"

"Three different viruses?" Ingrid said scornfully. "I don't believe it. Those viruses were genetically engineered to produce three different effects."

"Engineered by whom?" Jake said.

"How should I know? More advanced members of their own species. Or another species entirely."

Jake said, "If other continents on Greentrees had populations with that level of technology, Scherer would have detected them in his mapping expeditions. Hell, you wouldn't even need low fly-overs—there'd be thermal signatures and such that our orbital probes would pick up."

This was unarguable; no one spoke for a moment. Then Robert Takai said quietly, "If Ingrid is right in her genetics—"

"I am!"

"—then someone *is* running an experiment here on Greentrees. A giant Petri dish. The most Occam-razor explanation for that, Maggie, is members of their own species who planted them here from some other planet."

"Nonsense," Thekla snapped, her sharp British clip enraging Ingrid further.

"I'm telling you—"

"—ridiculous idea that—"

"—Lucy's fossil record—"

"—Stupid reasoning from—"

"Stop!" Jake said. And then, more quietly, "Wait."

He surveyed them impassively; at least, he hoped he looked impassive. His stomach hurt. "Let me summarize what we've got so far. These are facts. There is no fossil record of the Furs in this area. The three Fur groups show three distinctly different sets of behavior. We're fairly certain the ubiquitous behavior in each group has been brought about by alterations to the brain, and we believe this was done by some sort of viral analog. All three groups have backslid in civilization and appear to be dying out, but for different behavioral reasons. Can we all agree on these facts?"

One by one, the thirteen people facing him nodded. So far, so good. Jake wasn't under any illusion that the consensus would last.

"All right. Now, the Furs might lack a fossil record either because they came from somewhere else on Greentrees or were brought here by someone. The brain tamperings might be deliberate or they might be natural, since after all these *are* aliens. The—"

"The tamperings aren't natural!" Ingrid said. Her face was red. Jake held up his hand, palm outward.

"Just wait a bit, Ingrid. Please. Now, if you put those varying interpretations of our agreed-on facts all together, you get four possibilities.

"One: the Furs came to this area from some other, equally primitive area of Greentrees and contracted disease or diseases that are killing off their species, so that we're looking at the tail end of natural evolution."

Maggie nodded vigorously. "Yes. Like Neanderthals. That makes sense."

Roy Callipare, the geologist, said, "I think so, too. Those drunken Furs don't even need a fancy virus to account for their state—they're just using the equivalent of opium or peyote, and using it badly." Thekla also nodded, looking justified.

"—Two," Jake continued, before Ingrid could attack Roy, "the Furs came from off-planet but contracted the viruses naturally. The Furs came here voluntarily, just as we did, to colonize. Then the colony or colonies were attacked by viruses over the last thousand years, and this pathetic remnant is what's left."

"Oh, God, not the 'lost space colony' scenario," Ingrid said. "How many bad vids has that spawned?"

"No, it makes sense," Liu Fengmo said, surprising Jake. "Why should the Furs not come to colonize and then degenerate?"

Lucy said, "Because there are no artifacts from when they were not degenerate!"

"Not near here," Fengmo said thoughtfully, "but on other continents, maybe. No thermal signature would be detected from deserted technology or cities half buried under vegetation. I believe this."

"And I," said Faisal and Robert, almost simultaneously. Robert quickly added, "Or maybe they developed a way to detect the virus, and the healthy Furs left, taking all of their technology with them."

William Shipley nodded slowly, then shook his head. Jake didn't stop to figure out what that might mean.

"A third combination of facts: the Furs' brains have been deliberately tampered with. That implies that they were brought here from somewhere by someone, since we've all agreed that Greentrees doesn't hold a civilization sophisticated enough to genetically engineer targeted viruses. So this means that the Furs were genetically modified either before or after being dumped here by—"

"Why?" Robert demanded.

"We don't know that," Jake said patiently. "Maybe it's a penal planet of sorts."

"Too expensive to use a whole different planet," Robert said. "Interstellar energy costs are huge, Jake."

"I know. I'm just tossing out possibilities. Maybe Ingrid is right and it's some sort of biological experiment to—"

"Thanks for that, anyway," Ingrid muttered.

"—improve their race, or do some radical social experiment, or punish some equivalent of families or clans . . . we can't possibly know."

"That's true," George said. "But I think—"

"Just a minute, George," Jake said. God, it was like herding cats. "There's just one more possibility, however remote. The Furs were brought here and tampered with by some other race. If there can be one unknown sentient species in space, there can be more than one."

There. He'd succeeded in setting forth all combinations of the facts, even if the last one, manipulative *über*-aliens, sounded completely ridiculous even to himself.

Ingrid said, "I go for Jake's third or fourth theory. These Furs were brought here from someplace else and genetically modified. I don't know who did it, or why, but this is not a natural phenomenon. It's *not.*"

"I agree," said Todd, loyal husband, with a glance at Ingrid that fairly begged for approval. He didn't get it.

"I agree, too," Lucy said. She didn't look pleased, Jake thought, to find herself on Ingrid's team, but her tone was firm. "Jake . . . what do you think?"

He said slowly, "I don't know yet."

Scherer surprised them all. "I know how I think. If someone—if anyone—brings the Furs here for the experiment, they come back. To see how the experiment goes. Maybe they come back soon. We must be prepared."

"Oh, God," Gail said, "this is getting way out of hand. If *who* comes back? We're not going to divert Mira City's resources into preparing for invasion by some hypothetical *über*-aliens who probably don't even exist!"

A half-dozen voices clamored at once. Ingrid won out. "Just because Greentrees might be a petri dish doesn't mean that we're in danger!"

"It doesn't mean we're not," Roy said soberly.

Shipley, very pale, said, "Let us suppose that if this is an experiment, the experimenters do return. What would be best is to prepare some plans to meet them, a protocol that will welcome them without arousing anger. These are fellow beings, with souls of their own."

Shipley was the worst person to have said that, Jake instantly realized. Because the suggestion came from the New Quaker, everyone visioned some sort of quasi-religious, pacifistic evangelizing, and everyone immediately wanted nothing to do with it.

George said, "Even if the Furs were an experiment, that's no guarantee the experiment is still in progress. Look how few Furs are left, how primitive and degenerate they are. I don't think anyone's been to check up on them for hundreds of years."

"That's because they're a lost colony," Liu Fengmo said. "If we become diseased and degenerate, no one from Earth may ever know it, either."

Jake thought of the nonexistent quee transmissions from the *Phoenix.*

"I think Fengmo is right," Robert said. "This is a lost colony, or an isolated and dying remnant of a native species on the way out. Whatever they are, they're no threat to us. We have far too much to do to create our own life here to devote too much effort to the mystery surrounding the Furs."

George burst out, "How can you say that about the only other sentient species we've ever found in the universe?"

Gail said decisively, "I think Robert's approach is the only sensible thing that's been said here all morning. We can study the Furs, but basically we just have to wait and see what information turns up about them. Or doesn't turn up. Meanwhile, Mira City comes first."

"Wait and see," Fengmo said slowly. "Yes."

"*Nein!*" Scherer said. "We must prepare to defend ourselves!"

Jake saw that his militarism was as unwelcome as Shipley's religion. And as easily dismissed: Scherer was a soldier, therefore he would naturally anticipate war. Robert Takai said, not troubling to keep the disbelief from his voice, "How would we prepare against aliens that use star systems as *test tubes*? How the hell would we fight them?"

Scherer didn't answer quickly enough. Jake felt the group solidifying against Scherer. They might argue—would argue, fiercely and endlessly—over the Furs' origins. That debate was not going to disappear. But they were scientists and administrators. Their basic attitude was going to be wait-and-see on anything more than talk.

"It's bad science," George Fox said, "to assume we know enough to proceed with any action. We don't, really. Not yet. We need more facts."

"Yes," everyone said in various ways, and Jake found that he, too, agreed. They just didn't have enough information for a solid conclusion. The mystery was not solved.

Maybe it never would be. In some ways, that was the most disquieting idea of all.

He and Lucy discussed it later and, to his surprise, she was not content with doing nothing.

"It's not paranoia," she told Jake. "It's *not.* I'm a paleontologist. I *know* the Furs didn't evolve anywhere on Greentrees, and they didn't come here in some crashed spaceship and then dwindle precipitously in numbers, either. They—"

He said gently, "You haven't examined all of Greentrees, Lucy. Only a few limited sites."

"I ran computer simulations—Jake, it bothers me that you don't believe me. It feels like you're questioning my professional competence."

She was always so direct. Like Donnie. "I'm not doing that, Lucy."

"My sanity, then. Or at least my mental stability."

He took a second too long to answer. She stiffened and walked away.

They made it up, of course. Their passion was still so new, still at the stage where it could override anything else. By mutual tacit agreement they didn't talk again about what George took to calling "the Petri Dish Theory." They talked about Mira City, they gossiped about the people they knew, they laughed and teased and made love. It was all right.

But Jake was aware that now there were two things they couldn't discuss.

"Jake, we have a problem," Gail said a few weeks later.

At least it wouldn't be a Furs problem. Gail continued to think that the entire Fur situation was irrelevant. "What's the problem?" Jake said, and saw from her face that it was serious.

He ran through the list of current problems he was aware of: a breakdown in the pipe-laying equipment, which Ben Goldman was having trouble repairing. The ravages done to the experimental genemod wheat crop by a handsome, voracious creature vaguely like a beetle. The maiming of a young Quaker in an industrial accident. The damage to several inflatables from a recent storm. The arbitration dispute—already!—between two people over some allegedly abused equipment on loan from one family to another. This last was Jake's domain.

He had set up the legal system on Greentrees to provide justice with as little expense in time and effort and money as possible. The model was the United Atlantic Federation penal code, but most disputes came under binding arbitration, not jury trial. Legal software was employed whenever feasible. Everyone on Greentrees except the Cheyenne had signed contracts holding them to this system, without appeal. Rudy Scherer was prepared to enforce it, if necessary. But almost all of the colonists, including the New Quakers and Gail's ecologically minded family and Faisal's benevolent dictatorship and the Chinese group, were peaceful people, not inclined to crime. The ethnic communities largely lived separately within Mira City, but each was also under the kind of close, constant community scrutiny that established strong cultural controls over behavior.

"What's the problem, Gail?" he repeated when she didn't answer. They sat in the Mira Corp office, almost as crowded as it had been on the *Ariel,* despite being so much larger. Everything not in actual use somehow ended up dumped here: bedrolls and recorders and rock samples and broken equipment and reports that someone was someday going to file somewhere.

Still Gail didn't answer. Jake looked more closely, and now he saw the stunned horror on her face. His chest tightened.

She said, "It's Nan Frayne. She killed a Cheyenne brave and Larry Smith insists she be punished by the tribal council. They'll probably put her to death."

# 10

William Shipley sat in the airborne skimmer with his face blank and his hands clasped so tightly together that the fingers were bloodless.

They hadn't wanted him to come. In fact, Jake and Gail weren't going to tell him about the trip to the Cheyenne. He wouldn't have even known what Naomi had done, or what might be done to her, if she hadn't comlinked him herself.

It had been right after Meeting for Worship. Shipley had emerged feeling the Light within, even though nothing remarkable had been said in the meeting. But the silence, the harmony, the meeting worshipping together, the presence of Shipley's children and their families and the rest of the congregation humbly waiting for Light—all this had lent its grace, and peace filled Shipley's mind and heart.

"Dad? It's Nan."

He'd stopped dead in the middle of one of Mira City's newly paved paths. Two more plants had been approved by the bio group for transplant, and the path was bordered on one side by a thin, bright line of flowers, purple and deep red, with alien-looking petals.

"I only have a minute before they notice," Nan said breathlessly. "I'm supposed to be in isolation but this old Cheyenne woman thought I should at least get to contact my family and she brought me a comlink. They're going to kill me, I think. I killed a man, a bastard who actually deserved it, no question, but Larry Waterfoot or whatever he's calling himself—"

The comlink cut off.

Shipley stood holding his link, paralyzed. Then he set off at a clumsy, puffing run for Mira Corp's office. Jake and Gail were both there, and the second that Shipley saw their faces, he knew that they knew what had happened.

"Doctor," Gail said, moving swiftly to pull out a chair. "Sit down. You're all red."

"I—" He couldn't go on.

Jake said, "We know. Larry Smith just linked. Dr. Shipley—"

Gail said, "Did Nan call you? How?"

"Yes," Shipley got out. "I don't know how. She said an old woman thought she should contact her family—what happened? Do you know? Oh, please tell me!"

"Easy, Doctor," Jake said. "Yes, we know. Larry Smith comlinked us. We're leaving for there as soon as Lieutenant Halberg refuels a skimmer."

"But . . . but what happened?" He heard his own pitiful wail and tried to pull himself together. It would not help Naomi if he gave way to grief.

Gail and Jake exchanged looks. Jake, always better at handling people, nodded. He leaned toward Shipley.

"Doctor, it's still a bit unclear. The good news is that Larry comlinked us at all. That means he hasn't really made any firm decision about Nan or he'd just carry it out. There's every reason to hope that when we talk to him in person, the situation—"

Gail said, "Oh, cut the soft positives and tell the man what happened," and Shipley was grateful for her bluntness.

Jake said, "Nan was apparently living with the Furs. She—"

"With the Furs?" Shipley said. "Those aggressive ones in the Cheyenne territory? How did she—"

"We don't know," Gail said. "Somehow she got them to accept her. She didn't have a comlink with her or, it seems, anything else. The Furs have been making night raids on the Cheyenne, small skirmishes at the edges of the camps. The Cheyenne were ready for them, posting guards and so forth, and then each time the Furs ran away. So far nobody else has been killed, although two braves were injured. But apparently some young braves decided to carry these war games into enemy territory. They attacked a Fur village.

It happened to be the one Nan was staying at. Five Furs were killed, and Nan somehow killed a brave. The Cheyenne then wiped out the entire village with a laser gun."

Jake said somberly, "They weren't supposed to have any laser guns, according to tribal law *and* their Mira Corporation contract. That should give us a negotiating edge with Larry."

Shipley was too distraught to see how. "And Naomi—"

"The braves brought her back with them and turned her over to the tribal council."

A sense of unreality was settling over Shipley like stone dust. Tribal council, night raid, braves . . . *Naomi.* It was like something out of a bad vid about the nineteenth century.

"Do you know," he heard himself saying, "that the frontier Quakers in what was then America could frequently visit Indians safely even when the tribes were at war with the whites? It's true. Nonviolence . . ." He stopped.

Gail said kindly, "Doctor, this is a shock. Of course it is. Just sit quietly for a minute."

He said, "I'm going with you."

Jake said, "I don't think that's a good idea. We'll comlink you from the Cheyenne camp."

"I'm going! This is my daughter!"

Again Gail and Jake glanced at each other. Gail shrugged.

Jake said, "I don't think you'll be permitted to see Nan."

"I understand," Shipley said. He felt calmer now; he had something to do.

But what? Sitting in the skimmer, Shipley closed his eyes and tried to open himself to silence. If only he could have taken this to meeting! So often the truth emerged only when many minds gave a part of it, guided by the Light. But there was no time now for meeting.

And what could be done, anyway? Naomi had killed. No matter what the meeting did, no matter what Jake did, that couldn't be changed, or ignored. William Penn had seen that with the clarity of the Light, centuries ago: "*A good end cannot sanctify evil means, nor must we ever do evil, that good may come of it.*"

It didn't matter what justification Naomi thought she had for fatal violence. She had severed a soul from life.

Lieutenant Halberg landed the skimmer in the same place outside the camp that he had used before. Evidently this was the Cheyenne aircraft landing stage, another thing that was not supposed to exist. Larry Smith waited there with three others, two men and a woman, each considerably older than he was. The Threadmore coveralls were gone. All four wore tunics of some animal skin over synth pants and boots. Their hair, black and brown and dirty blond, was tied back and trimmed with feathers and stones.

As they climbed out of the skimmer, Shipley felt a warning hand on his arm: *Say nothing.* Shipley nodded at Jake.

"Hello, Blue Waters," Jake said.

"Hello, Jake."

"I'm sorry we meet under such circumstances. Can we go somewhere to talk?"

"We can talk here. There isn't much to say." Smith's sunburned face was set in rigid lines.

"If you don't mind," Jake said apologetically, "Dr. Shipley is feeling a bit faint. Can we get out of the sun?"

"You shouldn't have brought him," Blue Waters said, but he conferred in low tones with the other Cheyenne, and led the way toward the camp. Lieutenant Halberg stayed behind, looking unhappy at Jake's order to remain with the craft.

*Good,* Shipley thought with the part of his mind still working rationally. Get a nonthreatening foot in the door. Jake was good. Shipley let himself hope.

Much of Cheyenne life seemed to go on outdoors. Shipley saw people clumsily weaving baskets out of what he recognized as red creeper tendrils, tough and pliant. Two men laid strips of meat over a low, smoky fire. The odor wafted lazily in the warm air. In the distance a group of small, half-naked children ran and shouted happily.

Shipley, Jake, and Gail were led to a teepee occupied by two young women who sat sewing. The old woman said something to them that Shipley didn't catch and they left, wide-eyed. Everyone sat on green Arab rugs with gold borders, as out of place here as a VR set. Seven more people crowded into the teepee, and Shipley found himself jammed between Gail and the old Cheyenne woman. Jake sat across from them, undoubtedly to keep attention focused away from Shipley. The air was pungent with human and food smells.

Jake said, "First, Blue Waters, members of the council, thank you for agreeing to see us. I know that by contract you didn't have to, and I deeply appreciate it."

Two Cheyenne nodded, but not Blue Waters.

"I was thinking as we rode up here how little I actually know about your culture. I was expecting to see that your group had broken into smaller tribes. Wasn't that your original plan?"

"We will do so eventually," Blue Waters answered. "When we better understand this environment."

"And each tribe will be nomadic hunters, is that right?"

"Each tribe will live in harmony with the land, taking its gifts but not exploiting it."

"I wish I'd learned more," Jake said. Blue Waters crossed his arms across his chest. "However, one thing I do remember is that the chief personally bears accountability for the entire tribe. He must answer to the spirit of the land itself—have I got that right?—for the conduct of his people. That has to be a great responsibility, Blue Waters."

"It is. Can we—"

"Strong leadership is an admirable thing—we could probably use more of it at Mira City," Jake said ruefully. "If we'd had it, maybe this whole awful incident with Nan Frayne wouldn't have happened."

Shipley's breath caught, a deep painful wad of air he couldn't seem to expel. Blue Waters said nothing.

"I blame myself," Jake continued. "I shouldn't have let her stay here in your territory. *That* was a breach of contract, and I want to give you my apologies. I mean that, Blue Waters. This was our fault, not yours."

Shipley watched Blue Waters uncross his arms. He placed one hand flat on his knee, and now Jake did the same. Jake said, "You have the right to deal with Nan Frayne according to your tribal customs. That's absolutely clear. But let me ask you this—what would it take for you to turn her over to us instead, in return for the promise that if one of your nomadic tribes ever commits any crime in Mira Corp's territory, even straying in inadvertently and in the indefinite future, we'll turn them back to you?"

"I can't do that," Blue Waters said.

"Why, specifically, can't you?" Jake's tone was genuinely interested.

"We have a tribal council. The decision is not mine."

Jack looked confused. "Yes, but . . . you're solely responsible to the spirit of the land, right? The living spirit that's suffused into everything in nature?"

"Yes . . ."

"Well, I think I see what you mean. Dr. Shipley here is a New Quaker. His group governs by consensus, too. But each Quaker, as I understand it, is responsible for his or her individual conscience."

Jake looked questioningly at Shipley, and he managed to nod in agreement.

"And you're the same," Jake continued. "Group decision, but of course you as chief bear responsibility. Strong leadership." He smiled admiringly.

Blue Waters frowned.

"So let me repeat . . . what would it take for you to turn Nan Frayne over to us? What do *we* need to do? What can we do to keep relations peaceful while we both adapt to this environment?"

Blue Waters looked at his fellow Cheyenne. Some signal passed between them that Shipley couldn't read. Blue Waters said, "We've made our decision."

"I know you have, and you have that right," Jake said. "But then, if in the future some Cheyenne do stray into Mira Corp's territory—your children, for instance, who may grow up less respectful of the boundaries than the first generation . . . how many kids did you say you have, Blue Waters?"

"Three. But, Jake . . ."

"Shipley here has four. None for me or Gail, worse luck. Anyway, in the future—"

He kept at it an hour. Never blatant, always deferential. He admired what was honestly admirable about Cheyenne culture as Blue Waters slowly revealed it to him, and missed no chance to draw parallels with the New Quakers. The ideal of a simple and dignified life. The natural world as a wondrous benefaction, a holy gift. The constant awareness of the mysterious splendor behind every simple act of eating, moving, gazing at the sky.

Jake also asked Blue Waters' advice, repeatedly acknowledged his tribal sovereignty, tried to get the other three Cheyenne involved in the discussion. Eventually he succeeded in this. Then he doubled back, subtly pointing out how releasing Nan Frayne fit with the admirable things he'd learned about the Cheyenne. Releasing her was consistent with the kind of people the tribe was (or wanted to be). He stressed the reciprocity of leniency for their children, or their children's children. Blue Waters must look out, Jake said, for future generations; that fell under his mandate of strong leadership. By degrees Jake got Blue Waters to agree to something small, then something larger, and then somehow Blue Waters was the one coming up with a plan, and then all at once everyone was standing and Naomi was free.

"My God, Jake," Gail said when the three were alone, and her tone was not entirely admiring. "I hope I never have to oppose you on anything important."

"Shut up," Jake said, and for a second Shipley saw the raw edge of the man, scraped by the price he paid for his persistent manipulation.

Naomi was led up to them by two Cheyenne women. She wore only a blanket wrapped loosely around her thin body. Her hair was filthy and matted and she looked like she hadn't slept in days. She smelled dreadful.

"H-hi." Her voice quavered.

"Naomi—" Shipley reached out to his daughter.

"Don't touch me," she said, sounding more like herself. "Don't . . ."

"I won't," Shipley said helplessly.

At the skimmer, which Jake got them to as quickly as possible, she climbed in the backseats with Gail. Shipley had no choice but to lumber in beside Jake. Nan's reek filled the small cabin.

As soon as they were in the air, Naomi began to talk. Words tumbled out of her, unstoppable, and Shipley realized she was the closest possible thing to hysterical.

"I killed him, I killed the bastard, and I'm glad. I ran the spear through him from behind, it went in easily but then struck something hard in front, maybe the breastbone, Dad you'd think I'd know being the daughter of a doctor you fell down on my education. But nothing new there, is it? I heard the noise of those stupid braves attacking, 'braves' what a joke of a name they had fucking *laser cannons* with them! I jumped out of bed and yelled to warn my Furs but you can't make too many sudden moves they misinterpret it as aggression so Ninchee—"

"Who's Ninchee?" Gail said, with a gentleness that startled Shipley.

"My friend, she's the reason the Furs let me go to them. I sneaked away from Piss Water's laughable camp and took off all my clothes so I wouldn't look too much like the fake Cheyenne, and I found the Fur village and Ninchee found *me.* That's not her name of course but it's as close as I could come their vocal chords are different. Of course. She found me when she was foraging for food and of course she would have killed me except I'd learned from the sick Furs how to look harmless and passive—"

"The sick Furs? You mean the first Fur village we found?" Gail said, still with that unexpected gentleness.

"Yes, of course, what else, from some fucking computer program? So I went into passive mode and I think Ninchee might have killed me anyway except I'm female and small and maybe she thought I was a child. I think she did, they're very tender with children, there were two kids in one of the teepees the hunting Furs attacked a few weeks ago and they killed the adults but not the children, and afterward carried them outside so they wouldn't see—which is more than humans would do for the Furs! They're aggressive yes but who can blame them it's their planet not ours and they have no use for the fucking stupidity on nonviolence. 'Nonviolence'! You're such a fool Daddy it's not that kind of universe and so when those braves attacked with lasers, I went a bit nuts, I think, I pushed in the spear from behind, only it hit some kind of hard thing in front, maybe the breastbone, Dad you'd think I'd know being the daughter of a doctor, and I killed him. Dead. Gone. Blood . . ." She started to cry. The crying made her angrier.

"Fuck this!" Naomi screamed. "Fuck it! So what if I killed him there was enough other killing going on, all the time, stupid fucking Cheyenne it wasn't my Furs' fault ever—"

*"My" Furs.*

Gail said quietly, "No, it wasn't the Furs' fault. Nor yours. God, you must be exhausted, Nan."

"I'm fine, don't try to coddle me! And I never said it was my fault, you can't guilt me like that or not guilt me by saying you are . . ."

She went on, but Shipley heard her voice slow down, heard it drop in pitch until it was almost inaudible. Occasionally he heard Gail's soothing tones, also inaudible. He didn't dare turn around to look.

Just before they reached Mira City, the backseat fell completely silent. Slowly Shipley twisted his big body. Naomi lay asleep in the curve of Gail's arm. The older woman held her protectively, despite Naomi's gagging stench. When she felt Shipley's gaze, Gail raised her eyes. In them was a puzzled wonder.

"She really cares about them," Gail said. "The aliens. She really . . . cares."

Shipley was unable to answer. He saw Naomi, filthy and maimed, in Gail's arms. He saw Naomi, a cooing infant, cradled in the arms of her dead mother. He saw Naomi, a laughing toddler, in his own arms. He saw Naomi, manacled and shouting obscenities, struggling forcefully in the barely restrained arms of a court bailiff. Shipley could only shake his head.

"I agree with her about the violent nature of the universe," Gail said, and even through his grief and anger and relief, Shipley registered that Jake stared stonily ahead.

# 11

Gail sat at a meeting of her disputatious, high-minded family and tried to concentrate on the discussion, which concerned homesteading by Rick and Amali.

The question of land ownership, which was intimately tied to the question of capitalism, was a complicated one on Greentrees. For three years, by contracts signed by all colonists, there was no individual ownership of land except for the subcontinent set aside for the Cheyenne, who agreed to confine themselves to it for the next hundred years. That should be no hardship; the area was huge. The rest of the planet's largest continent was held in trusteeship by Mira Corp.

For three years, everyone but the Cheyenne were theoretically required to live in Mira City. This was the estimated length of time needed to establish a working relationship with the Greentrees ecology. By keeping everyone close at hand and proceeding carefully with the necessary scientific studies, Mira Corp hoped to avoid loss of life to poisoning, crop failure, natural disaster, and territory fights. More important, Greentrees would be protected from damaging exploitation before her ecology was understood.

After three years, sections of land would be assigned, using the satellite maps, with much area set aside as public parks and much as wilderness preserves. One equal section of land would be given to every adult, drawn by lottery. These could be homesteaded, mined under close regulation, or sold to each other for whatever the market could bear. Ecological standards would prevent any land use that was determined to present "significant ecological danger," as determined by a board of ten elected officials. Anyone who didn't choose to homestead was free to stay in Mira City, and enough land had been allotted within "city limits" for considerable expansion, everything but initial "inflatable-use properties" buyable from Mira Corp, which in turn was required to use the monies to pay for police protection, roads, water and sewage facilities, and other municipal concerns. These, however, were to be kept to a minimum. Child education, medical help, and cultural behavior, including neighborhood upkeep, were to remain the responsibilities of individuals or individual groups.

"In other words," Jake had explained years ago on Earth, "we're going to start out as a commune crossed with a scientific research station, and end up as capitalism crossed with frontier community spirit. All underlaid with libertarian contracts." No one had had the slightest idea if this confabulation would work. No one could think of anything better.

So far, which was less than six months on Greentrees, the system had worked fine, at least in part because Greentrees had turned out to be an even more benign and fertile place than anyone had hoped. Also, of course, it had been only six months. Still, there were problems. Gail and her family were looking at one such problem now.

In addition to its broad outline, Mira Corp's charter included many amendments and exceptions. One of these provided for people who wished to leave Mira City before the three years were over. They had two choices: live elsewhere but understand that they could not own the land, no matter how much they developed it, or move to an entirely different continent, across an ocean. The second wasn't really feasible. The shuttle, skimmers, and rovers all belonged to Mira Corp.

"We know we won't be establishing a permanent home," Rick Sibley argued. "But we want to do ecological work at some other place besides here. It's a big continent, people, and not homogeneous! Specifically, Amali and I want to work on the coast—*here.*"

Gail peered at the continental map that brightened the wall-screen. Damn, she was going to need another corneal adjustment soon. Getting older was not for cowards.

A red dot burned along the western coast, where a river from the nearby mountains joined the sea. Rick said, "Detail," and a smaller map of the area appeared. He began to talk about ecological niches. Gail tuned out.

She was an anomaly among the extended Cutler clans, the Sibleys and Statlers and Richmonds and deBeers. For two centuries they had produced scientists, organic industrialists, and passionate Earth advocates (and look how much good that had done them). Rick was an ecologist who had held a post at Harvard; his beautiful Malaysian wife Amali had a Ph.D. from Oxford on marine life computer models. Gail had a degree in business. Science, to her own early horror, bored her.

She'd outgrown the horror, and the shame that followed it, largely due to the scathing perspective Lahiri had provided. The world—any world—needed administrators to support its scientists and do battle with its ecological exploiters. Gail knew she was good at it, as long as she didn't have to absorb extraneous details.

She wasn't being good at it at this moment, however. She was too preoccupied with Nan Frayne.

Gail prided herself on her judgments of people. They were pragmatic judgments, and she utterly lacked Jake's manipulative finesse in moving people around like so many chess pieces. But usually she was pretty sharp in assessing a person's basic capabilities and limits. She had judged Nan Frayne as a waste of oxygen, a spoiled whining piece of crumpled tissue, with about just that much durability or practical use. She'd been wrong.

"So I think Amali and I should go there," Rick concluded. The vote of the family board was nearly unanimous, only Paul deBeers dissenting: "There's enough work here before anyone goes out hotshotting someplace else." Uncle Paul had always been cantankerous.

"Now, about Aunt Tamara," Sydney Statler said. "She fell and broke her hip and we need to have more nursing care than just the medic 'bot because . . ."

When the meeting was finally over, Gail walked toward Dr. Shipley's house. Halfway there she stopped, turned around, and went back. So what if she'd been wrong about Nan Frayne? Did she,

Gail, have to be right every single time about every single thing?

" *'Hubris'—isn't that what Lahiri always used to accuse you of?*" How had Nan known that?

It didn't matter how. Damn the bitch anyway. Gail had better things to do.

"Mr. Holman. Ms. Cutler. I need to see you."

Gail hadn't heard Rudolf Scherer come up behind them. She and Jake stood arguing with Robert Takai, Mira Corp's energy engineer, beside the half-finished dam across the river. It would create the reservoir to supply Mira City.

"I told you, Jake," Takai said heatedly, "that we need double the capacity you want. Water reserves—"

"We can't, Rob," Jake said. "I told *you*, the ecological study says 'Take this much and no more.' Maggie's team—

"Mr. Holman. Ms. Cutler. I need to see you."

Gail said, "Not now, please, Captain," but Jake apparently heard something in Scherer's voice that Gail did not.

"Is it important, Captain?"

"Very important."

Takai made an exasperated noise, somewhere between a sigh and a snort. Gail and Jake followed Scherer out of Takai's hearing. The area around the dam site was a mess of excavated soil and rock, heavy 'bot machinery, an extruder monotonously producing carbon monofilament cable. The construction crew's clothing lay strewn about; they'd removed it in the noonday heat. The ecotech's water-sampling console hummed, unattended. Two women argued fiercely over some detail of software interface for the dam backup computer. Wildflowers had been trampled underfoot.

Scherer said, "There is a ship in this star system."

At first Gail thought she hadn't heard correctly, that Scherer had said, "There is a slip in this star system." She'd almost answered, "What kind of a slip?" when Jake said levelly, "A ship?"

"Yes. It is detected two hundred AUs out by the all-sky search which we maintain for the large-blue-shift objects. Its trajectory brings it to Greentrees in sixty-eight hours. It is—"

"Whose ship?" Gail burst out. "From Earth?" It was possible that in the seventy years since the *Ariel* had left, Earth had launched another ship to Greentrees, with a faster drive. That was actually provided for in international law; the first country on a planet had claim only to the first continent it colonized. But Earth had been in such horrendous condition when the *Ariel* left, had been disintegrating so fast ecologically, politically, economically . . . and then there'd been that last quee message, about what should have been the shattering news of sentient alien life: *WGA disbanded. Geneva under siege. Cannot help with alien invasion. Proceed at discretion.*

Scherer said, "I think the ship is not from Earth."

Gail and Jake gaped at him.

"I think," Scherer continued, and now even Gail could see the tremendous tension he was holding in, at what cost she could only guess, "that it is some other thing. The ship moves at eighty percent of c, and—"

"So it isn't coming here," Jake said, relief in its voice. "After all, Captain, when the *Ariel* reached ninety-nine percent plus of c, we immediately had to start decelerating. This ship, if it's two hundred AUs out, can't possibly decelerate from eighty percent fast enough to stop at Greentrees."

Scherer said, "It decelerates, by our preliminary estimates, at roughly one hundred gees."

Silence.

Jake said, "That isn't possible. Unless . . . oh, then it's robotic. Unmanned."

Un-aliened, Gail thought, and suppressed an insane desire to giggle.

Scherer said primly, "We think yes, but we do not know for sure. The current rate of deceleration brings it to a halt at this planet. I advise we take all the possible precautions."

Gail blurted, "What are those? Do we have a protocol for the arrival of an alien ship?" So it was happening, what they'd talked about as impossible in that other meeting that now seemed unreasonably long ago.

"Yes, of course," Scherer said.

*My God.*

"The *Ariel* abbreviation is now empty of personnel," Scherer continued. "I leave her so, but I arm her to the maximum for the remote firing. I suggest a blackout for Mira City, in as many electromagnetic frequencies as possible, and a beacon we place far from Mira City. If the probe or the aliens wish to make contact, they go first to the beacon. This makes the opportunity for the further assessment of the situation. This assessment may or may not include if we try to determine the enemy's immediate intentions."

Jake said, "They are not 'the enemy,' Captain Scherer. We should not go in with that assumption!"

Scherer didn't answer.

Gail said slowly, "It *is* whoever planted the Fur colonies here, isn't it? They're coming back to check on their exiles or criminal colony or whatever Greentrees is."

"That's also an assumption," Jake said. "We'll do better if we don't make a priori assumptions."

Scherer said, "The beacon must illuminate in as many frequencies as possible. It must stand at least a thousand kilometers from Mira City. It must be heavily armed."

"I think," Jake said, "we need to call a meeting of the Board of Governors. Now."

The Board adopted all of Scherer's ideas. "We are constrained to do so, since we have none of our own," Faisal said. His usual urbane detachment had vanished. Liu Fengmo had said nothing at all; his smooth brown face creased in concern.

Dr. Shipley said, "Well, I have an idea. It's one I tried to have discussed before. Captain Scherer, please listen."

Scherer was already giving orders for transporting material to the beacon site, assisted by a shaken Robert Takai. At Shipley's words he looked over impassively.

"Who will be at the beacon to greet the aliens?"

Gail blinked. She hadn't even thought, hadn't even considered—

Scherer said instantly, "No one must wait at the beacon. The remote human presence only."

"I'm sorry," Shipley said, "but that isn't acceptable."

Gail and Jake looked at each other. What the hell—

Jake stepped in. "Acceptable to whom, Doctor? What are your thoughts on this? I do want to remind you, however, that this is not your decision."

"It's partly my decision," Shipley said. His forehead glistened with sweat. "Please, Jake, Gail, Faisal, Fengmo . . . we need to discuss this."

"We do indeed," said George Fox, currently the science representative on the Board. George, uncharacteristically, had said nothing throughout the first part of the meeting. Now he was again coming to life, although still pale. "This may be the first human contact with aliens at our own level of technology, or better!"

Gail said quickly, "Captain Scherer says there can't be any life aboard, not at a deceleration of a hundred gees." The idea of superintelligent aliens made her feel panicky.

"Not life as we know it," George said. "But who knows what's on that ship? Captain, can you tell how big it is?"

"No," Scherer said. "Not yet. No one must wait at the beacon site. It is too great the risk. A telepresence is sufficient."

Scherer's unbending orders were beginning to annoy Gail. They must have had the same effect on Jake because he said with sudden irritation, "This Board meeting is still in session. Sit back down, everybody, except for you, Robert. Keep on getting that stuff to the beacon site. All right, there's a motion to discuss human presence at the beacon site. Captain Scherer has disagreed completely. Dr. Shipley, what is your thinking?"

Shipley spoke carefully, consciously choosing his words. "We did not expect to find the Furs here, but we did. Human contact with the second Fur village has cost the Furs many lives. Our scientists, at least most of them, think the Furs came from somewhere else besides Greentrees. These new arrivals, whether they're on that ship or only represented by some sort of telepresence, may have some connection with the Greentrees Furs. It seems logical to think they do, unless we posit Greentrees as some sort of galactic crossroads, which doesn't seem likely.

"We've killed some of these beings' members, or pets, or experiments, or whatever they may be. Maybe they can detect that before they land. Maybe they already know it, through the cessation of some signal or something from here. Also, the beings will undoubtedly realize that our beacon site is heavily armed. We will be giving every possible indication that our intention toward them is violence.

"Is that really what we want to do? Before we even meet them?"

*He makes sense,* Gail thought, and resented it.

Scherer said, "We wish to tell them that we are able to make a defense."

"But, Captain," Shipley said, with what looked to Gail like a desperate patience, "how will they know it's a defense and not an incipient attack? It presents to them only violence."

"Assuming they perceive things as we do," George said. "They might not. They might not even be able to be communicated with, for all we know. Life takes diverse and strange forms!"

"George, you sound like a textbook," Jake said, but nobody laughed.

Shipley said, "Someone must be at the beacon site, in person, to offer peace. To at least look peaceful. Unarmed, open. I offer myself, on the grounds that everyone else here is necessary to Mira City."

Gail said sharply, "You are chief physician for Mira City, Doctor. For another two and a half years."

"But you have many other physicians. There are no other leaders of Mira Corp besides you, Jake, Faisal, and Fengmo. We Friends, remember, don't have leaders."

"I want to go with you," George said abruptly.

Scherer began, "No one must—"

"I'm a biologist," George said. "I may be able to spot ways to communicate with them, based on knowledge of different life forms, that—"

Jake said, with sudden violence, "George, you haven't been able to communicate with the aliens we've already got. The only one who succeeded at that is Nan Frayne."

A little silence followed his words.

Liu Fengmo spoke for the first time. "I think Dr. Shipley is right. He should go to the beacon."

Scherer said, "It is too great risk. A telepresence—"

They argued about it for another half hour. Gail said little. It was amazing how she could already predict how the voting would go. Was it because the outcome they were going to get was the best possible one, or because everybody was coming to dislike Rudolf Scherer's unbending self-righteousness? God, not the latter. Let them all be more rational than that.

She studied Liu Fengmo. The Chinese were the least troublesome contingent on Greentrees. There were only 539 of them, all from the same neighborhood in Redlands, California, UAF. When the *Ariel* launched, about half had been recent immigrants from China, slipping through some loophole in both countries' constantly shifting administrative policies.

China had been badly battered by Earth's ecological ills: violent weather patterns and global warming and various bio-disasters. Liu's people, both China- and UAF-born, were the kind who survived by playing possum, meek and nearly invisible in the interstices of urban life. Used to having almost nothing, Greentrees seemed to them a cornucopia of riches handed to them by Liu, whom they revered less like a patriarchal philanthropist than some sort of minor god. They had followed him unquestioningly to Mira City, a polite and silent retinue who worked hard and played little, at least publicly. Gail seldom saw Chinese adults after the workday ended. They stayed with their own inside their ugly little inflatables. Even their children were quiet and controlled.

Jake said that history argued that the next generation would be much different. Gail was not concerned with the next generation; her interests lay here and now.

George said, "Nan Frayne should go to the beacon site, Jake. She's the only one who's communicated with any Furs at all."

Jake pulled at the skin on his face. He must, Gail thought, be much more agitated than he looked. "How badly was she hurt by the Cheyenne, Dr. Shipley? Can she travel?"

"She should not," Nan's father said quietly. "She has sustained contusions, a minor fracture, and malnutrition. In addition, she is still . . . excitable."

Gail looked at him sharply to see if he seemed to be conscious of ironic understatement. He didn't.

"I agree," Jake said, and Gail heard the relief in his voice. Nan was always a wild card; Jake already had too many of those in this hand. "And she hasn't learned very much of the Fur language, anyway. What she did say is that the two groups have different languages, so perhaps the starfarers have yet another one, unless . . ." He didn't finish his thought. Gail suspected he hadn't had any coherent ending in mind.

It was finally decided that William Shipley and George Fox

would be at the beacon site, if and when the aliens, if there were aliens, landed there. The contact, if there was a contact, would be surveilled by the others at Mira City. The attack, if there was an attack, would be repulsed by one of Captain Scherer's soldiers, who would accompany the greeting committee. The alien examination of the *Ariel,* if there was an alien examination of the *Ariel,* would be—

Gail gave it up. Too many variables. No, too much tension.

She went to draft a nonthreatening announcement to Mira City that they were expecting company.

# 12

He had lied to the Mira City Board of Governors. No, not lied . . . just left out a piece of the truth. There was no way to tell it to them, no way they could hear it just now.

Shipley sat in the main room of his new house, hands on his knees, head bent. This room served primarily as a gathering place since most dining was, at this stage of the city's growth, still communal and heavily dependent on ship's stores. No private kitchen facilities had been installed anywhere outside the medina. No one minded; most colonists were thrilled to have any private place in which to sleep, relax, and arrange the few precious possessions brought from Earth. The inflatables had begun to be superseded by permanent foamcast buildings. Shipley's had been one of the first constructed because it connected to the "hospital," a much larger structure than the house, dominating it like a looming round hill beside a polished boulder.

The foamcast furniture was sturdy, unadorned, and sparse. The circular walls bore no art. New Quakers made their own decisions about how much color and decoration they wished in their homes, but the basic principle of simplicity, nondistraction from the spiritual, held. Two bedrooms and a bathroom, all opening off the main dome, completed Shipley's house. Through one closed door he could hear faintly the murmur of Lucy Lasky's voice as she visited Naomi, still confined to bed. When Naomi had finally let her father examine her, he'd found two broken ribs, contusions, and cuts over much of her torso.

How could Shipley have told the Board the exact truth? How could he have said, "My daughter took a human life. I am troubled in my mind over this. My responsibility is personal. There must be no more violence between humans and aliens, and I must act to see that there is not"?

Jake and Gail would not have understood. In their world, the acts of grown children were not the responsibility of their parents. They divorced how a child was raised from how she acted afterward—as if you could bend a twig west for years and then complain you didn't have an east-pointing branch!

But his responsibility for Naomi's act would still have been easier for Jake and Gail to accept than Shipley's other reason for going to the beacon site to meet the aliens. *I have been guided by the Light of Truth to give a testimony for peace.*

They would think he was crazy. Their opinion wouldn't matter, but it would matter that they wouldn't have let him go. And he must go. He must do what he could to prevent any more violence. A call from the Light was not merely a private belief; it was a call to action.

Gail came in without knocking, a good measure of how agitated she was. With her came a gust of sweet evening air. Shipley heard the faint cry from the medina of an imam calling the faithful to prayer. The notes floated in, drawn out and somehow plaintive, until Gail closed the door behind her. "Doctor, have you told Nan about the beacon and the ship?"

"No," Shipley said, "and I asked Lucy not to tell her. Lucy's in there now." Another spiritual problem; it was wrong to withhold the truth from an adult. But if Naomi knew that more aliens were coming to Greentrees, she would insist on being there, despite her injuries or Jake's orders. Shipley had just got his daughter back. He didn't want to lose her again to another group of strange beings. Or, more accurately, to her own strange impulse to join them.

"Good," Gail said, nodding. "I think it's better she not know yet. Can I . . . can I go in?"

Gail's attitude was oddly diffident. Why? Shipley found himself too distracted to concentrate on the question. "Yes, my dear, go right in."

"Hello, Gail," Lucy said. Naomi said nothing to Gail but went on talking to Lucy. Gail left the door open, and Shipley heard his daughter's voice sounding too high, too fast for the painkillers he'd given her. She was speeding along on older, more systemic endorphins.

"And they've combined the best of hunter-gatherer with domesticated crops. Lucy, they're so much more advanced than the passive Furs we first discovered that you wouldn't believe it. They make jewelry. Back in the woods, they're carving an enormous stone statue of a god—at least, I think it's a god—and they press oil out of those little bluish berries and store it in clay jars. My old Furs couldn't do any of those things."

*"My old Furs."*

Lucy said thoughtfully, "The two groups have had maybe a thousand years to differentiate themselves. It only took a few centuries for the original settlers in Polynesia to develop societies at different levels of advancement on different islands. Tonga had sophisticated art, weapons, and social organization. All Chatham reached was primitive handheld clubs. But, Nan, that was due to different environmental conditions on different islands—minerals and food supply and soil fertility. Both sets of Furs that you lived with have exactly the same resources available to them."

"Except," Naomi said excitedly, "the passive Furs have George Fox's brain virus."

"Maybe," Lucy conceded, "but even if it *is* a a virus that developed early on, the whole tribe would have died out by now, given how little they can care for themselves. And if developed recently, the tribe should already have more art, agriculture, and toolmaking. It still doesn't add up."

"Maybe," Gail said, "the virus got progressively worse."

Naomi said contemptuously, "What do you know about it?"

"More than you think," Gail retorted, and Shipley's breath caught. Was she going to tell Naomi about the new aliens? But no, Gail didn't lose control like that. She asked Lucy, "Have you told her about the third group of Furs, the ones that look permanently intoxicated on some sort of native plant?"

"Not yet," Lucy said. "Nan, don't try to sit up! Your father said to stay flat!"

"The fuck with that! What third group of Furs?"

"I brought you pictures," Gail said.

A long silence. Shipley got up and moved toward the bedroom. Naomi sat up in bed, studying the printouts intently. Finally she raised her head and looked at Gail. Something passed between the two women that Shipley couldn't read, some intense look that led Gail to speak.

"Don't ever talk to me in that tone again, Nan."

And Naomi, incredibly, said softly, "I won't. I'm sorry."

Shipley felt dizzy. What had just happened? He saw again the image of a just-rescued Naomi on the skimmer, filthy and maimed, asleep in the curve of Gail's arm. Despite the gagging stench, the older woman had held Naomi protectively. When she'd felt Shipley's gaze, Gail had raised her eyes, and in them had been a puzzled wonder.

Now Gail's gaze was locked with Naomi's. A long moment spun itself out, taut as piano wire. To Shipley's astonishment, Naomi suddenly smiled, a smile so humble and sweet that it didn't seem to belong on his daughter's face. When had he ever seen Naomi smile like that? He had never seen Naomi smile like that.

Gail said, "I've just made an executive decision, Nan. There's something we weren't going to tell you, but I think that was wrong. You have a right to know, and we may need you. Not now, but farther down whatever road it is we're going to be traveling. We may need your ability to communicate with Furs.

"An alien ship is on its way to Greentrees. It will be here in less than forty-eight hours."

Just before the skimmer left for the beacon site, Captain Scherer made one more try at changing the plan. "This is wrong," Scherer said, his jaw hard as diamond. "It is a mistake."

Shipley, Jake, Gail, George Fox, and Lieutenant Halberg turned to him. They stood beside the skimmer, outside the electronic perimeter of Mira City. The settlement had been shut down as much as possible. No lights shone, no construction machinery clanged or hummed. Within the walled medina, the new minaret soared silent and empty. No children ran through the rest of the unpaved streets. Shipley realized that for the first time in months he could hear the river without standing directly beside it. It swirled around the half-finished dam, babbling and singing.

Jake said, "Why is this a mistake, Captain Scherer?"

Gail snapped, "We already know the captain's opinion."

Jake said mildly, "Let him have his say, Gail."

Scherer surprised Shipley by speaking with something close to passion. "There is on Earth a long history of the small military force that defeats the much greater one—but *only* if the small force acts quickly, to retain the element of the surprise. One example: at Cajamarca, Francisco Pizarro, with 168 Spanish soldiers, conquers the Incan emperor Atahualpa, with a force of 80,000 soldiers. How can Pizarro do this? He takes the emperor prisoner before the Incas can assess the Spanish as enemies. The same thing occurs over and over in the human history, and we must learn from this. Our optimum strategy is to take these aliens prisoner before they can assess our strengths, and next we use the prisoners as some bargaining points with the force on their ship."

Jake said, "You're assuming that we're going to be in an adversarial position with the aliens."

"I do not know if we will be so or not, Mr. Holman. Nor can you know. But it appears they do some experiments on some sentient life. That is why the best tactic is to prepare."

Shipley said, "Prepare for what, Captain? Prepare for war and you will surely get war. Prepare for peace and there is a chance it may come."

Scherer didn't even glance at him.

Jake said, "You're saying we need to prepare for the worst possibility."

Gail cut in. "Jake, we don't have time for you to go through your people-handling skills of agreement and persuasion. We just don't have time. Captain Scherer, you have your orders. Now let's get moving."

Scherer appeared to have heard Gail no more than he had Shipley. His eyes stayed fastened on Jake, whom he clearly regarded as the true authority here. Gail flushed angrily.

Jake said, "I think we better stick to the original plan, Captain," and Scherer's face went, if possible, more wooden than before. "But I do appreciate hearing your views."

Shipley, Halberg, and George Fox climbed into the smaller skimmer. As it lifted, Shipley saw the others heading toward the bunker newly built for the telepresence equipment. Jake and Gail would hear, see, practically smell everything that happened at the beacon site, and they could project their holos there if necessary. Although Shipley couldn't imagine what circumstances might make that necessary.

He bent his head, closed his eyes, and tried to clear his mind to silence. George Fox made this impossible. The biologist seemed unacquainted with the solace of quiet.

"I wonder about Scherer sometimes, Doctor. The military mind. See adversaries everywhere, and you create them. See potential allies and you might create *them.*"

Never had Shipley been so unwilling to hear the New Quaker philosophy voiced by an outsider. Lieutenant Halberg in the pilot's seat in front of them—was he sitting even more stiffly than before?—leveled the craft twenty feet above the ground. Shipley stared at the back of Halberg's head without answering George.

"Take plants," George rattled on, oblivious. "The plants in any given ecosystem risk being eaten by the animals. Sometimes, it's true, plants develop defensive mechanisms like toxins or odors that discourage herbivores from eating them. But just as often, plants have developed evolutionary strategies to form *alliances* with animals. Verbena provides hummingbirds with nectar, and in return the hummingbirds unwittingly crossfertilize the plants by transferring pollen. Or take the cocklebur, *Xanthium strumarium . . .*"

George was evidently the sort of person who subdued nerves by chatter. Shipley thought of quoting to him his Quaker namesake: "*Listen to the still small voice within.*" He decided against saying this.

"Or consider the lowly dandelion—"

The beacon site was four hundred miles northwest from Mira City. On a rising swell in a high flat plain, Robert Takai's robots had assembled a low tower of foamcast laced with extruded carbon monofilament cable. The tower pulsed a short sequence of prime numbers from an array of electromagnetic devices in wavelengths not excessively absorbed or scattered by the atmosphere: visible light; infrared, reflective, short wave, and thermal; microwaves; and radio waves. It drew power from a nuclear generator underground. Also underground was the computer. A monitor sat around the bunker, with sensors hidden in the area to transmit audio and visual. At the base of the tower stood a small bunker of foamcast shielded with lead.

Lieutenant Halberg landed the skimmer, dropped off Shipley and Fox, and then flew the skimmer a mile away, setting it down behind a low rocky ridge. Shipley had a moment of panic: what if Halberg just left them there and didn't come back? But of course he didn't. A few minutes later they saw him come into view, running over the purple groundcover. He was amazingly fast. Augments, undoubtedly. Not for the first time, Shipley wondered about the ages of the Swiss security team. Their bios and cell samples both indicated middle age, although all of them, thanks to genemods, looked younger. Usually it was the young who became adventurers.

But, then, Shipley himself was here, wasn't he?

"There it is," George said suddenly.

Shipley shaded his eyes with his hand and peered in the direction of the sun. He could see a faint glowing dot in the sky about thirty degrees east of the sun. "How much longer till they get here?"

"Projected time is twenty minutes."

Halberg disappeared into his tiny bunker. What did he have in there? Shipley wondered. Scherer had made a trip last night to the newly completed bunker. "For the safety check," he'd told Jake.

Twenty minutes was a long time.

What was Naomi doing? Resting in bed, Shipley hoped, but he doubted it. She had worked on Gail to let her join the Board in the Mira Corp's bunker, a larger version of this one, where they monitored the alien landing. Shipley didn't know if Gail had agreed, but he suspected she had. From her willful, completely unauthorized contact with the Furs, Naomi had built a sort of special, semi-authorized standing for herself with the Board. And, perhaps, with Gail as well.

Ten minutes.

Shipley thought of Naomi Warren Bly, founder of the New Quakers, for whom his daughter had been named. Naomi Bly had written in 2008, "No one knows how another person may come to the Truth of the Light. Treat each other with as much tolerance as your conscience allows." But how much tolerance was too much? And did Shipley's confused thinking at this very moment on this very point apply to Naomi, Gail, Scherer, or himself?

His knees felt wobbly.

Five minutes.

George Fox said, "Something's wrong. They're not coming in. We should be able to see more by now."

A second later Jake's voice sounded in the receiver implanted in Shipley's ear: "They're not coming in. The space data show they're moving at slow speed toward the *Ariel.* Could be docking speed."

Shipley and Fox looked at each other. George, of course, spoke first. "A party without the guests. Now what?"

The sky blossomed into brilliance, and back at Mira City, Jake and Gail started shouting. Shipley, leaning for support against the bunker, tried to understand what was happening. Finally, with horror, he did.

"*Captain—*" Gail screamed.

"Oh, my God—"

"Mueller—"

"No! No!"

Captain Scherer had not waited for the aliens to board the *Ariel* and learn about humans, thus destroying any tactical advantage of surprise. Scherer had destroyed the *Ariel* instead, hoping to take the alien ship with it. If Rudolf Scherer had had his way, Pizarro would never even need to meet Atahualpa to defeat him. The smaller outnumbered force could do it by remote nuclear explosion.

# 13

Jake threw himself at Scherer, yelling something he could never remember. The soldier turned. Jake saw the blow coming directly at his gut and tightened his stomach muscles, frantically trying to shift to the side to absorb the punch with his obliques. It must have worked because although he felt fiery pain, Scherer's gene-augmented blow didn't kill him. It did send him flying into the bunker wall. He hit the back of his head against the bunker, and waves of red and black washed over him. He shook his head to clear it and tried to stagger at Scherer again. Gail had picked up something small and heavy—what? Somehow Jake couldn't identify it, although he knew somewhere in his reeling mind that it was something ordinary, something he should recognize—and she tried to bash Scherer with it. He tossed her away as easily as a pillow. Gail slid down the bunker wall and lay still.

*Waves of red and black . . . not again . . . he stood over Mrs. Dalton's body in the library and watched her die, but not before he'd lifted her by the hair and . . .*

Scherer hit him again in the stomach. Jake went down, unable to breathe. The red and black receded, replaced by an awful noise that Jake dimly realized was himself. He couldn't breathe, he couldn't get any air in his lungs, he was going to die . . .

Gasping, in agonizing pain, Jake watched Scherer suddenly fall as if in slow motion, twisting as he went down. Saw the laser hole in Scherer's neck—saw it, improbably, a second before the blood started to spurt in wild jets. Saw Private Franz Mueller, Scherer's handpicked soldier, standing over the body, so ashen he looked made of salt. Then Jake couldn't see anything at all.

When Jake struggled back to consciousness, the scene had only minimally changed, and he realized he had only been out a minute or so. Private Mueller bent over Scherer. The soldier was crying silently. Jake, still trying to force air into his lungs, didn't know if Mueller would shoot him, too, if he moved. But Gail lay so still against the wall . . .

He dragged himself toward her. Mueller jerked up his head. Tears flew off his cheeks like tiny diamonds. "Mr. Holmar . . . do not. You are hurt maybe. I look by her."

Jake's heart paused while Mueller bent over Gail. But Mueller didn't hurt her, merely checked her pulse and pulled back her eyelids. "She is okay, maybe. I call for a doctor!"

Now Jake became aware of a clamor coming from the monitors. Painfully he turned his head. Shipley and George Fox, at the beacon site, were demanding, "What's happening? Jake? Jake!" George was ineffectually waving his arms, his usually cheerful face terrified.

Mueller said, "Lieutenant Halberg," and then a rapid speech in German. Jake had forgotten about Halberg. He wheezed into his own wrister, despite the sharp pain it sent through his lungs.

"Dr. . . . Shipley. Come back. Mueller . . . shot Scherer. Gail . . . unconscious . . ." Too late, he realized that he wasn't thinking clearly. There were dozens of doctors in Mira City, closer than Shipley. Jake tried to say this but no more words came out.

George Fox answered him. Fox's image on the monitor had stopped waving its arms. It stood stone still, gazing upward.

"Jake, we can't come now. Halberg says the alien ship wasn't destroyed by the blast. A shuttle is coming down now. It'll be here in less than ten minutes."

Shakily, Jake stood. He moved every part of himself: no broken bones except maybe a rib or two. He could stand, walk, talk. But he couldn't do any of it quickly, and sharp hot pains kept darting through his chest. Fortunately, Mueller did whatever Jake told him.

"Call for a doctor. Then bring me that surgical tape . . . good. Now wind it around my chest, tight . . . tighter . . ." It was torture to raise his arms out of the way, but once Mueller had taped the ribs, Jake had a little more mobility.

"Lay Ms. Cutler out flat and elevate her feet a bit . . . good. Turn her head to the side in case she vomits. Do we have a blanket?"

They didn't, but Mueller stripped off his own uniform jacket and covered Gail. Jake felt a quick flash of sympathy for the soldier, along with a flash of regret that they hadn't allowed more people in the monitor bunker. More people would have meant more clothing, more help. Lucy had wanted to come, and Robert Takai, and Nan Frayne . . . Jake and Gail hadn't wanted the distraction. Ha! Consider the blasting of the *Ariel* and death of Scherer as distractions!

Halberg said over the monitor, "The alien mother ship remains in orbit. Damage, if any, unknown. Shuttle lands in four minutes." The lieutenant's voice wobbled slightly, a first as far as Jake could remember.

Mueller said, "We must bury Captain Scherer. Soon right away."

It seemed a strange statement under the circumstances—couldn't Mueller see that they had other things to do "soon right away"? Jake chalked it up to nerves. Mueller had just shot his commanding officer. And he hadn't called for a doctor.

"Mueller—a doctor!"

"Dr. Shipley comes."

"No, not Shipley! Someone closer! Call Faisal."

"No one else comes here," Mueller said, not looking at Jake. It took a moment for Jake to realize why. Mueller was trying to contain his crime, confining knowledge of it to those already aware. Unexpected empathy pierced Jake . . . *Mrs. Dalton, lying on the library floor . . .*

"Damn it, call for a doctor!" Jake didn't dare leave his post at the monitor for the beacon site: what might happen next? Mueller ignored him.

Gail stirred and moaned.

"I'm here, Gail," Jake said. "Don't try to get up. Just lie still."

"I see them," George Fox shouted. "Here they come!"

A peculiarly shaped craft screamed through the atmosphere and set down a few hundred yards from the beacon tower. It resembled a horizontally positioned egg with a long, flexible tail that whipped around for a few moments after landing. Almost immediately a door slid open in the end of the egg opposite to the tail, and a short, steeply pitched ramp lowered itself.

Jake braced himself for an attack of Furs, blood-hungry as the ones battling Larry Smith's Cheyenne.

A long moment passed. Then a small platform, no more than a foot square, rolled down the ramp. It was covered with a clear dome that appeared sealed to the ramp, and it was going far too fast to be stable at the ramp's steep rake. The rolling cart hit the ground, teetered, and nearly tipped. But it righted itself and rolled out of the way just as a second cart started down the ramp.

Inside the dome appeared to be something very complicated, filling the dome with dull red-brown . . . somethings. Jake leaned closer to the monitor, as if that would create a higher resolution. He realized that the inside of the dome was slightly cloudy, as if with steam, which was one reason he was having trouble seeing inside.

George Fox said, "My God, I think they're—" and the dome on the first cart shattered.

"No!" Dr. Shipley cried. "Don't fire! Halberg—"

This time Jake saw the laser beam shoot from the bunker toward the cart. It hit it again. The second cart was rolling frantically back *up* the ramp.

"Oh, the—" Shipley said before George Fox yanked him to the ground. The big man fell heavily, ungracefully. Jake actually shook the monitor, which sent piercing pain through his chest. Another laser beam shot out from the bunker and hit the shuttle, its door now closed. As far as Jake could see, the beam had no effect on the shuttle.

"Halberg!" he screamed. "Cease firing now! Stop it, you son of a bitch!"

Another laser beam. Gail moaned, or maybe it was Shipley at the beacon site. Jake couldn't even tell. He couldn't see George Fox. Fuck it to hell, Halberg was going to kill all the aliens if he could, the aliens that Scherer had already tried to kill in orbit—

"Jake," George's voice said, shaking. "He's dead."

For a moment Jake thought he meant Shipley. But the Quaker was rising painfully to his knees beside the bunker. There was no more laser fire, and Jake realized that George meant Halberg was dead.

"I fried him with my side torch," George said, and now his voice definitely shook. "We carry torches to burn off brush in the wild . . . red creeper . . . I didn't . . ."

"It's all right, George," Jake said, which was idiotic because it wasn't all right, of course it wasn't all right, it was the farthest from all right that it could possibly be.

Shipley was on his feet. Slowly he started toward the shuttle.

"No, Doctor, don't, it's too dangerous, they'll kill you!" Jake said. Shipley must have heard him but he kept walking anyway, unsteady but determined, holding his hands in front of him with palms upturned, demonstrating that they were empty.

Behind Jake, Mueller made a sound. Jake wouldn't have been surprised if Mueller, too, had started shooting, killing him or Gail or both. But Mueller didn't fire. Neither did the shuttle. Shipley crossed the hundred yards of open ground until he stood beside the shattered dome on its little cart. By the time he reached it, George Fox had caught up with Shipley. Both men stood beside the silent shuttle, looking down at the broken cart.

For the first time, Jake noticed that the flexible tail on the shuttle had stiffened and bent to point directly at the two men. Never had he seen anything he was so certain was a weapon. But the tail didn't fire.

William Shipley said to the thing twisted among the shattered pieces of dome, "I am so sorry. I am so very, very sorry."

George said, a little of the natural excitement returning to his voice, "Jake, this thing is dead. But I think it is—was—a flora-analogue. With leaves and vines . . . yes. I'm sure. This alien wasn't a Fur. It was a *plant.*

"And so was the other one that rolled back in when we started shooting."

Nothing was simple. And yet it all seemed to be decided quickly. Later, Jake would realize he had made a dozen decisions, one after the other, quickly and without hesitation. At the time he was barely aware of what he was doing; he just did it.

The aliens did not emerge from their shuttle. Nor did they fire on George and Shipley, who didn't touch the dead alien but did stay gazing at it for a long time. Jake had ordered George to leave the remnants alone. Let the aliens have their own death rites, if there were any, if they chose to. Jake just hoped the death rites didn't include racial revenge.

Neither Shipley nor George could fly the skimmer. "I don't want to leave anyway," George said. He was recording everything he could about the dead alien. Were its fellows watching? Would they object? How the hell did Jake know?

"I don't want to leave, either," Dr. Shipley said, although with less enthusiasm. "You have other doctors in Mira City for you and Gail, Jake."

"Yes." He had said the same thing to Mueller. But that was before humans had killed the first star-faring alien they'd ever met. "But I don't want news of this to spread too far. The rest of the Board knows, of course; they're linked to my monitors. But they don't want panic, either. Faisal will handle lifting of the blackout without causing a stampede of people out to the beacon tower. Fengmo is controlling his own people. And Gail and I don't seem to be badly hurt. Did you examine Halberg?"

"Only enough to determine that he's dead."

"All right. Look, I'm going to have Private Mueller fly the large skimmer out there—"

"Can he fly it?" George asked stupidly.

"Of course he can—all Captain Scherer's people can pilot anything. For God's sake, George. I'm going to bring Gail with me. I think the situation has changed. The aliens in the shuttle aren't retaliating, so maybe some negotiation might be necessary—"

"With a *plant*?" Faisal's voice said over the link.

"I said a 'plant-analogue,'" George said. "It's obviously not a plant. There are weird projections and what might be a slime-trail locomotion device, like on snails . . . I can't be sure of anything unless I examine tissues."

"Absolutely not!" Jake said.

"I know," George said unhappily.

Shipley said, "Are you positive Gail can be moved?"

"She's moving now, Doctor. She's sitting up—she's standing."

"Then bring her here carefully," Shipley said, and started instructions for transporting Gail. She interrupted these angrily. "I don't need a stretcher, I'm fine. Just what *happened* at the beacon?"

"Tell you in a minute," Jake said. "Private Mueller, please go get the other skimmer and bring it here. Private?"

The soldier stood gazing down at Scherer's body. His tears had dried, but there was a strange, unreadable expression on his face. Fear? That, and something else Jake couldn't identify. He said, "Private Mueller . . . Franz . . . you will not be court-martialed. You acted correctly. I will tell Lieutenant Wortz." Who was now ranking security officer.

Mueller didn't respond.

"Private Mueller!" Gretchen Wortz's voice from Mira City. Yes, of course, she was waiting with the Board and the other scientists, ready to defend the settlement if necessary.

If possible.

Mueller responded to Wortz's voice. "Yes, ma'am."

"Follow every one of Mr. Holman's orders. Mr. Holman, you have only Private Mueller by you in security. I come also."

Jake said harshly, "I think we've had enough contributions from the security team already." After a moment he added, "I'm sorry, Lieutenant. Stay where you are. We don't know what the aliens will do with regard to Mira City."

"Yes, sir," she said, and Jake heard in her voice some strange counterpart of the complex look on Mueller's face. He didn't have time to examine either.

Mueller left in the rover to get the large skimmer from its concealed location a few miles away. Jake said, "Faisal?"

"All goes well here, Jake. Do not worry about Mira City. Fengmo and I have things organized. May Allah be with you."

"Can He negotiate with aliens?" Jake asked, and cut the comlink. He bent over Gail. "How are you?"

"Fine," she said, crossly but unconvincingly. "Except for my arm."

"Well, I've got broken ribs. So don't give me a bear hug and we'll both be fine."

"Jake . . . what will they do?"

"How the fuck do I know?"

She ignored this. "They approach our ship in orbit and we blow it up, trying to destroy them as well. They land and we immediately kill the first alien out the door. If the positions were reversed, I know what I'd do. I'd assume enmity and blow away the beacon tower and everything anywhere around it before I was attacked again."

"Yes," Jake said.

"So why aren't they?"

"Maybe they don't have the firepower."

Gail snorted. "They come in at a huge fraction of light speed and decelerate at a rate that should have squished them all into puree, and they don't have the technology to demolish George Fox while he stands there gazing hungrily at their dead comrade? I don't think so."

Jake didn't think so, either. "Gail, they're *aliens.* How are we supposed to know what they think?"

"We didn't have much trouble decoding what the Furs thought on the Cheyenne subcontinent."

Jake didn't answer. Gingerly, careful of his ribs, he walked back to the console and accessed the space satellite recordings. He wanted photos of the alien ship in orbit.

It was the weirdest-looking thing he'd ever seen. A thick flattish disk, with a slender tube projecting from one side. The end of the tube bulged outward. It looked like a deformed drinking straw stuck into a cow pie. He couldn't get any idea of the scale. He called Faisal back.

"Faisal, I need a physicist. There isn't one on the Board, but surely—"

"Of course we have physicists, Jake," Faisal said, some of the urbane amusement back in his voice. "Just not on the Wellcome Trust team. I will send you one of my people, Karim Mahjoub, very good, studied with Nigel Fearling at Cambridge. And Karim has excellent English."

"Good. Actually, he can just report in from Mira City, he's probably already accessed the sat pictures."

"Yes, but I think he would prefer to be with you. Where the action is," Faisal said, wryly proud of this colloquialism.

"But—"

"I will inform Karim," Faisal said, and the link went dead.

Nothing was happening at the beacon site. George still stood gazing at the dead alien. "Jake, there's a bit of leaf or something that was torn off and landed a little away from the body. Can't I just—"

"No! Where's Shipley?"

"In the bunker. He's examining Halberg, for some reason."

"Dr. Shipley?" Jake said. "Please answer. Lieutenant Halberg *is* dead?"

"Yes," Shipley said. "Jake, you're coming here now?"

"Yes. Why? Is there some new information?"

"I'm not sure yet," Shipley said. "Please come soon."

What new information could there be about Halberg? Suddenly Jake didn't want to know. The crucial thing right now was the alien shuttle. It sat immobile, unknowable. Unvengeful.

So far.

# 14

Gail kept cradling her left arm in her right. Curtly she refused Jake's offers of a sling, comfort, anything else, so he shut up. When Mueller arrived with the skimmer, she climbed in unassisted, a laborious and painful-looking process. Before she'd finished, a rover could be seen and heard on the horizon. Faisal's physicist.

Four figures got out of the rover.

"No," Jake said. "Absolutely not. Good God, Ingrid, what the hell do you think you're doing?"

"I'm senior geneticist," Ingrid Johnson said. "I need to be there. George does systemic biology, not genetics. I need to be there when the aliens land."

"So you brought Lucy and *Nan Frayne*?"

Lucy said, "Jake, don't be angry. We were all together, waiting for news, when Faisal called for Karim. I want to be at the site, too."

"The last thing we need is a paleontologist!"

"I know," she said humbly. Her eyes said, *But I need to be where you are,* which was the stupidest reason for letting her come that he'd ever heard. Or not heard, since only her gaze conveyed it. And Nan Frayne . . . !

Nan still looked rat-chewed, her hair cut ragged to remove the filthy mats, in places so short that the scalp showed through. Her face and body were gaunt. But she stood stolidly, looking defiant . . . as if that were anything new.

"Listen, Jake," Nan said, "you might need to negotiate with these people. That's what I do, remember? I'm the only one who does it. The—"

Jake, Mira Corp's negotiator, said coldly, "You negotiate with Furs. Sort of. These are not Furs, and you are not going."

Nan's gaze looked past him to Gail, standing in the doorway of the skimmer. "Gail—you're hurt!"

"Broken arm," Gail said. "Go back to Mira City, Nan."

"No."

Something exploded in Jake. "You mangy brat, I'm not your saintly father. Get in that rover with Lucy and drive back to Mira City or I'll have Private Mueller shoot you down where you stand." He turned and walked toward the skimmer, pushing Gail inside. Ingrid, having not been mentioned in Jake's rant, climbed in meekly after him. Karim Mahjoub followed. Franz Mueller got in and closed the door.

No one spoke until they were in the air. Then Gail, leaning back in obvious pain against the skimmer seat, said quietly, "It didn't do any good, you know. Nan and Lucy know where the beacon site is. They'll drive a rover there."

Jake said, with conviction, "Not Lucy."

Gail merely smiled.

Jake had been afraid the sight of the skimmer's landing might provoke some reaction from the alien shuttle, but it did not. Nothing at the beacon site had changed. Karim Mahjoub disappeared instantly into the bunker to analyze any new data from Mira Corp's space satellites about the orbiting ship. Dr. Shipley came out from behind the small structure, his face stretched with tension.

"George?" Jake called, across the hundred yards to the shuttle. "Anything?"

The biologist sat cross-legged beside the dead alien, waiting for . . . what? He said, "I can't judge the rate of decomposition at all. But no Greentrees insects are drawn to the body."

Jake didn't see the significance of this, but Ingrid said, startled, "Are you *sure*?" She went to sit beside George.

"All right, come away from there," Jake said. It had been one thing for George to sit in front of the shuttle before Jake arrived;

maybe it had inhibited the aliens from emerging before Jake got there. But now that he was present, he wanted to give the aliens every chance to try contact again.

Reluctantly George and Ingrid retreated from the shattered cart. Jake looked closely at George. The shakiness the biologist had shown right after shooting Halberg was gone, but George was still pale.

Ingrid said, "If there really isn't any insect activity in—what? an hour—then it could be—" Jake tuned her out, and led George away from her.

"George, are you all right?"

His voice was flat, devoid of his usual cheerful certainty. "I had no choice, Jake. I had to kill Halberg."

"I know you did. Can I—"

"No. Just leave me alone and let me work." George turned away, and Jake let him go. Probably he was right. Work would help.

Shipley deftly set Gail's arm and stuck patches on her neck. Immediately Gail looked orders of magnitude happier. Shipley said, "Now you, Jake."

"Something's on your mind, Doctor. What?"

"Let me see to you first." He taped Jake's ribs and stuck patches on his neck. The pain floated away from Jake. But he felt tired, very tired. Different drugs from what Gail got?

"All right, Jake," Shipley said, very low. "Come with me. Just you."

He led Jake around the bunker, leaving Gail, Ingrid, and George in intense conversation. Karim was still inside at the computer. Dusk was starting to fall, long shadows that preceded the abrupt equatorial. The air took on that tart sweetness Jake had noticed before during Greentrees twilights. Something that flowered at night, George had said, but he hadn't yet identified the plant. Its sweetness was vaguely disturbing.

Lieutenant Halberg's body lay on the ground, covered with a light tarp. To Jake's surprise, Mueller was already digging a grave, frantically shoveling soil.

"No," Shipley said simply.

"I bury our officer," Mueller said. He didn't stop shoveling.

"It's too late, Franz," Shipley said. "I already know."

Mueller stood still, and this time there was no mistaking his expression: fear.

Shipley said, "It's all of you, isn't it? All seven had it done?"

"I know not anything . . . what you say . . . is wrong. Very."

"No. I'm not wrong. Franz, you have to let me take a tissue sample. And not blood or skin, either. An organ sample."

Jake burst out, "What the hell is going on here?"

Shipley didn't take his eyes off Mueller. "An organ sample *and* a cerebrospinal fluid sample. Do you feel it, Franz? Tell me the truth. You know what it can do, and you killed Captain Scherer because you saw it in action. Samples, Franz."

For an impossible moment, Jake thought Mueller was going to raise the shovel and bash Shipley with it. But then he let out a heartbroken sob and dropped the shovel. "I want not to die, Doctor!"

"No one is going to kill you, Franz. You know how it works. Raise your shirt, son."

Mueller did. His body was magnificent, toned and muscled, broad shoulders tapering to a narrow waist and flat belly. Jake watched Shipley put the black metal box against Mueller's torso, at the front below his rib cage, and then at the back at the base of his spine. The medico hummed softly.

"I'll know soon, Franz," Shipley said. "Stop digging. Go sit over there and collect yourself."

Mueller looked uncertain and Shipley, to Jake's surprise, repeated the instructions in German. At least Jake assumed it was the same instructions; Mueller trudged to a narrow bluish tree out of earshot and sat under it, his head down on his bent knees.

Shipley said, "I think I should sit down, too. It's been . . . a day." He lowered his soft bulk to the ground. In the gathering darkness he looked like some monstrous outgrowth of the alien purple groundcover.

Jake stayed standing, waiting. Dread slid down his spine.

"I started an autopsy before you came, Jake. Rough, but enough to confirm what I suspected. Halberg, and probably Scherer—in fact, probably Scherer's whole Swiss team—are rebuilts."

Jake said instantly, "Not possible. We did the most extensive security checks available! Not to mention medical tests. We went into every medical, financial, and criminal possibility for all seven of them, we—"

"I suspect they had it done after your check and before the *Ariel* launched. Although of course all the arrangements had been in place for decades."

"Subsequent medical checks—"

"It doesn't show up in blood or skin samples."

"But, Doctor, the cost alone—"

"I can't explain that part for you, Jake. I can only explain the medical aspect. But are you going to tell me that you have never heard of anyone's suddenly and unexpectedly acquiring a fortune that was not traceable?"

For a moment, Jake thought Shipley knew. About Donnie, about Mrs. Dalton . . . but that wasn't possible. It had been a lucky guess. Rage filled him that Shipley could put him through this. The sanctimonious old—

"My autopsy on Halberg only got as far as a few abdominal organs," Shipley said, as if he hadn't noticed Jake's reaction. Which, of course, he must have. "But a few organs are enough. You probably already know a lot about rebuilts, but let me explain them anyway."

Jake's rage grew. Shipley was manipulating him, talking to give Jake time to collect himself. No one directed Jake Holman's emotions. It was Jake who was the negotiator, the manipulator. The one in charge.

"A rebuilt body starts with a cloned cell," Shipley said. "The DNA is removed and altered, then inserted into a harvested egg. A baby is grown in either an artificial womb or a surrogate mother. When the clone is born, it's a perfect copy of the donor except for the genetic alterations, done *in vitro*, which are all to the brain. The child is an idiot. It can breathe and digest, but it will never walk, talk, feed itself, or be toilet-trained. Still, he or she can smile, laugh, recognize people, respond to sunlight or music or hugs.

"When the child is in mid-teens, it's killed for its youthful organs, which are then transferred, all of them, into the original person. Who, for reasons we still don't understand, thereby extends his lifetime to twice what it would have been. Somehow the aging process takes its cues from some, or all, of the body's organs."

"I know about—"

"Of course you do, Jake. Rebuilts are illegal in every country on Earth. Partly because of the ethics involved, and partly because somewhere around thirty percent of rebuilts develop mental illnesses. The brain-body interaction is an enormously complex one. A brain paired with organs it did not grow up with, even cloned organs, sometimes reacts weirdly. Different genes get expressed than would otherwise, or they get expressed in different quantities, or they fail to get expressed. The neurotransmitter mix in the brain is affected. Sometimes subtly, sometimes not. The result can be the whole range of psychochemical disturbances, from depression to schizophrenia. The most common disturbance is paranoia.

"Mira City hired a security team of rebuilts, and so far two of them have gone paranoid. Enough so to try to murder the 'Other,' which paranoids see as a threat. Aliens are the ultimate Other."

Now Jake did sit down. He seemed to see nothing, and to see everything that had happened. Shipley continued, "When it was just a small group of aliens with spears, living in thatched huts, they were no real threat, merely a curiosity. But with superior technology . . . well, the rebuilts saw that much differently."

Jake said, in a voice he didn't recognize as his own, "Mueller? Wortz? The other three?"

Shipley raised the medico and pressed a button. Data raced past on the miniature screen. "No. No cerebrospinal protein anomalies in Franz. Not yet, anyway. The condition can develop at any time, but it can be controlled by medications intended for whatever mental disturbances develop. Most of the time, anyway."

Total darkness fell. Someone switched on lights and the area around the tower and the bunker was flooded with brightness. Jake went on sitting, until Shipley touched his arm and he looked up, startled, as if he'd never seen the old man before in all his stupid, futile, misguided life.

# 15

As soon as Shipley told Gail about the Mira Corp's security team being rebuilts, she thought, *That's what Nan had on Rudy Scherer.* Nan Frayne, with her dubious criminal connections, had somehow heard about what the Swiss had done and had been using the knowledge to squeeze special treatment out of Scherer. Gail looked curiously at Shipley. Did he guess? No. He hadn't put his daughter together with what the soldiers had done. The bliss of moral innocence.

Her second reaction was to feel all the horror that Shipley wasn't voicing. Clones, human beings living their individual lives, feeling pleasure and pain and enough other emotions to be human despite their mental limitations. Then one day killed, mined for organs like so much dead rock for veins of ore . . .

Gail shoved away the sickening images in favor of the practical. "How do we find out if the other Swiss are affected? And what do we do if they develop the condition later?"

"We monitor cerebrospinal fluid for significant proteins and we medicate appropriately," Shipley said.

"Will they agree? What if they don't?"

"I don't know," Shipley said. He looked exhausted. "But if Lieutenant Wortz agrees, I imagine she can order the others to comply."

Gail nodded. This was something for Jake to take over. She said, "Doctor . . . why don't you slap some of those patches on your own neck? With all due respect, you look like you need a booster."

He smiled, and Gail realized that New Quakers must not use

such things. Well, more fools them. "Then at least go lie down for a bit. Ingrid and George have put up the inflatable that came on the skimmer."

"Yes, I will. But, Gail . . . promise to call me if anything significant happens."

She hesitated; a promise to Shipley somehow felt more serious than to anyone else. "All right. I'll call you."

"Thank you." He gave her his gentle smile and lumbered toward the inflatable.

The area around the beacon was starting to look like a ramshackle town, Gail thought, a miniature version of Mira City's initial mess. Floodlights from the tower bathed a ragged quadrangle of groundcover torn up by all the activity. On one side of the quadrangle sat the bunker, with Mueller creating a cemetery behind it. On another side sprawled the inflatable, which could sleep all seven of them jammed together on air mattresses, assuming all of them actually slept at the same time. Gail doubted this would happen.

Various equipment cluttered the third side of the quadrangle, including the portable stove off the skimmer, on which Ingrid was heating something while arguing with George. George seemed to have recovered from shooting Halberg; at least he didn't look as if he were dwelling on it. Gail approved. Don't regret the unavoidable.

The fourth side of the quad was empty, and the most significant of all. A floodlight had been angled to illuminate the long space between the human activity and the silent lopsided-egg shuttle.

She was heading back around the bunker when Karim Mahjoub came out. "Ms. Cutler, I have some things to tell everyone about the ship in orbit."

"Anything critical that we need to know this very minute?"

He seemed taken aback. To him, everything in physics was critical. "Well . . ."

"Then wait a few minutes." She rounded the bunker.

Private Mueller had finished his grave. He looked up at her. "Ms. Cutler, I like have . . . *ein Begräbnis.*"

A funeral. Now. But she saw his face and said, "Maybe Dr. Shipley could say a few words."

"*Ja.* Just some few words. And Captain Scherer . . ."

She had forgotten the body in the monitoring bunker outside Mira City, had actually forgotten the panicky fighting and the sickening moment Mueller had shot his commanding officer. Blame it on Shipley's patches. "Private Mueller . . . Franz . . . wouldn't you rather wait until Lieutenant Wortz can conduct a proper military funeral?"

Mueller's eyes darkened. "We have not the military funeral for a treason, ma'am."

Of course. Scherer and Halberg had both disobeyed Jake's orders. God, the torment this man's beliefs must be putting him through. She said gently, "Wait here. I'll get the others."

Shipley was not yet asleep. "Just five minutes, Doctor." Obligingly he heaved his bulk up from the mattress. Gail rounded up Ingrid, George, and Karim. "Where's Jake?"

George said, "He went to walk around the shuttle, see if he could see anything."

"Alone? You let him?"

George said, "How was I supposed to stop him?"

Gail ignored that. "George, can you manage this? A funeral for Lieutenant Halberg?"

George's answer both was and wasn't relevant. "Nothing we do here is the same as before." Gail nodded and went to find Jake.

It was the first time she'd approached the alien shuttle. It gave her a sudden chill. What were they doing in there, the plant-things? Were they mourning their own dead? Gail avoided looking at the smashed cart and the dead alien beside it.

She found Jake standing on the far side of the shuttle, about ten feet away from it, beyond reach of the floodlights. In the darkness she couldn't see his expression.

"Jake, this isn't safe. Come back. Private Mueller wants to have a brief service over Halberg's grave. I know, I know, this is hardly the time. But he's so torn up inside, I thought that five minutes of prayer from Shipley might make him feel better."

Jake didn't answer.

"Jake? Are *you* all right?"

"What would be all right in this situation, Gail?"

His listlessness angered her. "Who knows? Not me. But if George can rally, you can. After all, you didn't kill anybody. I'm just trying to do the best I can for these people here, and right now that means a dumb military service for Halberg."

"A service is a stupid idea. Let Wortz handle it on remote."

"Mueller doesn't think she will, because to his mind Halberg committed treason. So did Scherer. They disobeyed a direct order from the commander-in-chief, who is you."

That roused him. "I'm not a commander-in-chief, for God's sake! I'm an ex-lawyer turned space entrepreneur turned colonist!"

"Not to the Swiss. Get your balls over there, Jake. We need you. This isn't like you."

He stepped forward, and she saw that his face looked ravaged. "Jake—what *is* it?"

"Nothing. Let's go have a military service." He pushed past, leaving her to follow around the impassive shuttle.

Shipley stood so long with head bowed over Halberg's grave that Gail had a sudden misgiving: Didn't Quakers worship in silence? Was Shipley ever going to say anything at all?

She stood with George Fox, who seemed composed enough, considering. They stood far enough back from the grave that they could see past the bunker to the shuttle. The others crowded closer, ringing the mound of fresh earth. Someone had gathered a bouquet of wildflowers and put it on the raw soil. Mueller? Apparently even these aloof soldiers, these rebuilts, could act sentimentally. Gail wouldn't have suspected it.

She tried to summon personal memories of the dead man. But Erik Halberg had always been so aloof, so correct and formal, that nothing came to mind. She hadn't known him at all.

Finally Shipley spoke. "We know that God does not require of us more than is possible to a human being living a normal life. Men may act wrongly, but it is not up to us to judge their actions so much as it is to search our own. We cannot try to change others without examining our own hearts, and so being willing to change ourselves.

"We cannot know what was in Erik Halberg's heart when he fired upon that poor alien being. We cannot know if the things done to Friend Erik's body had affected his brain so that he was unable to stop himself—even if he wished to. All that is for God to see. The most we can do, guided by the Light of Truth, is to ask ourselves what this action will lead us to, and what is the right thing to do next.

"Erik Halberg was, by all accounts, a conscientious man. His comrades respected him. There must have been much in his life that was guided by the Light, as there is much in any life that will listen in simplicity and silence. We honor that in Friend Erik, the good within him. What matters in human life is often not what we think about something, but the best that can be thought about it. Let us remember the best in this man."

*Hardly a eulogy,* Gail thought. *Talk about damning with faint praise!* She caught Ingrid and George exchange a raised-eyebrow glance, but Mueller seemed satisfied. He suddenly sang out, "Aaaa . . . men," in such a sweet, high voice that Gail started. Where in his unknown history had that come from?

*"Danke, Herr Doktor,"* he mumbled to Shipley, emotion reverting him to German. Shipley nodded wearily.

Jake said, as Gail had ten minutes before, "Doctor, go lie down."

Karim was at his elbow, "Please, Mr. Holman, the ship in orbit . . ."

"Yes," Jake said. It looked to Gail as if Jake were making a huge effort to pull himself together. His face smoothed from anguish to forced rigidity, and he gave the young physicist a ghastly smile. "All right, Karim, let's hear it."

They moved to the front of the bunker. Instinctively, without anyone suggesting it, George, Ingrid, Jake, and Gail sat in a semicircle, facing the shuttle. After a moment's hesitation, Karim sat facing them, his back to the alien craft. George moved slightly to get a clear view around him.

"I've looked at all the data from the space sats," Karim said. As Faisal had promised, his English was excellent, with a slightly guttural accent that lent his words authority, despite his youth. Gail estimated his age as thirty, although slim and clean-shaven men always looked younger than they really were.

"My conclusions," Karim continued, "are of course only tentative. This is wholly alien technology. But I want to tell you my thoughts about the ship."

Gail looked for Mueller and was startled to see him standing beside the bunker, behind them and to the left, holding a gun. He had put himself on guard duty. But a gun . . . oh, my God, were they going to have a repeat of the shootings? She turned to Jake, who was already ahead of her. He whispered, "Shipley says Mueller's okay."

"I know that!" she whispered back.

Jake patted her arm: *Mueller is safe.* Gail wasn't so sure. Jake seemed to have regained his assurance just as she was losing hers.

Karim continued, oblivious. "The ship resembles the embodiment of a theory that has existed in physics for two hundred years but remained only a theory. It's called the McAndrew Drive, after the Scots physicist who first proposed it, Arthur Morton McAndrew. Put simply, it tackles the problem of accelerating at more than, say, three gees without pulping the people aboard into jelly.

"Theoretically, you could accelerate at, for instance, a hundred gees without feeling it at all, if you could balance the force of acceleration with an equal pull of sufficient gravity in the opposite direction. They would cancel each other out, and the passengers would feel as if they were in free fall. That's what I think the alien mother ship does. See, it is shaped like this."

Karim held up a data storage device, a thick flat crystal disk with a hole in the middle. He stuck a long twig into the hole, gripping it at one end.

"You see, the living quarters are inside my thumb. The quarters are a capsule that can move freely up and down along this shaft . . . like this, closer or farther away from the disk.

"The disk is made of some material we can only imagine, a material with enormous density, trillions of tons in a disk a hundred meters or more across and perhaps one meter thick. To balance that much gravitational force, the life capsule—that's my thumb, remember—starts well away from the disk. As you accelerate the disk away from the passengers, you move the life capsule closer, so increased gravitational pull always balances the increased acceleration. Of course, the life capsule must change shape, bowing at the edges, as it moves closer to the disk, to compensate for force differentiation."

Karim peered at them, as if to decide whether they understood.

Gail didn't. She kept watching Mueller from the corner of her eye.

George said, "But where do you get the energy to power the drive? I'm no physicist, but wouldn't you need a lot more than you could carry, even if you started consuming the disk to convert mass to energy?"

"Yes!" Karim said, beaming at George as upon a particularly bright pupil. "So we don't know where the ship gets its energy! My guess would be from the vacuum. The vacuum state yields a very high figure for its own energy whenever you try to reconcile general relativity and quantum mechanics, as you already know."

Gail knew no such thing, but didn't really care. The alien ship was here. The shuttle was here. The dead "leafy" body, which under the floodlights she could just make out at this distance, was here. How they all arrived didn't matter. They were here.

Once again, the weirdness of the situation overtook her. Sitting on an alien planet, waiting to possibly be wiped out by beings to whom this planet was also alien . . . *Lahiri, this is not what we'd planned.*

George and Ingrid were asking questions about tidal forces and matter-antimatter reactions. Gail heard a faint rumble, little more than a suggestion of noise. She might not have noticed it at all if she hadn't been listening for it. But, no, it was merely thunder, very distant. It was far too soon for the other.

Figure an average of fifty miles per hour in the rover, pushed at top speed, assuming fairly even terrain. All right, forty miles per hour. Four hundred miles. No stops. Lucy and Nan wouldn't be here until just before dawn.

". . . and can accelerate and decelerate at a maximum of a hundred gees," Karim finished. "That's what we clocked it at coming in. If I'm right, that ship could reach 99.9 percent of c fast enough to cover interstellar distances in what we would consider a few days. Shipboard time, of course."

Because they would come, Lucy and Nan. Jake had ordered them not to. But, as Jake himself had pointed out, he was not a head of state nor a commander-in-chief. He was an ex-lawyer turned space entrepreneur turned colonist, and nothing about this colony was going as planned.

---

In the middle of the night, Gail woke abruptly. Instantly her heart started to jackhammer. She'd heard someone outside the tent. Mueller and his weapons . . .

Mueller lay asleep beside her, with the heavy oblivious sleep of youth. Now Gail remembered the plan to have one of them always awake, watching the shuttle. There was a rotation schedule. But two places were empty: Ingrid and George.

She already knew what they were doing, but she crept out of the inflatable anyway, gingerly crawling over Jake. Outside, the floodlights still shone on full. Ingrid and George had set up their equipment, which must have come on the big skimmer, beside the cookstove. Ingrid looked up, guilty and so immediately on the offensive.

"For God's sake, Gail, don't come creeping up scaring people like that! Go back to bed, you have a broken arm, Shipley said to take care of yourself. The last thing we need is the burden of an invalid."

Gail ignored this attempted diversion. "Jake told you not to do that. Both of you."

George said pleadingly, "It's only a piece of . . . appendage that was scattered away from the body. We didn't touch the body itself. It's still there, just like Jake said. We only ran analysis on this small piece. And—"

"He told you no, George. We don't know what death rituals these aliens may or may not have!"

"Gail, will you listen a minute? We ran analysis. It's not DNA-based life."

It took a moment for George's words to take on meaning. "Then you have a piece of something that isn't life! Synthetic clothing or something—"

"No. It's cellular, even though none of the subcellular structures look even remotely familiar. And we can't be completely positive that the part we've identified as the nucleus-analogue is that. But we think so, and Gail . . . *it's not based on DNA.*"

She said stupidly, "All life in the galaxy is based on DNA. Everywhere."

"Everywhere we've been so far," Ingrid corrected. "But not this. This is *really* alien life!"

As if the Furs weren't. All at once Gail's head hurt. "So where are these viney-things from?"

"How should we know?" George said. He looked as if he not only hadn't slept, but might never sleep again. Exultant, with a faint underlay of hysteria.

Ingrid said, " 'Vines.' That's a good name for them."

Gail glanced at the shuttle. "Has it done anything?"

"No," George said. "Gail, the cell walls—"

"I don't care," Gail said, and stalked back to the inflatable, leaving the two scientists staring after her as if it were she who was the actual alien.

By the time Nan and Lucy arrived, everyone was calling the aliens "Vines."

The rover pulled up at dawn, Nan at the wheel and Lucy asleep until the vehicle stopped. From the look of her, Nan was evidently on the same sort of accels as Ingrid and George. Nan's hair stuck out in ratty patches, her skin was still rubbed raw and bruised, and one front tooth was missing. She grinned, higher than clouds, at Gail. Their eyes met.

Gail was astonished at the feeling that rushed over her. She stood still in the middle of the quadrangle and let herself feel it.

*Oh, my God, no. Not her.*

Friend William Shipley's daughter.

Ex-con.

Willful, self-centered bitch. No matter how much she was "changing" as she "found her calling."

Blackmailer of Rudy Scherer.

*Not her.*

Nan seemed to know, or guess, what was happening. She stared steadily at Gail, assessing. Lucy woke up, looked around dazedly, and shook her head. Nan went on staring, and then she smiled at Gail, a smile so humble and beseeching, so unlike Nan Frayne, that Gail felt her legs carry her toward the rover.

"Hello, Nan. Lucy."

"Hello, Gail," Nan said softly, and that was all it took.

# 16

He had slept fitfully, dreaming vague, monstrous shapes without names. People came and went in the night; standing guard, he supposed. It wasn't until almost morning that he fell into anything like restful sleep, and when he awoke, Naomi had arrived on a Mira Corp rover with Lucy Lasky.

"Good morning, Dr. Shipley," Ingrid Johnson said. She seemed buoyant and uncharacteristically pleasant. "Nothing happened with the shuttle during the night. It's still just sitting there."

Jake, who did not look buoyant, said, "We've hauled water in the big skimmer for rudimentary washing. It's in the tank."

"Naomi is here, isn't she?" Shipley said. Lucy stood with her back to Jake, eating something George had apparently heated on the stove. George looked calm; he had apparently come to terms with shooting Erik Halberg. Or perhaps he was one of those people who never had to come to terms with their own actions.

Jake said shortly, "Yes. Nan and Lucy have arrived," and strode off to the skimmer.

Shipley said to Ingrid, "Where is Naomi? Do you know?"

"She might be asleep. They brought another inflatable—it's set up over there."

Shipley hadn't even noticed the second, smaller inflatable, set up to the right of the bunker. He didn't approach it. George was handing out steaming cups of coffee, and Shipley took one.

Surprised, George said, "That's the first time I've ever seen you take caffeine, Doctor."

Shipley didn't answer. It seemed too much effort to explain that no, ordinarily he didn't want the artificial animation, the distraction from his own inner silence, that even a minor stimulant like coffee provided. But this was not "ordinarily." He was already cut off from silence by emotional agitation, as unwelcome as physical spasms. Too much was happening. At least the coffee was hot.

He drank half of it and knew it was a mistake. The exhortation to simplicity was there for a reason. His heart thumped and skipped.

He was discreetly pouring the rest of the coffee onto the ground when Naomi, not asleep after all, came around the bulk of the larger skimmer with Gail, both of them lugging sacks.

"Morning, Dada," Naomi called. "Getting to look like a fucking used-vehicle lot around here, isn't it?" She gestured with her free hand at the two skimmers and the rover, and laughed.

She was on something a lot stronger than caffeine.

"Naomi—"

"I know, I look terrible," she said cheerfully, "but I'm actually all right. And my appearance isn't exactly critical at this point in human history, is it?" She half turned and winked at Gail, who frowned. Naomi did look terrible, Shipley thought, but she also looked something he'd never seen in her before: purposeful.

Jake appeared. "What's that, Gail?"

Gail set down her sack. To Shipley, she looked ready for battle. "Some equipment Nan and Lucy brought with them."

"What sort of equipment?" His tone was too level.

Gail took a step forward and looked straight into his eyes. "Let's have this out, Jake. I know you told them not to come, and they did, and you're riled as hell. But they're here now and they have some good ideas about the shuttle. You owe it to the situation to at least listen."

"I owe it to the expedition to send them back to Mira City. Which is what I'm doing."

"Like the autocratic goon you are," Naomi said.

"Nan—" Gail said.

"Shut up, Gail, I know she's your girlfriend now but that doesn't mean—"

"Why, Jake," Naomi taunted, "what happened to your famous diplomacy and tact?"

"You worthless bitch—"

"Jake, don't you dare call Nan—"

"Stop!" Shipley roared, and the three of them, along with the rest of the camp, fell silent.

Weariness washed over Shipley. *Girlfriend.* They all looked at him in astonishment: William Shipley, physician, New Quaker, who never raised his voice or gave orders. Laughable plastic icon. Believer in primitive mumbo jumbo. Lord, he was tired. The coffee had only made it worse.

He said, "I want us to join in a Meeting for Silence. All of us. Now."

He didn't even say please.

Something about Shipley's outburst seemed to have restored Jake's smoothness. "I think that's a good idea, Doctor. We could all use a moment of silence to pull ourselves together. Come on, let's sit down. George? Karim?"

Jake had named the two most amiable and least angry people in camp. They sank easily to the groundcover. Karim smiled up at Shipley, and with a soft grunt Shipley lowered himself to the trampled purple ground.

After a moment Ingrid sat, too, followed by Franz Mueller. Lucy moved unobtrusively to sit near Jake, a small cross-legged figure. She bent her head.

That left Naomi and Gail. Shipley tried to clear his mind, to ask nothing, to be demanding of nothing. Let the good come, whatever it might be. His task was, simply, to wait.

Gail and Naomi sat on the ground, holding hands.

No one spoke. A few people shifted restlessly: Gail, Franz. But into the silence came the sound of animal song, the shrill and oddly sweet flutings of what George had called a reptile-analogue. A small breeze, cool and fragrant, ruffled the groundcover. It still bore a faint tang of night-blooming flowers.

No testimony came to Shipley, nothing that moved him to speak aloud. But slowly the silence cleared him. He felt it sinking into him, that silence, palpable and warm as sunlight. His stomach unknotted. Peace crept into him, precious spiritual sustenance, in shared silence with this most unlikely congregation.

Shipley wasn't sure how much time passed. Probably longer than anyone thought. Time could lose its meaning, in profound silence. When someone finally spoke, it was George Fox. In a low, quiet voice the biologist said, "The shuttle door is opening."

They came out one by one by one, each on a small rolling cart. Again the incline of the shuttle ramp seemed too steep for the carts, which plunged down, teetered, then righted themselves. The three carts then stood in a still row.

They *were* plants, Shipley thought—and were not. His eyesight was in better shape than the rest of his aging body. Through the clear dome over each cart he could see clearly the central trunk, a reddish-brown cylinder maybe a foot in diameter, a yard high. It looked tough, like hide or wood. Off it sprouted many appendages—tentacles? branches?—that in turn sprouted flat, fleshy-looking, irregular ovals of tissue, maybe a hundred of them. Leaves. Or fingerless hands. A few of the leaves/hands on the ends of the longest tentacles/branches did seem to have fingers. Or maybe they were just deeply serrated leaves. Or maybe they were other, more flexible plant-things, like vines. Nothing on the aliens made for easy analogues with Earth life. Or with life on Greentrees, for that matter. These creatures lacked discernible heads, eyes, legs. Some of the branches/tentacles/vines lay coiled loosely on the floors of the carts.

None of the humans moved until Shipley, as slowly as he could, turned his head slightly to look at Franz Mueller. The soldier had a gun beside him on the ground, but he made no move to touch it.

Jake, too, was checking on Franz. When he was satisfied, he began to rise, as slowly as Shipley had turned his head. "Nobody else get up," he said quietly. "Let's not panic them again."

Naomi shifted, and Shipley was afraid she was going to flout his orders, make a scene, wreck the moment. But all she did was push her sack toward Jake.

"The Chinese-English translator," she said softly to Jake. "A long shot, but who knows?"

"Not yet," he said, and moved carefully forward.

As he started toward them, the aliens began to wave their leaves/hands/protuberances. Jake stopped.

Slowly one cart rolled forward.

Jake moved again, matching its pace. Shipley suddenly thought, irrelevantly, that one of Jake's negotiating tactics had always been to match his opponent's body language. That would be very difficult here.

At a glacial pace, alien and human moved forward. Eventually they met, halfway between shuttle and camp. Then they simply stood, Jake looking at the alien, the alien perhaps looking back. Or not.

Another cart began to inch forward.

Gail said, "George. You go. You're the biologist."

George Fox needed no urging. He got up so eagerly that Gail hissed, "Slowly!" George made himself move more slowly.

It took ten minutes for George and the second alien to meet. The third cart began to move.

Ingrid Johnson started to rise. Gail said, "No."

Ingrid began angrily, "But I'm—"

"The wrong person for this," Gail said, keeping her voice low. Nonetheless, did one of the aliens turn its trunk slightly toward her? "Dr. Shipley. Go."

Surprised, he rose. Yes, it felt right. This was what he was supposed to do.

Up close, the alien looked even stranger. Its body was not made of flesh, or wood, or chitin, but of some substance different from all of them. Shipley was twice as tall as the creature would have been without its low cart. He gazed down at the top of the alien, a slightly waving mass of branches and tentacles and protuberances that, he could now see, were perforated with hundreds of tiny holes. The nonprotuberance body parts, trunk and "vines," were covered with what looked like brownish slime.

Shipley heard himself say, "Jake, let's sit down. As we were when they came out."

Jake and George sat. *In silence,* Shipley thought. It was the motionless silence that had led the aliens to open their doors. The quietude and peace. Humans were so seldom quiet. So seldom still.

"Just sit," he said softly, and marveled at himself for usurping Jake's authority. Jake didn't seem to mind. George looked as if he could sit there, gazing hungrily at the aliens, forever.

But could the humans behind them, Naomi and Karim and the others?

They did better than Shipley would have imagined. It was half an hour before he sensed two more people creeping up behind him and sitting down. He didn't have to turn to know that they were Ingrid and Naomi. Whatever the others in the camp were now doing, presumably under Gail's direction, they were doing it quietly.

Another half hour passed.

Shipley could feel the second stage of silence taking him. First, the sweet shared peace. Then, sometimes, if one was fortunate, the deeper meaning. He had never found words to adequately describe it. The closest he had ever come was in a poem by Andrew Marvel, whose life had been the reverse of tranquil:

*Meanwhile the mind from pleasure less*
*Withdraws into its happiness;*
*The mind, that ocean where each kind*
*Does straight its own resemblance find;*
*Yet it creates, transcending these,*
*Far other worlds, and other seas;*
*Annihilating all that's made*
*To a green thought in a green shade.*

Now Shipley, a green thought in a green shade, had no idea how much time was passing. A deep joy pervaded him. Not the Truth of the Light, but something else, something of such beauty and humble gladness that—

"Pheromones," George Fox said. "They're drugging us. No, don't get up, it's okay. Very light."

Shipley stumbled upward, and his transcendence shattered.

The other four stayed where they were. Shipley staggered back to camp and said to Gail, "George says they're using pheromones on us. To make us feel things . . ."

"What things?" Gail demanded.

He couldn't say to her, *I thought I had touched my own soul.* Instead he said, "Happiness."

She frowned. "Artificial happiness? Like fizzies?"

But he had never tasted fizzies.

Lucy said, "That doesn't sound right, Doctor. Ingrid and George's tests said the aliens aren't DNA-based. How could they produce pheromones that affect our DNA-based systems?"

Shipley didn't know. Shame flooded him, that he had not been able to tell the difference between a genuine religious experience and a drug.

Gail said, "Should we go take them out of range? Whatever that is!"

"George says not. He seems to think it's just a . . . a light effect that humans can handle. Like caffeine."

But Shipley could not handle caffeine.

Gail frowned. "Well, all right . . . I guess he's the expert. But if it goes on too much longer . . . do you know how long you were just sitting there, Doctor?"

"No. But I'm going back."

"You are? *Why?*"

He couldn't explain. Because of the shame. Because in some way Gail could never see, he still felt he was meant to make this contact, with these aliens. Because his own soul directed him to, and that was the only genuine prompting of the Light that he'd received for days. But Gail wouldn't have understood any of that, so Shipley said the easiest thing. "Because Naomi is there."

Gail nodded, too disciplined to blush.

Shipley started back toward the shuttle. But Lucy put a hand on his arm. "Doctor . . . what do you think they want?"

"So far, they merely seem to want to sit with us."

"To sit with us," Gail repeated.

"Yes," Shipley said.

"Well, no harm in that, I suppose. But no gain either. Do you know you've been sitting there for six hours?"

Shipley hadn't. He shook his head. Gail then said, "Just sitting there without saying or doing anything—weren't you *bored*?" and he turned to stare at her in astonishment, this alien who did not understand the first thing about him at all.

Eventually the humans got hungry. Ingrid must have slipped away and then come back without Shipley hearing her, because a sandwich and bottle of water were quietly pushed toward him on the groundcover. He ate and drank both slowly, as did the others. This led to bathroom needs, and one by one the five people left softly and returned just as softly. The aliens didn't react, nor show any similar needs of their own. The joy-producing pheromones had stopped soon after they began.

By twilight, nothing had happened. Naomi slowly pulled her translator out of its sack. Jake didn't object, so she put it in front of him, turned it on, and returned quietly to her place.

"It's set to assimilate their language," she whispered, "and to put together a lexicon and grammar as soon as possible."

"They're not using any language," Jake pointed out.

"Maybe they will if we do."

"If this thing is so good, why didn't you use it with 'your' Furs?"

"They'd have smashed it," Naomi said.

Jake raised his voice, although it was still a pleasant low tone. "Hello."

Was there a response from the aliens? Shipley thought he saw slightly more branch/tentacle waving, but he couldn't be sure.

"Hello. We are humans." Slowly Jake pointed at himself and then at Shipley and George, seated beside him.

Nothing.

"Hello. We are humans. We are glad you are here."

Again the sweet, treacherous, drugged simulation of joy slipped into Shipley's mind.

"That's a positive response," George said. "Keep on talking, Jake."

"Hello," Jake repeated. "We are humans. We are glad you are here."

Naomi said from behind Shipley, "Hello. We are humans. We are glad you are here."

"Hello," George said, "we are humans. We are glad you are here."

Ingrid repeated this, and Shipley felt he had no choice but to do the same.

Regret washed over him. Silence as a form of communication was at an end.

# 17

For an hour, people went on speaking to the aliens, simple sentences about the trees, groundcover, sun, their bodies. Pointing and smiling accompanied the words. None of it seemed to make the slightest difference. Jake felt like an idiot.

He dozed off sitting on the "grass"; he hadn't had much sleep the last few nights. Beside him, George said urgently, "Wake up, Jake. Something's happening."

It was dusk again. One of the carts rolled toward the dead alien. Jake felt every muscle in his body tense. Was it going to come now, the retaliation?

The cart stopped beside the shattered dome. From his angle of vision, Jake could just make out a slot opening in the cart bed. Something snaked slowly out.

"Oh, bless my ears and whiskers," George breathed.

The tentacle slowly—how slowly! These creatures did nothing in haste—didn't resemble the vines inside the dome. The tentacle was slimy and viscous, like a slug but more so. It crept leisurely along the ground and over the dead alien. Then just as leisurely it crept back and slipped into the slot in the cart. The slot closed. All three carts rolled up the ramp and the shuttle door closed. It was full night.

George, Ingrid, and Shipley crowded around the body. "Glistening with residue," Ingrid said.

"I think it's dissolving," George said. "They left behind an acid or toxin or maybe a bacterialike organism."

Shipley said, "It might be infecting the environment."

"Get away from there," Jake said sharply. "No samples, Ingrid, George—*none.* We have no idea what the significance of that is to these . . . creatures."

" 'Vines,' " George said. "We should call them 'Vines.' Actually, Gail suggested the name. I have some speculations I want to talk about, Jake."

"At camp."

Gail and Karim had prepared food more elaborate than the usual synth instabake stuff. Jake suspected Karim was responsible for this; Gail had never been much of a cook. There was a casserole of actual vegetables from the farm Thekla was pioneering. The food revived Jake, who hadn't realized how hungry he was.

"Are the vegetables all right?" Karim said. "Thekla worries that the different soil will affect the taste of Earth produce."

"It tastes wonderful to me," Shipley said, "although I don't know if it's the vegetables or this wonderful sauce." Karim beamed.

Food didn't matter much to George. After a few hasty mouthfuls, he said, "Okay. Listen. I'd like to put together what we saw. Jump in when you want to disagree or augment me."

"That bioarm that dissolved the dead alien—"

"That did what?" Gail said, startled, and George had to backtrack to describe the event for those who'd remained the hundred yards away in camp.

"Anyway, the arm that came out of the cart resembled a biofilm, a colony of bacteria that can develop properties far more sophisticated than a single bacteria. Terran biofilms produce a coat of slime that protects them from some antibiotics. They also develop complicated chemical signal systems and complex architectures of tubes and water channels to distribute nutrients and oxygen. And they're mobile, creeping along on pili.

"Now, here's my reasoning: the Vines don't breathe our atmosphere, the domes over them argue that. They can't interact directly with the Greentrees environment. But they do have traces of that same slimy substance on them under the domes. An extension of that, controlled by the Vine, could seal itself inside the slime, protected from contamination by gas or solid outside the dome. It could also deposit on their dead fellow some chemical to dissolve its poor misplaced body."

"A death rite," Shipley said.

Lucy said, "But why did it take so long? We killed the Vine yesterday." She glanced around for Franz Mueller, but he was at the stove, not listening.

Ingrid said thoughtfully, "The Vine might have needed that long to synthesize the bioarm. They seem to do everything very slowly."

George was gathering enthusiasm. "They're not DNA-based, so—"

"There goes panspermia as a galactic theory," Ingrid said.

"—so even though they're something like animals and something like plants and something like bacteria, we can't assume too much analogous function. But at least that triple hybrid is a way to begin thinking about them."

Gail said tartly, "And do these thoughts include what they might do to us? If they do everything so slowly, maybe they take revenge slowly, too."

Jake had been thinking the same thing. "Tomorrow we should resume sitting there just the way we did today. Remind them that we're trying to make nonviolent contact."

Ingrid said, "You don't know that's how they're interpreting what we're doing. You don't even know they're aware we're there at all."

"Oh, great," Gail said. "Knocking at the door of aliens that can't hear. That's a good use of time."

"It is, though," Nan Frayne said, and Gail made a face.

Jake said, "Anything on your translator program, Nan?"

"Of course not. They have to make sounds before sounds can be analyzed."

Gail said, "I've been thinking. Perhaps a team should sit here and meditate with the aliens. But it doesn't need all of us to do that. Faisal has been comlinking all day, Jake. He's doing a good job of running Mira City, with Fengmo's help, but there's a lot of corporate information they just don't have. I think I should go back tomorrow, with maybe Lucy and Karim and Nan and Dr. Shipley."

Nan said angrily, "I'm not leaving!"

"Nor me," said Karim. "As long as there's a chance I might get inside that shuttle, I want to stay."

Shipley said, "I, too, would like to stay, although I don't think I can sit all day on the ground again. These old bones are too stiff. I could stay in camp."

Lucy said nothing. Jake hadn't spoken to or looked at her; he was still angry she'd come to camp against his direct orders. She flushed and looked at the ground.

Gail said, "You mean I'm the only one leaving?" She looked directly at Nan, whose brows rushed together in a deep scowl.

Nan said shortly, "Looks that way. Unless you decide to stay."

Gail scowled, too. "I have obligations."

Nan shrugged. *Battle of the Titans,* Jake thought. Two strong-willed lovers; it would never work. They would kill each other. This thought made him think more kindly of Lucy, usually so pliable. Although not about being here at camp.

Gail said stiffly, "Then Lucy and I will return to Mira City tomorrow," and Lucy didn't contradict her.

George was still theorizing. "Terran plants are amazing biochemists. They produce a huge array of complicated molecules, not only to sustain themselves but to manipulate animals. Scent to attract pollinators. Toxins to repel predators. Even methods of regulating other species' reproduction . . . Did you know that there's a certain tree that includes in its leaves a molecule that prevents caterpillars from ever turning into butterflies? A way of limiting leaf-eaters."

"So maybe now we're all sterile," Gail said.

George ignored her sarcasm. "I'm thinking of that intoxicating scent the Vines released when we started talking. They *wanted* us to go on talking. They synthesized and released, probably from that same slot in the cart as the biofilm, a molecule that would please us. But we're DNA and they're not! Think about that a minute. They knew enough about us to create that molecule after a day's exposure to us, and without any direct physical contact!"

Ingrid said, "They could have been sampling the air from the second the shuttle landed. The air swarms with DNA life."

Jake said, "Or they could have been here before." The idea had just occurred to him, and it was appalling. "George, can you make a guess at the relationship between the Vines and the Furs, other than both having come to Greentrees from somewhere else?"

"No," George said.

"But the Furs are DNA-based."

"Oh, yes. They're similar to Terran mammals. Not to any one species, but they're bipedal, warm-blooded, brain encased in a cranial membrane, and so forth. In fact, remarkably like us, which suggests there may be one basic optimum configuration for evolving DNA-based sentience."

"What if," Jake said slowly, "the Vines are here because of the Furs? They're obviously much more advanced than Furs or—"

"Plants are advanced?" Gail said skeptically.

George said, "It depends on what 'advances' you value. We value language, writing, all that. But plants evolved on Earth earlier than we did, and have adapted to more niches. In fact, you could argue that plants have domesticated us and not the other way around. For millennia humans have improved plant species by artificial selection. We also carry their genes farther distances than they could themselves, and we nourish them for their flowers and fruit and grains. In one sense, we're the plants' servants. We've functioned to help them reproduce, conquer disease, and multiply. *We* serve *them.*"

"I'm going to bed," Gail said abruptly.

If she expected Nan to follow her, she was disappointed. But Shipley said, "Me, too," and Jake saw how haggard the old man looked.

George was unstoppable. "In fact, if plants hadn't developed flowers, humans might not exist. The majority of large mammals could only occur after fruits and seeds concentrated and multiplied the world's supply of food energy. Without flowers, the world might still belong to reptiles. Flowers created us, and they developed shapes and scents pleasing to us, and we in turn serve them. They enslave us with beauty and sweetness, just like women."

Nan snorted. Despite himself, Jake looked at Lucy.

"And these Vines," Ingrid said, and there wasn't quite the enthusiasm in her voice that there'd been in George's, "intoxicated us once. Already."

Karim said, "And as toolmakers they're also better than we are. They have that ship that can accelerate/decelerate at rates we can only dream of."

Private Mueller suddenly appeared. "Mr. Holman, I think we must have the guard again tonight, all the night."

"Yes," Jake said, "I think you're right."

He left George and Ingrid still talking botany and walked a little way toward the grove of tall narrow trees, hoping that Lucy would follow. She did.

"Jake, I'm sorry that I disobeyed your orders and came here."

"No, you're not. And I'm not either, not anymore."

He put his arms around her and she leaned against him. She felt delicious in his arms. "Ah, Lucy, how can I tell you what to do, you or anybody else? This is an unprecedented situation. Where in the Mira Corp charters do I look up 'Director's Behavior During Silent First Contact With Alien Plants'?"

She laughed. "Do you think they're going to blow us all away, Jake? Is this our last night alive?"

"If so, let's make the most of it." His hand moved to her breast.

"But you don't really think—"

"I think tomorrow will be exactly like today," Jake said. "More sitting, more meditating, more futile chattering. And nothing will happen."

Her voice dropped, grew huskier. "Then maybe we should—"

"Jake, Lucy," Ingrid's voice said, "I'm sorry to bother you . . ."

"Then don't!" Jake snapped. God, couldn't he have even this one moment of unanticipated sweetness?

Ingrid emerged from the shadows, her tone hardening. "Gail said to get you. Faisal just comlinked. There's a quee message from Earth."

"Repeat it once more," Jake said, not caring if he sounded redundant. He was finding it hard to concentrate.

Faisal spoke slowly and clearly from Mira City. " 'Third Life Alliance in charge in Geneva. War continues. Resources strained but hope to launch small scientific ship to Greentrees late next year to meet aliens. Meanwhile preserve good relations with aliens at all cost.' "

Jake pulled at the skin on his face. *Preserve good relations with aliens at all cost.* Right. And the quee referred to the Furs; no message had as yet been sent to Terra about the Vines.

Lucy said, "Who are the 'Third Life Alliance'?"

"We don't know," Gail said. "Whoever came to power, I guess."

"But will they still be in power late next year?" George said.

Ingrid said, "It doesn't say who this Third Life Alliance are conducting a war *against.* Quee messages keep getting shorter and shorter."

"Preserving resources," George said.

Lucy's voice was troubled. "So the new scientific expedition can't arrive for at least six years, ship time? Seventy-two years to us?"

"Not necessarily," Karim said. "It's been over seventy years since we left Earth. There might have been great scientific advances. They might have some new faster drive or space-time shortcut."

"Not if they've been using all their resources fighting wars," George said.

Everyone fell silent. Finally Faisal's voice said over the link, "Jake? Should I answer?"

"No," Jake said, "not yet. Let's wait until we see what develops here with the Vines."

"As you say," Faisal said neutrally.

Jake felt Lucy's small hand steal into his. The thin fingers were warm, but he knew his libidinous mood was not returning this night. He was suddenly exhausted, and all he wanted was sleep.

By dawn the dead alien's corpse had disappeared. The underlying groundcover didn't appear affected except for the parts blocked from sunlight by the shattered cart, but George and Ingrid immediately began taking samples.

"Either go back to camp with those or sit still here," Jake said. "The—"

"Here they come," Nan said.

The shuttle door opened and the three carts tumbled down. Jake, George, Ingrid, and Nan sat in the same positions as yesterday, Nan turning on the Chinese-English translator. "I had a thought in the night," she said. "This thing picks up the vibration range of the human voice, but that's all. What if the Vines are trying to talk to us in that range only dogs can hear, what's it called—"

"Ultrasonic," Ingrid said.

"Then if they are, or some other range, we wouldn't even know if a—"

"Hello," a Vine said.

Jake's head jerked back so fast his neck snapped. For a moment he couldn't see. His chest pounded. When his vision cleared, he saw that the others were looking at him.

"H-hello," he said.

"Hello, Jake Holman." The voice was level, uninflected. Mechanical.

"*They've* got a translator," Ingrid said, "working off everything we said yesterday. My God, it must be biological, maybe membranes vibrated by chemical signal . . ."

"The human eardrum is biological," George said. "Hello!"

"Hello, George Fox."

Jake repeated what yesterday had been canned prattle and today was amazing truth. "Hello. We are humans. We're glad you're here."

Instantly the sweet mild intoxicant filled him. That was their preferred way of communicating; the translator was just for the benefit of the humans. The scent was distracting. And this was, after all, a negotiation . . . His old skills rushed in, reassuring him.

"Please do not send us scents. We want more to talk." Always start strong, establishing dominance.

"Yes," a Vine said, and the intoxicant lessened, dissipating on the slight breeze until it disappeared.

"Thank you," Jake said. Should he apologize for the death of the Vine? Not yet. Stay in a strong position. But not too strong. Most humans, Jake knew, were not open to new information because they were made too uncomfortable by feeling ignorant; better to just close your mind entirely. Were the Vines the same way? Best to proceed on that assumption until he knew different. Don't seem overbearing.

The Vine said, "We are surprised to find you on this planet."

*Me, too,* Jake thought. He said, "We came . . ." How long ago in Greentrees rotations? The "month" was a meaningless concept when you had three moons. ". . . half a year ago." Close enough.

"You come from world what?"

"It's called 'Earth.' " That gave away nothing.

"Where?"

"Far away," Jake said.

"We come from world a hundred light-years away."

*They're being very open,* thought Jake, followed instantly by, *they're lying.* Too far. Even at c they would have needed a hundred years to get here, not even including acceleration or deceleration, although Karim had said they could do that frighteningly fast. But Karim had also said their orbital ship was small, how could it sustain even cold-sleep life for that long? Although—

The Vine's next words knocked the hazy calculations out of Jake's head. "Other aliens here not you come from very closer."

"Other . . . other aliens?"

"Look like you. Same genes."

The Furs. *All you bipedal warm-blooded DNA types look alike.*

It knew the word "genes." Had someone used that word here yesterday, or had the Vines been listening to the camp from a hundred yards away?

What did they know about us?

He said, "Same genes, yes. Where do they come from?"

The slot in the bottom of the cart opened. The bioarm slithered out. Instinctively Jake recoiled, then made himself sit still. The arm spread itself into a flat, irregularly shaped blob. It began to change color.

"It's *drawing,*" Nan whispered.

Most of the blob turned dark. Scattered across it were light dots. Jake said, "I don't—"

"It's the sky," Nan said. "The same one you've been looking at every night, dummy, the constellations as seen from Greentrees!"

Jake didn't notice constellations. One "star" started to glow redly. The Vine said, "The enemy's star system."

*Enemy?*

"They kill us," the Vine said. "Like you kill one of us, but they do not stop like you stop. They kill us on our planets. We cannot talk with them like we talk with you. They do not sit with us in the sun. They only kill."

"Your people are at war with the other aliens. The ones with our genes."

"Yes. Long war. Eight thousand Greentrees years."

Jake's mind reeled. He willed it steady and sorted through this information overload. Ingrid said, "Time dilation . . ."

"Yes," the Vine agreed in its mechanical voice. "They kill us and kill us."

Jake risked, "And you kill them."

"No."

"You do not kill them."

"No. You are sorry you kill one of us."

Jake said, "Very very sorry."

"Yes. We see. You sit with us in the sun."

The bioarm turned monochromatic and slithered back into the cart slot. Jake said firmly, "We are not your enemies."

"Yes, you are not," the Vine agreed.

"We are not the other aliens' enemies."

"Yes, you are not."

At least that much was established. Maybe Mira City could remain neutral, a noncombatant in whatever was going on between these two powerful species . . . except that the Furs on Greentrees had looked anything but powerful.

A war that had gone on for eight thousand years.

Nan said, "The other aliens . . . we call them 'Furs.' "

"Furs," the Vine repeated. Impossible to know if it understood the word's root meaning.

Nan continued, "The Furs on this planet, on Greentrees, they are your enemies?"

"No," the Vine said. "Yes."

The humans looked at each other.

The Vine said, "The Furs who live on another star system they kill us. The Furs on Greentrees do not kill us."

"Oh," Nan said. "Why not?"

"They have not weapons to hurt us," the Vine said logically.

Jake said, "Why did the other Furs leave these Furs here on Greentrees, without weapons?"

Now it was the Vines who were silent. Minutes passed. Were they communicating? Each Vine was sealed in a separate dome. They could be signaling by minutely waving fronds or whatever their appendages were . . . but could they actually see? Nothing on them resembled eyes.

Finally the same Vine, clearly their spokesperson, said, "The other Furs not leave these Furs without weapons on Greentrees. The other Furs not bring these Furs to Greentrees. These Furs are experiment in your genes. To win the war.

"We made the Furs on Greentrees."

It went on all day. At noon Jake couldn't listen anymore. Something in him reached saturation. George and Ingrid were asking biology questions, and the Vine was answering them partly in words, partly in bioarm drawings. The "talking" Vine seemed to have endless patience, just as the two silent Vines seemed to have an endless capacity to sit, silent, moving only when necessary to stay in the sun.

Jake rose, every muscle stiff from sitting so long on the groundcover. He badly needed to pee. He said courteously, "I must go now. George and Ingrid and Nan will stay to talk, if you agree."

The Vine said, "We agree. A little more talk. But then we sit together."

Oh, God, Jake was making a breach of protocol by skipping the sitting-together part. He was about to say he would rejoin them soon when the Vine said, "You must go, Jake. You are a mobile."

A what?

"You are all mobiles, are you all mobiles? We think yes. Mobiles must run and walk and go. On our world our mobiles do not talk. They do not sit together with us. We love them as mobiles. You humans"—George had taught them the word—"are partly mobiles, partly Vines."

"Yes," Jake said, because it was instinct with him to agree with strong statements and then work to modify his agreement later, according to negotiating necessity. But what had he agreed to? That humans were "partly mobile and partly Vine."

*"We love them as mobiles."*

George said eagerly, "Tell us about the mobiles on your world."

"No, it is not mobile time," the Vine said obscurely.

"Then tell us—" Jake left.

Gail and Lucy had not set out for Mira City, after all. Jake could hardly blame them. Talking Vines were a lot more compelling than mute Vines. "You heard?"

"The sensors are all still in place out there," Gail said. "My God, Jake, what does it mean? A war? They 'made' the Furs on Greentrees?"

"I know as much as you do," Jake said wearily. "We need to hear how George and Ingrid put it together. And you, Lucy. Societies we can't examine directly are your bailiwick, too."

It was a peace offering, and Jake saw that she accepted it as such. He was suddenly very glad she hadn't gone back to Mira City. Last evening's rage had evaporated in the unanticipated bout of lovemaking in the middle of the night, when Jake had slept off his first exhaustion. People, he knew, did sometimes fall into sex when danger was running high. But he had never done so before. His own behavior bewildered him. Lucy smiled at him, and the smile warmed his confused mind.

She said, "I have some ideas, unless of course they get modified by whatever gets said this afternoon. The Fur societies may be at different technological levels for some good reason. I'm going to bring the plant-sitters something to eat."

"After that could I talk to you a few—"

"Mr. Holman!" It was Karim, looking determined. "May I please get aboard that Vine shuttle? Will you ask permission of the Vines?"

Jake gazed at the young physicist. Everybody had a different slant here. Karim looked not the slightest bit interested in the Vine biology that so captivated George and Ingrid, nor in the alleged creation of Furs that fascinated Lucy and Nan, nor even in being caught in the crossfire of some sort of interstellar war. Karim was after the alien physics, and he had the single-minded look of a bloodhound on the scent. All that was missing was the baying.

"I don't know, Karim. They haven't offered to let us inspect the shuttle close up."

"We haven't asked."

"True. But it would be a mistake to push them."

Karim said, "They seem ready to answer any questions we ask, and they're giving us far more information about them than we're giving them about us. Do you have any reason to think they might refuse to let me go inside the shuttle?"

He would have made a good lawyer. "Let me think about it,"

Jake said. Karim moved off, looking unhappy. "Lucy, where are Mueller and Dr. Shipley?"

Her thin, pretty face grew somber. "They're taking a walk. Franz is having a very hard time with what Scherer did and Halberg did and he himself did. Dr. Shipley tested Franz's cerebrospinal fluid again, and then he said he and Franz were going to take a walk."

Gail said bitterly, "Let's just hope Mueller doesn't shoot Shipley."

Jake understood the bitterness; she was having a hard time herself with what had happened. She and Jake had hired the Swiss security team. He felt guilty, too. He said, "How did they all elude the background checks? Did you ask Nan Frayne?"

Gail accepted the connection that his question implied. Lucy moved tactfully away, out of earshot. "Dr. Shipley was right. Scherer had arranged for all the . . . the rebuilt work to be done after we'd finished our checks and before we launched from Earth. Of course, they'd started the clones years earlier. Mueller and Josef Gluck, the youngest, were barely out of their teens. Scherer had served under their fathers. It was a multigenerational pact."

Jake asked, "Funded how?"

"Nan didn't know. Wherever the money came from, Scherer was very careful covering it up. In fact, I was surprised to learn that hidden fortunes were possible in this comlinked age."

*Oh, they were possible,* Jake thought, and carefully kept his face from giving anything away. "How did Nan learn about it?"

Gail looked briefly away. "In prison. A chance encounter. She has a varied history, that one."

"Gail . . . are you sure you know what you're doing, choosing Nan?"

"Of course I don't know what I'm doing," Gail snapped. "What makes you think any of us know what we're doing? We're awash in aliens while simply trying to survive on an alien planet. Which reminds me, Thekla has a problem with the genemod wheat. She wants to talk to you."

Jake found he was glad to comlink Thekla, back at the Mira City farms. It made things seem almost normal.

Almost.

# 18

Shipley came back from his walk with Franz Mueller more troubled than when he'd left. The soldier had insisted on carrying a weapon and on staying within sight of the group by the shuttle at all times. As a result, the walk had comprised a large semicircle, with Franz paying more attention to the aliens than to the conversation.

The only time Shipley felt he'd had Franz's attention was when he said quietly, "You didn't want to have the cloned organs put in, did you?"

"Yes, I did want!" Franz almost shouted. A moment later he turned stony. "Captain Scherer make the clone for me, when I am still nineteen, twenty years old. My father and Captain Scherer. My father commands the unit Captain Scherer serves. Captain Scherer saves my father's life, in the fighting at Rio de Janeiro . . . you remember the fighting at Rio?"

"I've read about it," Shipley said. Food riots, about as brutal as urban uprisings could get. It made painful reading; what had it been like to live it?

Mueller continued, "They swear the *Blutpakt.* All of them alive after the fighting swear the *Blutpakt.*"

Shipley nodded. These were—had been—increasingly common on the Earth the *Ariel* had left behind. The word might be German or Italian or Bantu or Chinese, and the details differed, but the intent was the same. In a fragmented and lonely century, with globalization bringing neither strong kinship ties nor strong religion, a blood pact meant completely reliable loyalty. The members could count on each other for help, protection, companionship, continuity, no matter what else happened in their life. They lived near each other, took care of each other. They were what a community should be, had perhaps once been.

Was a New Quaker meeting only a milder version of a *Blutpakt,* cemented by different means?

No. A meeting did not create, nurture, and murder innocent cloned human beings for a chance at extended life.

"Franz, you could have had a *Blutpakt* without becoming rebuilts."

He didn't answer, staring fixedly at the shuttle.

Shipley said, "You feel terrible about shooting Captain Scherer. Don't you also feel terrible about killing your clone?"

"No. The clone is not a human, it is the clone. Doctor, *Entschuldigen Sie,* but you are not a priest. I am Catholic when I am a boy, but I am not Catholic now. And you are not a priest."

True enough. Shipley had started this walk to see if he could make Franz feel better, ease some of his guilt. Somewhere Shipley had gone off track. But the image in his mind, of a teenage Franz Mueller drooling and smiling, then strapped down and butchered for his heart, his liver . . . Shipley shuddered. The image didn't seem to horrify Franz the way it did him.

"Franz, I must, as a doctor, ask you some questions."

"Ask."

Shipley ran through an artful list, designed to elicit not only information on Franz's physical state but his emotional one as well. When he was finished, Shipley knew no more than when he began. Franz was not sleeping well, but then, who was? He was jumpy, given to mood swings, uncertain about the future, wary of the Vines. But he did not seem depressed, delusional, paranoid, manic, or schizophrenic. He was merely the callous and confused product of a callous and confused age, thrust into a situation that would confuse a Buddha. Or a George Fox, original version.

George Fox, current version, seemed the least confused person in camp. He hurried in at midafternoon, carrying a clanking nest of empty canteens like robot dogs on strings. "Karim! Where's Karim, Doctor?"

"Latrine, I believe."

"The Vines said he can go aboard their shuttle!"

Beside Shipley, Franz Mueller tensed. "I go, also."

Jake said, "No."

At first Shipley thought that Jake was forbidding Karim access to the shuttle. However, Jake addressed only Franz. "No weapons aboard the Vine shuttle, or anywhere near them in person. They're friendly to us, and we want to keep it that way."

Franz said, "With respect, Mr. Holman—they *seem* friendly."

"Appearances are enough for now. No weapons."

"I can go if I leave weapons here?"

Shipley saw Jake hesitate before he turned. "Doctor?"

"Franz does not seem mentally unbalanced in any way." But he was augmented, surely, in ways Shipley couldn't imagine, and was capable of doing a great deal of damage even without visible weapons. *Say no, Jake.*

"Yes, *if* you leave all weapons here. And if you stay just outside the shuttle, watching Dr. Mahjoub as he goes in."

"*Ja,*" Franz said solemnly.

Shipley watched the two of them set off toward the shuttle. A path was becoming beaten into the purple groundcover. Behind him Lucy Lasky said suddenly, "Everything has a suspended feel, doesn't it? Like we're all hanging over a . . . a huge chessboard and we don't know what moves will come next."

*More like hanging over an abyss.* Shipley didn't say this aloud. He watched the growing group around the Vines, Karim and Franz added to George and Ingrid and Naomi. He wished he could find a moment of inner silence: quiet, peaceful.

Unsuspended.

The Vines again went inside their shuttle at dusk, and Karim dropped his bomb. "It's not theirs."

At first no one but Shipley heard him. George went on talking about the observed properties of the bioarm, interrupted often by Ingrid. Shipley said to Karim, "What isn't theirs?"

"The shuttle," Karim said and this time he raised his voice. "The shuttle doesn't belong to the Vines. It's not theirs."

Jake turned slowly to stare at Karim.

Shipley said, "Whose is it?"

Karim shrugged. "I can't tell that. How could I know? But the inside is not configured for them. There are *seats,* molded up from the floor and not removable. What would the Vines need with seats? And the control console is too tall for their height. They've built a step up to it, and they've built little racks to hold their carts while they're inside, but both are alterations to the original hull, built out of different materials."

He had the total attention of the entire camp.

"There's a slime coating over the entire inside, but it doesn't cover the controls. I didn't get to see the engine, of course, but what I could deduce about it from guessing at the controls just doesn't seem . . . right for Vines."

George said urgently, "Karim, what do the molded seats look like?"

Karim made a vague shape in the air.

"I mean," George said even more urgently, "do they seem made for a bipedal creature not quite our height with a place for a thick powerful tail?"

Shipley saw immediately what George meant. It made him a little dizzy.

"Yes!" Karim said. "I didn't realize it . . . but those seats would fit Furs perfectly! So would the height of the control console! It's a Fur ship!"

"Or was," Ingrid said.

Shipley caught sight of Naomi. His daughter stood very still, and he felt the conflict within her. She had championed the Furs. She was fascinated by the Vines. The two were at war, and the Vines may have taken over a Fur ship, but not one built by any Furs on Greentrees.

She looked straight at him and snapped, as if the interstellar war were his fault, "Get away from me!"

He didn't move. After a moment Naomi did, to the other side of George, who was so caught up in theorizing that he hadn't noticed the exchange between father and daughter.

"If the Vines are telling the truth," George said, "then they've been at war with the original Furs for millennia. Time dilation at a huge fraction of c would make that possible, wouldn't it, Karim? Especially since that drive you mentioned, what did you call it—"

"The McAndrew Drive," Karim said. "Yes, it would let them accelerate and decelerate really fast, so the shipboard time would be very small compared to the lapsed time on their two planets. Or on Greentrees."

"So the Vines have a bio-based technology," George rushed on, "and the Furs have physics-based tech. Like this shuttle. And if they're at war with each other . . ." He seemed to run out of statement.

Lucy said, "There's never been an historical case where a lesser technology defeated a greater one for very long."

Ingrid said, "But which here is 'greater'? Biotech or physics tech? We don't know enough about either one, as these aliens practice it, to decide."

Shipley said quietly, "It also depends on your definitions of 'great' and 'defeat.' " No one heard him.

Karim tried to say something, but Ingrid was louder. She said, "The Vines said they *made* the Furs on Greentrees. I think they mean it literally. They created several groups of Furs in different colonies, and then—"

Naomi said angrily, "How could anyone 'create' entire adult members of a species not even based on the same gene stuff?"

Ingrid ignored Naomi, the nonscientist. "—and then the Vines altered each colony differently. One colony was made incurious and inadaptable. One made permanently intoxicated. The Cheyenne-territory colony made, I don't know, maybe—"

Lucy said, "A controlled experiment. But why?"

Jake said, "To find a bioweapon that would incapacitate the Furs on their home planet."

"And also—" Karim began. Naomi cut him off, snarling, "That's dumb. Why not just kill the Furs on the Fur home planet?"

No one spoke. Into the silence Shipley said wearily, "Because they don't practice killing."

His daughter turned on him. "They're not fucking *Quakers*. Dad! Keep your anachronistic religion out of this!"

"No," Jake said, "Dr. Shipley's right. Look at the evidence. We blew up the Vine ship. They didn't blow up ours in retaliation. We killed the first one of them off the shuttle. They didn't fire back. We—"

Ingrid demanded, "How do you know they even have weapons?"

Karim said, "They have weapons. Also, they—"

George said, "There's no species I know of that doesn't have some defensive measures, even if it's running away. Of course, that's Terran animal species, which these are not. Although plant defenses—"

Ingrid said, "I'm still bothered by the idea that the Vines could create an adult society of Furs without—"

Karim shouted, "Will you listen to me!"

Everyone stared. Karim, the polite young Arab and junior scientist, never yelled. He said, "I keep trying to tell you. The Vines said to me during my shuttle inspection that tomorrow they're going to the Fur colonies on Greentrees. They invited us to come along. They're perfectly willing to explain what they're doing, I think. After all, they've explained everything else we've wanted to know.

"All we have to do is *ask.*"

An alien, plantlike society that practiced nonviolence.

That's what Shipley had said to Jake. But it wasn't really true, was it? If everything speculated about in camp this evening was true, Shipley thought, then the Vines practiced a kind of violence equally as horrifying as the rebuilts' kind. Rebuilts manipulated genes, the stuff of life, to create living sources of spare parts. Vines manipulated genes to create ways of destroying their enemies' brains, rendering them so passive they couldn't even care for themselves. How nonviolent was that?

Shipley couldn't sleep. He'd crept out of the inflatable somewhere between midnight and dawn, leaving the others breathing deeply after hours of excited talk. Lucy Lasky was on guard duty. She nodded to him but asked him no questions, for which he was grateful. Gail or Ingrid would have told him to go back to bed, or stay in camp, or otherwise remain where, even asleep, he couldn't escape human noise. Chatter. Snoring. Crying out in nightmares Shipley didn't want to know about.

He walked away from camp, avoiding the directions of both the shuttle and the small inflatable occupied by Naomi and Gail. It wasn't really dark; two moons and a glory of stars shone in a clear sky, and the light signal continued to flash from the top of the tower, beacon to any Vines that might be left in the mother ship. Although Karim had said it was small for an interstellar ship, that living pod bulging from its stick above the high-density disk. These four—now three—Vines might be all that the ship had contained.

Shipley didn't want to think about what Karim had said, what any of them had said. He wanted silence.

The purple groundcover, ghostly silver by moonlight, wasn't broken by boulders or fallen logs. Shipley had brought an inflatable stool with him, so lightweight he hardly noticed carrying it but strong enough to support his bulk. He inflated it and sat down heavily, facing away from camp. Something small scurried away from him in the groundcover. He ignored it; his boots were practically impenetrable. The sweet night scent of Greentrees wafted around him.

Truth, simplicity, silence, conscience. Those were the New Quaker tenets. "The truth shall make you free," the Bible said, and it was right: truth set one free from deception, meaninglessness, emptiness, egocentricity. The truth was the best that was in each person, the inner light that could blossom into joy. The New Quakers had departed from Earth because there seemed no Terran society left that didn't value lies, image, scams, celebrity, and cynicism over truth.

So why was he having such a hard time hearing the truth inside him?

The Vines had deliberately refused the chance to kill humans in retaliation for the killing that had been done to them. They had answered, as far as Shipley could judge, every question the humans asked with openness and truth. They had demonstrated, as finely as any Quaker in history had ever done, that it was possible to offer to aggressors a potent nonviolence and so turn them into allies. It was as if the Vines had read the George Fox of six hundred years ago: "*Take away the occasion of war.*" Shipley couldn't imagine a more eloquent peace testimony than the ones these strange aliens had offered humans.

And yet they were at war with the Furs. Hadn't the Vines offered the Furs the same nonviolence as they'd offered to humans? Perhaps they had, and the Furs had refused to respond, redoubling their own attacks. If those space Furs were anything like the ones that Naomi had stayed with near Larry Smith's Cheyenne, Shipley could believe it.

A truly nonviolent group would then have refused to retaliate, even if it meant death. Better death than participating in evil. But the Vines had, apparently, not reacted that way. Instead they had brought DNA samples of Furs, or Fur embryos, or something, to this remote planet, had engineered multiple colonies of Furs, and had begun experimenting on them, using living beings with the same cold-blooded lack of regard that Franz Mueller had expressed for his murdered clone.

Was any of this even true? It was the result, after all, of the Vines' word—if "word" was the correct term—combined with theorizing by George, Ingrid, and Lucy.

On the other hand, the theory fit Occam's razor: it was the simplest explanation that was consistent with observed fact and didn't leave out any facts.

Simplest? A plant-run controlled experiment in eugenic horror on an alien planet—that was the simplest explanation?

Shipley put his hand on his chest. Lately he could feel his heart skip beats, despite the mechanical regulator. It hadn't done that on Earth seven years ago, seventy years ago. He slapped another patch on his neck and his chest quieted. Still, no organ lasted forever, no matter how you conserved it. You could only replace it, like Franz had—

He was going around and around in unproductive circles. So he stopped thinking and let the silence of the night fill him. Gradually, his agitated mind calmed. Shipley sat there a long time, until his legs were stiff and his truth came to him somewhere before the brightening dawn.

It wasn't a large truth. No great light shining on the problems of the Vines, or the Furs, or Naomi, or Franz. But Shipley was grateful for the knowledge that did come to him, because it said clearly what he must do. There was no greater blessing than to know you were acting in accordance with right.

It was right for him to go with the Vines to each Fur colony. He would be needed. He didn't know for what, but he would be needed. His part in this—whatever "this" actually was—was not yet over.

At peace, Shipley lumbered to his feet. He stretched, feeling his old bones creak, and started back to the sleeping camp.

# 19

Gail said, "You're very hard on your father," and immediately regretted it. Now they would have yet another fight, and they'd already had two in as many days. Neither woman was the type to back down.

But Nan only rolled over on her belly and said, "Let me tell you a story from when I was a kid."

Gail squinted at her in the dim light. It was sometime after midnight, but they had left the screened top of the inflatable open and cool starlight turned everything silver. Gail, chilly after the heat of lovemaking had worn off, lay wrapped in a blanket. Nan, who never seemed to get cold or hot or hungry or tired, lay naked, her negligible ass a slight mound in the long taut length of her body. Gail could see the scars, some old and some new, which Nan seemed to pay as little attention as she did to any bodily need except sex.

"When I was eight or nine," Nan said, "I wanted a cat. Not just any cat, a genemod cat I saw advertised on the vids. My mother had died a few months before, and I really wanted this cat. It was bright blue and it had huge silver eyes and big ears like an elephant and it could talk. Not really, of course, but there was an audio program wired in its throat to respond to different tensions on the vocal chords, so that when it made a low contented purr there also came out words saying 'I'm so happy' or some such shit."

"I remember them," Gail said. She'd thought them hideous, but then when Nan had been eight or nine, Gail had been twenty-eight or -nine.

"I wanted this cat with everything that was in me. I tried to wear my father down. I talked about the cat at breakfast. I talked about the cat at lunch. I talked about the cat at dinner. I'd stand outside the bathroom while he was in there peeing, and shout through the door about the cat. I emailed him holos of the cat. I was relentless."

Gail had no trouble believing this.

"The weird thing was, I could have afforded to just go buy the fucking cat. I had money my grandmother had given me over the years, quite a lot of it, in a bank account. But I wanted *him* to give me the cat. To show that he knew how much I wanted it, or that he approved of my desire, or some such fucking thing."

*To show that he loved you,* Gail thought. She put her hand on Nan's bare ass. Nan didn't seem to notice.

"But he wouldn't buy me the cat. Instead he'd sit me down and talk to me gently about simplicity, and nonviolence, and the truth of letting natural creatures be what they were instead of altering their genes just for the vanity and egocentricity of humans. He'd go on and on, always patient, never losing his temper. And I'd get more and more insistent about wanting the cat. I spray-painted a picture of the cat on his doctor-office door. I threw tantrums in public. I even traced the outline of the cat on his bed in my own shit."

*Oh, my God,* thought Gail. *Poor Dr. Shipley.*

"The more I pushed, the more he talked to me patiently and dragged me to silent Meetings for Worship and tried to do stupid things like read me bedtime stories. But I didn't stop asking for the cat."

"It was a power struggle."

"You bet your talented fingers. So one day he comes home with this kitten. *Not* the cat. Not genemod. An ordinary, wide-eyed, puking-cute kitten, gray with white stripes. And that's supposed to settle me. Do you know what I did?"

"What?" Gail already knew she wasn't going to like the answer.

"I took my money out of the bank and I took the kitten to a geneshop on the Indian reservation. They were legal there, you know, it wasn't U.S. land so—"

"I know," Gail said. "Go on . . ."

Nan rolled over, shaking off Gail's hand, and she lay on her back, looking up through the mesh screen at the stars. "I couldn't make the kitten over into the cat I wanted, of course. But I had them insert fluorescent genes under her skin so she'd glow blue. I had them add growth hormone to her ears. I had them do . . . other stuff. And then I brought the kitten home and showed it to my father. 'See?' I said. 'A genemod cat, and everything I got done to make her this way will kill her in a month or two.' "

"Nan—"

"Don't go soft on me, Gail. Or flay me, either. I flayed myself enough. I hated what I'd done. But I didn't hate it as much as I wanted to get back at my father. And I *really* didn't hate what I'd done as much as I hated his reaction."

"Which was what?" She couldn't guess. Unimaginative, Jake sometimes called her.

"Dad cried. He had the kitten 'put to sleep' before it could suffer, and he cried for the kitten. And for me. But he never yelled at me, or punished me, or told me what a fucking shit I was."

Nan's voice held fury, which confused Gail. She said nothing, waiting.

"Don't you see?" Nan lashed out. "I wasn't worth getting angry with! He'd already written me off as evil, beneath anger or contempt, and so he didn't spare me any! The bastard had already dismissed me as hopeless!"

Gail lay quietly. She saw that it wouldn't help to say anything, but that she was going to say it anyway. "There might be other ways to interpret his behavior, Nan."

"You can't resist defending him, can you?"

"Oh, rot. I attack Dr. Shipley's ideas sixteen times a day, and you know it. But I know that all parents make mistakes. That's why I'm profoundly glad I never wanted to be one."

"Me, neither," Nan said, and seemed to lose interest in the entire subject. "Are you really going back to Mira City tomorrow?"

"Yes."

"The situation here doesn't really interest you, does it? Two races of aliens, a space war—"

"*Hypothetical* space war," Gail said. "God, it sounds like something from bad vid. No, it doesn't interest me all that much. I know that's hard for you to understand, because the puzzle of it fascinates you. What fascinates me is running Mira City. Making all the pieces of that puzzle come together every single day: managing the water and food supply in and the wastes out and the buildings going up and the courts developing and the crops adapting to Greentrees. What do I have to work with? How can I best use it? What else do I need and where can I get it?"

To Gail's surprise, Nan nodded. "I can see that. Sort of. For you, anyway."

Gail smiled. "A gracious concession. We're not much alike, dear heart."

"Nothing alike."

"So why—"

"Oh, God, not this," Nan said. "Every lover I've ever had has run this program on me eventually. 'Why us?' Why not? And don't go thinking that by that I mean we're just a one-night's roll-and-tickle, Gail. I like you. I just don't want to analyze why. Ask me something else."

"All right," Gail said belligerently. "How did you know that Lahiri used to accuse me of hubris? How did you know about Lahiri?"

"Somebody overheard Jake mention her to you once. As for the hubris, I guessed."

"Good guess. But I don't want you to mention her again."

"Okay. My turn to ask something. Why are you partners with a dribble dick like Jake?"

Gail said judiciously, "I don't know that his dick actually *dribbles,* having never tested it out," and was rewarded by Nan's giggle. "However, I like Jake. He put up his part of the money and he does his part of the work and he does it well."

"His part of the work is manipulating people," Nan said.

"Oh, and you never engage in that behavior yourself."

Nan grinned at her, a wicked grin Gail could see clearly. The sky must be brightening. But the next moment Nan stopped grinning and said soberly, "There's something gnawing at Jake."

"I never noticed it. What?"

"That's why I like you," Nan said, and the grin was back. "You never notice anything complicated about people. I don't know what's chewing Jake. I don't care, either. Gail, don't go back to Mira City tomorrow. The place can stumble by without you for one more day. Come with me to the Fur colonies with those Vines."

Gail was touched. Nan had put aside the sarcasm, the fencing, the nasty strike-before-you-get-struck pose. She was asking as simply and straightforwardly as if they'd been lovers for years.

"I guess Mira Corp can wait one more day. But one more thing—"

Nan leaned over to kiss her, and Gail forgot the one more thing. This battered, vulnerable, bedeviled, relentless, untrustworthy girl . . . Gail hadn't ever expected to feel like this again. It was worth giving up one day of water supply and waste management.

The next day she wasn't so sure. George, who either had slept well or didn't need much sleep, woke everybody well before dawn. "We need to eat, pack up, be ready to go when the Vines are."

"Go where?" Gail said grumpily. "Do your aliens furnish an itinerary, George?"

"I'll ask when they get up. Meanwhile, I've been working out a theory"—he looked at her face—"but I'll tell it to somebody else."

"Good idea."

Lucy, apparently another person at ease with morning, was ladling out bowls of hot noy, a nutrition-maxed soy synth, high fiber, that actually tasted pretty good. Gail took a bowl of noy and a cup of coffee. She consumed them standing up, shivering a little in the predawn chill and assessing who was in what shape.

Dr. Shipley looked terrible, as if he'd hardly slept. He was clumsily helping Mueller carry equipment out of the soon-to-be-abandoned tower. The beacon was being left on, presumably in case more Vines from the mother ship, if there were any more Vines, wished to come downstairs. Ingrid and Karim were taking down the large inflatable, and Nan the small one. That left only Jake. Gail didn't see him until he came up behind her.

"I just talked to Faisal and—"

"He's up already?"

"And had his morning workout. Not everybody's an unathletic slug, Gail."

"Ummmm," she said, too groggy to bicker.

"Faisal said everything's running smoothly in Mira City. They don't need us."

She said, "You don't look like you think that's good news."

Jake shrugged. "Nobody's ever indispensable, but I suppose we all would like to think we are. Anyway, the arrangements here are all set. Finally. I wanted Mueller to drive the rover back and report to Lieutenant Wortz, but he said no so—"

Gail choked on a mouthful of coffee. " 'Said no'? Since when does our security team override your orders?"

Jake gazed at her seriously. "Since never. But I also talked to Dr. Shipley, and he wants to stay close to Mueller until he's sure Mueller isn't going to have some sort of stress-and-rebuilt psychotic reaction to everything he's done."

"Good God, Jake, do we want to take that sort of person with us when we have aliens along who are capable of who-knows-what? *Two* sets of aliens. Why don't you send Shipley and Mueller both back to Mira City in the rover?"

"Because Shipley won't go. He says he has to make a peace testimony. And I won't send Mueller alone, without supervision."

A peace testimony. A psychotic reaction. Aliens. "When did the loco weeds start controlling the garden?"

"Since always. Anyway, you have your own personal loco weed you're bringing along. Nan's no worse than Dr. Shipley."

Gail said, "Interesting that you're defending him. I thought he made you uneasy."

"Can we stay with the topic here, Gail? Mueller, Shipley, Lucy, and I are going in the small skimmer, and the other five of you in the large one. Karim can pilot. He's had experience."

"And what about the rover?"

Jake pulled at his face. "It's staying here for now. We may need it after we return from this fact-finding expedition."

"Is that what it is? Seems more like a sideshow. Listen, Jake, I'm going for only one day. If the Vines are conducting a guided tour for longer than that, the small skimmer is going back to Mira City, with either Mueller or Karim piloting. Can we agree on this?"

"Yes," Jake said, and suddenly he looked very tired. "I may go with you. I'm not really any use here, you know. George and Ingrid and Nan are the only ones actually equipped to make contact with the Vines. The Vines don't seem like a threat to us, and no negotiation with them seems necessary. They just tell us anything we ask."

She said slowly, "Doesn't that make you suspicious?"

"Of what?"

"I don't know," she admitted. "But so little reticence just doesn't seem . . . prudent."

"And how many prudent plants do you know? But Karim did say something to me this morning . . ."

Gail felt cold. Whatever Karim had said, she wasn't going to like it. "What?"

"He said that if the mother ship is a McAndrew Drive type of thing, and it's drawing energy from the vacuum to power an acceleration that matches the gravitational force of—"

"Skip the technical details," Gail said. "What's the problem Karim sees?"

"The Vines have a huge amount of energy available in that drive. If they're really at war with the Furs, why don't they just attack the Fur planet with the plasma drive? It would make a formidable weapon, Karim says. Why 'create' colonies genetically identical to their enemies and then work at creating molecules to keep them alive but harmless?"

"Oh, God, Jake, I don't know. Maybe they want slaves. Or trading partners. Or zoo animals. How can we tell what creatures so different from us might want?"

"We could ask them. And I intend to."

"You do that," Gail said. "Meanwhile, let's get this circus in the air."

Someone, probably George, must have arranged things last night with the Vines, because they didn't appear. Instead their shuttle lifted off just after dawn, a silvery egg with a long tail. It looked, Gail thought, like one of the one-celled creatures with a flagellum that she vaguely remembered from school biology software. God, she had biology on the brain. George's influence.

Sitting beside Nan, Gail watched Greentrees flash by below them. Even though Karim hadn't taken them very high, the planet looked different from its appearance at ground level: less alien, somehow.

The pointy trees and strange animals and red creepers weren't distinguishable. Instead Greentrees offered sweeping savannas, winding rivers, placid blue lakes. If you ignored the foliage's being dull purple instead of green, it might almost have been Earth, an Earth primal and pristine as if twenty thousand years of human history had been undone.

Which might not be a bad thing, Gail brooded. She seldom let herself think about Earth. Earth was Lahiri. It was also the physical and social ruin that humans had made it, now apparently even worse than when the *Ariel* had left. The *Ariel*, that Rudy Scherer had blown up rather than let fall into alien hands, and this even before Scherer knew who the aliens were and what they wanted. Had it really happened because Scherer was a rebuilt? Or because there was something ineradicably violent and destructive in human beings? The same something that was steadily destroying humanity's home world.

Gail didn't usually think so negatively, or so abstractly. And she wasn't going to let herself do so now; there was no percentage in it. One more day of this weird atmosphere full of talk about alien warfare, and she'd be back home at Mira City, occupying herself with the useful and practical concerns that would keep Greentrees from becoming another Earth. That was what made sense.

Determinedly she turned to George. "Did your leafy friends tell you how far until the first stop on this tour?"

"I think we're here now," George said. "That looks like a Fur colony. But it's not one of the three we already knew about!"

"Stop salivating, George. Maybe they'll let you have a turd to analyze."

He said seriously, "A turd would be good."

Gail was nervous about being attacked by wild Furs, but she needn't have worried. The three aircraft set down near each other, and immediately Furs came racing toward them. But they stopped—or were stopped—at some barrier Gail couldn't see.

"A force field of some type," Karim said excitedly. "But then why didn't they use it around their shuttle at our camp? No, of course, it's probably not impenetrable to the energy weapons Mueller used. But then later, when we made first contact? No, they had decided to risk it because of all that quiet sitting Shipley made us do the day before."

This was going to be easy, Gail realized. The scientists were going to ask and then answer all their own questions. She didn't have to say or do anything.

The Vines disembarked with the usual precipitous rolling of their carts down the too-steep ramp. Karim guessed, "That's because the shuttle wasn't theirs. It wasn't designed for those carts. I'll bet they captured it from Furs."

The Furs clustered at the invisible barrier didn't look as if they could create shuttles. Neither were they the impassive, incurious clods from the first Fur colony the humans had discovered.

Nan said breathlessly, "They're not disabled, not intoxicated, I don't think they're as warlike as my Furs on the Cheyenne subcontinent . . ."

No, they didn't look warlike. In fact, many of them had children clinging to their backs. Maybe even most of them. And there was something else, something about their size or coloring or something . . .

George said, "They're all female. Every one of them. Look at their backs—no crests."

Ingrid said, "The males could be out hunting. Or have some sort of ritual sequestration. Or—"

"Or this colony *is* all female," Nan said harshly. "To see if they're more controllable that way. Another phase of the genetic experiment."

Gail looked at her. Nan wore a complex expression: distaste, sorrow, the anger that with her never lay far below the surface. So that's how it was going to go. Nan had been fascinated by both alien species, but now she was choosing the Furs. Her first contact. The experimented-upon. The underdog.

George was babbling excitedly. "On Earth there's a species of mite, *Brevipalpus phoenicis,* whose members are all haploid. Eggs develop without fertilization. The genome contains an incorporated bacterium that feminizes any males. There's an evolutionary advantage: the mites don't have to divide energy resources between two sexes, so the species can survive with a lower rate of reproduction. Also, it avoids all the costs of sexual reproduction with competing X- and Y-chromosomes."

Ingrid said, "These haploids, if that's what they are, seem to have all sorts of energy. The colony seems to be flourishing. There are three new structures that I can see going up over there, and look at all those healthy-looking offspring!"

Lucy, recording furiously, said, "I wish we could go into the village to see how the levels of tools and art compare with the other Fur encampments."

The Vines rolled their carts right up to the barrier. A bioarm, which still gave Gail the creeps, snaked out of one cart and fastened itself on the invisible wall. Three or four Furs, jabbering, crowded close. Something seemed to be happening, perhaps some exchange of bodily fluids. Gail shuddered.

She said to Nan, trying to lighten her own mood, "A colony of all women sounds good, but if there's never any sex . . ." Nan didn't even hear her. Like Ingrid, George, and Lucy, she was so involved with the two alien species in front of her that her own kind might not have existed.

Gail wandered back toward the assembled aircraft. Karim was again peering into the open door of the Vines' shuttle—did he have their permission to do that? He must have at least had Jake's, since Jake stood beside Karim, talking earnestly.

Then, more quickly than she'd expected, it was over. Everyone clambered back into his, her, or its transport. Gail wished she gone in the other skimmer. Nan was ignoring her, and George didn't seem able to shut up.

"I talked to Alph. He said—"

"Alph?" Gail demanded. "Which Vine is that? And how do you know it's a 'he'?"

"I don't," George said. "I'm just calling them Alpha, Beta, Gamma."

"That's what we called the moons."

"So what? I told you, they don't use sound-wave communication among themselves, it's all an exchange of chemical signals. Their real names would be totally meaningless to us. I talked to—"

"If they communicate by exchanged molecules," Gail said, feeling belligerent, "then how do they communicate across great distances?"

"I asked them that, too. Alph said—I think this is what he meant—that they don't. Most Vines are interconnected somehow, so a chemical signal just goes on and on until everyone 'hears' it. Or maybe they're all so interconnected only one part of the organism needs to hear it. I think communication must be very slow on their planet."

That figured. Gail remembered the Vines sitting in the sunlight, doing nothing, for hours and hours. "But what about communication through space? To the mother ship?"

Karim, at the control console, said, "They have Fur technology for that. I would bet it's Fur technology. Maybe before they got it, they didn't have any space program."

*"I talked to Alph,"* George repeated forcefully. "They do have a bio-based technology. They'd never left their planet until the Furs started the war. But now they have a few outpost colonies, and this group of Vines comes from there. It's much closer than the hundred light-years from Greentrees to their home world. Both places have some feature I couldn't understand, except that I got the impression it was very, very important.

"And another thing—they're hoping to find a genetic way to render the Furs harmless without killing them. Killing is anathema to Vines. That may be philosophical, but I think it's equally likely to be biological. If you're essentially one large, loosely connected, slow-moving organism that's self-sustaining with sunlight and water and your own decayed moltings, there's no evolutionary advantage to selecting for murder. It would be like killing yourself."

"You sound," Nan said in a deadly quiet tone, "as if you approve of the Vines."

George was too excited, or too uninterested, to pay attention to Nan's tone. "Of course I approve of them. Apart from how interesting they are biologically. An intelligent, nonviolent, planet-conserving species . . . what's not to like? If humanity had been like the Vines, Earth wouldn't have been wrecked."

Nan said, "Oh, there's nothing to not like, George. Nothing except the fact that your Vines are experimenting with other sentient beings, DNA-based beings like yourself, creating them just to destroy them while they develop an efficient method of genocide. Nothing to not like."

"I don't think—"

"Obviously not," Nan said coldly. "The Vines are no better than Scherer's crew, creating clones to slaughter for biological advantage."

"The difference, and it's crucial—" Ingrid began hotly, and Gail tuned out. God, she was sick of these arguments about aliens. She pulled out her comlink and opened the channel to Faisal.

He didn't answer. Damn, Gail had thought he was more responsible than that; he'd agreed to keep his link beside him at all times. She comlinked Robert Takai, Mira's chief engineer.

Takai didn't answer.

Neither did Thekla Barrington at the farm.

"Lend me your comlink," she said to George, who passed it over without pausing in his expostulating.

She couldn't link Faisal on George's handheld, either.

Gail sat chewing her lip. It probably wasn't anything. She'd lost track of which side of the planet they were on. Of course, the satellite system theoretically made comlink possible from anywhere on the planet, but if one comsat was malfunctioning, and the skimmer just happened to be out of range of the next one, it was possible that there would be a gap in geographical coverage. Wasn't that possible? She would have asked Karim, but he was busy piloting.

It was probably just a comsat glitch. That's all it was.

# 20

In the other, smaller skimmer, the flight was completely silent. Mueller piloted, and since all Jake could see was the back of Mueller's head, Jake couldn't assess the soldier's expression. Shipley sat with his head back against the seat cushion and his eyes closed, sleeping or meditating or praying or whatever it was he did. Lucy sat beside Jake, gazing out the window.

As the skimmer touched down at the second Fur camp, Lucy said, "Oh! This is the intoxicated one!" Jake, who hadn't been there before and had only seen the vid of the tipsy Furs, didn't recognize the place. But Lucy's comment cheered him. Why should that be?

He searched for the answer and found it: because he was unnerved by the earnest, cosmic, pacifist Vines, and also by Shipley's quick understanding that they *were* pacifists. Some drunken hilarity among a DNA-based species promised a welcome contrast.

George Fox was already off the large skimmer, waiting impatiently for the Vines to emerge from their shuttle. "I wonder if the Vines will erect a temporary electronic wall around this village, too. What do you think, Jake?"

"Haven't a clue," Jake said.

Ingrid said, "Possibly not. These Furs don't look like they're going to be rushing us anytime soon."

This was true. As they walked cautiously toward the village, Jake saw that it was in a dilapidated state. Roof beams hung at a crazy angle over huts with half the thatch missing. One stone hearth was not only broken but scattered, as though someone had hurled all the rocks gleefully in various directions. Weeds covered the one garden patch he could see. There were no Furs in evidence.

"Sleeping it off?" he said to George.

George frowned. "That psychotropic molecule shouldn't produce much of a hangover. At least, it doesn't in us."

Jake refrained from saying the obvious. A pair of Furs staggered around the corner of a hut and lurched toward them.

Instantly Mueller had a weapon in his hand. Shipley, whom Jake hadn't noticed getting out of the skimmer, laid a hand on Mueller's arm. It wasn't necessary. The Furs staggered a few more paces, then collapsed into each other and hung on, making a noise from wide-open mouths. Laughing? Jake didn't know, but he had a clear view of the aliens' impressive teeth and he backed away. The Furs seemed oblivious of the humans. They laughed (if that's what it was) until they fell over, at which point the male started groping the female's belly and the female passed out.

George said, "That looks like a lot of university parties I once went to."

Ingrid said, "Don't anthropomorphize, George. My cat behaves the same way with catnip."

"We didn't include catnip in the plants we brought with us," said George, "but maybe we should have."

"Jake," said Gail's voice behind him, and he turned. One look at her face and he knew something was wrong. Before he could ask what, a Vine cart—only one—tumbled down the shuttle ramp. Maybe Karim was right about the shuttle being captured technology; the pitch was way too steep for the cart. However, the cart didn't stop at the bottom of the ramp. It rocketed toward the humans at a speed Jake never would have suspected those carts could do, and Mueller raised his gun to fire.

"Franz, no!" Shipley said. "Look, it's stopping! It wants to tell us something."

The single cart lurched to a halt directly in front of Jake, who made himself not flinch. The uninflected mechanical voice said, "Jake, you go away. Now. All humans go away now. The enemy is here. Our ship is destroyed."

Lucy gasped. Karim pulled out some piece of portable equipment and began keying furiously. Gail said, "I can't link Mira City, either. My God, did they take out the comsats, too?"

"Yes," Karim said. "I just got the automatically beamed data, the comsats are all gone. Wait, there's one left—there it goes!"

Jake said rapidly to the Vine, "Are Furs doing this? The Furs you're at war with?"

"Yes. They will find your city. If you go up in your skimmer they will find your skimmer. If we go up in our shuttle they will find our shuttle."

"Heat signatures," Karim said. "How good is their detection equipment? Can they find these colonies?"

Ingrid said, "*We* found them from the air."

The Vine said, "First they will go to your beacon."

"My God," Gail said. "What will they do to Mira City?"

"We do not know. They are not at war with you."

Dr. Shipley said, "What will they do to *you*? And to these colonies?"

"They will kill us. We do not know what they will do to these colonies. We will wait in our shuttle."

The cart rolled backward toward the shuttle. Jake called, "Wait! Don't you have weapons on that shuttle? Fur weapons? They'll come in an identical shuttle, won't they? Can't you destroy them in the air?"

The Vine didn't seem to hear. It sped toward the shuttle and up the ramp.

Mueller said, "The large skimmer has some armaments. Not too many. I try to hit the Fur shuttle before it lands."

"Wait," Shipley said. "Before you try violence—"

Jake said, "All of you be quiet. Now."

They were. He saw that they expected him to take charge, give orders. He needed more information.

"Franz, Karim, what weapons is the skimmer carrying?"

Karim answered. "Lasers, both pinpoint and wide-scan. Also some handhelds: guns, tanglefoam, a focused EMP transmitter, and a focused beta-wave incapacitator, short range. Nothing really heavy."

The handheld weapons would be no good. "What are the chances of taking the Fur shuttle out, if it comes to that, with the laser?"

Franz said, "How can we know? It is an alien tech."

Karim added, "All I've had is one brief glimpse at a Vine counterpart to the shuttle, and with time dilation, it may already be hundreds of years out-of-date."

Jake said, "Then, all of you, what are the chances the Vines are telling the truth here?"

Nan said hotly, "I'm glad at least somebody sees the possibility that they're not!"

Lucy, very pale, said, "Why wouldn't they be?" Lucy, the innately truthful. *We see the world as we are, not as it is.*

Gail said, "We'll know soon enough, if another shuttle appears here."

"No," Jake said, "We'll know another shuttle has appeared. We won't know just from its appearance who's aboard, or what their intentions are." Heads nodded. "Therefore, we need to be prepared for various contingencies. Mueller, you stay in the skimmer and be prepared to deploy weapons, but not until I give you the signal. The comlinks are out, so it will be visual—a raised arm, like this."

Mueller said, "No. Maybe you are not able to raise your arm. If they incapacitate you."

Everyone started talking at once. Gail said sharply, "Quiet! Let Jake think, for God's sake!"

Jake tried to think. Mueller would have to decide on his own whether to attack . . . No. Impossible. Mueller was a rebuilt who had already killed his own captain. But he'd done that to protect Vines. "Karim, can you operate the weaponry in the skimmer?"

"Yes," the physicist said.

"Unacceptable!" Mueller snapped, sounding so much like the dead Scherer that Lucy jumped.

"Franz, it is acceptable because I need you to protect me personally. I'm staying here to greet the Furs, as head of Mira Corporation with legal claim to this planet. Franz will cover me from some secure place. The rest of you are going to retreat into the forest until we know what's happening. Leave someone fairly nearby to report back to the rest. Leave . . . Nan. She's the most used to Greentrees' wilderness." And that would keep her from insisting on hanging around here.

Nan looked hesitant, then nodded. She'd be close enough to observe. But Gail said instantly, "No, not Nan. A scientist, who at least has a ghost of a chance of decoding what they're looking at!"

"I'm staying," George said.

"No, you're not," Jake said, putting into it everything he had of authority.

Ingrid said uncertainly, "But if . . . if you all get killed here and we're in the woods and we can't use the skimmer, how will we get back to Mira City? We must be hundreds of miles away!"

"I don't know, Ingrid," Jake said. "This is not a plan with multiple scenarios to cover every contingency. We'll have to see what happens. But I do know that for any species in the universe, from Terran chipmunks on up, encountering two beings is a lot less likely to provoke fear and violence than encountering a whole crowd of beings."

He saw that they all had noticed the "two beings." He'd already forbidden George to stay. Gail, the alternate leader for Mira City and never very patient with aliens, was unlikely. Karim, who must be romantic, looked enviously at Lucy, but the others understood.

"Thank you, Jake," Shipley said. "I'll be glad to stay."

Under Gail's efficient direction, as much life-support equipment and supplies as they could carry were removed from the skimmer and apportioned among Gail, George, Ingrid, and Lucy. Nan found herself a watching place from the cover of some trees and augmented it with more branches and leaves. Mueller did the same on the opposite side of the clearing. Nan had high-resolution zoom goggles, but Mueller refused them, saying simply, "My eyes do this." Augments.

Before he left, Mueller checked that Karim knew what he was doing with the skimmer's limited weaponry. To himself Jake admitted surprise that Mueller had agreed so readily to turn the skimmer over to Karim. Perhaps the soldier was going to be scrupulous about obeying orders, in order to separate himself from what the other rebuilts, Scherer and Halberg, had done. That would be a plus.

Lucy, her slight body stooped under her burden of equipment even though Gail had given her less than the others, waddled up to Jake. "We're going. Good luck. I love you." He'd been afraid of an overwrought farewell, but she knew better. A brief dry kiss and she left with the others.

He was suddenly pierced with the intense desire to see her survive.

Within half an hour the place was eerily quiet. The three aircraft, human and otherwise, sat in the overgrown clearing that might once have been a tended farm. The two village Furs still lay heavily asleep, or possibly dead, between two dilapidated huts. Jake saw no other Furs until a trio of children emerged from the forest.

"Dr. Shipley, look," Jake said quietly. Shipley had been sitting on his ubiquitous inflatable stool, eyes closed. He opened them and his gaze followed Jake's discreet gesture.

The children walked with the same drunken gaits as their elders. They spied the humans, opened their mouths, and emitted sounds similar to the ones Jake had labeled "laughter." One slapped the ground over and over with his tail; the others may have needed theirs for enough balance to stay upright at all. Holding on to each other, the trio lurched forward.

*Don't shoot, Mueller,* Jake pleaded silently. *Please don't shoot these kids.* Mueller didn't, either because he had more restraint than Jake gave him credit for or because the Fur children veered off toward the village and disappeared into a hut with only half its roof intact.

*Kids.* That's how he'd thought of the young Furs: as "kids." They seemed—were—so much closer to humans than the Vines. Were the Vines telling the truth? What was going to come roaring at them out of the sky?

And when was it coming?

"Waiting is often the hardest part," Shipley said tranquilly.

What the hell kept him tranquil in this unprecedented, absurd, dangerous situation? Jake didn't really want to know. Religious mumbo jumbo. It was on impulse that Jake had let Shipley stay, but he'd known even then that the impulse was sound. Shipley had seen that the Vines were pacifists. He didn't panic. He'd handled Mueller well, and seemed able to handle anything except his horrific daughter.

Daughters. Sons. Brothers.

He was not going to think about Donnie now.

But he wasn't quite disciplined enough to avoid it. Not even traveling 69.3 light-years to Greentrees had gotten him away from thinking about Donnie. Mrs. Dalton.

"Jake," Shipley said, and Jake was grateful for the interruption, "what are you going to say to these Furs?"

"Are you so sure it's Furs that will be arriving?"

"I think so. I believe the Vines. What will you say to them?"

"That depends on what they say to us. Or if there's time to say anything before they cut us down."

"Yes," Shipley said. "But if there is time, may I communicate? I would use gestures. They're unlikely to speak English, you know."

Of course they weren't going to speak English. Jake hadn't been thinking. The Vines had listened, or rather their translator device had, to a day of deliberate, nonstop human dialogue before it could construct a program to translate. If that was indeed what it had done. George had been frankly skeptical of translation from chemical communication by exchanged molecules to sound-wave human speech, but there was no denying it had happened. What would the Furs have, if anything?

Shipley said quietly, "We could still get Naomi back here. She apparently learned at least a limited way to communicate with the Greentrees Furs."

"Who aren't the space-faring Furs," Jake said. "Let Nan stay where she is." A loose cannon if he ever saw one.

Shipley touched a button to inflate his three-legged stool, lowered himself onto it, and again closed his eyes. Praying? Well, fine, if it helped him. Jake had no such consolation. He scanned the sky until his eyes ached.

Three hours later, when he wished he'd had the foresight to keep some of the skimmer rations for himself and Shipley, he saw it.

It started as a faint white spot against the white-blue sky. The spot grew, became a light. A roar—God, it was coming in fast!—and he lost sight of it for a minute. When he found it again it was a craft, floating down gently toward the clearing. A silver egg with a flexible tail. Identical to the Vine shuttle already sitting there.

Jake tensed, in case the Vine shuttle fired, or the new shuttle did. It didn't happen. Instead the shuttle door opened immediately, the ramp descended, and an alien strode down the ramp.

A Fur.

Dressed only in bands of cloth that crossed its hairy body at several points and held . . . things, the alien was identical to the Furs drunkenly asleep a hundred yards away. To the Furs sleepwalking passively through their dying village. To the Furs that had attacked Larry Smith's Cheyenne. To the female Furs that had mobbed the invisible fence, thriving babies clinging to their backs. Except this Fur, a male, walked as if he owned the planet. He threw back his head and roared, then kept walking toward Jake and Shipley. He showed no fear of them or of the other shuttle.

Shipley stood. Jake prepared to die. Either this warrior—there was no other applicable word—would kill him, or Mueller would kill it and then its fellows would kill him.

Several things happened at once.

While the Fur was still twenty yards away, Jake felt something bump his chest, something invisible and diamond hard. Shipley, standing a bit closer, was bumped by it first and staggered backward, tripping over his stool. A burst of laser fire exploded from Mueller's position. It had no effect whatsoever, seeming to evaporate into the air twenty yards from the Fur in the direction of Mueller's position. Mueller fired again. No result. The tail on the Fur shuttle whipped around and pointed toward Mueller, and there was no more human fire.

The Fur walked up to Jake and Shipley, and Jake continued to feel the hard barrier against his chest. It must be a version of the force field the Vines had put between themselves and the all-female Fur village. But portable. The warrior Fur was encased in a movable shield that could withstand whatever Mueller had been firing. Could it withstand Karim's arsenal in the skimmer? The Fur didn't look fearful of either craft behind him.

He stopped five inches from the humans, threw back his head, and roared again. A part of Jake's dazed mind noted that sound penetrated the shield just fine.

Jake said, "I am Jake Holman. I am a human. Hello." Slowly he raised one hand, palm up to show its emptiness, pointed at himself, and repeated, "I am Jake Holman. I am a human. Hello."

The Fur roared a third time. Jake saw that he was looking beyond the humans, to the unconscious, filthy Furs lying on the ground in the village. The warrior's teeth, long and sharp, flashed in the sunlight. *Teeth evolved for tearing flesh,* George had said. Carnivores or omnivores.

Two more Furs raced down the shuttle ramp. They were dressed, or undressed, the same as the first Fur. The ramp was, Jake noted irrelevantly, the right pitch for their stride. The male carried a dark metallic oval device, the female a greenish stubby stick. She pointed it at the Vines' shuttle, and as easily as that, the shuttle door slid open and its ramp descended. She charged inside.

Jake felt sick. That Fur was going to kill the Vines, shatter their domes and burn them, just as Mueller had. And he could see no reason why he and Shipley wouldn't be next. Why hadn't the Vines done something? Their shuttle wasn't weaponless, but they hadn't even tried to defend themselves.

The Fur with the black metallic egg had reached his leader. He set the egg down on the grass and the leader roared again. He jabbed a hand at Jake and Shipley. Jake stared dumbly. What did the thing want?

Shipley said, enunciating clearly, "I am William Shipley. This is Jake Holman. We are humans. Hello."

Jake said, "You think it's a *translator*?"

"I don't know," Shipley said. "Yes, wait, I think it's a translator. The Fur has stopped roaring at us."

It was true. The terrifying alien had gone impassive. In the brief silence it pointed to the egg and then to Jake and Shipley. "We are humans," Jake said. "Hello. We came to this planet to live. We came from far away. We—" He stopped.

A Vine emerged from the shuttle, its cart clearly pushed so hard from inside that it tumbled over on its side. The cart righted itself, but another cart was thrown through the air from inside the shuttle, hit the first one, and knocked it over. The third cart careened down the ramp, followed by the female Fur.

She picked up the cart closest to her and pushed it away from the other two. Then she fired. The domes shattered and the burned goo that had been living Vines oozed over the metallic carts. The Fur did something to her weapon, fired again, and the carts shattered. She picked something out of the wreckage and strode away, not so much as glancing at the one living Vine left behind.

When she reached the other two Furs, she stopped and made a complicated gesture at the leader, a simultaneous head jerk and foot stomping. A salute? Jake saw that the thing she'd plucked from the shattered cart was another translator egg.

She set it on top of the first, and the two did something to join together. Not melt into each other, not join with cables, not anything Jake could name. One minute they were two black eggs side by side on the dusty purple groundcover, and the next they were a double egg that reminded him of a malformed potato. No one moved. Jake looked at Shipley, who gave a tiny shrug.

After at least two silent, motionless minutes, the lead Fur said, or growled, or chittered—it sounded like an unholy combination of all three—to the egg. It then said, in the same uninflected mechanical voice Jake had been hearing for three days, "What are you? Why are you with our enemy? Did you create these"—the translator hesitated—"blasphemies?"

A word it must have learned from Shipley. There was no other possibility. And multiple questions—the worst kind to fire at a witness on the stand. But there was no judge to intervene. Jake was on his own.

"We are humans," he said as calmly as he could. "We did not create these blasphemies. They were here when we came from our home planet. Our home planet is far away from here. We came to this planet half a year ago only."

The translator spat out some gibberish; certainly *it* was highly inflected. The three Furs listened. They then jabbered among themselves. Then the leader said to Jake, through the translator, "Open your craft. Tell the humans inside to all come out."

This was the test, then. But of what? If Jake refused, surely it would be interpreted as a hostile action. Or would refusal fit with some sort of ritual warrior behavior, as with Japanese samurai or Larry Smith's original Cheyenne? If Jake agreed to let them examine the inside of the skimmer, would that be interpreted as a peaceful gesture or as cowardice? If the Furs saw the level of tech that the skimmer had, would they then be convinced that humans had had nothing to do with the Fur "blasphemies"? Or would they simply kill Karim, as they had already killed Mueller and two of the three Vines?

There was simply no way to know.

Jake's hesitation, as these questions tumbled through his mind, lasted no more than a second. But Shipley stepped into the tiny pause.

"We will open the skimmer. We will tell the one human inside to come out. We have nothing to hide from you or from the others. We are beings of peace and truth."

Damn him! Jake was speechless, half from rage and half from prudence. Every negotiating instinct in him said not to contradict Shipley, that above all the humans must present a united front. But his blood boiled. How dare Shipley usurp his leadership with his namby-pamby Quaker nonviolence!

The Fur was nodding. "Good. Go." And Jake, having no choice, gave the signal he and Karim had agreed upon for Karim to open the skimmer door and emerge, unarmed. The three Furs all turned to watch. Jake turned his body away from the translator and said softly to Shipley, "Do that again and you're dead."

"I'm prepared for that, if necessary," Shipley said. "This is the right thing to do, Jake." The serenity in his voice enraged Jake further.

The skimmer opened and Karim emerged. He started toward them, ashen but not faltering, a young man risking his life when most of it still lay ahead of him. The female Fur who had stormed into the Vine shuttle now disappeared into the skimmer.

Karim reached Jake and Shipley, was briefly inspected by the Furs, and then was ignored. Jake took Karim's arm and unobtrusively turned him away from the translator. That was the best he could do. He whispered, "Karim, stay calm and quiet. That egg-looking thing is a translator. You saw them kill the Vines and Mueller?"

"Mueller's not dead," Karim said, but before Jake could ask more, the Fur leader turned back to the three men.

"Yes. You did not make these blasphemies. Sit." He strode away.

Sit? Shipley was already settling heavily on his stool. The female Fur emerged from the skimmer. They must have some form of communication among themselves not clearly evident, Jake realized. The leader had received his lieutenant's judgment on the skimmer tech before the lieutenant had emerged.

She walked from the skimmer to the Furs' own shuttle and disappeared inside.

Karim said, "We're inside the field now!" The young physicist was following instructions to sit but was doing it in a very peculiar way. He revolved as he lowered himself, his arms extended, so that he looked like a slowing top. His fingers remained bent, as if at some barrier. Jake put out his own arm and discovered that they were enclosed in a circular, invisible wall just large enough to hold the three of them comfortably.

Karim said, "They said to sit down, Jake," and Jake sat.

"How do you know Mueller's not dead?"

"I was still receiving his heat signature. The skimmer detectors can pick up a single body at that short distance, you know. Mueller's thermal energy wasn't fading. He's probably just knocked out somehow."

So the Furs hadn't killed a human who had fired on them, despite what they'd done to the Vines. That was encouraging. Jake started to say, "Do you think *their* equipment can detect Mueller's heat signature, or Nan's—" at the same moment that Shipley leaped off his stool, crying, "No! No!"

At first Jake didn't see what had anguished Shipley. The two male Furs stood quietly, impassive. Karim grabbed Jake's arm and turned him toward the Fur shuttle.

The tail was rising, snaking around until it pointed at the Fur village. A beam came out, a shimmery disturbance of the air rather than any actual color. It moved very, very slowly—surely electromagnetic radiation couldn't move that slowly? The beam widened as it went. One broadening side passed within ten feet of the humans' invisible cage. The beam hit the Fur village, and the village disappeared.

Jake blinked. One minute the village had stood, and the next it was gone. All of it: groundcover, ramshackle huts, cold cookfires, drunken passed-out Furs. Three Fur children.

Karim stared in disbelief. Shipley stood with his head bowed, his face a mask of pain. A cold, demonic impulse blossomed in Jake, one he'd known before. Donnie. Mrs. Dalton. It was the impulse to hurt the already hurting, who were in no position to strike back.

"You did that, Doctor," Jake said. "You taught them the word 'blasphemies.' That's what you do with blasphemies. You destroy them. Congratulations."

The moment he said it he regretted the words with a pure, hard intensity that was almost a prayer.

# 21

Karim said, "They're back. Two of them, anyway."

The three Furs had gone inside their shuttle, to confer or radio their mother ship or, for all Jake knew, to take a coffee break. During their absence, Jake had said to Shipley, "I'm sorry." He hadn't been able to bring himself to say any more. Shipley had nodded, face averted, and said nothing.

The two Furs, the leader and the other male, strode toward the humans' invisible cage. Jake was struck all over again by their contrast to their impassive clones and their drunken clones. Truly, behavior made the species.

Karim, who had been watching not the aliens but the aircraft, said, "Oh . . . no!" Jake spun around to look.

The weapon/tail on the Furs' shuttle was activating again. It snaked up in its eerily hypnotic rhythm until it pointed to the Vines' shuttle, beside which the remaining Vine still stood silently on its cart. The very slow beam was emitted from the tail, widening as it went. From Jake's vantage point, it passed within a yard of the cart. Then the shuttle no longer existed.

Karim cried, "But it was originally their own!"

"Contaminated," Jake heard himself say. Karim had said the inside was coated with slime, presumably part of the Vines' self-sustaining life-support system. They couldn't stay in their domed carts all the time.

The tail snaked through the air again.

"No," said Karim, but this time it was a whisper. The leisurely beam was sent out, and the skimmer disappeared.

The two Furs had reached Jake. At his feet the translator said, "We go now. We return later. You humans will be here."

"All right," Jake said, because it seemed expected that he reply. "How long will you—" But the Furs had turned and were striding back to their shuttle. A few minutes later, it lifted. Jake watched it until it became part of the bright morning sky.

Karim said unsteadily, "The cage is gone." He walked through what had been a clear wall. Shipley remained sitting on his stool, head bent.

Jake breathed deeply until his head felt clearer.

"All right. We know that they're coming back, but we don't know when. How do they know we'll still be here?"

"Where would we go?" Karim said. "No, that's not it. We could probably hide. Their thermal-signature detectors can't operate over too great a range or they'd mistake large mammal-analogues for us. My guess is that we're still in a cage, but a much larger one."

"Find the limits," Jake said. He raised cupped hands to his mouth and yelled, "Nan!"

"I'm here!" she called back. "Coming!" A moment later he saw her break cover and run toward him, carrying her recording equipment. Jake waited to see if Karim's "larger cage" would stop her from reaching him. It didn't.

"Nan, leave that stuff here and go see about Franz Mueller. If you can get to him."

She nodded and was off again. Whatever else the girl might be, she was useful in a physical emergency.

Jake said, "Karim?"

"It's curious," he said. "The wall is right here on this side, but it seems to veer off to take in a wide territory in the direction Nan was hiding." Karim was feeling with the flats of his palms along nothing.

"You look like one of those old-time mimes," Jake said, despite himself, but didn't wait to see if Karim smiled. He started toward Mueller.

Nan and Mueller came out of the woods, the soldier leaning on the wiry girl. Nan called, "He's very dazed."

"Dr. Shipley!" Jake called. "We need you!" It was good to give the old man something to do besides brood.

Nan sat Mueller on the ground and Shipley lumbered toward him. She came up to Jake and said, "That energy-wall-thing curves right behind him. It's weird. They calibrated it to include him but then stop."

He studied her carefully. Nan had championed the Greentrees Furs, thought of them as "hers." Now their older, meaner big brothers had shown up. How did she feel about Furs now? Her face, taut around the eyes and with a stony set to the mouth, made Jake decide this wasn't the time to ask. Like her father, she needed to be kept busy, too.

"Nan, Karim's tracing the wall clockwise. Start right here and do the same thing counterclockwise. If we're in a cage, let's see how big it is."

Now the hardest thing. Jake walked over to the one Vine left alive. "Alpha?"

"Beta," came the calm, uninflected voice that was, under the gruesome circumstances, the most awful thing Jake had ever heard.

"I'm so sorry for your loss. Our loss, too. For what happened to your . . . your brothers."

"We do not have their death flowers," the Vine said.

Jake had no idea what it meant.

"We do not have their death flowers forever."

"I'm sorry," was all he could think of to say. Along with everything else, the pronoun disconcerted him. Did Beta think of itself as plural? "Can I . . . can I do something for you?"

"Yes. Later."

"All right," Jake said, wondering what he'd committed himself to. "I . . . all right. May I ask some questions now?"

"Yes."

He sat, to bring himself level with the Vine. Behind its clear dome it looked as alien as ever. The projections that might have been vines or tentacles or semisolid biofilms, slimy and purple-red, sprouted off the scaly-looking trunk. Two or three of the fleshy leaves/hands/sensory organs/who-knew-whats seemed randomly distributed. The Vine stayed motionless as it "talked," and if words hadn't been coming out of the translator Jake would have had no way of knowing if "Beta" were as dead as his colleagues.

"Where do you think the Furs have gone now?"

"They destroy our other Fur colonies."

The other "blasphemies." Shared genes apparently meant nothing to the aliens. Nor did compassion, even for those made in their own image.

"Will they destroy the Fur colony on the subcontinent?" He had no idea if the Vine understood the term or not, but he plunged ahead. "The big colony of healthy Furs. Many Furs and more being born all the time. They seem healthy."

"Our control," Beta said, surprising Jake. On second thought, he realized that the Vine must have picked up a lot of English scientific terminology from the long hours of conversation with George and Ingrid. Or, at least, the translator program had.

"Yes, the control group. Will the Furs destroy them? Even though you made them healthy as a control?"

"Yes."

The single syllable chilled Jake. No mercy. He didn't bother to ask about the colony of parthogenetic females.

"How will they find all the control Furs? They have many villages and Nan says many of them go long distances to hunt."

"They will find enough of them. They will destroy all or almost all females. Females do not hunt often. The others will die out in a generation or two."

"Beta . . . we have humans living in that area, too. Around a thousand. Will the Furs destroy the humans?" Larry Smith's Cheyenne, on their quixotic, ridiculous mission. Jake stopped breathing.

"We don't know if they will destroy humans."

"Including us?"

"We don't know. Fur thinking is very strange to us. Like yours."

Jake thought about this. Karim joined them. "Jake, the wall clockwise curves around where the village was and then goes west, widening at a very slight angle. From watching Nan, it seems to do the same thing counterclockwise, although she wants to go on checking. It's a very large cage, and I think it's shaped the way it is for a reason."

"What reason?"

"I think it's meant to enclose all nine humans. Gail's group as well as us."

Gail's group. Lucy. They hadn't gotten away, after all. On the other hand, if they were outside the invisible cage, where would they get away to? Mira City was four hundred miles away, through unmapped wilderness filled with alien predators.

"If I am right," Karim continued, "then they've probably encountered their end of the wall already. Or will soon."

"Send Nan after them."

"She's already gone."

Without orders. Jake couldn't afford annoyance now. "How's Mueller?"

"Dr. Shipley says he'll be fine. He just was knocked out for a while and he's still dazed. I have a theory the Furs were using some sort of . . ."

"Not now," Jake interrupted. "Tell me later. Beta says he thinks the Furs have gone to destroy the other experimental colonies as completely as they can."

Karim digested this. Something moved behind his dark eyes, and his skin had a mottled look.

"Sit down, Karim," Jake said, before the young man was driven to ask. "You might have some good questions to ask Beta, too."

Karim sat. "I'm so sorry about your brothers," he said to Beta, and bowed his head. Faisal's people had such good manners.

"We do not have their death flowers," Beta said. It was still eerie to hear grief expressed in that mechanical monotone.

"No," Karim agreed.

"We do not have their death flowers forever."

"No," Karim repeated politely.

Jake said, "May I ask more questions, Beta?"

"Yes."

"What do you think the Furs will do after they destroy all the experimental colonies?"

"They will talk to their ship."

"For orders, yes." That made sense. "And then?"

"They will find the other experimental colonies."

Jake and Karim looked at each other, puzzled. Jake said tentatively, "Other colonies? What other colonies?"

"On the other planet. By the other star."

Karim let out a long, low whistle, a surprising and oddly musical sound. Instantly Beta said, "Make the noise again."

Karim looked at Jake, who nodded. Karim repeated his whistle, then threw in eight bars of the "Tales from the Vienna Woods."

"I didn't know you could whistle," Jake said. People were endlessly surprising.

"Again," Beta said, and despite the translator's mechanical, emotionless tone, Karim must have felt encouraged. He whistled more of the waltz, then a complicated piece Jake didn't know, and finally a few random bird calls, clearly showing off. When he stopped, he glanced sheepishly at Jake.

Beta said, "It brings light to my soul."

Clearly Shipley's phrase. But Jake was oddly touched. In its grief, the Vine had found some sort of comfort in human music. Maybe there were some sort of birds on that native planet where Vines sat dreaming silently in the sun. The Vines communicated by chemical signals, but perhaps that didn't mean they were entirely unaware, in some peculiar manner, of sound.

Karim said shyly, "I'll whistle more for you later, if you like."

"Thank you, Karim," Jake said. "Beta, what other colonies do you have by another star? More experimental Furs?"

"The same experiments. Different environment. We don't know the Fur planet. We never go to the Fur planet."

Jake tried to put it all together. "You mean, you made the same kinds of experimental Furs twice, in different environments? To learn which kind of genetic alteration would most make them harmless? Two of each experiment?"

"Four," Beta said.

*Four.* Four planets capable of supporting DNA-based, oxygen/carbon/nitrogen-breathing, sentient life. Like Furs. Like humans. How far did they have to go to look? How long had this experiment been going on? Jake of course understood the way that relativistic time dilation made hundreds of years pass on planets but only a few on shipboard, which was how the Vines could experiment with Furs for generations. But the same hundreds of years must be passing on both their home worlds. What kind of species could sustain a war for thousands of years?

Humans had once, in a much more constrained arena, fought something called the Hundred Years' War.

Karim burst out, as if he were unable to contain the question any longer, "Why didn't you just blast all over the Fur planet with the vacuum drive on your mother ship?"

"We don't do it."

The pacifism thing again. Or maybe it was something else. Jake said, "Did you make your spaceships? The mother ship you had in orbit?"

"The mother ship was made by Furs. We use it. They have many. We use many. We think about the ships at home, in the sun."

Karim said to Jake, "If it's all stolen tech, then of course the Furs can counter it. But . . . how did the Vines—" He turned in embarrassment to Beta, "How did you capture so many Fur ships? How did you get the tech to . . . to think about in the sun?"

Beta was silent. Jake thought it wasn't going to answer, but then he saw that the cart's slot was sliding open and the bioarm slithering out. Beta was going to make a drawing of some sort, and it was going to take a while.

Jake twisted to look behind him. Mueller stood on the groundcover, doing deep knee bends. He looked fine again. Dr. Shipley lay stretched full length on the ground, his arm flung over his face. Jake hurried over.

"He sleeps," Mueller said. "Mr. Holman, I have my weapons. But against the Fur shield they did not work. Why?"

Now Jake remembered the way Mueller's laser beam had simply disappeared before it hit the Furs or their shuttle. Another mystery.

"I don't know, Franz. You can ask Karim, but I don't think he'll know, either. However, I'm going to tell you something very important. The Furs are going to return, and I don't want you to attack them *unless I clearly give a verbal command.* Attack will only endanger our position. Do you understand? I warn you, disobeying this order will be considered equivalent to treason."

"Yes, sir," Mueller said unhappily. Jake, feeling like a fraud for applying military structure when he wasn't military, gazed down at Shipley. The old man snored heavily. Well, sleep was probably good for him. No one knew what lay ahead.

When Jake returned to Beta, the bioarm had flattened itself into a slimy slab and colors were forming as various cells pigmented. He waited until the process was finished, another ten minutes.

Karim said, "It is a satellite array. In enormous orbits, covering an entire star system!"

Jake looked at the bioarm. He saw a large center circle, four widely spaced smaller circles that might have been planets, and hundreds of tiny dots quivering all over the drawing. He said doubtfully, "I don't think they're satellites, Karim. Their tech doesn't lean that way, and how could they have captured that many satellites from the Furs?"

"Not satellites," Beta said. "Us."

Which cleared up nothing. Jake looked carefully at the picture, memorizing it. He now noticed that the second smaller circle had a single fine filament extending into space, not unlike a tail. "Beta, is that second planet from the sun your home world?"

"Yes."

"What is that . . . string? Tail going into space?"

"Not the tail," Beta said. "The ramp."

"Oh," Jake said, clueless.

Shouting sounded from the east. Jake sprang up, straining to hear. Nan?

Beta said, "Jake Holman."

"Yes?"

"Can William Shipley sit with us?"

"I'll get him," Jake said, surprised. But before he could ask any more about this, Nan burst from the woods and ran toward him at top speed. Jake walked to meet her.

"Jake! They're on their way back, Gail and the rest. The wall stopped just east of them, within *feet.* So since the Furs knew just where they were, Gail decided they may as well be here."

"Thanks, Nan," Jake said. The girl's face and arms were covered with scratches and bruises, none of which she seemed to notice. There were leaves caught in her chopped hair.

Coming up to Nan, Karim said, "Is George coming? I have something to describe to him."

"Of course George is coming, did you think they cooked him and ate him? Stick to physics, Karim."

Jake went over to where Shipley still lay asleep. Kneeling, he shook Shipley gently until he woke. "Doctor, are you all right? There's a request for you."

Shipley heaved himself up, looking toward the woods. "Someone's hurt?"

"No. It's Beta. The remaining Vine. It asked me if you would come sit with it. I think it's grieving." Or something.

Shipley looked toward the encased alien. Something moved behind his eyes. "Are your people Jewish, Jake?"

"No. Why?"

"Did you ever hear of sitting kaddish?"

"No," Jake admitted.

Shipley was silent a moment before saying quietly, "It never ceases to amaze me how human the Vines seem."

It had never ceased to amaze Jake how unhuman they seemed.

Shipley walked off toward the Vine. Watching him, Jake thought about Beta's asking specifically for Shipley. Shipley had been the one to first suggest the humans just sit quietly beside the Vines' shuttle, back at the beacon tower. He had been the one to teach the Vines a sentence like "It brings light to my soul." Quakers, like Vines, sat silent together, thinking or dreaming or whatever went on in their minds.

And he, Jake, thought the Furs were closer to humans. The Hundred Years' War. Might makes right. Tech means physics, and physics means weapons.

Disquieted, he walked toward the woods to meet Gail, Lucy, George, and Ingrid.

George said, "Not satellites. *Spores.*"

He studied a replica of the drawing Beta had made on the bioarm. Everyone but Shipley sat around the fire Gail had made. She'd grabbed a portable heater from the skimmer, but she was probably saving it in case . . . in case what? In case they were caged here a long time, or had to make their way to Mira City. Jake didn't believe that would be possible, but it was like Gail to plan for it anyway.

The abrupt Greentrees night had fallen. All afternoon had been spent putting together a camp from what they had. It was a pretty primitive camp because they didn't have much. Gail had taken from the skimmer only what could be carried, and she had concentrated on food. There was a one-person inflatable brought to protect the food from weather and predators. They had five blankets woven with thermal fibers. They had dried food and a communal pot to cook it in and some spoons, plus the water-clean machine and a large inflatable tank to keep the sanitized water in. The cage didn't encompass a river, but Nan had found a muddy pond and all of them except Shipley had taken turns with the numbing work of filling the cooking pot, carrying it the mile to the clearing, and dumping it through the cleaner until the tank was full.

Jake hadn't been able to eat much. He half listened to George, half scanned the darkness for Shipley where he still sat with the Vine. Jake had never seen such darkness; the sky had clouded and the only light came from the fire. Gail was also saving the flashlights. The air was turning chill and damp, and if Shipley sat there much longer he would be stiff as glass. Jake hoped like hell it didn't rain.

George said, "Sure, it could be, Karim. Their tech is bio, not physics. They can create molecules we never dreamed of, with near-perfect control. So they create some sort of bacteria-analogue that eats at whatever metal the Fur hulls are made of. Or some other vulnerable external part of their ships. Make them self-replicating at a very fast rate. They—"

"Where are they going to get the energy for that fast replication?" Ingrid said.

"From the sun, where the Vines get it."

"They'd need water."

"Ingrid," George said, not patiently, "how do we know they need water? We don't know what they need. They're not DNA-based."

"Even so," Ingrid argued, "they have to get building-block chemicals from somewhere to live and to replicate. And how did they get up there in the first place?"

George pointed to the drawing. "See this thin filament coming up from the planet? It could be a space elevator."

"Could be," Karim conceded. He took the drawing and squinted at it as if the crude representation could actually tell him something.

Lucy said, "A kind of panspermia. Only not creating life—puncturing ship hulls. Until the Vines can get up there and appropriate the craft."

Ingrid said, "I see more holes in this theory than I can count."

Karim said, "I know. But don't forget, Ingrid, there's not only alien biotech behind this . . . this star-system shield, there's some alien physics as well. We can't get energy out of the vacuum to power our ships."

"If that's what they really do," Ingrid said.

Jake got up and stretched. Lucy looked up at him inquiringly, but he smiled down and gestured for her to remain. He wanted to bring Shipley into the makeshift camp. The old man had been sitting there, without even dinner, for hours.

Shipley was just getting to his feet when Jake stumbled toward him through the darkness. He could barely make out the bulky lines of Shipley's body.

"Doctor? Gail says to come and eat." Gail, not Nan. Nan hadn't once asked after or moved toward her father.

"Yes. Beta is asleep, or whatever they do."

Jake wondered how you'd tell. He groped for Shipley's arm. "Let me guide you, Doctor."

"Just a minute, Jake. I want you to know something. Beta gave me its death flower."

"Its what?"

Shipley guided Jake's hand to a small packet wrapped in what felt like layers of tightly wound groundcover. "This. It's a death flower. A small piece of Beta that the bioarm pushed through the slot. If any opportunity arises, I'm to give it to any other Vines we encounter. If anything happens to me, will you do it?"

A complex emotion seized Jake, one he didn't dare analyze. He said instead, "You swore a deathbed oath to an alien?"

"New Quakers don't swear oaths," Shipley said. "Our word should always be good, making any additional requirement unnecessary. But yes, I said I would do this. Beta expects to die when the Furs return. If I can't, will you—"

"No!"

Shipley tried to peer at him in the darkness. Jake heard himself breathing harder, felt it slipping back over him. Donnie. Mrs. Dalton. Dying requests. *No.*

"Jake—"

"Ask Gail. Or George. And come back to the camp before you get hypothermia. You're shivering already."

"Jake—"

"I said to come!"

Silently, Shipley stumbled after him to where the humans huddled, like a primitive tribe without even cave or teepee, around the precious fire.

Soon after sunset the rain began, cold and relentless. Shelter was primitive. Gail had assigned the tiny storage inflatable to Shipley and insisted he take it. "Don't argue with me, Doctor, I've got too much to do to indulge you." Shipley had submitted. Jake figured he was the only one actually dry, if not warm. As compensation, the physician had refused to take one of the five thermal blankets.

Jake and Lucy shared one, Gail and Nan another. Mueller had also refused a blanket from, Jake suspected, a tough-soldier stance. Or maybe Mueller had unknown augments and genuinely didn't need it. Ingrid, George, and Karim each lay wrapped in the other three. All of them shared a crude lean-to Nan had directed them to make, with large forked branches driven into the ground as supports and layers of branches slanting to the ground as roof and windbreak. It was mildly effective except when the wind changed direction suddenly and cold rain blew in slantwise. Everyone slept fitfully.

A pressure built in Jake's head. He recognized it, and its intensity, and its end. Fear drenched him, colder than the rain.

"Lucy," Jake whispered in her ear, inches from his mouth. He breathed in the sweet, fecund smell of her dirty hair.

"I'm awake."

"Come outside with me."

"Now? Outside?"

"It's stopped raining." It hadn't, really, but it had slowed to a pervasive, miserable drizzle, and it was no more wet out there than in the shelter. Or so Jake told himself. This sudden need to talk to Lucy scared him with its strength. It was Shipley, Shipley and his deathbed oath to the damned alien, Shipley and the memories he'd released . . . Jake couldn't wait anymore. If he waited, he would explode.

Lucy rose, stepping over Ingrid and Karim in the dark. Jake groped for her hand and hung on blindly.

He led her through the drizzle to nowhere in particular, and ended up beside the invisible wall behind the spot where the skimmer had once landed. Twelve hours ago, fourteen? It seemed days. Somewhere in the wet blackness Beta sat under his dome, its sides streaming with a water he could never touch. Jake pulled Lucy to a sitting position with their backs against the wall, the thermal blanket a hood over both their heads.

"Jake, what *is* it?"

"I have to tell you something."

He could feel her waiting.

"I have to tell you something, but it isn't easy to say. I just need someone—you—to know the truth before I die."

She said gently, "We won't die."

God, she was brave. He tried to match her courage. "Maybe not. Maybe I want you to know anyway. To know what kind of a person I am." *And then you won't love me anymore.* But that was a risk he felt impelled to take.

"I had a brother. Twelve years younger than I. He was . . . wild. Our parents died when I was nineteen and Donnie was seven. We were poor, and there wasn't anybody else, so I raised Donnie. No, that's not true . . . Donnie raised himself. I was too busy with college and then law school to do more than buy groceries and give him lunch money. By the time he was ten Donnie was spending most of his time on the streets, with predictable results."

"Jake, that wasn't your—"

"*Just listen,* please. Donnie had a police record by fourteen. I had just passed the bar and I tried to be home more but it was impossible. Atlanta, where we lived, got worse and worse and Donnie would disappear for days. So I forcibly put him in a pseudo-military school in Virginia, one of those places where they supposedly outfit troubled kids for careers in space. Motivation, discipline. Goals, all the crap I still believed in then.

"And it seemed to be working. He made new friends, not street thugs but kids from respectable families. He started spending his time with Hobart Sullivan Dalton III."

Jake waited, but there was no reaction from Lucy. The rain picked up again.

"You didn't ever hear about the Dalton murder? Twenty-five years ago?"

"Jake, I was five years old."

She still might have heard of it, but he let it go. "The Daltons were a wealthy family. Beyond wealthy. They were what people meant when they said that the rich had taken so much they'd drained both poor and the Earth itself. Anna Standish Dalton was a widow and Hobart was her youngest son. The two older kids were good little vampires but Hobart had decided it was more fun to kick his relatives than to enjoy his advantages."

Lucy said, "Like Nan Frayne."

"It isn't the . . . never mind. Maybe. Hobart and Donnie teamed up and stole inside the school, outside the school, anywhere they could. The school expelled them. Donnie came home and I gave him hell so he disappeared into the high-tech slums of northern Virginia with Hobart. He emailed every once in a while, and eventually I had a jumper follow the electronic trail and track him down. It took me a couple years to get to it because I was having my own troubles. My wife and I were in the middle of a nasty divorce."

"Your . . . wife?"

"Rania." Strange to think that Rania had been dead and buried for decades now, back on that shadowy Earth lost in time dilation. "We didn't have much money, but she wanted it all. I didn't want to give it to her. We spent enormous amounts of time fighting each other, and Donnie got lost in the smoke of battle. But when I found him in Virginia, I took an aircab up there and checked into a hotel and started the utterly futile process of arguing him back to a straight life. It was like arguing with the wind. I could see that Donnie, and Hobart, too, were both using neptune and it was already destroying them. They were gaunt and crazy-eyed and filthy. I wouldn't give Donnie any money for the drug, and I gathered that Mrs. Dalton wouldn't give Hobart any, either. He didn't come into any money of his own till he turned twenty-one."

This time when he paused, Lucy stayed quiet.

"I decided to go see Mrs. Dalton to discuss the boys, and I told Donnie I was going that same night. I took a robocab to the estate. I was just approaching the front door of the suburban, still out of sight of the surveillance vids, when the gate burst open and Donnie ran out. He was hysterical. I made him tell me what had happened. When he had, I thought quicker than I ever had in my life. I was a state's attorney, Lucy. I knew how these things worked."

Jake's mouth felt dry, despite the rain. He licked his lips. Lucy was very still.

"I made Donnie change clothes with me. Boots, coverall, face mask, gloves. I told him to walk back to the city, get as far as he could before the police caught him, and not to resist arrest when they did. Hobart had taken the surveillance system down, and it was still out. He knew, or had gotten, the codes. I walked right in. I thought I might see servants, but I didn't.

"Mrs. Dalton and Hobart lay in her study, where Donnie said they were. Probably he'd fired first, and his gun was still in his hand. She'd been quick, though, maybe even simultaneous, and her gun was right beside her. Maybe Hobart hadn't expected her to use it. It's one thing to shoot your mother. It's another to have a mother kill a child, even a child that's just forced her to open her e-account and transfer a million dollars to you.

"When I went in, I planned on simply taking something, anything, that might help in Donnie's defense. I knew he'd be caught. Forensics is too damn sophisticated; he'd have left fibers and God-knows-what all over the place. I did, too, but it was all from Donnie's clothing. They'd know someone else had come in, but they wouldn't know who. Not an inch of me was exposed. I picked up an e-tablet, thinking I'd check out later whose it was, what if anything it said. Then I noticed that Mrs. Dalton was still alive. And I saw something else."

Lucy made a movement and Jake put a restraining hand on her arm. If she interrupted now, he didn't think he could finish this.

"She'd been shot maybe ten minutes ago. I was pretty sure she was dying, but her heart was still pumping. That meant her blood was still flowing. As long as the blood flows anywhere, it flows everywhere, including through the capillaries in the eye. And Hobart had already forced her to open her e-account for a transfer. I—"

"No . . ."

"Yes. I dragged her by her hair to the terminal and shoved her retina against the scanner. It authorized a money transfer. I dropped her and transferred ten billion dollars to the Bolivian secret account I'd set up to keep assets away from Rania, and I left the house. It was a major conjunction of circumstances that had come together, like a major conjunction of planets, and just as rare. To me it meant that I was intended to defend Donnie. I took the money, which was still only a fraction of the Dalton estate, to hire the best lawyers I could to defend him. The cops would suspect where the money came from, of course, but they wouldn't be able to prove anything. They wouldn't be able to put me on the scene. My practice and my life would be ruined but it seemed to me, in the fever of that moment, that my ruin was right, too, because I owed it to Donnie. I'd failed him and it was my job to make it up to him. Lucy, I left that house in a glow of unholy virtue, illuminated by my own inner light."

"Jake?" Gail called from the direction of the shelter. "Lucy?"

Jake said, "Only it didn't work out that way. There was no defense. Conjunctions of circumstances last only an instant, you know, and then the planets move on. Donnie went straight to a neptune den in the city, took an overdose, and died the next day."

Gail, more insistent: "Jake! Are you out there? Are you all right?"

"I was never even a suspect. The cops assumed either Hobart or Donnie had transferred the money before the shooting. Bolivian accounts were absolutely secret and absolutely secure. If they hadn't been, half the transnationals might have collapsed. That ten billion dollars had just disappeared off the face of the Earth, for all anyone could prove."

"Jake—"

"Just a little bit more. I waited five full years. Then I spent one billion of the ten to have the best criminal jumper in the world create a rich uncle to leave me the other nine in his will. By the time he finished, my Swiss uncle Johan had a lifelong e-trail, friends, old retainers, everything. Then I started Mira Corp and looked for investors as eager to get off the stinking corrupt planet as I was. My first investor was William Shipley, upright leader of a New Quakers sect that wanted to live a purer and more idealistic life somewhere else."

"Jake!" Gail called, and now there was real fear in her voice.

"We're all right, Gail. Leave us alone!" Jake yelled, but instead of calling back an embarrassed apology, Gail must have started toward them. Jake saw a flashlight bobbing toward them in the dark.

"You know the rest, Lucy. And now you know it all. You're a pretty pure and idealistic person yourself. Can you still say you love someone who's done what I did?"

He couldn't see her face. She was silent, and in her silence Jake saw why he'd told her. Not because of Beta's deathbed request to Shipley, that Shipley had the damned gall to pass on to Jake. Not so that someone knew the truth about Jake before he died. Not even to test Lucy's emotion for him. No, he'd told her in order to destroy that emotion. *And then you won't love me anymore.* And he would be free of the burden of living up to it.

"Lucy?" he said gently, almost caressingly. Still she didn't move or speak. And then Gail had reached them, oblivious, organized, officious Gail, shining her flashlight into both their faces and saying, "Hey, you two shouldn't be out here alone in the rain. Is something wrong?"

"No, Gail," Jake said wearily. "Nothing's wrong except that we're caged in the rain by enormously powerful war-crazed aliens intent on genocide. Other than that, things are exactly as they were before."

# 22

Shipley woke stiff in every muscle, even though he'd lain on the cushioned inflatable floor in the only dry shelter. It took him a while to crawl out and stand. He flexed his knees and then his shoulders, which helped not at all, and felt in his pocket. It was still there.

Gail had given him a waterproof, e-sealed plastic box the size of his palm to keep Beta's "death flower" in, replacing the pathetic wrappings of Greentrees groundcover. Shipley didn't know what she'd dumped out of the box to free it. Whatever it was, Gail would have efficiently stored it somewhere else. She stood now directing breakfast, which was being cooked over the portable heater. Maybe there wasn't enough dry wood after the rain. The sky was still overcast.

Everyone else seemed to be up and doing something. Shipley looked for Naomi but didn't see her. He headed for Beta.

The little Vine's cart stood beside a curve of the invisible wall. After much discussion, humans still had no idea why one Vine had been left alive, even if only temporarily. For future torture, if necessary? Shipley shuddered.

Nor did he know how to tell if Beta were awake, assuming the Vine had any other mode. Beta had talked of "dreaming," but Shipley didn't know if that referred to sleep, meditation, or some unknowable alien state.

"Hello, William Shipley," the translator said in its flat voice.

"Good morning, Beta."

"Sit with us in silence, William Shipley."

He'd brought his stool. Pressing the button to inflate it, Shipley lowered himself to the plastic and bent his head. His stomach rumbled but he ignored it.

Silence. Peace.

He wasn't sure how long he sat there. He was not moved to speak. Beta was.

"William Shipley, we die this day."

"If the Light chooses," he said, because he had to say something.

"Death is sadness to us."

"But only sadness," he said, and this time the words were not simply to fill the space. Something moved in Shipley, deep and heartfelt, and he closed his eyes in gratitude.

"Yes," Beta said. "The death flowers will grow. They have grown two times. They can grow three times."

"So you told me last night, Beta."

"You must tell Jake Holman."

Shipley opened his eyes. "Tell Jake about the gene library? Why?"

"The Furs may kill you, William Shipley. They may kill all humans. Or they may kill some humans. You are not like us. You are like our mobiles. You are like the Furs also. The Furs have a leader, one who speaks first. You have a leader, one who speaks first. If they leave any human, they will leave the leader. Tell Jake Holman about the death flowers. Tell Jake Holman where the death flower planet is. He will return our death flower to us."

It was the longest speech Shipley had ever heard from a Vine. How many of George's "chemical signals" had been required to fuel the translator? Shipley realized that Beta had been preparing this speech all night. How long could the Vine go inside that dome, without outside refueling of . . . something? George had guessed that the closed ecosystem might be self-sustaining for a while, but not indefinitely, or all the slime wouldn't have been needed inside the Vines' shuttle.

He said, "I will tell Jake Holman," and the inner silence, the precious inner peace, vanished. "Beta—"

"Thank you. We will sit in shared silence."

There was nothing else he could do.

They were still sitting there, Shipley and the Vine, when the noise began, mounted, became light in the sky.

"They're here again," Jake called. "Everyone in!"

Shipley didn't move. Beta said nothing.

The Fur shuttle set down where the village had stood. Immediately the ramp opened and all three Furs stepped out. The female walked over to Beta, while the other two strode to the humans, clustered behind Jake.

Shipley stood. "No, please, listen to me first—"

The Fur ignored him. She had no translator; to her he'd been spewing gibberish. He took a step toward her but she ignored that as well. There was something in her hand.

Behind him, Karim began to whistle, sweet and slow, one of the songs that Beta had so enjoyed the day before.

"Good-bye, William Shipley," Beta said. The Fur fired. The Vine and its little cart disappeared.

"Good-bye, Beta Vine," Shipley whispered.

The female Fur waved Shipley toward the others. He stood numbly beside Naomi. The leader said through the egg-shaped translator on the ground, "You. Step here."

He meant Jake. Jake hesitated, then moved to the place indicated, a few yards from the others. The other male Fur grabbed his arm and began cutting off his clothes with some instrument held in his furry hand.

"Hey!" Naomi said angrily and leaped forward. Gail tried to grab her but missed. It didn't matter; Naomi hit an invisible barrier. They were caged again.

Naomi started cursing, a stream of words so foul that Shipley stared in shock. Gail said sharply, "Stop it, Nan! The translator doesn't know those words anyway, so the only one you're upsetting is Jake." Naomi subsided, leaning into the wall, her face a silent snarl.

The Fur continued shredding until Jake stood naked. Gooseflesh rose on him in the cool morning air. Shipley looked away until the Fur ran a curved dark object over Jake's body, front and back. When he'd finished, the leader said, "What are you?"

"I am a human," Jake said. He stood with his arms defiantly at his sides, refusing to shield himself. His genitals hung limp and pale.

The leader swatted him on the shoulder, hard enough for Jake's face to register pain. "What are you?" The question, repeated in the emotionless translator voice, sounded obscene.

Jake tried again. "I am the leader of the humans."

Evidently this was what was wanted. The female pushed Jake aside. He lurched sideways but didn't fall, encased in a second of the invisible walls.

The other male reached toward the huddle of humans. The closest one was Naomi.

"No!" Shipley cried, in a shrill reedy voice he didn't recognize as his own. Gail's was much stronger.

"Nan, don't struggle. Do you hear me—don't struggle. You'll only end up dead or maimed!"

Shipley's eyes blurred. But for perhaps the first time in her life, Naomi listened to someone. She stood sullen but quiet while the Fur cut off her clothing and ran the curved rod over her. It was a weapons' check, Shipley realized. He looked away from his daughter's naked body.

"What are you?"

Naomi growled, "I am the messenger for the humans." The female shoved her beside Jake.

The invisible barrier must open and close when the Furs wanted it to, Shipley realized. Naomi . . .

George was next. The middle-aged botanist was slightly overweight, and his doughy body was striped with suntanned and white parts. He stood stoically, not resisting.

"I am a scientist of plants."

"I am a scientist of evolution." Lucy, her naked body so thin that her ribs showed below the small breasts. Did the translator understand the word "evolution"? Yes. Lucy was pushed beside George, Naomi, and Jake.

"I am a scientist of stars and planets." Karim, his hard, brown body barely held in control, something dangerous moving behind the dark eyes.

"I am a scientist of genes." Ingrid, for once not arguing.

"I am a soldier." Mueller. Shipley would have expected him to go sooner. Or did soldiers hold back, looking for a chance to attack? If so, Mueller hadn't found it. The rebuilt spoke as flatly as the translator itself. White welts marked the scars on his body where the cloned organs had been transplanted into him.

Only Shipley and Gail left. The whole obscene procedure reminded Shipley of something, pulled at the edges of his stunned mind. Some point in history, when humans had stripped other humans and forced them to identify themselves, forming lines of those who would live and those who would die . . . He couldn't remember. He couldn't think. And there were no lines here, just a clump of naked, shivering people behind a wall they couldn't see.

Belatedly, Shipley tried to step in front of Gail, but she elbowed him aside. While she was stripped, Shipley watched Naomi. He had never seen such a terrifying look on any human face; he would not have known a human face could look like that.

"I am an administrator," Gail said. The translator was silent; it had learned English by way of Vine, and Vine was unlikely to include a word for "administrator." The second male slammed his fist into Gail. She staggered sideways and he caught her bruised arm in a cruel grip.

She didn't crumble. Obviously in pain, she said, "I am a keeper of names."

Something changed on the leader's furred face, until now as still as stone. His gaze jerked to her. The translator at his feet said, "You are the keeper of names and birds?"

Birds? Shipley thought he hadn't heard right. But Gail was quicker. She said firmly, "I am the keeper of lists and birds."

The leader let out the roar he had only before given on first landing. The second male dropped Gail's arm. Then all three Furs dropped to their knees, the powerful balancing tails folded under them.

The genuflection—if that's what it was—lasted only a moment. Then the Furs were standing again, balanced on their tails. The translator said, "We honor the keeper of names and birds. You may die now, if you choose to die now for birds and the morning sky."

Gail said shakily, "I do not choose to die now."

"You will tell us when you choose to die for birds and the morning sky."

She said, "I will tell you when I choose to die for birds and the morning sky."

The leader roared again. Gail was led, but not shoved, to the others. Shipley was dazzled by her presence of mind.

Then it was his turn. He stood quietly, staring at the ground, while the clothing was cut from him. The sudden air on his chest and genitals felt colder than he expected. Shame, primitive and undeserved, flooded him. The curved rod was run lightly over his body, and stopped at his hand. Voluntarily he opened it to show the sealed metal box.

"I fix broken human bodies," Shipley said. He doubted that "doctor" had been in the Vines' lexicon; with their exquisite mastery of genetics, the Vines probably repaired themselves. "This is my device to fix humans. I must have it to fix humans."

The Fur took Beta's death flower from him and tossed it onto the pile of shredded clothing. The female raised her weapon and fired, and all of it vanished.

Beta's genetic identity would never make it to the hidden library. Beta was gone forever. Shipley still couldn't recall where he'd read about the double line of naked prisoners, those to live and those to die, their ancestral lines ended with them. He wished he could remember.

He wished even more that he had known Beta's actual, true name.

The nine humans were herded aboard the shuttle. Either it had been built in two sections or it had been altered overnight, because the part they occupied was completely separate from any access to anything else. A featureless half-egg-shaped box, it contained nothing but thick padding on the floor. The temperature was much colder than outside.

"Cargo hold?" Ingrid faltered. "If it's not pressurized . . ."

"They're too smart for that," George said. "Their planet is probably colder than ours. Look at that fur."

Karim said, "Lie down, everyone. Now. This thing doesn't have a McAndrew Drive, and there's going to be acceleration."

To fit, they had to squeeze tightly against each other. Shipley found himself between the wall and a red-faced Lucy. She was so tight against him that he felt her small nipples harden with the cold, and then felt himself redden stupidly.

"Lifting," Karim said, unnecessarily. Apparently the scientists eased their fear by oral reporting.

A weight slammed into Shipley's chest. He couldn't breathe. His eyeballs burned, and his body turned to lead, and still he could not force air into his lungs. He felt himself on the edge of blackout, and then it was over and he was gasping, his lungs on fire.

"Not too bad," George gasped. "No more than six gees, and *fast.*"

Jake said, "Everyone all right? Doctor?"

"Y-yes," Shipley said, and a part of his mind registered that Jake's voice came from the other side of the tiny cabin. Not from the other side of Lucy.

Karim sat up. "Gravity. We're not in free fall. How the hell do they do that?"

Jake said, "Will that gravity burst come again, Karim? Should we stay lying down?"

Karim said, "I don't see why it would if we're going to dock with the mother ship."

Jake didn't say to lie down again anyway. Shipley saw why: sitting, they had at least a few inches of space between them.

But it was cold, so cold. They moved together anyway, wordlessly, shivering. Lucy's slim body felt like ice. Shipley, fatter, estimated his body temperature to be as much as three degrees above hers. He put his arms around her, and in a few minutes they were one mass of flesh, rattling with the bone-piercing cold.

Fortunately, it didn't last long. A gentle jolt, and the door slid open. The lead Fur and his two lieutenants stood there. Roughly they pulled the humans from the shuttle, which seemed to be encased in a close, dim bay of some kind. They were pushed through a door, which closed behind them. Mercifully, it was warm.

Another bare room except for floor matting. Two metal eggs sat on the floor. One was a translator, the same one as on Greentrees or a different one. The second, open at the top, was filled with water. The door closed.

"No food," Ingrid said.

Jake said, "Is everybody all right?"

Ragged yeses.

"Okay," Jake said. "We don't know where they're taking us, or why, or how long the flight will take. But we're not dead yet. That's something."

No one answered.

Gail said briskly, "Wherever we're going, we don't have to sit here doing nothing on the way. Karim, didn't you say that this ship had a . . . a Somebody's Drive? So that it can accelerate and decelerate really fast and so get between star systems much faster than we can?"

"Yes," Karim said. "The McAndrew Drive. There's a disk of superdense material that—"

"Good," Gail said. "So we won't have those gees when the ship leaves orbit?"

"Shouldn't have. In fact, we may have left orbit already."

"Good," Gail said, nodding. "Then this floor padding isn't really necessary. Let's see how much of the cloth we can get up and tear or bite or something into strips. Maybe we can make some sort of minimal clothing. We don't know what the temperature will be where we're going. And it will keep us busy."

Ingrid was looking at Gail as if Gail had lost her mind. But Jake said, "It's a good idea, Gail. All right, let's start."

"Wait," Shipley said, and his voice came out a high quaver. He tried again. "Wait. Please."

Everyone turned toward him. He had to be careful. If he called it a meeting for worship, or even a shared silence, no one would participate. There would be noise, chatter, argument, scientific speculation. Would it be untruth to call it something else?

No. And the need was great.

He said, "Before we start making clothes, could we have a time of silence for Beta? A . . . a memorial?"

He scanned the faces. Jake's full of strain, Gail's impatient. Lucy's and, surprisingly, Karim's soft with sudden compassion. Mueller, impassive as always. Ingrid and George indifferent.

He didn't dare look at Naomi's. Naomi, with her scorn for him, her unholy glee in causing hurt. He wasn't strong enough just now to withstand her, as he had withstood her her whole life, trying to show her a better way. He was so tired. Beta was dead, and Shipley had failed in the last thing the Vine had asked of him. If Naomi turned her cruelty on him now, Shipley realized with fresh horror, he didn't think he could keep from breaking down.

Jake said gently, "Of course, Doctor. We can have a few moments' silence for Beta. He was . . . he was always gentle."

Ingrid scowled. Shipley blocked out the sight by closing his eyes and bowing his head. He didn't know if the others did the same, but at least no one spoke. Shipley tried to clear his mind, to clear the way for peace and light, if they would come. It was hard. They were all there, tolerating the silence but not sharing it, impatient to get on with the decisions and actions they relied upon instead. It wasn't a meeting for worship. It wasn't a meeting for anything, not even a remembrance of Beta. It was an interruption he had pushed onto them all from his own arrogance, his own mistaken attempt to give when he needed instead to receive, a futile and pointless imposition that brought no one anything, not even himself . . .

Then Karim began to whistle. A moment later Shipley felt the touch of small callused fingers, and Naomi's hand stole into his own.

# 23

Gail didn't know how long she'd been asleep. She was jolted awake by the opening of a door.

A Fur stood in the doorway, staring impassively at the humans jerking abruptly awake on the ship's deck. A few, hard sleepers, didn't hear the door and slept on, oblivious. The Fur—which may or may not have been one of the three they'd seen before, the Furs all looked alike to Gail—registered no reaction at the bands of gray cloth torn up from the deck matting and now wrapped around human bodies at various points. Most people had simply tied their allotment around their hips, covering their genitals. Lucy and Nan were small enough that their share stretched over their breasts as well, a primitive sarong.

"Come," the Fur said, through the translator egg he carried. The smooth egg shape had now sprouted a handle. *Convenient,* Gail thought. She shook George awake.

The nine humans followed the Fur through the same narrow featureless corridor, or perhaps a different one, to the shuttle. Again they were herded into the claustrophobic space. Gail, the last to enter, felt a Fur tentacle on her arm and jumped.

"Keeper of names and birds, you may die now, if you choose to die now for birds and the morning sky."

Not a sky in sight, morning or otherwise. Not to mention birds. Gail said as firmly as she could manage, "I do not choose to die now for birds and the morning sky."

The Fur let her go and she climbed into the shuttle.

"Lie down," Jake said sharply. "Possible acceleration." He had barely finished talking when Gail felt the gees pressing down on her. She endured it, having no choice, not fighting. After a few moments it passed.

"Everyone?" Jake said. "Doctor?"

Nan answered. "He passed out. But he's breathing." She watched her father, and Gail watched Nan.

Nan had held his hand during the pathetic, mawkish "memorial silence" for the dead Vine, but let go of it immediately afterward and hadn't glanced at him again. Whatever was going on with Nan, Gail wished the girl would get over it. Nan should make up her mind to either behave decently toward Shipley or ignore him. Just as Nan should make up her mind about the Furs. She'd championed the experimental Furs on Greentrees and she hated the callous Furs here. This seemed clear enough to Gail, and reasonable, but Nan apparently complicated it in her own perverse mind. For some reason she needed a unified set of reactions, and it was tearing her up, and Gail couldn't see why. Gail felt herself growing impatient with Nan's anguish about aliens. It was self-indulgent.

And Jake, too, had something weird going on between him and Lucy, something that had started during their night talk in the rain. Lucy wouldn't meet his eyes or sit near him, not once during the day and a half aboard the Fur ship. If it *had* been a day and a half; the lights never dimmed and all they'd had to go by was their own internal clocks.

Why couldn't any of them, Nan and Shipley and Jake and Lucy and probably even Franz Mueller, still brooding over having killed Scherer, recognize what was genuinely important here? Survival was what mattered now. The rest was just self-absorption. Gail wanted to shake them.

Her belly rumbled. God, she was starving. No food had ever been offered on the ship. Lucy and Nan, with no extra body fat, already looked gaunt in the face. The others, more comfortably padded, just looked hungry.

"Deceleration," Karim called, and everyone braced themselves against the only thing possible, each other. Gail's bones were rattling when the shuttle stopped.

What was outside?

The door opened. Jake had positioned himself to be the first out, followed by Mueller. Gail went last, behind Shipley and Karim, the old man leaning on the young physicist.

A different planet. Expected, of course, but still a shock. Her body felt heavy, sluggish. She looked around and blinked.

They stood on a wide plateau beside a steep mountain. In one direction rose red rocky slopes, half covered with greenish vegetation. After so long on Greentrees, the red stone and green flora looked strange, wrong. Plants should be purple.

In the opposite direction she could see for miles, a vista of rugged terrain. Valleys, rivers, more mountains. The sun low in the sky was small and very bright, and the shadows had knife-sharp edges and strange coloring. Was it the same sun? Yes, they hadn't been traveling long enough to have left the Greentrees star system.

A slow, cold wind blew. The air, which raised goose bumps on her skin, smelled pungent with . . . something. Something rotting. Gail took a step forward. The ground pulled at her. The sky was naked of birds . . . too much gravity? Despite herself, Gail felt tears prick her eyes. The scene was too alien, austere and wild and unwelcoming. Angry at her weakness, she blinked the tears away.

To her left stood a large triangular stone building, the rough reddish stones mortared together in no particular patterns, and some much smaller outbuildings. Smoke rose from a hole in the roof. It smelled acrid. Something brightly colored was tied to poles beside the building, but Gail had no idea what it was.

Two Furs had also exited the shuttle. One addressed Jake as if the others didn't exist. "This is another planet where enemies made our people as blasphemies. We will leave you humans here. The enemy will come here to visit the blasphemies. They will take you in their ship if you ask them to take you in their ship. They will take you to their planet.

"You will not tell them we have found this world. You will not tell them we have found the other world where you were. You will tell them you were left here by other humans to die. They will take you to their planet.

"On their planet you will be under their shield. You will destroy their shield so we can attack. You will not tell them why you will destroy their shield. You will tell us where you are and what you do on your—" and the translator barked an untranslatable sound.

Simultaneously, the Fur handed Jake a flat metal tablet that Gail recognized instantly. The screen from the portable version of the Mira City quee sender/receiver, severed from its energy source. It had been transported to the beacon site in case some final, fatal confrontation occurred and that had been the last chance to quee Earth about the fate of the Greentrees colony. The Furs must have taken it from the human skimmer before they blew up the craft.

The Fur said, "If you do not do all these things, we will destroy Greentrees and your city and all humans on Greentrees. If you do not do all these things, we will find Earth and destroy it. Earth will not be hard to find." The Fur turned to go.

"Wait!" Jake said. "We have questions!"

The Fur turned back, without change of expression. At least not as far as Gail could tell.

Jake said, "How do we destroy the shield? We don't know how to do that!"

"Then you must learn how."

"But . . . we have no weapons!"

"You must learn how," the Fur repeated.

Gail said, "The quee you gave us . . . our sender-to-you-of-information"—she pointed to the tablet in Jake's hand—"it has no power! It will not send to you without power!"

"We put power into it," the Fur said. "It will send to us, Keeper of Lists and Birds."

"But—"

"If you do not do all these things, we will destroy Greentrees and your city and all humans on Greentrees. If you do not do all these things, we will find Earth and destroy it."

Gail watched Jake pull himself together. "You have said, Leader, that we must destroy the shield from the enemy planet. But think about this for a minute. We do not have such advanced technology as you. You know that from our shuttle, our weapons, our quee power source, which was so much bigger and more clumsy than yours. You are clearly superior to us in technology. So if you cannot destroy the shield, how can we humans, who—"

"If you do not do all these things," the Fur said, "we will destroy Greentrees and your city and all humans on Greentrees. If you do not do all these things, we will find Earth and destroy it." Once again he turned, impervious to Jake's flattery or logic. Gail felt panic rising in her.

The first Fur disappeared into the shuttle. The second spoke directly to her.

"Keeper of Names and Birds, you may die now, if you choose to die now for birds and the morning sky."

"I don't choose to die, damn it!" Gail said, before she could stop herself. The Fur didn't react. It disappeared into the shuttle, and a second later the shuttle began to lift. Gail felt the heat shock, much less than from a human craft but still perceptible, and threw herself on the ground with her arms over her head. By the time she got up, unhurt, the shuttle had gone.

"All right," Jake said, stopped, started again. "We need shelter and food. I'm going to knock on the door of that charming chateau and see if we can get an invitation to tea. Franz and George, you come with me. Gail, take everybody else . . . somewhere. Behind that boulder, I guess, or into that ravine. And take this."

Nan said, "I'm going with you, Jake. I lived with Furs on Greentrees." He didn't argue, either because it was too much trouble or because he thought she might actually be useful. Gail considered both reasons specious. These Furs—if they turned out to be Furs—weren't the same as the ones on Greentrees. And it was a leader's place to enforce his own decisions.

"Give me the quee," she said to Jake. Often, although not invariably, she had been the one to use it both aboard the *Ariel* and in Mira City. He handed it to her. Detached from its clumsy and large base, it felt unnaturally light. Could there really be enough power in there for a quantum-entanglement energy link with whatever counterparts the Furs had on their ship? And how were the crazy aliens going to read the English writing she would send? None of it made any sense. Nothing had made any sense since the first Fur colony had been discovered on Greentrees.

"All right, everybody," she said, "let's go."

The rough ground, red rocks mixed with low prickly plants bearing pungent dark blue berries, hurt her bare feet. And God alone knew what pathogens they were stepping in, or breathing in. If exposure didn't get them, disease might.

Don't think like that.

"Dr. Shipley, can you manage?" she asked. The old man looked both terrible and ridiculous, his huge belly hanging over the strip of gray cloth tied around his hips, his gray-haired chest prickling with gooseflesh from the cold. Every line in his face sagged.

"Yes, I can, Gail. Thank you." Lucy and Karim helped him down the slope behind the boulder. At the bottom, Gail saw, was a sort of indentation in the cliff wall. Less than a cave, more than an overhang. It would do.

They slipped and slid down the slope, pebbles clattering away under their feet. Gail's body felt too heavy. She stepped on something sharp and cursed. But inside the not-quite-a-cave they were protected from the wind, and the rock was even warm from sunshine. She sat down gratefully.

Immediately Karim began to talk. "I think that's an F-class star, maybe an F7 or F8. I would guess from the level of glare that we're much farther from the primary than Terra is from Sol, so we're not getting nearly the energy. The gravity seems about a third more than Terra. The air pressure is greater, that's why you're having trouble breathing. The—"

"Karim," Gail said, "is any of this information of practical use to us?"

He thought a minute. "There's probably more UV, X rays, and charged particles than we're used to. We should try to stay out of the sun."

"Great," Gail said. "The sun is the only thing keeping us from freezing."

"And don't move too quickly. It's going to take a while to adjust to this denser air pressure."

Gail examined the bottom of her foot. Whatever she'd stepped on hadn't broken the skin.

Lucy said, "I saw some garden plots behind that stone lodge. I could go get some food. If the Furs can eat it, maybe we can, too."

Ingrid snapped, "You don't even know if Furs are the life form here."

True enough. Without information, without their technology to test new plants and excavate tunnels and protect them from predators and cure them of mishaps, they were helpless. Near-naked infants with nothing to do but wait.

Fortunately, the wait wasn't long. George reappeared, looking excited and ridiculous in his inadequate gray loincloth. "Gail! Everybody! Come on up, there's food in the lodge."

They scrambled up the small slope, Lucy and Karim helping Dr. Shipley. The old man was puffing badly. On the plateau, the cold wind hit them again. Gail was glad to enter the stone lodge.

Inside was warm, smoky, and crowded. An open hearth burned in the center of the room, the smoke ascending through the hole in the roof. Wooden beams were hung with unrecognizable bunches of plants and hunks of what looked like meat inside clear membranes. A dozen Furs sat huddled together on one side of the fire, half of them children. As usual, Gail couldn't read their expressions, but there was no mistaking their postures. Gail had seen that shrinking in dogs, in cats, in cornered mice, as well as in human beings. These Furs were terrified.

On the other side of the fire, eating something grayish-green, sat the rest of the humans except for Nan. She crouched with the Furs, carefully matching her body posture to theirs, growling softly at one of the adults.

Jake said, "They seem scared witless of us. Ingrid thinks the viral alteration in this lot might be something analogous to the human trait of novelty avoidance. Anything new scares them into paralysis."

Gail said, "Should you be eating that?" Her mouth watered from just seeing it.

George said seriously, "We don't have much choice. Either we eat or we starve. The Furs made this, it's a sort of dried plant mush, I think. There are piles of it in that hole over there. They didn't object when we took some."

Nan said acidly from the other side of the fire, "They wouldn't object if we took everything they owned. Don't you understand? They've been mutilated, in their brains and in their survival instincts, so that the Vines can create Furs who are so afraid of them they'll do anything to avoid new objects, experiences, or beings. It's experimental rape."

So Nan had resolved her conflict about aliens. She'd found a new group of victims to champion, and the Vines were again the evil dehumanizers. So to speak.

Gail peered into the hole George had indicated. It was lined with more clear membranes and filled with chunks of the gray-greenish food. She picked up a piece and licked it. Slightly bitter, but not repulsive. Her belly was having contractions from hunger. She chewed on the chunk and sat close to the welcome warmth of the fire.

"If we all die in the night," George said, "that will solve the issue of what to do next."

"We're not going to die in the night," Gail said. Now they had food, shelter, possible mentors. There was something for her to work with.

"Gail," Jake said, "wake up. They're gone."

"What?" She lay on the lodge floor, wrapped in a blanket made of some grayish pelt she couldn't identify but which itched. It also smelled strange. Neither smell nor itch had kept her from sleep. After three nights featuring rain, tension, and cold, falling asleep in this itchy hide in this smoke-filled space had seemed like the greatest luxury imaginable. So, of course, it hadn't lasted.

"They're gone," Jake repeated. "The Furs. All of them."

She sat up. The lodge was full of pale watery light: dawn. Everyone lay asleep except Jake, Karim, and . . .

"Where's Nan?" Oh, God, she had gone with them, the little idealistic fool . . .

"Outside. Karim wanted to see if the charged light from the primary produces auroras. He left without noticing whether the Furs were here or not, but Nan woke up when she heard him and she noticed right away. She woke me."

"And you woke me," Gail said, trying to hide her relief that Nan hadn't traipsed off to live with the natives. "Why?"

"Because while Karim was stargazing he thought he saw an object moving among the stars. It might just be a comet or meteor, he said. But it also might be a ship."

*"Already?"*

"Presumably," Jake said dryly, "the Furs plan well. Gail, if there *is* a ship, and if it's Vines, and if they indeed rescue us, we have to decide what we're going to do."

"I know," Gail said. It had actually been a kind of luxury to concentrate on simple survival. Food, water, clothing, shelter. It kept the larger issues at bay. Genocide, treachery, planetary sabotage, the destruction of Mira City. Nobody should have to make decisions that big.

She said softly, "We couldn't do it even if we wanted to, Jake. We don't have the faintest idea how."

"Really?" he said bitterly. "Not even you? The keeper of lists and birds?"

"Go fuck yourself," she said, and felt a little better. "Are there auroras out there?"

"Spectacular ones. All over the sky. I suggest you catch them now, before the sun rises."

"No," Gail said. "I'd rather get everybody up and breakfast organized."

They ate quickly, silently, a necessary task rather than the slavering relief it had been last night. Even Mueller ate, although reluctantly. He seemed to shudder when the alien food touched his lips. Ingrid threw another log on the dying fire. Several people sat wrapped in their itchy blankets. Gail, George, and Lucy had already started to hack and tie theirs into something more closely approximating clothing.

Gail waited for Jake to begin. He looked better than she expected, reasonably rested and fed, but controlled desperation tautened his face.

"All right, here are our options as I see them, people. Either the Vines come for us, like the Furs said, or they don't. We can't control that. What we can do is pick one of three choices. We can disappear into the wilderness and hide from any aliens, Vines or Furs, that show up. Survival would be problematic because we don't know this planet at all, and we don't have our technology to get to know it safely. But since we would be so low-tech, if we move far enough, probably no aliens will detect us. After all, they're only using a tiny fraction of the planet for the experimental colonies. That's choice one."

George said, "I don't put our survival chances very high. We have no idea what predators, insect-analogues, or poisonous plants we'd encounter. And even if we do go, if what Karim saw *was* a ship, the Vines might be here pretty soon. Who knows how many colonies they have here or in what order this one is to be checked on?"

Gail said, "That doesn't rule out choice one, though."

Jake said, "Choice two. Do what the Furs said. Go with the Vines, tell them we've been marooned here by our own people, get under their planetary shield. Then hope we can figure out a way to destroy the shield."

No one spoke.

"Choice three. We meet the Vines and tell them the truth, including what the Furs want us to do. Then we hope they can help us."

Nan burst out, "Help us do *what*? They can't destroy anything, or they would have already destroyed the space-faring Furs' planet. They'll sit and talk about it all, talk is all they know how to do. And meanwhile, the dominant Furs will just wipe out these colonies on this planet, the way they did on Greentrees."

*Oh, Nan,* Gail thought. Siding again with the underdogs. Even at the expense of her own kind. Aloud Gail said, "A key question here is whether we really believe the Furs will destroy Mira City if we don't cooperate. The threat to destroy Earth might be just bluff, but Mira City is accessible to them."

George said somberly, "They'll destroy the city."

Karim said, "I agree."

Gail said, "Then our choice is clear." She didn't look at Nan. "We have to do what the Furs told us to do. Maybe we can figure out how to destroy the shield from within, maybe not. But if we don't at least try, five thousand of our fellow human beings will die. More if they can kill Larry's Cheyenne."

George said, "As opposed to an entire planetful of beings on Vine!"

"Who are not our people," Gail said steadily. She felt very clear on this. "Our loyalty is to human beings."

Franz Mueller said, "*Ja.* I say this also," startling everybody. He seldom said anything.

Ingrid, looking troubled, said, "I don't see any possible way we could destroy a shield we don't even begin to understand. So even if we got to Vine, we would still be ineffective, and the Furs would still destroy Mira City. If not Earth."

Jake said, "But if we don't try to destroy the shield, we *know* they'll take out Mira City."

Nan burst out, "But the chances are overwhelming that either way we can't stop the destruction of Mira City! But we can save these poor creatures here from either being murdered or experimented on any more! If we slip off into the wilderness and find them, over time they'd get used to us. We could teach them. Together we could survive!"

Gail said, "No. Mira City comes first, even if the chance is slender. God, Jake and I and George and Dr. Shipley are all on the Board of Governors! Do you think we can just sell out our own people to maybe save our own lives?"

Ingrid said, "We'd save our own lives if we went to Vine. Even if we don't bring down the shield, we'd be safe under it, since it works."

Gail said, "Our loyalty to Mira City comes first."

Nan said hotly, "Don't be such a species chauvinist, Gail! The experimental Furs are sentient, too! How is putting our kind above theirs different from all those times in history when one group of humans decided a different group was subhuman and felt free to experiment on them or kill them off?"

Jake said, "Calm down, Nan. And everybody else. We need to discuss this rationally to make the best decision quickly."

"It's not merely a rational issue!" Nan retorted. "Lives are involved!"

"Yes," Ingrid said. "Ours."

Gail said, "Isn't your husband back in Mira City, Ingrid?" and Ingrid clenched her fists and glared at her.

Karim said, "The shield—" He was cut off by a clamor of voices.

"Mira City—"

"The Furs—"

"—best chance for survival—"

"The Vines—"

"Loyalty—"

"Stop!" Shipley cried, and tried to get to his feet. He staggered and fell. Lucy tried to catch him, and under her slight weight they both crashed to the ground. Shipley sat up, his blanket slipped off his shoulders, a fat old man trembling but determined to speak.

"Stop. Please. Listen."

"Go ahead," Jake said. And to everybody else, "Let him talk."

Gail looked at Jake's face. He hated having to let Shipley speak. He still disliked and distrusted the New Quaker. But Jake was fair. Gail knew what it cost him, and she nodded. Shipley could speak.

But she doubted it would change anything. They needed a practical plan, not a religious philosophy. She just hoped Jake gave Shipley no more than two minutes. If not, she would interrupt him herself.

This was too important to leave to eccentrics.

# 24

Shipley took a precious moment to gather his thoughts. But then he found he didn't have to. The words flowed out of him, through him, with all the clarity and simplicity of truth. It was the Light in him speaking, and he merely needed to open himself to it and be grateful to be so used.

"We've spoken of loyalty to humankind, to Mira City, to other sentient species more abused than humans, to our own lives. But there's another loyalty involved here, too. There's a loyalty to the truth. It's the truth that makes us free—free of deceit and arrogance and fear. Truth is the best that is in each of us. That's the definition of truth: the part of us that's naturally drawn toward the good. If we act from truth, then something wonderful can happen."

He drew a quick breath, afraid to stop talking in case Jake cut him off, equally afraid that if he didn't breathe deeply, the constant drag of this planet on his old lungs and heart might keep him from talking at all.

"If we act from truth, then the way is open to reach the truth that is in others. Only when we're truthful with others can any joint action call on the best that's in *them,* as well. The Vines are truthful people. We've seen that, in the way they answered all our questions without hesitation, and with answers that have all proved accurate. We know they're brave people, from the way Beta died. They're good people, not the aggressors in this war of theirs.

"If we act from truth with the Vines, if we *tell* them the truth, then together we have two species' resources to decide what will best serve us all. If we don't tell them the truth, if we lie, we cut off that possibility. We lose all the advantages of truthful cooperation. And we also cut ourselves off from the best that's in ourselves.

"Please, Jake, Gail—tell any Vines that come the whole story. Everything. Then the way will be clear for decisions based on reality, not lies. Trust those good people. Trust ourselves."

He ran out of breath, out of words. His lungs ached, but he looked hopefully at their faces. The Light had come through him so strong, so clear . . . surely they would be convinced!

Then Naomi said flatly, "Sure the Vines are good people. Good people who experiment on other races in order to create biological weapons."

Shipley felt his own face contort. His daughter.

But the decision was not, after all, Naomi's. He gazed at Jake and Gail, hoping, pleading in his mind.

"Does anyone agree with Dr. Shipley that we should tell the Vines everything? Agreements, just for the record?"

Lucy raised her hand. Lucy, with the idealism he had seen on the *Ariel*, even through her temporary madness.

After a moment, Karim also raised his hand. "They may have science we do not know about yet, that can help us out of this if we're honest with them."

Naomi said harshly, "I vote to disappear into this planet."

Jake said, "This isn't a democracy, Nan. I'm asking for opinions only to guide my decision. Do—"

"This isn't your stinking corporation, Jake! You're not CEO out here!"

"—the rest of you believe we should try to carry through the Furs' orders, as our best chance to save Mira City and maybe even, if they're not bluffing, Terra?"

Ingrid nodded vigorously, followed by Franz Mueller, George, and Gail.

"I think so, too," Jake said. "That's five. Nan, even if this were a democracy, we have a majority. We tell any Vines that show up that we've been dumped here by our own people as punishment for some crime. Aboard the Vine ship we try to find out every single thing we can about that shield. We keep in touch with the Furs by quee; Gail, you can do that. And once we're on Vine, we try to destroy the shield in order to save the humans on Greentrees.

"To keep consistency, I'll be the only one who ever talks to any Vines about Greentrees or our supposed crimes or pretty much anything not completely innocuous. If Vines ask you about anything, refer them to me."

Ingrid said, "How do we know the Vines that are supposed to come here haven't already been told all about us by quee?"

Karim said, "Because the Vines don't have quee. Beta told me."

"Then how do we know the Vines that come here won't first have gone to Greentrees and found their Fur colonies destroyed, and then guess what the Furs' plan for us is?"

Jake said, "It doesn't matter if they went there first, because I'm going to say that when we were dumped here by our own people from Mira City, we'd never seen any aliens except the degraded Furs on Greentrees. We're going to be enormously surprised that the space Furs even exist. And they won't guess what the Furs have told us to do. The Vines will believe that we're outcasts from our own kind."

Ingrid demanded, "How do you know?"

"Because," Jake said, "they're a truthful race."

Shipley got up and went outside.

He lumbered over the rough ground to a rock away from the lodge and sat on it, his back to the building. Now he wasn't aware of the cold, hardly aware of the pull on his muscles and pressure on his lungs. They were going to use the Vines' own goodness against them, building lies on the scaffold of the Vines' truthfulness.

He bowed his head and closed his eyes. This was wrong; he could feel its wrongness in his very bones, a life-destroying cold. But they were going to do it. Lie now and, if they could, kill later. Kill an entire planetful of sentient creatures.

He berated himself for not convincing them. There was so much more he could have said! He could have told them about the many Old Quakers who were moved by the Light to go among the American natives of five hundred years ago, for trade or friendliness. About the many times the natives, who were capturing and torturing other emissaries, had accepted the Quakers, offering them no violence because the Quakers brought no violence. About the power of a sincere peace testimony to change a situation. About

John Woolman visiting violent Indians "that I might learn something from them." Of Dr. Lettsom and the highwayman, of Caydee Umbartu and the West African Rebellion . . .

Shipley sat on the cold rock a long time. No one approached him, not even Lucy. He knew his mind was muddled now, the clarity and truth of the Light having departed. But in his confusion one thought stayed visible, sharp as a sword in his mind.

Jake had said he would lie to the Vines. That's what he would do. But Jake had not asked, because it had not occurred to him as a possibility, what Shipley would do. Jake had not asked whether Shipley, acting out of his own conscience, would tell the Vines the truth anyway. But, then, it wouldn't have mattered if Jake had asked.

Shipley didn't know the answer.

An hour later, Naomi disappeared. It was Gail, of course, who noticed, as she noticed everything. "Dr. Shipley, have you seen Nan?"

She would only have asked him as a last chance, he realized. Cold clutched his belly. "No. Isn't she . . . isn't she with the group that went to get more firewood?" Gail was preparing for a long stay in the lodge, in case.

"No. They're back. She returned with them but now she's gone."

They stared at each other. Shipley got shakily to his feet. "She's gone to find those Furs. The primitive ones she displaced from this lodge."

"God, she's a pain in the ass!" Gail exploded. "If it weren't for—" She didn't finish her sentence, instead stomping over to Jake, who was inexpertly tying together a garment out of blanket. "Jake—"

Shipley's legs suddenly wouldn't support him. He sat down again, but only for a minute. *Naomi . . .*

"A party's going to look for her," Gail reported. "Franz, Karim, and Lucy. Lucy thinks she'll retrace the steps the firewood group took because it's the most obvious path for the Furs to have taken, and then go on from there. Lucy will be the runner. If they're gone more than two hours, Lucy will come back here to find out if the shuttle's returned yet."

"I'm going, too," Shipley said.

"Doctor—"

"As far as I can, anyway. What if she's hurt? Or someone else gets hurt?"

"Lucy's used to wild paleontology sites, Franz is a trained soldier, and Karim keeps himself in terrific shape. You—"

"Are a fat old man. I know. But she's my daughter. Gail, I'm going."

Gail said nothing. Shipley joined the others, his blanket clutched around him. He knew how he must look. Franz Mueller said, "We go. Herr Doctor, if you cannot match our pace, we leave you."

The pace, fortunately, wasn't too quick, since every time they reached a plausible place for Naomi to have left the path, Franz split up the party to check for signs of Naomi's having passed that way: broken twigs, disturbed ground. Each halt gave Shipley, trying not to puff audibly, a chance to catch up. The main path must have been worn smooth by the Furs from the lodge. It led downhill along a mountain stream that must have provided water, bordered by strange-looking trees, or tree-analogues, that looked as if they'd provide firewood. Squat things, with broad drooping leaves, they reminded Shipley of sullen dwarves. The lower the search party descended along the path, the stronger was the pungent smell of rot and decay.

The path stopped when the stream joined a small river. By now they were perhaps a hundred feet below the plateau containing the lodge. Irregular reddish cliffs towered above them. On this side of the river was only a narrow strip of ground between cliff and river, but on the opposite bank the ground widened.

Franz said, "Karim, you cross the river. Look if she go there. Lucy, you go along this side of the river. I go above, up the cliff."

Shipley said, "Would Naomi have gone up there?"

Franz didn't bother to answer. Shipley looked at the cliff with trepidation. But, yes, there were some hand- and footholds, and Naomi, with her wiry body and the indifference to pain she'd had even as a small child, might have climbed it to better survey the terrain below.

Shipley sat on the ground beside a pool where the river deepened. What had she done? If they didn't find her, and the Vine shuttle landed, Jake would leave her here. And he'd be right to do it. Even if they did find her, how would he persuade her to go?

She'd never listened to him. Why hadn't Gail come? Because the mission to the Vines was more important, even to Gail, than one willful arrogant girl.

Shipley put his head in his hands. He didn't see the animal until it was almost upon him.

Something made a noise, somewhere between a growl and a croak. Shipley looked up. It was crawling out of the river, some sort of alien beast, brown and long and smooth-bodied, with curved brown teeth. It was coming toward him.

Shipley made himself freeze. Some Terran animals wouldn't attack unless you moved. But this wasn't Terran, and it kept on crawling.

Maybe he could outrun it. But not back up the mountain path; it was too steep. He'd have to run along this side of the river, on the narrow rocky strip of ground between water and cliff. Or maybe it would be better to back away slowly, hadn't he read once that had been the right way to escape from a bear? When Earth still had bears.

Slowly Shipley began to back away. He could hear his own breathing, loud and labored. The stones pained his bare feet. The animal crawled faster toward him.

He broke and ran. Within four steps he tripped, crashing onto the stones, crying out loudly. The animal seized his forearm and he felt its teeth sink into his flesh. He thrashed and rolled, trying to shake it loose. The pain was sheer agony.

"Fucking ass!" someone screamed and then somehow Naomi was there, hitting at the animal with a stick, trying to grab its jaws and force them off his arm. It wouldn't let go, and the blows of her stick had no effect whatsoever.

Pain blurred his vision. But there was something *above* him, something jumping off the cliff . . .

Franz Mueller. The soldier leaped off the ridge. In the air he did a three-quarter revolution, a not-quite-full somersault, that landed him in the center of a thick clump of bushes with his back facing down, body folded into a vee. Within seconds he was up off the bushes. He seized a stick and jabbed rather than struck at the animal. It released Shipley.

He tried to roll away, couldn't. Naomi yanked on his unhurt

arm. She was amazingly strong; he felt himself being pulled upward and tried to help by stumbling to his feet. She dragged him away, even as he tried to look for Franz and the animal.

He was still jabbing at it, precisely and quickly, dancing out of reach of its jaws. Shipley saw the final jab go into a hole in its head. Franz had blinded it.

Silently the creature slithered back into the water.

Naomi gasped, "He's hurt. Get his other side . . ."

"*Nein.* I guard the rear against another animal. Here come Karim. Go up the path. Where is Lucy?"

"Here," Shipley barely heard. The world was wobbling. He was losing blood from his arm, must make a tourniquet. Pathogens . . . many animals carried a huge number of pathogens in their mouths . . . He couldn't tell them any of this. Arms were pulling him back up the mountain path, stumbling and lurching, and he couldn't speak. His vision blurred.

"Another animal comes. Go faster," Franz said, and then he saw or heard nothing.

He woke on the floor of the lodge. Gail, Jake, and Naomi sat beside him. One of them said, "He's back."

"Dr. Shipley?" Gail, leaning over him, her face concerned. "Can you hear me?"

"Y-yes."

"Good. You're going to be all right." He could see honesty compel her to add, "We think."

"Tourniquet?" His voice came out a whisper.

"Franz made it. He knows what he's doing."

So Franz had survived. Shipley said a grateful prayer. "He j-jumped."

"Ass-right he did," Naomi said, her voice full of admiration. "And fought off those things as well."

"Lucy?"

"Fine," Gail said briskly. "No one was hurt except you. I think that if we're here much longer, Franz had better start giving us all survival lessons."

Jake said, "If we're here much longer, a lot of things will have to change."

Shipley heard the anger in Jake's voice. Naomi . . . he meant Naomi's running off that way. She'd endangered three other people. And now Naomi would angrily counterattack, and the whole painful ritual, familiar to him since her childhood, would start over again. She'd find the something hurtful, and then while you were bleeding from that and trying to hold on to patience and charity, she'd find something even more hurtful, more targeted to the vulnerable soft areas everyone possessed . . .

"I know, Jake," Naomi said. "Dad, I'm sorry. This was my fault."

For a moment he thought he hadn't heard her right. But her face, still defiant with its set lips and angry eyes, showed something else as well. Shame. She *was* sorry.

"N-Naomi . . ."

Jake said, "Don't try to talk. It can wait until later. Naomi, I think you'd better leave now. We'll sit with him. Go find Karim and Lucy and Franz."

To apologize to them, Gail meant, for risking their lives as well. And, astonishingly, Naomi got up and went.

Gail said, "I can't—Doctor? What is it?"

A sudden spasm of pain shot up his injured arm. Toward the heart . . . Shipley waited, but the spasm subsided and his heart didn't stop. He whispered, "Pathogens . . ."

"I know," Gail said. "George says there's no way to know what you took on with that bite. But he also said that the same thing that protected us on Greentrees is probably operating here. Any microbes you took aboard simply can't proliferate using our DNA or nourish themselves with our cells. The genes are just too different, even if they are both DNA. He says all we can do is wait. You should sleep, if you can."

He did, fitfully. Between brief bouts of painful sleep, he half woke, and each time Gail and Jake were still there, talking softly. Did just a few minutes pass, or hours? He had no way to tell. But he heard bits of their conversation, coming to him among tangled dreams of the beast crawling out of the river, coming toward him, closing its fangs on his arm. The same dream, again and again.

Gail said, "—believe it. Will it last?"

"I think so," Jake said.

"But why now? She's hated him so steadily for—"

"She didn't hate him. Not really. You must know that, you saw her momentary softening when Beta died and Shipley was so upset."

"All right. She didn't hate him. But that 'softening' didn't last. Why do you think this will?"

"*She* risked for *him*," Jake said. And then, "Basic negotiating technique, Gail. You get the other guy to do you a favor of some kind. That makes him feel well disposed toward you, and in a much better frame of mind to give you whatever else you want. We feel good toward people we help, provided the help isn't too disproportionate. Not toward the people who help us. We resent those because then we're obligated. Nan finally got to give, on a big scale, for her father."

So that was it, Shipley thought, before he drifted off again. All these painful years, and he hadn't seen it, hadn't understood . . .

"He's still asleep," Gail said. But he wasn't, because he clearly heard the footsteps run across the stone floor of the lodge, clearly heard the excited young voice of Karim Mahjoub.

"Jake! You better come now! A shuttle is on its way down."

# 25

So it was time. Jake walked steadily out of the lodge behind Karim, who pointed to the mountain plateau—it looked too bleak to be called a "meadow"—beyond the lodge. "They'll probably set down there."

"All right. Tell Gail to get everyone in the lodge. We don't want to overwhelm them with nine humans all at once. You and George stand with me." Physicist, biologist, and . . . what was Jake himself? Leader? Negotiator? Would-be quisling?

He couldn't afford to think like that.

Karim said, "Not Franz? He'll want to be here."

He'd probably earned the right, Jake thought, but he couldn't see what good a soldier would do, even a brave, quick-thinking soldier. If this shuttle held Furs, humans had already received a demonstration of how useless human aggression was against them. If the shuttle held Vines, no aggression was necessary.

"No, not Franz. Tell him he's to stay with the rest on my explicit orders. As commander-in-chief," Jake added, and even Karim must have caught the bitterness in his tone because the young physicist glanced at him, startled, before running off.

*All right, Holman. Get a grip on your sarcasm. No more theatrics.*

He watched the shuttle come down, the now-familiar dull metal egg that didn't blacken during reentry nor scorch the ground where it landed. Fur technology. By the time the door slid open and the ramp descended, Karim and George stood beside him, both dressed in crude tunics cut from blankets, looking like unwashed primitives less able to care for themselves than the degraded aliens they'd dispossessed.

Vines or more Furs?

It was Vines, rolling down the too-steep ramp in domed carts, indistinguishable from the Vines that had died on Greentrees. Was there a translator in one of those carts? If so, it wasn't programmed yet for English. If not . . . he'd consider "if not" when he had to. Jake stepped forward.

"Hello. I am Jake Holman, a human. We are peaceful. Hello."

The carts stopped, and then two of them fled back into the shuttle. The third stayed put.

He approached very slowly, Karim and George matching his pace, and just as slowly sat on the rocky ground ten feet from the Vine. It was going to be Greentrees all over again. Sit with them in shared silence, as Shipley had taught him. Then, tomorrow or the next day, begin to talk, softly and persistently, until the translator had enough English vocabulary and grammar for the Vine to reply, and the Vine had enough trust in humans to open a dialogue. Continue that conversation as trust increased on both sides.

Then tell them the lies that might lose them a planetful of their own people.

It all went exactly like that.

At dusk the Vine rolled back inside its shuttle and closed the door. Jake, chilled to the bone despite the extra blankets Gail had brought everyone and more worn-out by just sitting than he could have thought possible, stood up stiffly and went into the lodge. The fire was welcome. His hands and feet had lost all feeling.

"How is Dr. Shipley?" he asked Gail.

"I don't know. He sleeps a lot and he doesn't complain, but other than that I can't tell. I don't know what to look for. Eat, Jake. All we're risking is that chunky stuff, but it's a little tastier heated."

A grill woven of green wood spanned the fire, covered with the greenish-gray food that Nan was turning with a pointed stick. Jake accepted one in a crude wooden bowl and ate it with his fingers. Nan wouldn't meet his eyes. She looked more chastened than he would ever have thought possible.

Karim said, "Dusk lasts much longer than on Greentrees, which argues that we are not near this planet's equator. I wonder if this season now is winter or summer?"

George said, "Summer, I'd say, judging from the number of plants in 'leaf' and even in flower."

"Then it's a good thing we weren't dumped here in winter. I'm frozen through."

Jake said, "From now on, everybody be careful what you say even if you're inside the lodge or far away from the shuttle. We don't know what they can or cannot hear. Everybody understand?"

Nods, including a reluctant one with a touch of her usual sullenness from Nan.

Franz said, "We need some schedule for the guard duty. Jake, maybe you and the other watchers sleep, not do the guard duty."

Watchers. So that's what he was. Mueller's suggestion was a good one. He needed to stay as alert as possible.

"All right, Franz. Good idea. You arrange the guard duty schedule." At least he could give him that. It felt good to transfer at least a small part of the responsibility to someone else. And Jake desperately wanted to sleep.

It didn't happen. He slept a few hours, then woke and could not will himself to oblivion. When he heard Ingrid come in from guard shift and Lucy go out, he waited until Ingrid snored softly, and then he followed Lucy.

The planet's one moon shone among unfamiliar stars. A slow cold wind blew. The sweet night odor of Greentrees had been replaced by a thick, fetid reek. Lucy stood against the sheltered side of the lodge, two blankets over her crude tunic, her feet wrapped in a third. Jake, barefoot, said, "Lucy," and she jumped.

He moved into the welcome shelter of the lodge. The motionless Vine shuttle was clearly visible, but in the shadows her expression was not.

"Lucy, since I told you about . . . what I did, you've stayed completely away from me. Are you thinking about it, or have you decided that you don't want to have anything to do with me?"

She said nothing, which told him everything. He said quietly, "You're very hard."

She cried, "I can't help it!"

And maybe that was true. Maybe people could give only so far, support the weight of only so much. Add more, and they collapsed. People were what they were. Shipley was a pacifist not from belief but from temperament; the belief was unknowingly embraced to match the temperament. Nan was a rebel, Gail an organizer, Mueller a soldier in the same way: temperament first, belief afterward to justify inevitable actions. Maybe even the Vines and the Furs could not transcend their basic nature, just as lead could not become gold. Lucy was a woman with a passionate belief in doing what was ethical. She was righteous, or self-righteous if you wanted to look at it through that lens, but either way she could not accept what she considered unethical without violating something in herself so deep, so essential, that you might as well call it the "soul" and be done with it.

And what was he, Jake?

"I'm sorry," Lucy whispered.

"I know you are," Jake said, and went back inside to try again to sleep.

The next day passed as he had expected, with a rotating band of humans sitting on the ground and talking nonstop to the domed Vine, hoping like hell that it did indeed have a translator in that cart. George said yes, of course it did, it would have needed to talk to its experimental Furs. Jake doubted this. He kept the rotation moving, three humans outside at a time, watching that nobody got too cold. At least the reek of last night had vanished with a shift in the wind.

By afternoon Shipley was definitely worse. He muttered in some kind of delirium, indistinguishable words. His big body felt clammy. Nan tended him silently, doing whatever Gail told her to, but there was little except keeping him warm and hydrated.

Jake joined the group outside, gesturing for Ingrid to go back to the lodge. She left gratefully. Karim had been talking about stars and planets; Jake motioned him to silence.

"Visitor, I want to tell you something important," he said, enunciating slowly and clearly, choosing the simple words they'd agreed to use for the benefit of the translator program, whatever it was. "One human of us is sick. His body does not work correctly. Something is wrong with his body. An animal of this planet attacked him. The animal bit his arm." Jake touched his own arm. "He is sick. We do not have our tools to fix his body."

Jake stopped talking. After several minutes he thought he had failed to force the pace. But the delay was only the Vines' characteristic leisurely way. Eventually it spoke, the first words it had said. "Where are your tools to mend the sick human?"

It had programmed the vocabulary. The voice was the same flat mechanical one of the Fur translator; this must also be captured and adapted technology. Jake said, "Our tools to mend the broken human are on another planet. Humans made a colony on the other planet. We lived there before we came here."

"Why you come here with your tools on the other planet?"

It didn't yet have the verb tenses. Then Jake realized what had just been asked, and he forgot about grammar. This was it. Time for the lie to begin. His chest, already heavy under the planet's gravity, felt like stone. He hoped that Karim could keep his face neutral. Although what did it matter—the Vines probably could not read human faces. All Karim had to do was not talk.

Jake said to the Vine, "We humans came here without our tools to mend people because we came here without any of our tools. We were left here by the humans on our planet. They did not want us to be with them on that planet. We were left here to die."

"Why?"

"Because we want to build different things from the other humans. There was a war. We lost the war." If there was one thing the Vines should understand, it was war. They'd had thousands of years of it.

The Vine remained silent a long time. Finally it said, "We are at war."

"With whom?" His heart thudded in his leaden chest.

"With people like the people that lived in this lodge. Where are the people that lived in this lodge? We made them. We do not see them."

"They ran away when we came," Jake said truthfully. "They were afraid of us."

"Yes. They are afraid of all things new. We made them afraid of all things new."

These Vines were going to be just as honest and open about everything as Beta had been. *You might as well call it the "soul" and be done with it.*

The Vine added after one of its long pauses, "Bring the sick human to here. We look at the sick human."

"Yes," Jake said. "Karim, stay here."

Slowly Jake walked back to the lodge. The others were clustered around the fire, braiding some foliage into rope. Gail hurried to meet him.

"Gail, the Vine wants to see Shipley. It's possible it can do something to help him. George says they're biochemists, after all."

"It spoke to you?" George, his face eager.

"Yes. Nan, we need to bring your father outside to the Vine."

She glared up at him. "To experiment on? The way they did with the Furs?"

"To maybe save his life. I don't have time for any dramatics from you. If it hadn't been for you, he wouldn't be in this state in the first place."

Nan flushed. Gail said, "Ingrid, get Karim in here. Franz, can you and George and Karim together—"

"Not necessary," Mueller said. He bent over Shipley and lifted him. He then carried him—not even slung over his shoulder, *in his arms*—outside.

Gail said to Jake, "Did you know he could do that?"

George said, "Short-term muscle augments. It gives a burst of strength. My God, what else can he do?"

Jake didn't know. But this wasn't the time to ask. "George, you and Nan come outside. The rest stay in here, and I'm going to send in Karim. We're still trying not to confuse or frighten the Vine with too many humans." He'd rather have Karim than Nan, but he knew it was pointless to forbid her. Her devotion to Shipley was now as exaggerated as her neglect of him had been before. The girl had no moderation.

Mueller had laid Shipley on the ground directly beside the Vine. Jake was irrationally glad to see that Mueller was at least puffing. Shipley had to weigh at least 225 pounds, and the gravity here was maybe a third more than Terra.

The Vine said nothing, but the slot in its cart opened and the bioarm snaked out and toward Shipley. Nan took a step forward. Jake put a warning hand on her arm, and she halted, scowling.

Slowly the bioarm reached Shipley. It engulfed his hand. Jake watched, repelled and fascinated. What could the thing tell from just the hand? Was it taking skin samples? Going underneath the skin, through pores or something? Inserting some sort of microscopic needle? George was practically salivating in his hunger to study this.

As much as fifteen minutes passed. Jake was getting chilled. Nan said abruptly, "You're letting him get too cold!"

"Yes," the Vine said in its toneless voice. "This human must become more warmer. This human must become fix. This human must go in our shuttle to our ship."

Jake said quickly, "I must go, too. I am the leader." Surely they would have that word from Furs.

"Yes," the Vine said. And then, "All humans must go. All humans cannot stay on this planet. You are not made to stay on this planet. You will die. All humans must go with us."

That easy. Candy from a baby. Jake said, "Go where?"

"We can bring you to your other planet. We can bring you to different place on your other planet. Where other humans will not kill you."

"They'd find us," Jake said. "They have very strong tools. Technology. We will die there. We will die here. We want to live. Can we go to your planet?"

Long silence. The bioarm continued to engulf Shipley's hand. Finally the Vine said, "You will need different air. You will need different food. We can make for you different air. We can make for you different food. It will become very strange for you."

"I know," Jake said. "But we'll go anyway. Thank you. At least we'll be alive."

Until, and if, they could destroy the Vine shield.

They took Shipley up first, along with Nan, who would not leave him. Loading the physician into the shuttle, Jake thought that Nan was the only one of them who could enter it without gagging. The entire inside was coated with slime similar to the bioarm. In the enclosed space, the smell was fetid. If this stuff manufactured Vine atmosphere, how would humans breathe it? Presumably the Vines had that covered. More immediately, how would the rest of them force themselves into what seemed like the inside of someone's gut?

"We have a problem," Gail said to Jake. "If we were just dumped here by our own species and we're innocent of Furs, Vines, and space wars, how are we supposed to explain that we have a quee?"

The quee. Jake had forgotten about it. They were supposed to use it to keep in touch with their Fur masters . . . his mind recoiled from the word, but it was true. They were puppets of the Fur masters.

Jake took the quee from her hand and examined it. It seemed to consist of only the screen from all the ponderous equipment that had existed originally on the *Ariel*, later loaded onto the skimmer. The screen was surprisingly light, no more than three or four pounds. Could the Furs really have put sufficient power in it to contact them several times from light-years away?

He dropped his voice to a whisper. "It's not Fur design, whatever that might look like. It's a human artifact. If the Vines ask about it, I'll tell them that the humans who marooned us here left us this one contact with them so we wouldn't be cut off entirely."

"Do you think they'll believe that?" Gail said skeptically.

"How the hell should I know? But if they really are as interconnected as George says, then maybe the idea of total isolation is so horrific to them that they'll accept that we were given a lifeline." He handed the quee back to Gail, who knew better than to say any more.

When the shuttle returned, after a few hours, the inside had been cleaned out. Only one Vine rode back downstairs. It may or may not have been the one Jake had already talked to; they all looked alike. This alien sat under a dome, although not in a cart. There was no translator visible, and the Vine said absolutely nothing on the ride upstairs. Nor did it appear to pilot in any way. Karim looked hard at the unused controls, studying.

All seven of them could fit, although it was a tight squeeze. Gail carried the quee. Unlike the Fur shuttle, this one was heated. There was the same jolt and increased gees on acceleration, however. How had Dr. Shipley taken that? Without the translator, there was no way to ask.

A quick ride, the slight bump of docking, and they were there.

They exited the shuttle into what had to be an airlock. Small and bare, it nonetheless had seven items resting on the floor. Clear bowls with thick neck rings: *helmets.* "Put these on your heads," the airlock said, the mechanical voice coming from everywhere.

"My God!" George said. "I don't believe it!" He held the helmet close to his face and stared at it, smelled it, listened to it, fingered it, and, yes, tasted it. "I think the neck ring is filled with a life form of some type. It will presumably recycle or replace our air without the need to carry tanks or pumps. And the bowl—"

"I'm not putting that thing on," Gail said flatly.

Ingrid said. "You'd rather breathe methane or whatever it is they have on board?"

"Wouldn't be methane," George said. "I think the bowls are made of some sort of secreted substance, like an oyster secretes nacre to form a pearl. The entire thing must be biomanufactured out of living bodies that—"

"Shut up, George," Jake said. "This is not the time. Suit up, everybody."

He led the way, suppressing his shudder as he lowered the helmet over his head. He almost tore it off a moment later when he felt something warm and slightly moist touch his neck. He made himself endure the forming seal. The air he was breathing was fresh and sweet.

"George, you're next." By rolling his eyeballs downward he could just see the thin membrane in front of his mouth vibrate with his words. "Can you hear me?"

"Clear as middle C," George said happily. He put on his helmet. Life, Jake thought, would be much easier if everyone on this team were an exuberant biologist. Or maybe not.

Ingrid, Karim, and Lucy were next, all three scientists, each flinching only slightly when the neck ring sealed. Franz Mueller watched closely. He lowered his helmet warily, but once it was on, he nodded.

"All right, Gail. Now you."

"No," Gail said.

Jake saw that she was genuinely terrified. She'd never liked the idea of aliens, not from the very first. She had not gone to Greentrees expecting aliens. How was she going to live the rest of her life with them, on Vine?

Ingrid said, "Gail—"

"Shut up," Gail snapped. She picked up the helmet, closed her eyes, and lowered it over her head. Jake put a firm hand on top. Sure enough, when the neck ring sealed, Gail tried to tear off the helmet. Jake's hand prevented her. Through the clear bowl he saw her turn ashen, then faintly green.

"George—what if she vomits in there?"

"The bioforms will probably clean it up," George said uncertainly. Gail didn't vomit. Jake saw her calm herself, although her color remained doubtful.

"You're a trouper," he said to her softly. She glared at him.

The airlock door slid open. Jake led the way into the Vine ship. He stopped, too dazed to go forward.

George peered eagerly over his shoulder "Oh, my God!" he shouted. Jake stepped to the side, partly to let the others through and partly to catch Gail if, when she saw the ship, she either fainted or fled.

# 26

Gail faltered on the threshold, then made herself take a deep breath before she remembered that the breath was coming from slimy microbes in her neck ring. That almost made her gag again, but Gail forced herself to rally. She was going to be here awhile. It was only practical to get used to her surroundings. Jake stood hovering, looking ready to catch her if she did something stupid like fainting, which he ought to have had the sense to know she wouldn't do. Gail swept past him into the ship.

It was one large circular room perhaps a hundred yards across. All of it—*every inch*—was a zoo. No, a garden: much better to think of it as a garden. Seething slime, looking at least two inches thick, covered the entire floor and crept up the walls and onto the ceiling. Vines sat tumbled together in clumps, their branches or arms or whatever they were intertwined. You couldn't tell where one creature stopped and the next began. Runners ran across the slime to connect the various groups of Vines. The light was very bright, the room stiflingly hot and humid. Instantly Gail began to sweat under her blanket-tunic.

Not a garden. A hothouse out of some feverish nightmare.

"Gail?" Jake said. "You all right?"

She ignored him. Where the humans stood, the slime had drawn back, probably to keep from getting stepped on. The floor underneath seemed to be metal, but a metal pitted and corroded and irregular, maybe to give the slime purchase.

"Where are Nan and Dr. Shipley?"

"I don't know. I just got here myself," Jake said.

Someone said, "We can show you," in a flat mechanical voice. Gail looked down. A translator lay at the base of one of the Vines.

"Please show me," she said with as much firmness as she could muster.

Slowly some of the slime began to crawl to either side of a narrow strip. It took fully five minutes, but a path opened to the opposite side of the room. By the time it was completed, Gail had taken off her tunic. She couldn't help it; it was either undress or pass out from the heat. Underneath she wore a strip of blanket tied around her hips; Jake had made them leave behind the strips of cloth taken from the other shuttle in case the Vines identified the cloth as Fur.

Carrying her blanket and the quee, Gail walked through the parted slime (wasn't there an old legend about a sea parting for someone?). The path wound between clumps of Vines huddled silently, motionlessly together. George said they communicated by exchanging information-laden molecules. What were they saying now?

She tried not to tremble. Even the cold, bone-crushing Fur shuttle had been better than this.

At the far end of the room, beside the slimy wall, Dr. Shipley lay on the floor, naked except for the strip of cloth around his vast hips. Nan, who had dispensed with the cloth, hovered over him. She had laid their two blankets side by side to form an island in the slime, and Gail stepped onto it gratefully. "Nan? How is he?"

"I don't know. He sleeps more, but it's better sleep, I think. Or maybe just unconsciousness. I don't know what these plants are doing to him! They keep sending bioarms onto his body, and one long, thin one even down into his nose."

Gail shuddered. "They probably have to figure out his biochemistry before they can come up with any drugs. Remember, they've never seen humans before."

"You're talking shit," Nan said accurately. "You don't know what they're doing any more than I do."

True enough. Gail sat down beside Nan and began tearing a strip of cloth off her blanket. Nan might go nearly naked, but Gail was full-breasted and middle-aged, she bounced and sagged uncomfortably, and she wanted some sort of bra, even if it would be hot.

All at once, the floor under Gail began to curve.

She stifled a shriek and threw herself flat on the blanket, but of course it wasn't an earthquake. Nothing so explicable. The floor continued to bow, but . . . but . . .

It was a moment before she could identify what felt so weird. Nothing, including herself, was rolling downhill, even though her line of sight told her that the center of the circular room was rising. Or the edges were falling. Or something.

Slowly she stood. *Perfectly steady,* said her feet. *Perfectly flat floor.* But her eyes said, *This room is now convex.*

Karim came down the path, looking delighted. "Just as predicted! Wonderful!"

"What's wonderful?" Gail said tartly.

"The life capsule is adjusting its shape as it moves down the shaft toward the massplate. It *must,* in order to keep gravitational force equal everywhere in the living area to what it is over the gravitational center of the massplate. You see, as we accelerate—"

"Never mind," Gail said.

"Oh, but it's fascinating! Posit a living-area radius one-tenth the radius of the massplate. Then, at maximum acceleration, when the moving living area is closest to the massplate, you'd expect twenty percent bowing because—"

Gail turned her back on him. To Nan she said, "Food? Water?"

"There's water being made there." Nan pointed to what looked like a hard, clear cup nestled in the slime at a base of a huge Vine. "The water just *appears.* What do you suppose it's made of?"

"$H_2O$."

"Ha ha," Nan said sourly, but she looked slightly reassured, which made one of them.

"How are we supposed to drink it through these helmets?"

"I don't know," Nan said, but of course if there was a risk to be taken, Nan must take it. She picked up the cup and brought it up to her lips. As helmet and cup touched, the helmet bowed inward and fused to the cup. In a moment they were one, and the water—or whatever it was—poured into Nan's mouth. When she pulled the cup away, it separated from her helmet, which returned to its original rounded shape.

"They think of everything," Nan said, and her tone was not admiring at all.

A routine developed, bizarre though the idea seemed to Gail. Three blanket islands were created amid the constantly foaming slime. The largest was near the single Vine that possessed a translator, beside the airlock door. The second was about twenty yards away, for people who wished to sleep without talk. Sleeping in the helmets took some getting used to, but they managed it. The third island, dubbed "the infirmary," was on the far side of the room where Dr. Shipley lay unconscious. This site had been chosen by the Vines when Nan and Shipley first came aboard. No one knew the significance of its location, if there was one.

Permanent paths, narrow enough to walk single file, connected the three blanket islands. The paths led "uphill" as registered by line of sight, although there was never any muscular sensation of walking "up" or "down." Karim said, "That's because wherever you step, the force is perpendicular to the floor." He spent hours working out the calculations.

A separate path led to an unblanketed spot that the humans used as a latrine. This was shielded from view from the islands by a towering clump of Vines. Gail hated using it. She hated even more the fact that every time she returned, the spot was bare of waste. What did the slime do . . . eat it? She tried not to picture this.

Beside each path, several of the hard clear cups had appeared, with indentations for each in the slime. When a cup was put down, water slowly began to seep into the cup.

George was fascinated. "The cups are made of the same material as our helmets, some nonliving compound. Well, that's not so surprising. The Terran marine sponge *Rosella racovitzae* constructs glass fibers for skeletal support from the silica dioxide in seawater. Oysters make pearls, insects make chitin. Naturally, the Vines have conscious control over this process."

"Naturally," Gail said, but the sarcasm was swamped in George's enthusiasm. Gail sat with all the others except Lucy on the large blanket. Lucy slept on the other island, her small face pinched and drawn with something more than exhaustion. Nan and Dr. Shipley were likewise asleep, and Gail had gingerly walked the path, hoping desperately it wouldn't close up on her, to the big island, where George was trying to talk to the translator Vine. The process was hobbled by George's wanting to use scientific terms the translator program couldn't yet handle.

He said now, obviously dumbing down, "You make these cups for us."

"Yes," the flat "Vine" voice said.

Karim said shyly, "Do you have a name?"

"You call us 'Vine.' "

"Yes," Jake said, "we do. But do you, yourself, have an individual name? A name for just you?"

"We do not understand," the Vine said.

George said, "I don't think they have individuals. It's a . . . a group whole. Semidifferentiated but not psychologically separate. Like the organs in your body are differentiated but don't have individual consciousness."

Jake looked at him. George added hastily, "Of course, I'm just guessing."

Gail's stomach rumbled. She said, "Vine, can you make . . . humans need food, you know. Or else we die."

Jake looked as if she'd preempted his ritual "negotiating procedures" again. Well, too bad. She was hungry, and all of them, especially Dr. Shipley, were going to have to eat soon.

"Yes," Vine said. "Humans need food. We can make food for humans. We analyze you now. Then we make food for humans."

Analyze her? Now? What were they doing? Nervously Gail scanned her body, but she didn't see any of the slime on herself or edging over the blanket.

George said, "You won't see it, Gail. They can use flakes off our feet on the paths. And anyway, they have Dr. Shipley."

Vine said, "We will make food soon. We analyze now."

Gail's stomach rumbled again.

George said, "Vine, may I touch some of your . . . your slime? The thing covering the ground?"

"The thing covering the ground is us."

"Oh, sorry," George said. Naked except for his blanket loincloth, sitting cross-legged with his small potbelly resting on his thighs, he looked like an embarrassed Buddha.

Vine said, "We give to you slime to analyze." A piece of slime crawled onto the blanket and separated from the rest.

Gail drew back. So, she noticed, did Franz, whose aversion seemed as great as her own. But George put his hand down and the slime slowly inched onto his palm. He raised it to eye level.

"Amazing! Ingrid, look at this! It has pili—multipurpose, I'd guess, movement and chemical detection. But look at the internal structures! It's not really a biofilm, it's more like a . . . a sort of superflexible multicellular."

"It may be co-evolutionary with the Vines," Ingrid said. "Sentient, do you think?"

"If they don't fully differentiate among the plantlike forms, they may not with this, either. It's sentient in that it's a part of them."

"Well, if—" Ingrid began a long technical discussion, and Gail stopped listening.

A little while later, the slime—she couldn't think of it any other way, no matter what George said—began to foam alarmingly. Something was happening. The clear cups filled not with water but with a thick, gray substance.

Vine said, "Here comes food for you."

Gail said, "Absolutely not." The gray goo looked completely disgusting. Her stomach growled.

George said, "Vine, is this food made with the nutrients we need?"

"This food is made with the nutrients you need."

Ingrid said, "It's going to lack fiber. I doubt it will even satisfy hunger," but she picked up her cup.

George seized his and drank it down, his helmet flowing into a cup-accommodating shape. Gail shuddered.

"It's good!" he said. "Tastes like chicken."

"Chicken?" Jake said.

"It's an old joke, Jake. Never mind. It actually tastes sweet and tangy. Like lemonade."

Jake picked up his cup. He had a determined look that Gail recognized: Jake thought he ought to set a good example even though he didn't want to. But he raised the cup and drank it all, looking surprised afterward.

"Not bad, if you don't look at it. It *is* sort of like lemonade."

Ingrid said, "It includes hunger-suppressing hormones, I think. I don't feel hungry anymore."

Karim drank his and nodded approval. Gail could feel her mouth water from hunger. She picked it up, closed her eyes, and took a small sip. Jake was right; if you didn't look at it, it wasn't bad. Eyes closed, she drank the rest.

Jake said, "Franz?"

"*Nein!* Never!"

Gail lowered her cup and studied the soldier. He had paled and his powerful body, on display in the brief sarong, had gone rigid. Franz said, "The aliens manipulate our minds with this. I not drink."

George said gently, "If they wanted to manipulate our minds, Franz, they could do it with airborne molecules. They wouldn't need ingestion."

"I not drink!" He got up and stalked down the path to the infirmary blanket.

Vine said, "We can make for him a different food."

"This food is fine," Jake said. "Please don't be offended. Vine. He's . . . nervous. This place is very strange to us."

"Yes," it said neutrally.

Gail stood. "I'm going to check on Dr. Shipley."

*And on Franz.* A "nervous" rebuilt with possible surfacing paranoia struck her as a very dangerous thing. If Jake weren't so depressed with the necessary lies he was telling—and really, why should a negotiator balk at telling lies? This wasn't a side of Jake she'd seen before, and she didn't like it. If he weren't so preoccupied with that, he himself might have reacted to Franz's outburst. What was Franz doing now?

Nothing. He sat quietly on the infirmary blanket, staring at the wall. Dr. Shipley's eyes were open.

"He's conscious," Nan said. "They . . . delivered something into him. Some drug."

Gail heard the profound revulsion in Nan's voice, mixed with relief over her father. Gail sat down. She was conscious of her seminudity, and of Nan's, only in Shipley's presence. The big man was sweating profusely. "How are you feeling?"

"Better. Better than in a long while, in fact. They're medicating me quite effectively."

Gail smiled. "Well, you can ask Vine what the medication is, if you're willing to fight George for airtime."

Shipley sat up. He smiled at his daughter, then looked away. "Naomi . . . are there any clothes you could put on?"

"He's better," Nan said, with such a complicated mix of emotions that Gail would have laughed if she hadn't known it would enrage Nan. Instead she reached for one of the two full cups beside the blanket.

"Dr. Shipley, you should drink this. It's 'food' the Vines have prepared for us. It doesn't taste too bad, if you don't look at it."

"You drank that?" Nan demanded.

"Reluctantly. But I feel full now, and energized."

"I'd rather starve!" Nan said hotly.

Shipley took the cup from Gail, sniffed it deeply, sipped. "It tastes like lemonade."

"That's the consensus," Gail said.

"Dad, don't drink it!"

Shipley took another sip, then finished his cup. He smiled apologetically at Nan. "We have to eat, dear heart."

"I don't." Nan turned her back on them.

"It could have poison," Franz said.

"Franz," Dr. Shipley said, "we may be here a long while. You must eat sometime, and this is what there is."

The soldier only stared at him impassively. Gail started to say, "If we—" when Nan interrupted her.

"Gail! The quee's on!"

The quee had been left at the edge of the infirmary, as far as possible from Vine's translator. Although, of course, the other, closer Vines may have been able to hear anyway, or do whatever they did and transmit the news throughout the entire hothouse. Gail shot a warning glance at Shipley, Nan, and Franz: say nothing revealing. When she saw from their faces that they understood, she took the quee tablet from Nan.

It felt strange to be holding the tablet that, aboard ship and skimmer, had been fixed to its finite power source. But otherwise the quee's tech seemed the same. It buzzed softly to announce a message, its light glowing red. She slid back the tablet cover, holding the screen at any angle close against her body in an attempt, possibly futile, to keep any Vines from seeing the message. What would they "see" it with? With something, presumably, since they "saw" humans. Thermal signatures, maybe.

Quee messages themselves didn't emit thermal signatures, although the equipment did. The messages were fleeting fluctuations of quantum-entangled particles. The information was captured and stored for a long time, at least in the incredibly brief temporal measures of the quantum world, before anything appeared on screen. The Furs had entangled this one with a quee of their own, and apparently they had solved any translation problems. English letters appeared in glowing green.

*Are you aboard enemy ship?*

Gail opened the reply button. Transmission was by an alphabetic code. She tapped. *Yes.*

The screen blanked.

Aloud Gail said, as steadily as she could, "Our families back home send their hellos."

Somewhere in the tangle of alien foliage, Lucy screamed.

The infirmary was at the opposite end of the circuitous path from the sleeping blanket-island. By the time Gail reached it, behind Franz and Nan, everyone else was already there, crowding onto the three-blanket space amid the slime. No one looked frightened, and Lucy had stopped screaming.

"It climbed on me," she said, eyes wide.

Then Gail saw it. A thumb-high *human* clambering around everyone's feet. No, not human, but . . . but what? Gail stayed on the path, unwilling to get any closer. The tiny thing started to climb George's leg, pulling itself up by his plentiful hair. It had at least chosen the right person; George cupped his palm under the creature and gently picked it up.

For the first time ever, Gail saw the biologist speechless.

The two-inch-high creature *did* look human, or at least more human than anything Gail had seen in aliens. It was symmetrical, bipedal, with a recognizable head. The head had eyes and a hole that might have been a mouth. True, instead of arms there was a single long, flexible, sticky-looking tentacle coming out of its chest, and it had no genitals. But the proportions were the same as a human's, the skin looked soft and light brown, and all Gail could think of were the childhood stories her nurse had read her about fairies and elves.

The tiny thing chittered at George. "Hello," George said experimentally, but he got no answer.

"Look!" Ingrid said. More of the creatures were emerging from the foliage. Gail saw a broad, fleshy "leaf"—or hand or whatever it was—open at the base of a Vine. A chitterer ran out. The things swarmed near the humans.

Franz, his face set, pulled back his leg to kick one away from him. Jake said sharply, "Franz!" and the soldier settled for a firm push.

"Gail, let me by," George said. "I need to ask Vine about these!" The creature in his palm still chittered at him, looking completely unafraid.

Everyone trailed George to the main island, where he demanded, "Vine! What is this?"

Vine said, "Those are our mobiles."

An echo sounded in Gail's mind, something Nan had told her that Beta had said: *"You are all mobiles, are you all mobiles? We think yes. Mobiles must run and walk and go. On our world our mobiles do not talk. They do not sit together with us. We love them as mobiles."*

"Mobiles," George said. "Are they . . . can they think? Analyze?"

"They do not need to analyze," Vine said.

"Oh." Even George seemed at a loss. Finally he said, "Are they a part of your life cycle? Will this mobile become a Vine?"

"No."

"Was it once slime?"

"We were all once slime," Vine said, and Gail saw from George's face that this cleared up nothing. A dozen of the creatures had run onto the blanket and were trying to climb the humans. Franz pushed his away, stood, and stalked back to the infirmary.

Vine said, "They are curious. They will taste you. Then they will return to their work."

George clearly saw this as an opening. "What is their work?"
Vine said expressionlessly, "It is time for us to make love."

Gail stood and edged her way through the sitting crowd to the path. Vine and George were obviously settling in for another long conversation, and everyone except Gail looked fascinated. Even Nan sat with a chittering mobile on her palm. Whatever her revulsion for Vines and slime, this third being had evidently engaged her interest. Almost Gail could understand; the thing looked even closer to humans than Furs did, and unlike Furs, they responded rapturously to being stroked.

Dr. Shipley sat up in the infirmary. Franz sat at the opposite edge of the blanket, staring at nothing.

"Doctor? How are you feeling?"

"Abnormally well, thank you. What is happening over there?"

"Some tiny creatures have appeared that Vine calls 'mobiles.' It says they're part of their mating process."

"Really!" Shipley looked as interested as Nan. Gail sighed. Was she the only one who didn't care how, when, or if the Vines fucked themselves? Which was apparently what they were preparing to do.

"I think I can stand," Shipley said, and tried. He crashed back onto the blanket.

"Stay quiet. You're not well yet," Gail said crossly, before she remembered that she was talking to a doctor. Shipley smiled painfully.

"Yes, my dear. You're right. It's just that I feel so extraordinarily well after the Vines' ministrations. I want to ask how . . . but I can do that later, and hear about the mobiles later, too."

Franz said violently, "Tell the plants to keep those things off me, or I crush it. Tell them."

Gail stared. Franz did not apologize. Instead he said, "Nobody here remembers Mira City."

"I do," Gail said softly, and felt a sudden bond with the furious soldier. Everyone else *was* caught up in the mysteries of alien biology. Gail didn't understand. Mira City was never out of her thoughts, not for one minute. If Jake and Karim and George couldn't succeed in destroying the Vine shield after they landed on

Vine, it would be Mira City that would be destroyed. Five thousand human lives, including Gail's family. Plus everything she had worked for, believed in, staked her life on for fifteen years.

"*I* think about Mira City," she said, knowing she couldn't say more without compromising Jake's plan. But it was enough. Franz looked at her and nodded, mollified.

Shipley, however, was studying them both, all the acuity and perception restored to his keen old eyes.

# 27

Shipley came late to the discussion of mobiles, and had to piece together knowledge from what the others said, and from what he could observe. He told himself that he was medically interested, knowing that he was only distracting himself as long as he could.

No one willingly faces pain and betrayal.

So he studied the mobile that sat happily on his massive leg and marveled at the infinite variety of the universe.

The mobiles were pollinators, or something analogous to pollinators. They ran around from Vine to Vine transferring "pollen" on their sticky tentacles. The Vines produced some molecule that gratified some desire in the mobiles, although not food. George said, "Terran plants do the same thing, you know. Domesticated species, anyway. They've taught us to grow them, protect them, even engineer and hand-graft them, by gratifying our desire for the beauty and scent of flowers. We're just bigger, smarter bees." He paused. "Or bigger, smarter mobiles."

Naomi said, "Why don't they just drop pollen on themselves?"

"Self-pollination wouldn't mix the genes enough. Lots of Terran species have evolved ways to avoid self-pollination. Some make their ovule and pollen grains chemically incompatible. Others stagger the times when their stamens produce pollen and their pistils are receptive. Sex has great evolutionary advantages."

"Sex?" Naomi said, looking around for Gail, who wasn't there. "Vines are male and female?"

"Not necessarily," George said. The mobile on his palm tried to jump off, and he lowered it gently to the blanket. It ran off into the foliage. "You can have sex without different genders."

"I know," Naomi said, and Shipley kept his face still. She wasn't beyond wanting to disturb him.

"We call those gametes 'female' that retain other DNA-bearing organelles like mitochondria," George said, warming up, "and those gametes 'male' that don't. But maybe Vine gametes don't contain such organelles. They don't even use DNA."

Vine said, "I don't understand those words."

Before George could explain, Shipley said quietly, "I have another thought. If Vines mate by pollination, then any organism can be the carrier of any other organism's genes. Maybe that's why they never evolved to kill. It would be like killing your own offspring."

Naomi looked suddenly angry. Jake stared hard at Shipley, evidently thinking that he should not have mentioned any prior knowledge of Vines' pacifism, or anything else about them. George looked impatient, as if Shipley had carried the discussion offtrack.

But the Vine said, "Yes. Of course. We die, but we do not understand killing. Our enemy kills."

Jake said, still glaring at Shipley, "What enemy? What are you talking about?"

Shipley lumbered to his feet. He was not wanted here. And he could no longer distract himself from the decision he would have to make soon.

He walked gingerly along the path to the infirmary. It was empty except for Franz. Gail had gone to the sleeping island, finally exhausted enough to sleep. Franz had discovered that the mobiles would not come onto the infirmary island (had they been "told" not to by the Vines?) and now spent all his time here. He still refused to eat, as did Naomi. At the moment the soldier lay on the infirmary deeply asleep, his magnificent body finally as relaxed as a child's.

Shipley sat down, bent his head, and closed his eyes. He tried to clear his mind, but the image of Beta would not leave.

*"This is our death flower, William Shipley. Will you give it to other Vines so that Beta will grow again?"*

*"Grow again. Beta?"*

*"Yes." Beta said. "The death flowers of all Vines are safe on the secret planet. The death flowers will grow. They have grown two times. They can grow three times."*

*Jake said incredulously. "You swore a deathbed oath to an alien?"*

*"New Quakers don't swear oaths," Shipley said. "Our word should always be good."*

And Shipley's word had not been. The Furs had destroyed Beta's death flower, vaporized it as thoroughly as they had vaporized the gentle Vine itself. And now Shipley was compounding the lie by not telling these shipboard Vines, who had rescued and trusted humans, the truth that might save their planet.

Shipley, under Jake's direction, had become one of the people inside a Trojan horse. Deceive the enemy by pretending to be something other than what you were. Slip in behind his defenses. Destroy from within the walls.

Except that the Vines were not the enemy. By his silence, Shipley was helping to destroy friends. But if he was not silent, the Furs would destroy Mira City.

*"The truth is the way, and the way is the truth,"* early Quakers had said, and not only Quakers. How did that quote from Plato go? *"Truth is the beginning of every good thing."* No good things could result for the Vines if Shipley did not tell them the truth.

If he did tell them the truth, at least five thousand humans would perish.

If he didn't tell them the truth, there would be no chance of finding a better solution, one that might save everyone. And in addition, Shipley's own life and his faith would be a sham. "Let your life speak," he had smugly told Lucy, so long ago on the *Ariel.* A life must speak truth.

He could not speak the truth. Around and around it went, until Shipley's head ached and his eyes burned. He reached for his cup and drank the nourishing food provided by the Vines. He lay down in the rescue ship provided by the Vines, breathing the sweet helmeted air created for humans by the Vines, and tried to sleep. But still the question wrapped around his tired mind, strangling it, and no answer came.

---

"They're slavers," Naomi said angrily. "How can you doubt that?"

"I think there's more than one way to look at it," Gail said neutrally.

Shipley lay still. He had the sense that he had been asleep a very long time. Something in the food, or just the exhaustion of an old body recovering from injuries? Gail and Nan sat at the edge of the infirmary blanket, talking in low voices. Franz Mueller had gone; Shipley was alone with the two women. Naomi looked terrible: gaunt, with deep hollows in her cheeks. She had eaten nothing for . . . how many days had they been aboard this ship? Shipley didn't know. Behind Naomi loomed two large motionless Vines, unhearing. Perhaps unhearing.

Naomi said, "There's no other way to look at it! These fucking plants have enslaved these little mobiles, keeping them imprisoned in leaves until the Vines need their services as walking pricks! What else would you call that but slavery?"

Shipley heard Gail's effort to keep her voice neutral. "The mobiles don't seem unhappy."

"Oh, fuck, Gail, since the beginning of time there have been 'happy' slaves who didn't know better, in every culture that ever practiced slavery. You know that. It still isn't right."

"They're not human. You can't apply human judgments to alien biology."

"You know," Naomi said slowly, "it wasn't until just this moment that I realized you're a bigot."

Then Gail did lose her temper. "The hell I am! I'm just being reasonable. The mobiles are not just tiny human beings, no matter what they look like. They may not even be sentient. Nobody else is indulging in this brand of self-serving anthropomorphism!"

"Franz agrees with me."

"Oh, marvelous. A rebuilt who's getting more xenophobic every hour. Did you see him slash at that Vine when a frond accidentally brushed his leg?"

Naomi was silent. Shipley thought, *Slash?* With what? If Franz Mueller was showing signs of the same paranoia that had unbalanced Rudy Scherer and Erik Halberg, then Shipley needed to know about it. He tried to get up but a great lethargy seemed to press on his body.

Gail said, "Nan?"

"I don't want to talk about it." Naomi got up and stalked off.

"Well, I do!" Gail said. "I'm sick of your melodramatic exits on the supposed moral high ground!" She leaped to her feet and followed Naomi down the path.

Still Shipley couldn't seem to move. The vast room was quiet now. The dense biomass, or something else, deadened sound; voices from the other two islands didn't reach the infirmary. Nor did the Vines make any noise. And Shipley heard no chittering from the mobiles—did that mean that had all gone back inside what Naomi called their "plant prisons"?

Then Shipley did hear something.

The sound came just as the grogginess at last left his limbs and he could move again. A faint sound, thin but clear; perhaps it carried only because it was pitched so much higher than human speaking voices. A sweet sound, sharply evocative of another place, another time, another vastly different circumstance.

Karim Mahjoub was whistling the rondo from Beethoven's violin concerto.

*Beta, listening to Karim whistle Strauss and then Mozart. "It brings light to my soul."*

Light.

Shipley sat up on the coarse blanket. He had made his decision.

It was not an easy decision to carry out. He needed to be alone with Vine, the alien with the translator. No one knew whether the other Vines could hear, or understand, anything of human-Vine interaction. Perhaps they all, as one entity, shared everything. Perhaps not.

From three to eight humans usually occupied the main blanket-island, beside the airlock. Franz never went there, but George never left. The biologist even slept beside the translator, not on the sleeping island. "I don't mind the rest of you talking, I can sleep through anything," George said. What he meant was that he didn't want to miss anything.

Shipley joined the fluctuating group beside the translator. He needed to observe Franz, but the rebuilt would have to wait. This was more important.

"You're awake," Lucy said kindly. "Welcome back, Doctor. How do you feel?"

"Fine," Shipley said. "How long was I asleep?"

"Two days. Vine said you needed to heal."

Two days! No wonder Naomi looked so starved. Jake, too, had lost weight and looked hollow-eyed, although Shipley knew he was eating. Jake looked haunted by something unconnected with food.

That, too, would have to await more observation. For now Shipley needed to get Vine alone. But Vine never was.

George and Vine talked about molecule formation.

Ingrid, Vine, and George talked about genetic heredity.

Jake and Lucy pointedly did not talk to each other, a silence as loud to Shipley as accusations.

Karim whistled until his lips ached from puckering.

Naomi appeared seldom, but Gail darted back and forth between the infirmary and the main island. Another quee message, she announced, from "home," and in her voice Shipley heard the anguish that Vine, presumably, could not distinguish or interpret.

George and Vine talked about species evolution.

Jake left, came back, sat quiet as death.

Karim and Vine talked about the physics of the star in Vine's home system.

Finally, Shipley could wait no longer. He had no idea when the ship would reach its destination, or what would await them there. Nor did he know how long the Furs would wait before deciding the humans had reneged on their "bargain." Every minute mattered.

He rose ponderously. Lucy looked up at him. He said, "I think I should check on Franz," and walked off the main island, down the narrow, slime-free path toward the infirmary.

The path wound through clumps of Vines, patches of writhing slime. For perhaps a third of its length, the path was out of sight of both the main island and the infirmary. Shipley stopped at a secluded spot, beside a group of four Vines growing close together. He put his hand on the trunk of the closest one, not knowing if this was necessary to get its attention. Not knowing anything.

"Vine," he said softly, "this is William Shipley. I don't know if you can hear me, or detect me in some other way. I must talk to the Vine with the enemy translator. I must talk alone, without my fellow humans. It is very important. Please."

Shipley waited. Nothing. The being under his hand felt slick, coated with some version of the biofilm on floor and walls. A flashy "leaf" touched his wrist, perhaps merely blown by the slight breeze that was a constant in this strange place. Maybe even if the creature couldn't understand Shipley's words, it could pick up a sense of urgency from the chemicals in his palm.

"Please," he whispered again.

Nothing.

But when he went back to the main island, uncertain what else to do, everyone present had stood up in excitement. George, Ingrid, Jake, Lucy, Karim.

"Look, Doctor!" Ingrid said. "A new path!"

The slime was parting in a different direction. It moved slowly, half a slither and half a creep, creating another foot-wide ribbon bare to the floor. The new path disappeared into a grove of exceptionally thick, tall Vines. For a moment Shipley was afraid. What had he done? Images of the carnivorous plants of Earth, of red creeper on Greentrees, crawled through his mind.

George said with elation, "Vine says it has something completely new to show us about its culture!"

"Go now," Vine said in its flat, expressionless voice, and George didn't wait to be told twice. He charged down the new path, followed closely by Ingrid and Karim. Jake went more slowly, and when he did, Lucy started down the older path to the sleeping island.

"I'll see it later," she told Shipley in a constrained, unconvincing voice. "Too crowded." She tried a smile, failed, and set off toward the sleeping blanket.

Shipley was alone with Vine.

He sat down and began, hands locked together in front of him, and even though he whispered, his voice sounded loud in his own head.

"Vine, we . . . I must tell you a new thing. New, important information. Very important.

"We have known some of your people before. One gave me his death flower to take to you, so that you could put it in the secret library of genetic samples and it could grow again. But the Furs destroyed the death flower before I could bring it to you, and I am so sorry."

The Vine said nothing. There was no way to judge its reaction. Even so, Shipley felt his voice grow stronger and his heart lighten, lifted by the conviction that this was the right thing to do.

"We humans knew a group of Vines who came to our planet. They came to check on the experimental colonies of your enemy—we call them 'Furs'—that you had left on the planet. Not the planet where you found us, but your other colonies. Furs in a spaceship destroyed those colonies, and the Furs destroyed the Vines who came, and the Furs carried us to the planet where you found us. They told us to do a terrible thing. We are doing that terrible thing. We have not told you about it before. We have lied to you."

Shipley had saved that word for last: "lied." He had no reason to think that the Vines understood it.

"We told you things that are not correct, Vine. We said our fellow humans had made us leave our planet. That is not correct. The Furs brought us away. They put us where your ship would find us. They wanted you to take us to your ship. They wanted you to take us to one of your planets."

Shipley paused. At this point in his story a human, any human, would have said "Why?" Vine said nothing. Looking at its alien shape, at its flesh that was neither flesh nor wood nor chitin, the strange possibly intelligent slime coating it, Shipley was not thrown by its silence. He was saying truth, and from that only good could ultimately flow.

"The Furs wanted us to be on one of your planets. They want us to be under the shield you have created around your planet, the shield that captures their ships before they can attack you. The Furs told us to destroy the shield. If we do not destroy the shield, the Furs will kill all the humans left on our planet. Five thousand humans in one city, another thousand elsewhere. We lied to you to save our humans. We agreed to destroy your shield. But that is not the correct thing to do. The correct thing to do is to tell you the truth, and together we can make a plan to save your people and mine."

Shipley stopped. His heart was beating so fast he thought he might faint. He made himself take deep, calming breaths. Vine said nothing.

Hadn't it understood? Beta had seemed to understand so much! Was this Vine even now destroying Shipley's fellow humans, out of Shipley's sight and hearing, in retribution? Naomi . . . Why didn't the alien speak? Oh, God, had Shipley's vocabulary been too advanced, his sentence structure too complex? What did the thing think it had heard?

"Vine," he said desperately, "do you understand what I've said? Do you?"

The alien said, "What is the new information?"

Shipley gaped at it.

"I do not understand what is the new information, William Shipley. This is not new information. Jake Holman told us all this information before."

"That's right, Doctor," Jake's voice said quietly behind Shipley. "I told them all that information before."

# 28

Ludicrously, irrelevantly, Jake wished he had a vidcam. The look on Shipley's face . . .

The respite was only momentary. Breaking in on Jake's amusement was the anguish again, the anguish he would carry forever. Shipley had told the truth to the Vines, but so had he, Jake. Now Mira City would be murdered. No, not now, but soon, when the Furs finally figured out that the humans were not going to destroy the Vine shield from within because the humans were never going to be "within."

"They're not going to take us to any of their planets, Doctor," Jake said. "They're not fools."

Shipley stared at him, and then at Vine, as if he expected it to speak. It didn't, of course. Vines only spoke when they had something to say. Yet another thing that differentiated them from humans.

Shipley said quietly, "Why did you tell, Jake?"

"Same reason you did. To secure their help with some *über*-plan that will save everything."

"That wasn't my reason," Shipley said.

*Nor mine,* Jake didn't say. He didn't know what his reasons were, anymore. Expediency, hope, truth, cynicism, Lucy . . . It was all mixed up in there somehow. God, he was tired. It had been so long since he slept well.

Shipley said, "But you *did* tell them. You told Vine about the Trojan horse and—"

Jake sensed the attack before he actually felt it. Mueller behind him, standing on the path that led to the infirmary. Jake had half turned when Mueller grabbed him and spun him around the rest of the way.

"You! You tell them! You murder Mira City! *Scheisse!*" Jake felt Mueller's fist slam into his stomach, and then he couldn't breathe, no air was coming into him, only fire, his body was on fire—

Something yanked Mueller off him.

Jake collapsed, gasping, in more agony than he'd thought possible. From the corner of his eye he saw Mueller wrapped around with a . . . a vine. Two vines. Tendrils from Vine, tangling him in strong alien living ropes.

But Mueller, augmented, was stronger. With a roar he broke free of Vine and stomped on the broken tendrils. It was the stomping that saved Jake's life. In the long moment it took before Mueller again launched himself at Jake, something happened. Jake still couldn't breathe and he sensed himself losing consciousness, but not before he saw Dr. Shipley grab Mueller's left ankle. The rebuilt hadn't expected anything from Shipley; Mueller was off balance. Shipley's desperate tug tripped him. Mueller fell sideways and landed facedown beside the edge of the blanket.

He was only down a few seconds. With terrifying speed he leaped up, but in those few seconds his helmet had dissolved on contact with the ground slime. Mueller's face was smeared with slime. Wildly he tore at his skin, but his face, too, was dissolving. In Jake's pain-filled vision, the flesh, the eyes, the mouth of the rebuilt, were being eaten away . . . everything went black.

When he came to, air again filled his lungs. His torso ached but no longer burned. Gail hung over him, holding a cup. "You're back. Good. Drink this, Jake, I'm tired of dribbling it down your throat. No, don't *move,* damn it, you've got three broken ribs. Just drink."

He did, spilling half of the liquid over his chest. Almost immediately the ache in his body eased. Cautiously he turned his head. He lay on the main island. George sat beside Vine, but no one else was present. Jake could see the raw places on Vine's trunk where the thick tendrils had been ripped off.

"Mueller?"

"Dead," Gail said somberly. "George says it was probably a version of the same compound they used to dissolve their dead fellow back on Greentrees."

Greentrees. Another life.

George said, "Vine made you that painkiller."

"Vine?" The alien had killed Mueller. *We don't kill,* it had once told him.

George misunderstood Jake's question. "Vine will be okay. He can regenerate limbs, you know. It'll just take a while."

"And your ribs will be fine, too," Gail said. "Dr. Shipley bound them, and you're supposed to move as little as possible." She hesitated. "He blames himself, Jake. Apparently he tripped Franz and Franz fell into the . . . he fell. Shipley considers that he killed Franz."

"And so blames himself for saving my life," Jake said bitterly. Shipley's view was irrational. The fall had not killed Mueller; the slime had. "Does Shipley think it would have been better if Mueller killed me?"

"I don't know what he thinks," Gail said. "I never did. But he said that both you and he told Vine about our plan. That isn't true, is it?"

"It's true." She stared at him flatly. "Then I wish Franz had killed you. You've destroyed Mira City."

"Gail," George said softly.

Suddenly she wailed, "Why? Oh, God, Jake—*why?*"

The same question Shipley had asked. Before he could begin to answer, she slapped him across his helmet so hard that his head rolled to one side and pain shot through his ribs. "There!" she screamed. "I attacked Jake, too! So dissolve me, you alien bastard!"

"Gail!" George said. He rushed to grab her. "Don't!"

"I don't care, George! He's murdered them all, everybody in Mira!" She started to sob.

Vine said, "Wait."

Instantly George let go of Gail. "You're talking to us again!"

Jake, ribs still hurting, managed to say, "It hasn't—"

"Not a word," George said. "But he did make you the painkiller so I hoped—"

"George," Vine said, "be quiet, please."

Jake had never heard a Vine give an order. Or even a request, and which was this? In the toneless voice of the translator, it was impossible to tell.

George stood still, expectant. Silent tears rolled down Gail's cheeks. Jake lay on the rough blanket. Everyone waited.

Finally Vine spoke. "We will bring the other humans back now. We will talk to all humans together. We have an idea."

An idea. The alien had an idea. Jake struggled to sit up. Gail didn't help him, or even look at him. Nor did George, whose entire attention was on Vine.

The path to the infirmary was still clear, but the new path, the path to the "new thing" Vine had offered to show everyone, had vanished. When had that happened? As Jake watched, the path slowly reappeared. The slime crawled back from both sides. *The slime.* Jake tried not to recall Mueller's face.

George said to Jake, "The path closed after we got to the new bio event. It was . . . never mind, it doesn't matter. You'd already gone back. I think Vine hadn't counted on that; he wanted to keep us all away as long as Dr. Shipley needed to talk privately to him. But you overheard Shipley, didn't you?"

Jake nodded.

George continued, "After Franz attacked you, Vine brought just me back. Shipley was . . . is . . . well, you'll see. Vine wanted someone to explain to. Then I went to the infirmary and got Gail and Nan."

Jake said, "Where's Nan now?"

"With her father. Vine, do you want Dr. Shipley and Nan here, too?"

"All humans," Vine said.

*All humans left alive, anyway.*

"I'll get them," George said.

As soon as the path was wide enough, Karim and Ingrid and Lucy came thundering down it. Ingrid demanded, "What *happened*? My God, Jake, what did you do to Vine?"

Gail said bitterly, "Gave it a pruning."

"What—"

"Shut up," Gail said. "George will be back in a minute. He'll explain."

"Gail, you're *crying*," Lucy said. Gail turned her back to everyone.

Karim said firmly, "I'll get George." He disappeared at a run.

Jake closed his eyes. He wished he could go to sleep. He wished Franz Mueller had succeeded. Mira City . . .

"We are all here," Vine said. "We will sit in shared silence."

"Not now," Jake heard himself saying loudly. "We're humans. Vine, not . . . we can't wait like you can. Tell us your idea!"

A pause long enough to cause madness. Then Vine said, "Okay."

Jake opened his eyes and found himself looking straight at Shipley. The old man was ashen. He looked somehow collapsed, as if his great bulk had fallen in on itself. God, if this was what faith could do to a man as punishment for saving a life, then Jake was glad to be agnostic.

Nan hovered beside her father, her bones sticking out like chisels under her thin skin. Gail still had her back to everyone. Ingrid, outraged, said, "Will someone please tell us what the hell *happened*?"

In a low voice, George filled in events for her, Karim, and Lucy. Great, Jake thought, now everyone knew everything. Always good to have an informed jury.

Vine said, "We have an idea. This is our idea. We can save Mira City. We can save our planet. We can make no more killing."

"How?" Nan demanded. "How in the fuck can you do all that?"

Vine told them.

"No!" Nan screamed. "You can't!"

Jake said, "I'll volunteer to go first. Vine, get started. Now. Do me first."

He was energized. There was a plan. Or maybe his energy came from the drink Vine had made for him; Jake was beyond caring where the energy came from. For the first time since leaving Greentrees, Jake felt hopeful. So did Karim, George, Ingrid, Lucy, and Gail, although Gail's hope had an edge of hysterical fear that Jake didn't like. She had never trusted any alien, and now the entire plan depended on the most alien of them all.

That left Shipley and Nan. Neither would agree.

Jake had never understood Shipley. The New Quaker was still

torturing himself over Franz Mueller's death, as if it had been Shipley and not Vine who had killed the rebuilt. And now Shipley was tossing around inflammatory words like "genocide."

"We're not going to kill the Furs," Jake explained for the third or fourth time. "We're only going to make them less dangerous."

"Castrate them," Nan said furiously. "That's what it amounts to!"

"No," Jake said. "George, I haven't got time for this. Explain to them."

"I already explained," George said.

"Then do it again!" Jake strode off the main island toward the infirmary, where Gail kept the quee. As he left, he heard George say, "They'll be happier than before, the Vines said so, and isn't happiness the goal of life anyway?"

"No," Shipley said. "It isn't."

Shipley was right, Jake thought, although not in the way he thought. Shipley meant that the goal of life was some sort of spiritual attainment, some inner peace. Jake knew better. The goal of life was survival. Happiness was an incidental side effect. If this plan worked, everyone would survive. Humans, Vines, even Furs.

Unless something went wrong. The best way to guard against that was to plan carefully for all contingencies. And no one was better at planning than Gail.

She already had the quee on her lap, although she hadn't activated it. She was, he guessed, mentally envisioning what she would send, revising and compressing. Ingrid was with her. Jake said, "Where's Lucy?"

Ingrid said, "Vine wanted her somewhere. It opened a special path for her and closed it up afterward." Ingrid's voice held resentment: Why Lucy and not her?

Some things never changed.

Jake said, "How could Vine tell Lucy it wanted her somewhere?" The only translator remained on the main island.

"It opened a path and a tendril wrapped around Lucy's hand and tugged at her," Ingrid said. "Not by force," she added hastily, seeing Jake's face. "Lucy didn't have to go. She chose to go."

Franz Mueller, his eyes and flesh dissolving . . . But Jake couldn't think that way. He had to trust the Vines. There was no other choice. "Did the Vines take Karim, too?"

"Yes, but in a different direction."

To wherever the bridge was, Jake thought. Karim was going to get a crash course in flying a Fur ship. If that was possible. It should be—after all, the Vines flew Fur craft, and they didn't even have *eyes.*

To Gail he said, "I want you to get Shipley and Nan back here in the infirmary so I can talk to Vine alone."

Gail said flatly, "Nan won't go anywhere just because I ask her. She thinks that what we're doing, what Vine is doing, is nothing more than experimenting on advanced species for purposes of genocide. No better than what the Liberation Science Rebels did in Dakar."

Jake said, "Yes. That's why I want to talk to Vine without her."

"Why do you—"

Ingrid interrupted Gail. "Jake, I don't think you have to be beside the translator for Vine to hear you. Dr. Shipley must have asked it to get us all out of the way so he could speak to Vine alone, and he must have done it someplace else than the translator because that's where we all were."

"Yes," said Jake; he'd already figured that out. "I could talk to Vine anywhere. But it can only answer me beside the translator. Gail, if you can't get Nan and Shipley here, who can?"

"No one can budge Nan when she's got her mind made up."

"Then budge Shipley and Nan will follow. Go tell the doctor that Ingrid has collapsed and he should come immediately. Ingrid, collapse."

Ingrid opened her mouth to protest, thought better of it, and lay down on the blanket. Gail set off at a dead run.

When Shipley and Nan appeared, Shipley looked alarmed but also less tortured. It would do him good to have something else to think about beside Franz Mueller. For a short while, anyway. During the clamor around Ingrid, Jake slipped away and ran down the path to the main blanket, where only George remained. Running made his ribs ache even through the painkiller; he slowed down.

"Vine," Jake said rapidly, "Dr. Shipley and Nan will never agree to this plan. They will tell the Furs the truth." Just as Shipley and Jake had told Vine. "I think you should prepare a drug that will make them both completely unconscious but otherwise unharmed, and keep them that way as long as necessary."

George gasped but said nothing. Vine said, "Yes."

The first hurdle jumped. Jake said, "Shipley will drink anything you give him, but Nan won't eat and she barely drinks. How can you deliver the drug?"

"We can make the molecules in a gas. Everyone else must leave the infirmary blanket."

"All right. But a gas won't penetrate their helmets."

"This gas will penetrate their helmets."

That was a sobering thought. But Jake merely said, "Can you make the gas soon?"

"We already have those molecules."

*Prepared and ready to knock out the whole lot of us if we had run amok. Not a thing to mention.* Instead Jake said, "What are you doing to Lucy?"

"Experimenting on her," Vine said, and Jake's blood stopped in his arteries.

George said, "What experiment? Is she all right?"

"We do not know if any human will be all right with this plan. You know that. We create tests with Lucy."

Jake forced himself to say, "She's . . . she's nervous."

"That is why we create tests with her."

George said unconvincingly, "I'd rather you used me."

"Your nervous system is not as responsive."

Jake said, "How long until you begin with the rest of us?"

"We don't know. These are not simple molecules we must create. They must affect two different species in two different ways."

"Right," Jake said, and felt helpless again. He pushed the feeling away. He couldn't afford it just now.

He walked back to the infirmary. Ingrid sat up, trying to look like someone who had just come out of a faint. She wasn't a particularly good actor.

"Just stress, I think," Dr. Shipley said. "Although she shows no other symptoms of acute distress." He looked suspiciously at Jake.

Jake said, "Then if you're all right, Ingrid, you better come with me. Vine is ready to start infecting us. The—"

"Already?" Shipley said. "How could it create serum that fast? The molecules would be so complex that—"

Jake cut him off. "How should I know how Vine did it? He did. You had better make a choice, Doctor. You, too, Nan. Either come with us and get infected or stay here."

"What you're doing is *wrong,*" Nan said passionately, misguided idealist till the end.

"Ingrid?"

"I'm coming," she said, and left with Jake. When they reached the main island she said, "I'm ready."

"The infecting agent isn't," George said. "Not yet."

Ingrid turned accusingly to Jake. "You said—"

"I needed you out of there. Vine is knocking out Shipley and Nan for the duration. We can't afford their noncooperation."

Ingrid's mouth made a small round O.

Gail, holding the quee, looked uncertainly at the path to the infirmary. "They'll . . . be all right? Not harmed permanently?"

"Of course not," Jake said. "We're the ones running that risk."

George said, "What do we do now?"

"We wait," Jake said. "For the Vines to do their biochemical magic."

Lucy came back hours later. The time had scraped slowly by, largely in silence. Gail had gone to check on Shipley and Nan and found them both deeply asleep. It had taken all five of them, Jake and George and Karim and Ingrid and Gail, to carry Shipley along the path to the main island. Jake wanted the eight humans together at all times. He had carried Nan himself, her skinny starved body as light in his arms as a child. Carefully he laid her beside her father.

Ingrid said acidly, "Probably the first time in two decades that those two have been peaceful together for longer than an hour . . . look! There's Lucy!"

She came walking toward them over the slime, not on a path. Jake realized that none of them had ever done that. Her small bare feet sank two inches into the biofilm, but she didn't even look down. This was such abnormal behavior that Jake immediately feared the worst. But when Lucy sat down with them on the blanket, she looked and sounded normal.

"I'm done," she said. "I'm infected."

Jake said angrily, "Vine, I told you I wanted to be first!"

"No," said the expressionless translator. "You must make decisions. You must not get sick."

"He's right," George said before Jake could answer. "Someone has to stay uninfected in case we get . . ." He didn't finish.

Jake said, "I know that. Vine, I want to be infected. Gail will stay uninfected to make decisions as necessary."

Gail looked startled, then ashamed. But she didn't protest. Her xenophobia, Jake knew, was not ideological, like Nan's. It was biological. She would be of more use uninfected, and on the quee.

*Infected.* He looked at Lucy. She sat with her legs childishly extended in front of her, her torso covered with the improvised gray sarong. Her face was calm. Tranquilizers?

"Vine, tell us what to expect. For us and for the Furs. Tell us everything."

Vine said, "Lucy has drunk the best molecules we can make in this short time. We cannot dream in the sun about this, in the correct way. Soon we will have enough drink for Jake, George, and Ingrid. The molecules will infect everyone. The infection will be breathed out on the air. Our enemy breathes the same atmosphere as you do. When our enemy takes you on their ship, you will infect them. They will take the infection to their planet. The infection spreads very quickly."

"But what does it do?" Ingrid said. She stared at Lucy.

Vine said, "We created this molecule for our enemy. We tested it for two hundred years on our experimental enemy on the planet where we found you. You did not see that experimental colony. It was our best experiment. The enemy was happy. They sat dreaming in the sun. They made many offspring and cared for them. The offspring sat dreaming in the sun. But they did not starve. Everybody grew enough food and made enough shelters. But they did not make machines or ships. They did not like to move more than necessary. They were happy dreaming in the sun, in shared silence."

*My God,* Jake thought, *the Vines are going to turn the Furs into the closest thing possible to plants.*

Vine added, "Infected enemies will make many more offspring

than others. Infected offspring are sexually desirable to their own kind."

After a stunned silence George said, "Like . . . like flowers. Pheromones attract bees and even attract us, all for the purpose of increasing their reproductive advantage."

"Yes," Vine said. "Like flowers."

Ingrid said unsteadily, "That's what the molecules will do to the Furs. What will they do to us?"

"We do not know," Vine said. "You are carriers. We re-created the molecule to live in your body and be spread by you. That was difficult. We do not have the correct time to do more."

Jake said, "But if Lucy . . . what if this 'molecule' kills us?"

"We don't know," Vine said. "Lucy is still alive. But you must drink the infector right before you board the enemy ship. You will live long enough to infect them."

Vine wasn't cold-blooded, Jake reminded himself. It only sounded that way from a combination of translator expressionlessness and alien calm. Still, he didn't stop himself from saying sarcastically, "Well, your part's done. Shouldn't you Vines be getting into your escape ship soon, before we quee the Furs?"

Vine didn't answer. All right—let the plants time their escape when they would. They knew their own survival strategies best. Jake's concern was human survival, of Mira City if not of himself and his peculiar team here. Although, of course, he wanted to survive. He watched Lucy, who looked around at them all steadily, bravely. No symptoms of sickness yet.

How soon would symptoms come? You could infect one species with a disease designed for another, George had explained, and have the first species never get sick at all. Mosquitoes did not die of malaria. Mice did not die of Hanta viruses. Cats did not die of Corin's disease, the horrifying genemod bioweapon that had wiped out most of the African Mediterranean, leaving only armies of healthy cats.

On the other hand, George had added, some species did die of cross-species infections. He had declined to give examples.

"Gail," Jake said, "send the quee message."

She nodded. All of them, except the sleeping Shipley and Nan, watched as Gail coded in the message. It would instantly be received on the Fur ship and translated into whatever symbols their quee equivalent used.

**WE LEARNED CANNOT DESTROY ENEMY SHIELD. WE LEARNED LOCATION GENETIC LIBRARY ENEMY USED TWICE TO RESTART SPECIES. LIBRARY CAN BE DESTROYED EASILY. WE WILL TELL YOU LOCATION IF YOU AGREE TAKE HUMANS BACK TO OUR COLONY AND TO NOT DESTROY OUR CITY.**

George said, with a pessimism not characteristic of him, "They'll know it's a trick of some sort. It's obvious."

"We've been over this," Jake said. "They will suspect a trick. But they will also think we learned the location of the library, because they saw that the Vines cooperated with us on Greentrees. They'll believe the Vines will have told us everything we want to know. They believe the Vines are honest and open, and we're secretive and treacherous."

"And they're right," Lucy said.

Jake didn't contradict her. The Vines hadn't been completely open. They had not told the humans, not even William Shipley, the location of the genetic library. They were truthful but not stupid.

George said, "More important, the Furs think we're dumb. They may even believe that we believe they'll trade fairly with us: Mira City for the library."

Ingrid said, "There's no way to know what they believe."

Because they're so much like us, Jake thought. We hardly ever know correctly what each other believes. Shipley's religion, Lucy's moral squeamishness. Nan's passionate misanthropy, Gail's mother-hen capability . . . Where had any of it come from? Genes or upbringing or circumstances? Shipley had more in common with a plant than with his own daughter. They were all of them mysteries to each other.

"Here comes the answer," Gail said. Jake craned his neck for a better view.

BARGAIN AGREED. WE ATTACK SOON.

Jake felt as if Mueller had punched him again. *Attack.* Of course that was how the Furs would think of it. And this was a Fur ship;

the Furs knew it well. They expected the Vines to defend themselves.

He said, "Vine, we'll have to say that you all figured out that the quee was receiving from Furs and not from Greentrees, as we supposedly told you. That's the only way we can account for your escape. You better go to your escape craft now."

Vine said, "There is no escape craft."

"But you said—"

"No," Vine said. "We never said we have an escape craft. We do not. We have only a shuttle, slow and made for planetfall. We never said we have an escape craft. You humans assumed we have one."

Lucy said slowly, "You're not going to escape."

"We cannot. But our death is good. We will save our planet, and yours. This is our experimental work for a thousand years past. It is good."

"My God," George whispered.

Vine continued, "We will give you our death flowers. You must put them inside the quee. The enemy will not look there. They may let you keep the quee.

"Please give our death flowers to our people if you ever see them again."

# 29

The Fur ship approached more quickly than anyone could have predicted. Almost immediately after his request about death flowers, Vine said, "The enemy ship will be here in six hundred human breaths."

In Karim's absence, George was quickest with the math. "About half an hour."

"That *soon*?" Lucy said.

"The Fur ship must have already been close," George said. "How many of these McAndrew Drive ships do they have, anyway?"

Jake had no idea, and he didn't care. Not at the moment. Vine's announcement had stunned him. The sentient plants—and Jake couldn't think of them any other way, no matter what George said—were going to die. They knew that when they'd proposed the plan to save their planet and Mira City. It was the same debate that the humans had had before they boarded the Vines' ship. Both species were acting to save their planet-bound fellows. But there was one important difference: the humans had voted to destroy another species, and the Vines had voted (if voting was what they did) to take their own lives.

What did that say about the ethics of each race?

No time for ethics. Karim reappeared. Jake said simply, "Can you do it, Karim?"

"I hope so." The young physicist's usual enthusiasm for alien technology was subdued by the weight of what he was taking on.

Jake said, "Vine, give the rest of us the infecting drink. Karim, can you get the quee case open to put some packets inside? Without damaging anything in there?"

"I think so. What are—"

"I'll explain later. Vine, where are the death flowers?"

"You must collect the death flowers from us. Our brother will open paths."

"All right. Ingrid, George, Lucy, you go and . . . Lucy?"

"I'm fine," she said, getting to her feet. But behind her transparent helmet, droplets of sweat stood out on her pale face.

"Already?" Jake said to Vine. "She's sick already?"

"We don't know."

Because the "molecules" had been designed for Furs, not humans. Jake understood. He watched as three of the clear cups embedded in slime filled with a clear, yellowish fluid. Gail shuddered.

"The paths are opening," George said. "Let's go."

The thick slime was parting again, this time in many places, crawling into ridges on either side of five narrow paths. Jake said, "A path for you, too, Gail. Let's do it." He half expected her to object, but she didn't, although she looked almost as ashen as Lucy.

Jake walked down one path to the first clump of Vines, a grove of three. A tendril snaked toward him, "holding" a tiny packet of leaves, or flesh, or whatever it was. Gene-stuff. He said, "Only one packet? There are three of you here," but of course there was no answer. Yet they must be individuals, or else one packet would do for the entire ship. Were these three then one individual? With or without the "brother" slime? Jake would probably never know, and it didn't matter anyway. He took the packet.

It felt slick in his hand, and he had to force himself not to drop it. He moved on, collecting three more packets, and then his path brought him back to the main island.

Karim was already there, stuffing more of the tiny packets inside the quee. Vine said, "The enemy ship is docking with our ship."

Ingrid, George, and Lucy raced in. Lucy looked neither better nor worse. Karim snatched their packets and stuffed them into the quee. Jake said, "All right, drink!" He picked up a cup.

The yellowish fluid didn't have the lemonade taste of the food Vine had been preparing for them. No time for peripherals, Jake guessed. He forced down the bitter drink, gagging slightly.

Vine said, "The enemy is on the bridge of our ship."

Jake hadn't even been sure the ship had a bridge.

George and Ingrid finished the drink and set down their cups. Karim, of course, wasn't infected; the last thing they needed was a pilot who was sick as well as totally inexperienced. Immediately all the cups dissolved and the airlock door opened. A helmeted and suited Fur entered, a male who might or might not have been the same one Jake had encountered before. It was odd to see a Fur fully clothed. Another male behind him carried a translator egg, and a female carried one of their curved weapon-sticks.

None of them left the airlock. The leader snarled something and the translator said flatly, "Humans will come with us."

Jake had choreographed their departure to include action, not explanations. Karim took Shipley's sleeping bulk under the armpits and dragged him forward. George picked up Nan. Gail carried the quee. They all moved forward together into the airlock. Jake waited for the Fur to object to the unconscious humans, or at least ask about them, but he did neither.

Jake had warned everyone against good-byes to Vine. There were to be no clues to the Furs about the human-plant relationship. Vine, too, was silent.

The Fur translator said, "You were nine humans. Now you are eight humans."

Jake said, "The plants ate one human." Behind his clear helmet the Fur made some facial distortion, but there was no way for Jake to tell what it meant.

"Remove that alien helmet and throw it back."

The airlock was full of Vine air. Jake said, "Everybody, take some very deep breaths." He forced air into his own lungs.

The helmet came off easily. The humans threw it back onto the main island. Jake waited for the Fur to tell them to remove the strips of cloth from their bodies, but this time the alien did not. The strips weren't human-made; they were blankets stolen from the primitive Furs and probably too low-tech to be considered a threat.

Jake's lungs burned by the time the airlock closed and refilled. He gasped. And then they were aboard the Fur ship again, in the same featureless room with the floor mats they had torn up for clothing. So this *was* the same crew of Furs. They had simply followed the Vine ship, as Jake should have realized they would. That's why they'd reached it so quickly. He felt like a fool.

All three Furs entered the room with the humans. The leader said to Gail through the translator, "Keeper of Names and Birds, do you wish to die now for birds and the morning sky?"

"No," Gail said.

He turned to Jake. "Tell us where is the enemy's gene library."

"I must draw it," Jake said. "We don't understand what the enemy said. We just memorized it. I must draw it."

The leader bared his impressive teeth. A pan-stellar carnivore gesture, Jake noted impersonally. All three Furs still wore their close-fitting suits and clear helmets. How much air did the outfits hold? Jake saw no tanks or hoses. The Furs were not the bio-wizards the Vines were. The air supply in those helmets must be limited.

The second male set down the translator and disappeared. Time passed before she returned, carrying a round blank slate made of . . . something. No one said anything. The only sound was Shipley's snoring.

Jake took the slate and a curious curved "pen" that seemed to have no exposed point but that marked on the slate anyway. He began to draw constellations, very slowly. The constellations had been carefully displayed on Vine's bioarm. Vine had said they indicated a plausible false location for the gene library. Jake hoped it was as plausible to Furs as to Vines.

The ship rocked slightly, just once. Karim blinked hard.

The Furs did not remove their helmets.

Jake drew with agonizing slowness, finally stopping completely. "I'm trying to remember everything," he said apologetically to the translator. "I want to get it right."

*"You realize," George had said to Jake, "that after they think they have the location, they have no reason not to kill us."*

True enough. But not conclusive. Jake had been a lawyer for a long time; you never released a material witness until you had corroborated his testimony. He didn't know what the military analogue was for that judicial safeguard, but he was sure there was one. These creatures were soldiers.

And aliens.

He drew yet more slowly.

Shipley snored.

The leader reached up and removed his helmet.

Jake drew a few more meaningless strokes. The other two Furs removed their helmets. Carefully Jake moved toward the Fur to show him the slate. Jake didn't get too close, or make any sudden gestures. He just extended the slate, but not too far, and when the leader leaned in for a closer look, Jake breathed on him very gently, so that the soft puffs of air were almost like a discreetly blown kiss.

Lucy began vomiting about an hour later. Until then, there had been almost an air of celebration in the closed ship compartment. A very quiet celebration, since no one said anything overtly. The chamber was undoubtedly under surveillance. But people smiled at each other. Humans had probably infected the Furs. Humans were alive. Still. For now.

On the other hand, the female with the weapon had torn the quee from Gail and carried it away with her. Jake had no idea what they would do with it, or with the "death flowers" inside, if those were discovered.

"I wish we had some water," Gail said. "Last time they gave us water." She had torn more cloth from the floor matting, which was getting pretty scruffy, and cleaned up Lucy as well as she could. It wasn't very well. Lucy lay quiet, glassy-eyed, in a corner.

Ingrid said loudly, "She must have eaten some food gone bad." Gail rolled her eyes at this clumsy attempt at misdirection.

Jake became aware that his own insides were beginning to feel peculiar. A little sour, then roiling . . . He just made it to another corner before he vomited.

"Oh, God," he heard Gail say.

Things got strange after that. Vine was bending over him, only it wasn't Vine but Beta, covered with black flowers like horrific shiny orchids. "You murdered Mrs. Dalton," Beta said in Lucy's voice. Dr. Shipley was there, too, sitting in his damned shared silence, except that when Jake shook himself loose of Beta and walked over to the physician, he saw that Shipley wasn't praying. He was dead. "You murdered Mrs. Dalton," the corpse said, and Jake screamed back, "I was only trying to save Mira City!" Then Nan danced by, naked and writhing lewdly.

"Don't hallucinate out loud!" Gail said, leaning close to his ear. "What if they're listening?"

"All right," he answered, but it came out in Fur so she didn't understand and went away.

Fire danced along his arms and legs. He held the arms up to admire the colors in the flames: red and yellow and orange and blue and green and red and yellow and . . .

"I need water, damn it!" Gail bellowed at the ceiling. "At least give me some water!" Then, the next minute or hours later, "Oh, fuck. *Nan!*"

After that, nothing.

# 30

Gail had each one in a corner: George, Ingrid, Jake, Lucy. All vomiting in unison. God, the stench was awful.

And then Karim started to puke.

"You don't have it!" Gail cried, forgetting surveillance. "You didn't drink it!"

"I must have . . . have caught it from . . . one of them," Karim said, paling under his brown Arab skin like a suddenly peeled coconut.

Gail's spine froze. If Karim had caught it from one of the others, he might get too sick to fly the ship. And if Karim could catch it from an infected human, then so could Gail.

And then no one would be left functional. And Mira City . . .

Only activity kept her going. Now that there were five of them vomiting, she was fresh out of corners. She put Karim against the wall between Lucy and Jake. Dr. Shipley and Nan slept on, oblivious, in the center of the room.

The most she could do was tear cloth strips off the floor, or off their bodies, to clean up the sick ones, and to make sure none aspirated any vomit. Good thing she wasn't squeamish, at least not about humans. After what seemed an eon, all except Jake stopped puking and fell into a fitful sleep, and Gail thought the worst was over.

Then Jake, whose fever felt the highest to her unaided palm, began hallucinating aloud. "You murdered Mrs. Dalton!" he cried.

Mrs. Dalton? Who was she? Jake tried to sit up, his face twisted in horror, his body quaking with fever and fear. Gail pushed him back down again. "Jake, don't hallucinate out loud! What if they're listening?"

"You murdered Mrs. Dalton!" and then, "I was only trying to save Mira City!"

Gail tried to drown out his maunderings. At the top of her lungs she screamed, "I need water, damn it!" Which was certainly true. She kept on screaming it until Jake quieted.

To her surprise, the door opened and a Fur entered, carrying a basin of water.

Gail shrank back. An alien touch . . . But the Fur ignored her. It walked a few steps into the room, stopped, stared down at the basin, looked around, stared again at the basin, stopped again.

Gail had never seen a Fur behave like that. And it was unarmed. Furs always had weapons, or were accompanied by other Furs with weapons. This one stood motionless in the room. Cautiously Gail stood and approached it. She reached out and took the basin from the alien's hands.

Its lips drew back over its teeth. Oh, God, it was angry . . . but the lips quivered and the skin around the eyes did something. The powerful tail quaked. It looked like . . . these were aliens, but for a crazy moment Gail was sure that the thing was *laughing.*

The Fur turned and walked back toward the door in the same bizarre manner, as if it was having trouble remembering what it was supposed to do. Its tail quaked some more. It lurched out the door. Gail slammed the basin down, not caring that fully a third of the water sloshed onto the floor. She snatched at the door just before it finished closing and caught it in her hand.

Heart hammering, she waited for the door to be slammed on her fingers, or jerked open again in fury. Neither happened. After a long moment she stretched out her other arm toward Karim, who lay closest to the door. Her finger just reached a piece of vomity cloth she had used to wipe his face. Gail grimaced in disgust, folded the cloth several times, and wedged it in the door.

That Fur had been infected.

*"They'll be happy,"* Jake had promised. *"Dreaming in the sun,"* was the way Vine had put it. Maybe, but to Gail that alien had looked punch-drunk. Maybe that was just the first stage. Too bad

it hadn't been the first stage for humans, too. A bunch of giggling shipmates would have smelled better than a bunch of feverish vomiters.

She mopped up the precious water she had spilled by wringing out soiled cloths to use again. With the clean water left in the basin she did a better job of washing the five sufferers' faces. Should she give them water to drink? She had no way of knowing how safe the water was. Better not.

Creeping around the fouled cabin, she checked on everyone again. They were all alive. Lucy seemed a little cooler, but maybe that was just wishful thinking. Dr. Shipley and Nan still slept like the dead. How long were their induced comas supposed to last? Had Jake even thought to ask?

Shaking her head, Gail tried to think of something else to do. Inactivity was the enemy, always. If she kept busy, she'd be all right. But she couldn't think of anything else. Finally, all she could do was sit and stare at the propped-open door until, incredibly, she fell asleep.

She woke with a scream. Something was happening, something terrible. But it was only Nan, sitting up groggily in the middle of the floor. From some combination of fear and joy, Gail cried, "Oh, fuck. Nan!"

"I'm glad to see you, too," Nan retorted, looking around her. Her grogginess disappeared too quickly. Glaring at Gail, she demanded, "What has that rat-bite Jake done now?"

And it was going to have to be Gail who told her. Nan, who had hated the Vines from the beginning. Nan, who disapproved with passionate morality of biological experimentation on another species. Nan, who was capable of anything.

Gail crawled over to Nan and put her mouth very close to Nan's ear. "Surveillance," she breathed. "Can't talk now. Wait."

And there was nothing Nan could do but accept that. For once. It was almost a triumph.

Dr. Shipley didn't wake. After an hour in which nothing whatsoever happened, Gail couldn't stand it anymore. If the infection spread among Furs as fast as it did among humans, everyone on board was already diseased by now. She hoped.

"Come on," she said to Nan. "We're going."

Nan's eyes widened. "Going where?" Apparently she hadn't noticed the cloth holding the door open a fraction of an inch.

Gail took Nan's hand—how good the small scarred fingers felt!—and led her to the door. Carefully Gail pried it open. Nan made a satisfying sound of surprise. Gail said, "The Furs have been infected."

"You don't know that! You only know that five of us are deathly sick!"

"The Furs are infected, too," Gail said with more conviction than she felt.

The two women crept out the door. They stood in the featureless corridor by which they'd entered the ship. At the end, Gail knew, was an airlock; she didn't want that. The corridor branched to the right, and she led Nan that way. It branched again. Gail chose randomly.

As soon as she rounded the second corner she gasped and stopped. Two Furs lay writhing on the floor. Sick? Too sick to leap up and attack? Gail backed away frantically, but Nan caught her shoulder.

"Gail, they're mating!"

*"Mating?"*

Nan laughed. It did look like mating, Gail thought, in that the two seemed to be shoving hard against each other. What else were they doing? Suddenly Gail didn't want to know. *The infected ones will be sexually irresistible to other Furs.* Jake had told her. Well, it wasn't going to do humans any good if they wasted all that lust on each other. That was no way to spread the infection.

At least they weren't vomiting.

"Take this," Nan said. She'd spotted two of the curved weapon-things on the floor beside the oblivious Furs and had retrieved them. She thrust one at Gail.

"I don't know how to use it," Gail whispered.

"And I do? Take it!" Nan didn't bother to lower her voice. The copulating Furs never looked up.

Nan aimed the weapon and began fiddling with one end. Gail caught her arm. "You don't know anything about the settings! You could blow a hole in the ship!"

"I guess you're right," Nan said. "So what do we do with these two?"

Gail was only glad that Nan wasn't still posing as the champion of Furs. But Nan's next words dispelled that illusion.

"They'd be better off dead than made into these experimental caricatures," she said bitterly.

"We need these experimental caricatures. Don't be a moron, Nan. Let's just . . . just go on."

They crept carefully past the frenzied copulators, who didn't seem to notice. Nan said, "That must be some fuck."

Gail ignored her. What was she doing, brazenly thrusting into the enemy's part of the ship? But what kind of enemy was more interested in sex than war?

A good enemy to have.

The corridor led to a large room. Before she saw anything else, Gail saw that the floor of the room was made of some thick, clear material crossed with gray struts in an irregular pattern. The floor was bowed at the edges, and under it a short way from the center was a mass of dark stuff connected by a short thick pole.

"So it is a McAndrew Drive," Nan breathed, but Gail scarcely heard her. She had caught sight of the Furs in the chamber.

There were five of them. They all sat on the floor, their balancing tails spread out behind them. Two looked up as the humans entered, and Gail caught her breath. But the Furs didn't move. They merely gazed quietly at the humans, as if they found them interesting contemplative objects.

"Get . . . get their weapons," Gail said unsteadily.

Nan complied. No Fur objected to having the guns, or whatever they were, taken from them. But one arose just as Nan disarmed him, and Gail gave a little cry. Nan leaped back. The Fur ignored her, walking over to a storage cabinet. It removed something and began unconcernedly to eat.

So they could feed themselves. What else? Or was this only the first stage of the illness, as the humans had had a violent first stage, and would the infected Furs act differently later on? Gail had no idea.

Nan had staggered on that last leap backward. Now she lurched over to Gail, saying unsteadily, "A little light-headed . . ."

"Of course you are. You refused to eat anything for days!" Gail snapped, just as Nan fainted.

Wonderful. Just what Gail needed. Tranquilized aliens, puking shipmates and a starving Nan. Not to mention that Gail hadn't the vaguest idea what she herself was doing.

She slapped Nan awake and made her eat some of whatever the Fur had taken from the storage bin. Nan had always been willing to eat the food of Furs, who killed humans. It was the food of Vines, who helped humans, that Nan refused. But this was no time to reflect on the perversity of human nature.

"I think we need to pen them all up in some one room, before they . . . change in some way."

"Change in what way?" Nan said.

"How should I know? The only room that I'm sure locks is the one we were imprisoned in. We need to get all the humans out of there and put in all the Furs we can find."

Nan stared at her as if Gail were crazy.

"Well, do you have a better plan?"

"I might, if you'd tell me the whole story of what the fuck's going on!"

"I'll tell you while we drag our people out here. Come on, let's get going."

Nan took it better than Gail expected. Too well, in fact. Gail would need to think about that later.

By the time they'd dragged the five sick humans plus Dr. Shipley onto the bridge, Gail's arms ached. Nan, weakened by self-willed starvation, trembled. But Karim, at least, seemed better. Maybe he had the strongest constitution, or maybe catching the thing from another human led to a milder case than being directly infected. How would Gail know? She didn't know anything.

Karim stared at her with some recognition in his dark eyes, although he didn't answer her. The others seemed in some sort of fitful coma, unresponsive and still feverish.

"If we could only get your father awake!" Gail said. "He's the doctor, after all."

Nan stared somberly at her sleeping parent stretched out on the ship's floor. "It's genocide, Gail."

She didn't mean Shipley, Gail realized. She meant the infected Furs, sent home (if they could actually manage that) to turn the rest of their race into happy, copulating idiots.

"Nan—" she began, but Nan cut her off.

"You know what they're doing?" Nan said in the bitterest tone Gail had heard from her yet. She looked at the five quiet Furs, who had shown not the slightest reaction to having sick humans dragged into their midst. "They're focusing on higher qualities. They're dreaming in the sun. They're sharing silence together, waiting for the Light. They're having a fucking New Quaker meeting!"

Gail said quietly, "Are you going to resist us on this, Nan? Try to sabotage our plan?"

"No," Nan said wearily. "I've tried that twice, and look what happened. I know now I can't control everything that everybody else fucking chooses to do, even if I hate it."

*Not a bad definition of maturity,* Gail thought. But all she said was, "Let's get started finding all the Furs."

It was easier than she'd hoped. Gail and Nan didn't have to drag the Furs as they'd dragged the humans. They merely prodded with their stolen weapons, and the Furs obediently walked where they were pushed. There turned out to be only twelve of them aboard the ship, which was divided into many small rooms and narrow corridors. Gail finally realized that the total area was no bigger than the one large room on the adapted Vine ship. Furs and Vines apparently had different cultural ideas about how to use space.

All twelve Furs fit easily into the featureless room with torn matting. Gail had insisted on washing out the room once she located the water supply. The chamber was clean and stocked with food and water when she removed the cloth doorstop and the door locked on their captives.

"Now what?" Nan said.

"Now we look for the quee they took from us."

"Why?"

Gail didn't say, *Because the Vine death flowers are in it.* "Because it's the only one we can read. Eventually other Furs are going to notice that this ship isn't communicating, or whatever it's supposed to be doing."

"So what do we do about that?"

Gail had no idea. This had been Jake's plan, and either he was supposed to be directing it or else all the humans were supposed to be murdered already. Instead, she was in charge. "Just start looking for the quee!"

They found it in a storage cabinet. Gail didn't attempt to open it; she didn't know how. Karim would have to do that. She checked on each person. They were all still alive, and Karim at least felt much cooler.

Nan was still studying the quee. "I don't think this will help us. Isn't it quantum-entangled with this ship? Unless you know how to reset it, any other Fur ship is going to communicate on the quee that belongs on this ship."

She was right. Gail said wearily, "I don't even know what their quee would look like. And even if I identified it, it isn't rigged up with an English translator. Whatever other Furs say to these Furs, we wouldn't be able to interpret it anyway."

"Well, then, forget that," Nan said, tossing away the quee. It thudded to the floor.

Gail hadn't ever before felt so helpless. She knew herself to be a competent woman, a superb organizer. But how did you organize diseased aliens, sick humans, and a ship nobody could fly?

"Nan, are we moving now?"

Nan stared at her. "Of course we're moving now—we're at maximum acceleration. Look under your feet! The living quarters are as close to the massplate as they can get. Didn't you listen to Karim explain the McAndrew Drive?"

"No," Gail said. "But if we're moving, we need to change course."

"To where?"

"Greentrees. If the Furs discover that this ship isn't communicating properly"—*when they discover this ship isn't communicating properly*—"they'll come looking for it. They also might just go destroy Mira City, since they'll conclude that humans aren't keeping our end of the bargain. We have to be at Mira first, ready to destroy them."

Nan gaped at her. "Do you really think—"

"I don't think we have any choice! If only I could get Karim functional . . ."

"Maybe we don't need Karim," Nan said. "I have a better idea."

They rummaged through more storage cabinets, among oddly shaped objects that were total mysteries. Eventually Nan said, "I think this is it." She held up a curved reddish baton with a ball on the end of it. It looked to Gail like a bent scepter.

"It did look like that . . . Nan! Don't just experiment!"

"How else will I know? It wasn't a weapon, remember." She fingered the baton in various ways. "There . . . I felt a slight tingle. Try to approach me."

Cautiously Gail moved forward, hands groping in front of her. They hit an invisible wall. "It's here! But it's only a few feet high."

"Stay there while I experiment."

It took half an hour for Nan to master creating straight walls of various heights, curved walls of various degrees, and enclosed prisons of various diameters. "All right, I'm ready. Let's go."

Gail caught her arm. "Nan, listen to me. You had a special bond with Furs. When you see what the infection is doing to them, and I have no idea what that could be at this stage, are you going to get so angry that you don't help me with this?"

Nan pulled her arm away. "I'll always be angry over what the Vines have done. I voted against this plan, remember, before Jake decided to remove the competition by knocking me out. But you guys went ahead anyway, the Furs are infected, and I don't see any way to turn back."

"Sure you do," Gail said slowly. "Make sure these Furs never come in contact with any other Furs."

"The only way to do that is to kill them. I'm sure you're right that there's another ship speeding toward us this minute. They must know how to locate one of their own ships, and if they do, they'll free their own people. I could shove all these Furs out the airlock and they'd probably let me, but I won't kill them!"

*Like father, like daughter.* Gail studied Nan's face: furious and sorrowful and resigned. "Okay," Gail said. "Let's go."

The two women walked back to the imprisoned Furs. Gail

pushed open the door while Nan created a protective wall around her that also blocked the doorway.

It was a good thing she had; some of the Furs rushed Gail, teeth bared. And not in giggles, either. They weren't exactly attacking, Gail realized after a moment, but they were trying to escape. "Second-stage infection," she told Nan with a conviction she didn't feel. "They've recovered enough to be aware again of their surroundings, but look, they're not trying to . . . to get at me."

"So stop shrinking and turning pale," Nan said. "You're perfectly safe. I've got this thing under control. Take one from the back of the room—they still look completely drugged."

From the back. Easy for Nan to say, she was safe in the corridor. Gail felt a light push on one side. Nan was changing the shape of her prison, making it into an elongated oval that still blocked the door but now stretched into one corner, where a Fur sat on the floor, tail folded under, gazing at nothing. Other Furs were pushed aside by the growing wall. Gail kept one palm on its reassuring invisible surface. The surface blinked off for a fraction of a second, then blinked on and the corner Fur was inside the wall with Gail.

She felt the old stomach roiling and clammy skin. This was a creature that could kill her with one blow. Worse, it was alien. She made herself reach down and grasp one of its arms. She pulled and the Fur stood up.

"Good!" Nan said. "Now come forward."

The room was full of noise. Fur words or whatever they used. Gail tugged the obedient Fur toward the door. The others put tentacled hands on the invisible wall and tried to tell it something, but the Fur, still in the first stages of infection, merely made a strange rolling gesture with its head. Gail led it out the door. Nan closed it, and they had a pilot.

"How do we know this one can fly the ship?" Gail asked, belatedly.

"We don't for sure, but look at its chest-strap thing. Those are the same marks that were on the female shuttle pilot. In fact, I think it's the same Fur."

Gail looked at the alien, belatedly realizing from its crest that it was female. Then probably the room also held the same leader who had so ruthlessly enlisted humans as saboteurs, who had ordered their skimmer vaporized. Gail wasn't sure which one he was, either. Not that it mattered now.

"How are you going to communicate with it, since we can't find a translator egg?"

Nan didn't answer. She took the Fur by the hand and led it to the bridge. She sat it firmly in what Gail assumed that Nan assumed was a pilot chair. The Fur looked at Nan expressionlessly. Nan picked up the pen and slate on which Jake had drawn the false location of the Vine genetic library. (How had she figured out how to erase Jake's drawing?) She drew a star system with tiny humans, Furs, and Vines all standing on the same planet. The Fur did something with its face but made no move.

Nan drew a sketch of the Fur sitting in the pilot seat. Then she drew what even Gail recognized as a food container like the ones they'd seen in a storage cabinet.

She drew a thick black line through the food.

The Fur started to cry.

Gail said, "What—"

"George first observed that in a Fur child on Greentrees," Nan said. "In that thriving all-female camp. He speculated that a tearing mechanism of some sort is necessary to all creatures with eyes and without a nictitating membrane. To clear dust and stuff. But he thought even then that the tears might also be a distress expression. He said some mechanisms would be duplicated in different evolutionary paths from sheer chance."

"Oh," Gail said. She didn't remember what a nictitating membrane was.

The Fur went on crying, large tears rolling grotesquely over the matted hair on its face. Nan pointed again to the star system drawing, the pilot console, and the blacked-out food sketch. The Fur reached for some strange-looking protrusions in front of it.

"Or maybe," Nan said flatly, "her tears aren't a distress mechanism. Maybe that's joy. Isn't this infection supposed to make them happier?"

Gail didn't answer. Checking on her patients, another thought occurred to her. "Nan—the other Furs stayed docile only so long. What are you going to do when this pilot here goes into the second stage of infection?"

"Put her inside a wall."

"What if it just sits there and starves instead of piloting? Or if it flies the ship off on a different course from the one we want? We wouldn't even know that was happening!"

Nan scowled. Chagrin turned to anger. "Fuck it, Gail, I can't think of everything!"

"I didn't say that you could."

"You implied that I—"

"Forget it, Nan. We don't need your tame Fur, after all."

Karim was waking up.

"So you took control of the ship, just like that," Jake said.

"Don't make it sound so easy," Gail said. She felt so much more like herself when the others were around her. Everyone but Dr. Shipley had regained consciousness, although you couldn't say they were well. All of them except Karim still had high fevers. Their heads ached, they had muscle cramps, and every once in a while someone got dry heaves, although nobody had any stomach contents left to heave up. Even Karim, the first time he tried to stand, toppled over and hit his head on the deck. Blood to add to the vomit. Fortunately, the wound wasn't serious. Gail bound it with their dwindling supply of blanket cloth.

"How long until we reach Greentrees?" Ingrid demanded weakly.

"How would I know?" Gail said. "We're just passengers. Karim, are you going to be able to figure out this weapons arsenal in time?"

"No," Karim said. The physicist, seated in the pilot's chair, studied the array of weird protrusions in front of him. Jake had ordered the Fur pilot taken back to the "brig," as he called it. Gail didn't think the joke was funny.

" 'No'?" Nan said, before Jake could answer Karim. "You can't figure out the fucking weapons?"

"Nan, think about it," Karim said patiently. "The Vines didn't show me how to operate the weapons system aboard the ship they stole from the Furs. They didn't know how to operate it, because no Vine has ever used any Fur weapons. They just don't use weapons *at all*, remember?"

Gail said quickly, before Nan could begin on the Vines, "But you can't learn the weapons."

"No, Gail."

Jake said, "Then all this is for nothing. A second Fur ship can just blast us out of the sky."

"Not necessarily," Karim said. "Here's an important fact. Do you remember way back before we first reached Greentrees, when the *Ariel*'s computer registered another ship streaking past at an acceleration of a hundred gees? That ship came really close to us, but it took no notice of us at all. The reason is that when a McAndrew Drive is on, it's generating an intense cloud of plasma as it derives energy from the vacuum."

"So?" Nan said belligerently.

"So in the middle of that plasma cloud, the sensors can't operate. The Fur ship, or Vine ship, whichever it was, couldn't detect the *Ariel.* It didn't know we were there. The Fur fleet keeps track of each other by quee. Our quee wasn't entangled with theirs; it was entangled with Earth, and anyway ours didn't operate continuously, as theirs apparently do. So the other ship just never detected the *Ariel* at all."

Gail knew Karim's words were important, but she didn't know why. She looked from his face to Jake's and back again.

Jake said slowly, "So if we destroy our quee—both the one that belongs on this ship and our own that the Furs modified to communicate with them—then no Fur vessel will know where we are."

Nan said, "But we won't know where they are, either."

Karim said, "We will if we turn off our drive but theirs is on. And even though we don't have use of the Fur weapons, we do have this." He pointed to the huge disk below their feet.

"So?" Nan said. "That's not a weapon. And anyway, the other ship will have one, too."

"Yes," Karim said, "I know. But . . . listen."

# 31

William Shipley didn't know where he was.

The last thing he remembered was feeling very sleepy on the infirmary island aboard the Vine ship. But even lying on his back and gazing up at the ceiling, he could see this wasn't the Vine ship. This ceiling had no slime on it.

He didn't feel ill. In fact, he felt extraordinarily well. He turned his head to look around.

A metal room, not as large as the room he'd left filled with Vines and slime and paths. Left how? This room was clearly a bridge; he could see displays with totally meaningless symbols and protrusions and the back of what must be a pilot chair, and below his feet a short pole connecting the room to a black disk that could only be what Karim called a "super-high density massplate." Was he aboard another part of the Vine ship? He saw no Vines, humans, or Furs.

Carefully Shipley got to his feet. Several open doorways led off the bridge. He started toward one, but Karim's voice startled him so much he gasped aloud.

"Dr. Shipley! Hello!"

Karim sat in the pilot's chair, staring at the incomprehensible protrusions. Shipley said, "What are you doing? Where are we?"

"On the Fur ship," Karim said, not looking away from his protuberances. Some of them moved, seemingly of their own accord. Occasionally Karim touched one. "Gail took over the ship from the Furs. We control it now."

*"Gail?"*

"I'm sorry, Doctor, but I have to concentrate. Find Jake to explain, please."

"Where . . . where is everyone?"

"Destroying the quee."

Shipley shook his head to clear it. This didn't help. Nothing made any sense, nothing at all. He picked a doorway at random and started toward it.

He'd gotten only a few feet when he heard a tremendous crash. Karim didn't even jump. The physicist did something to one of his protuberances, and all at once the black massplate began to slide away from Shipley's feet. For a moment he thought the ship was breaking apart and he clutched at empty air, swayed off balance. Then he caught himself as he realized what was actually happening.

The ship was decelerating. The life quarters were sliding along the pole to keep the pull of deceleration balanced with the gravity pull of the massplate. He said, despite himself, "Karim . . . please . . . where are we?"

"Greentrees."

*Greentrees?*

Another crash, followed by shouting. Dazed, Shipley lumbered toward the sound, following it through a short narrow corridor.

George, Ingrid, Lucy, and Gail all stood crowded at the entrance of a small room. Inside, Jake raised a heavy piece of some unknown equipment over his head. He brought it down as hard as he could on a small tablelike structure bolted to, or part of, the metal deck. The table, already dented, caved in a little more. Jake shook with the recoil of the impact. It seemed to Shipley that he could actually see Jake's teeth rattle.

"Okay, Jake," George said, "my turn."

"Gladly."

Shipley said, "What—"

"Doctor!" Gail cried. "You're up! How do you feel?"

The commonplace question in the midst of lunacy finished Shipley. A wave of dizziness swept over him. He fought it off and tried again. "What are you doing?"

George said, "Oh, Lord, you need the whole story from the beginning. Jake, give me that thing, it's my turn."

Jake relinquished the makeshift sledgehammer and moved out

of the way. George smashed it down on the table. Over the deafening noise Ingrid shouted, "They're still all weak, so it's good you're here, Doctor. Don't let them rupture something inside themselves!"

Gail shouted crossly, "He doesn't even know what they're weak from! Come on, Doctor, I'll explain."

Gratefully Shipley followed her back to the relatively silent bridge. The massplate beneath his feet was now clearly a disk on a pole, moving away from them—or, rather, they from it. As soon as he could be heard, Shipley said, "Where's Naomi?"

"With the Furs. She's fine, doctor, don't worry."

With the Furs. *Don't worry.* Shipley put a hand on Gail's arm. Another deafening crash sounded from the other room. Gail said, "Come with me where it's quieter. I'll explain."

The explanation took a long time. As Gail finished, the others trooped back in, and George fainted.

"George!" Ingrid cried. "Doctor!"

George revived almost immediately. Shipley made him stay on the floor. Running his hands professionally over George's chest, taking his pulse, peeling back his eyelids to look at the whites, Shipley felt some measure of calm return to him. This, at least, was familiar.

"I'm fine," George said impatiently. "I want to get up."

"Your pulse is racing."

"I just destroyed an alien quee!"

From his pilot chair Karim called, "Are you sure it's destroyed?"

Ingrid snapped, "No, we can't know a hundred percent. It's alien tech! But we're pretty sure it's gone."

Jake said, "That just leaves the other quee. Karim, how long till we're in orbit around Greentrees?"

"Forty-seven furries."

Gail looked at Shipley's face and said, "Karim invented that name for the units measured on the Fur chronometer. The Vines taught him to read their numbers."

"It's in base six," George added helpfully.

Gail said, "Don't overburden him with stuff he doesn't need to know. Or me, either. Doctor, I'll take you to Nan, if you like. She's feeding the Furs. She's the only one that can manipulate the invisible wall."

Shipley stood, but at that moment Naomi entered the room from a different doorway. At the sight of her, half naked and scarred and starved-looking, everything that had happened on the Vine ship flooded back into Shipley's mind. Franz. The attack on Jake. Shipley tripping Franz. The slime eating at the rebuilt's face . . .

Naomi said, "Dad?"

Gail said, "Doctor, sit down. You're white as talc."

"I want . . . want to talk to Naomi."

The others tactfully moved off. Naomi took him by the hand and led him down yet another narrow corridor. It was featureless, but out of sight and sound of the bridge she sat on the floor and gently pulled him down.

For a long moment neither of them spoke. Then Shipley said, "Gail told me what happened."

"Yes," Naomi said. "It was wrong. It's wrong."

"But you're going along with it. With arranging for these infected Furs to spread their passivity to their home world."

"Yes," she said, but she didn't meet his eyes.

Shipley felt his stomach turn over, and then press upward into his chest. She was lying. She might fool Gail, but not him. Naomi was not going to go along with what she still saw as genocide to the alien race that, despite everything, she still championed. Because the Furs were the ones she'd befriended first? Because they shared DNA with humans? Or just because Naomi was, and always would be, in opposition to everyone else out of sure perversity? That was how she defined herself: lone rebel. The definition was more important to her than any external truth. Without that definition, she felt she was nothing.

Was he any different? He defined himself as a New Quaker, it was the heart, and soul of his existence, and without it he would be nothing either.

She was starting to look at him suspiciously. To divert her, Shipley said, "I killed Franz Mueller. I swore never to kill, and I did."

"Oh, Dad, you just tripped him! That wasn't wrong! The fucking Vines killed him!"

*No,* Shipley thought. Naomi didn't understand. His action had led directly to Franz's death. He was therefore responsible. But he let her talk on, passionate and convinced and true to her own perverse idealism. His heart was filled with painful love. *My child.*

When she finally ran out of words, he said simply, "I'd like to see the Furs. What they are now."

She jumped up eagerly. "Come on. I'm the only one that can use the wall to get in." She took him by the hand and led him to a door. Proudly she drew a small curved baton from the minimal clothing wrapped around her slim hips. She did something to it and then opened the door. A few Furs rushed the door. The rest sat quietly on the floor, raising their heads to look at the newcomers with, it seemed to Shipley, curiosity, but no alarm. Shipley walked in within Naomi's wall.

Peace filled him, unexpected and sweet as a clean breeze in a fetid sty.

"Naomi . . ." He couldn't say more. Instead he sat down beside the door.

"Dad . . . what the fuck are you doing?"

"Sharing silence."

He watched the expressions play over her face: impatience, the old scorn, a new tolerance. Still, he didn't think her acceptance of him would be strong enough to keep her here. So he said, "It's because of . . . of Franz. I need to just sit in silence with these people for a while. Please . . . sit with me, Naomi. Please."

She hesitated, and he held his breath. But she sat. He only learned why when she said, "You're different now."

"Different? How?"

"It seems like—well, like *you* need *me.*"

"I do. I always did."

She scowled. "I don't mean like that. I mean, like I'm the stronger one now. Since you killed Franz."

"Yes."

She stared at him hard, and he bowed his head at the lie he'd just told.

They sat there, in silence, for a long time. Finally he said, "Naomi, turn off the wall."

"Turn it off?"

"These people aren't going to harm us. You can see that. They're in some advanced stage of the infection. Even the ones that rushed up at first . . . look, they're all just sitting here"—*dreaming in the sun*—"and I want to genuinely share silence with them. Without barriers, even invisible ones."

"I can't turn off the wall. It's holding the door open, see? The door doesn't open from this side."

"Oh. Well, I'll hold it open. You can't believe these quiet people are going to escape." Shipley moved his bulk to sit half in, half out of the door.

Naomi said stubbornly, "If you're 'sharing silence,' what the fuck does it matter if there's an invisible wall or not?"

He said, "It doesn't. Never mind, dear heart. Leave it on."

She scowled again and, contrary to the end, turned off the wall.

Shipley reached quickly and grabbed the baton away from her. He threw it over his head outside the door as he lurched to his feet.

He only succeeded because she hadn't been expecting it. Immediately she screamed and leaped on him. She fought with absolutely no restraint, kicking, and biting. Shipley felt her teeth close on his shoulder and he cried out. But he outweighed her by 150 pounds, an impossible advantage to overcome. Backing up, his bulk blocking the doorway, he thrust her off and slammed the door, leaving her inside.

Heart in hard arrhythmia, he leaned against the outside of the door and wondered if he was going to have a myocardial infarction. He stared at the baton, forcing himself to concentrate on its curved hardness as his heart eventually slowed and he could breathe normally again.

The Furs inside wouldn't hurt her. Shipley was sure of it. They would never hurt anyone again. But Naomi would likely have ended up killing them, along with everyone else on board. Shipley didn't know what sabotage she'd planned of Jake's strategy, but he was sure that sabotage had been on her mind. He, her father, had seen it in Naomi's eyes. She'd been prepared to kill everyone aboard if necessary, including herself, in the service of her belief that bringing this infection to more Furs was genocide. For that belief, Naomi would have died.

*"Let your life speak."*

And he, Shipley thought, might have agreed with her up until the moment he entered that room. When he had, when he'd sat among the newly peaceful Furs, the Light had come to him as it never had before. Not blinding but deep, sweet with conviction beyond all doubt. These people were not the zombies he'd expected. The infection had not rendered them soulless. Instead, it had removed the bloodlust that Darwinian evolution had bred into them, and allowed a higher evolution to happen. This was the right next step for the Furs. It was their path: from war to shared silence, dreaming in the sun, at peace.

Naomi would never have seen that. She wouldn't have allowed herself to see it. And so he had thwarted her sabotage, whatever it was going to be. She would never forgive him, of course. Shipley had bought right action at the price of his daughter's fledgling love for him.

The price was not too high. And maybe it balanced Franz's death.

He closed his eyes, suddenly glad of whatever metal the door was made of. It was very tough. Through it he could not hear Naomi's pounding with her small fists on the other side.

# 32

The ship had stopped. Through the floor port Jake saw the long, long pole stretching from the life quarters to the disk at its other end. Beyond the disk, far below, he saw what he'd despaired of ever beholding again.

Greentrees.

The planet turned slowly below him, green and blue and white with clouds, the most beautiful thing he'd ever witnessed in his entire life. The ship was in high orbit, coasting along without power. With the plasma drive turned off, all the ship's sensors were operating. Now everything depended on how well Karim had been taught by the Vines to read those sensors.

George sat on the deck, prying open the portable quee. Karim gave him directions but never took his eyes off the strange alien displays. Karim only understood about a fourth of them, he'd told Jake. The Vines had had so little time to teach him.

"There, it's open," George said. He tipped the quee and several small, sticky packets slid out. Death flowers.

Lucy said quietly, "We don't know that we'll ever have a chance to give these to any Vines." No one answered her. She raised her big eyes to Jake, and it seemed to him there was a pleading expression in them. About the death flowers, or about something else? He looked away.

Ingrid said, "What do we do with the gene packets meanwhile?"

Unexpectedly, Dr. Shipley said, "Give them to me. I'll take care of them."

Silently Lucy gathered up the packets and handed them to Shipley. Everyone felt awkward around the New Quaker. He'd told them, quietly and without dramatics, why he'd imprisoned Nan with the Furs. Gail had gasped and, Jake suspected, cried when she was alone. The others had nodded, unsure what to say, and had left Shipley alone to, presumably, deal with his guilt over Nan. But Jake suspected that Shipley wasn't feeling guilty. The old doctor seemed to Jake to have a new peace about him, as if he'd settled something in his mind. Jake didn't want to know what. The convolutions of the religious mind, he told himself, were beyond him. Nor did he care.

Now Gail said, "Then if we're ready, let's launch the quee."

That part was easy. They put the quee in the airlock, opened it, and accelerated very briefly. The quee shot out and then followed them meekly in orbit, like a puppy on an invisible string, maybe a thousand kilometers behind. Jake saw the planet wheel out of view; Karim was positioning the ship.

Now all they had to do was wait.

Jake couldn't sit still, as the others were doing. Dr. Shipley sat with his head bowed and his eyes closed, presumably communing with the infinite. George, Lucy, and Ingrid sat talking in low voices, as if they feared they might distract Karim, who sat with utter concentration focused on his alien displays. Gail had disappeared.

Jake went to look for her. As he suspected, she sat with her back against the door of the Furs' prison. The Furs', and Nan's.

"Gail, she's all right in there. The Furs are harmless now."

"So Shipley says." She looked up at him with determined calm. "Jake, tell me again how this is supposed to work. I still don't understand it."

He sat beside her. The request was a welcome diversion. "Let me start by telling you what we can't do."

"Seems appropriate," Gail said dryly. "Since this whole mess began, we haven't been able to do much about anything."

"True enough. And now we can't hurry the Fur ship which, I'm pretty sure, will have been sent to destroy Mira City. The ship will get here when it gets here. It had communication from the Furs before we defanged them, and anyway it's homing in on our orbiting quee.

"When the ship gets here, we can't fire on it because Karim has no idea how to operate the ship's weapons and doesn't want to risk missing his one shot.

"We can't tell where the Fur ship will stop in relation to the orbiting quee. Undoubtedly it's going to stop outside weapons range, since it knows there's something weird going on with the ship and it also knows the ship's weapons range. We, of course, don't know the range, and so we can't tell how far out from Greentrees the ship will be when it stops decelerating and turns off its drive. We also don't know if they can fire their weapons with the drive on, or if it needs to be off."

Gail muttered, "We don't know much."

"But they don't know something important, either. They don't know that the orbiting quee *isn't* on our orbiting ship. Since the Quantum Entanglement Energy link is the only signal they're receiving, they probably assume it's coming from our ship, and furthermore that the Vines are operating the ship. They think we're way too stupid."

"Well," Gail said logically, "they'd be right if we hadn't had the Vines show Karim how."

Ignoring her, Jake said, "That means the Furs don't really know where our ship is."

Gail shifted her back against the hard door. Jake could hear the tension in her voice.

"You've made a lot of assumptions in there, Jake. What if they're not true?"

He didn't reply to that. She already knew the answer. They would all die. Instead he said, "Now here's things we can do. We can stay unperceived by the Furs until they turn off their own drive. We can accelerate at roughly a hundred gees. We can watch after the Fur ship comes into range of our sensors and record how fast it's decelerating. Maybe we can calculate, from its position and rate of deceleration, just where it will be when it turns its drive off."

"Maybe?"

Jake said quietly, "Karim can read the Fur displays on speed and position and interpret the Fur numbers. Sort of. He doesn't know how to use their computer. And he doesn't know at all how to access the computer on Greentrees with this equipment, or even communicate with Greentrees. So Karim has to do the calculations manually between the time he sights the Furs' ship and the time they turn off their drive."

Gail was silent a long moment. Then she said, "I'm going to check on Dr. Shipley. He's taking Nan's . . . action very hard."

*No, he's not,* Jake thought as he watched Gail walk away. *You are.*

While Dr. Shipley had achieved some sort of inner resolution Jake didn't understand and didn't want to understand, Gail was tormented by Nan's intended betrayal. Gail was the most forgiving, maternal person Jake had ever known (although her feelings for Nan could hardly be called maternal). But could she forgive this? How far did love extend?

As if on cue, Lucy rounded the bend in the corridor that Gail had just left.

"Jake . . . could we talk?"

It was the last thing Jake wanted to do. But Lucy had already sat down facing him, her small face with its big eyes intense as ever.

"We might not survive this," she said bluntly, "but either way, there's something I want you to know."

"Lucy, it's not—"

"No, please, Jake, listen. It's important to me. I said after you told me about . . . about Mrs. Dalton that I just couldn't go on being with you, that I couldn't help myself. That was true, then. A deliberate murder so horrible . . . *I couldn't help it.* But I don't feel that way now. You risked so much, Jake, you were so brave . . . I mean about telling Vine we'd planned to destroy their planetary shield. You told him even before Dr. Shipley did. It was the most heroic thing I've ever seen."

He said flatly, "So I've redeemed myself in your eyes."

"I wasn't going to put it that way, but . . . well, yes." She leaned forward and closed her eyes.

He could smell her, a powerful feminine smell, and the scent went straight to his groin. Her face moved close to his. Before their lips could touch, he made himself push her away.

Her eyes flew open. "Jake?"

Anger, blessedly, lent him the firmness he needed. "You say I've redeemed myself with you, Lucy. But you haven't redeemed yourself with me." Her mouth made a small pink O.

"You don't understand, do you? You think that because I told you something about myself that you couldn't stomach, you had the right to push me away. You're right; you did. But now you've decided that my subsequent actions cancel out that long-ago murder and so I'm fit to love again. But, Lucy, I don't want a love as fickle as that. What I told you was twenty-five-year-old history, but you still couldn't accept it. Couldn't accept me. Now you decide you can, that I've somehow met your idealistic code and the balance sheet of my desirability is in the black again. What would it take for me to slip back into the red? How much disapproval of my acts would you need to decide again I'm unfit to love you? In, out, in, out . . . I don't want to live that way, always on trial with you. Always awaiting the next verdict. I'm sorry, but I don't want it.

"I don't want you."

He couldn't have been more brutally frank, Jake knew. He didn't regret his frankness. Lucy got up unsteadily and walked away. He watched her disappear around the bend, and closed his eyes wearily.

He was still sitting there, some unknowable time later, when Ingrid appeared and called to him, "Jake! Come here! Karim's sighted the Fur ship!"

A hush like an empty cathedral. It occurred to Jake that he would prefer to die amid human noise, not this cemetery quiet. But no one dared disturb Karim.

The young physicist sat in his borrowed pilot chair, on his lap the slate and alien pen Jake had used to draw for the Furs the supposed location of the Vine genetic library. Karim scribbled furiously in small, crabbed handwriting. Every twenty seconds or so he glanced up at his displays, presumably to make sure nothing had changed. His shock of dark curly hair cast a bobbing shadow on his intent face. He was naked except for a wide strip of rough cloth around his hips.

Calculating by hand. In base six. Under more pressure than even Jake, no stranger to tense situations, could imagine.

Jake peered at the displays from a respectful distance, but they meant nothing to him. Squiggles and lines and peculiar beehive-looking things in three dimensions. Did Karim really know what he was doing? *"A lot of assumptions,"* Gail had said, and she was right. Oh, so right.

"Okay," Karim said. "I've got it. Let's go."

He dropped the slate and reached for the weird protrusions on the console. Jake saw his fingers tremble.

There was, as usual, no feeling of motion. But the life quarters slid closer to the disk; they were accelerating.

Jake couldn't tell how far out they went. It took only a few minutes, acceleration and deceleration, and then they stopped. He knew this not only because the massplate was at maximum distance from them, but also because Karim suddenly became compulsively talkative, his voice clipped with strain.

"Okay, we're here. I cut the drive. We're just floating here. The disk is pointed toward the place I expect the Fur ship to turn off its drive, based on its velocity and rate of deceleration. We're close to it, very close. They can't detect us, of course, until they turn off their own plasma drive because their drive is creating such a furious mess of ionized gases."

"Karim," Jake said tentatively. He wasn't sure if it was better to offer Karim reassurance or to let him rave.

"It'll look like a bright ball trailing a pendant of purplish blue—" Suddenly Karim's tone changed. "And there they are."

Jake strained his aging eyes. Yes, there it was, coming toward them just beyond the edge of the black disk, a moving brightness with a long tail, getting brighter every second . . . It disappeared behind the edge of the heavy-density disk. Jake felt irrational panic. How would Karim see it?

But of course Karim wasn't going by sight. His hands touched two of the strange Fur protuberances and his gaze never wavered from his displays. He was going by timing, expressed in the alien units Jake had so sardonically called "furries," waiting for the symbol to come up that Karim had calculated was the right moment. The exact moment the Furs would turn off their drive and detect the human ship, which had once been one of their own. No, Karim was actually waiting for a moment just before that. Karim had to have the ship in motion by then . . .

It happened so quickly that Jake wasn't sure it had happened at all. And then he was, and a queer disorienting sickness washed over him . . . *they had missed.*

The Fur ship had turned off its drive. A few carefully calculated seconds before, Karim had thrown his ship into its maximum, near-hundred-gee acceleration. Disk first, the human vessel had hurled toward the life quarters of the Fur ship, which had been moving out along its own pole during the entire deceleration, to balance its own heavy-density disk. It was now at the very end of the pole, at its farthest distance from its disk. Karim had been supposed to smash his disk into the life quarters at maximum acceleration, killing everyone aboard. But just before their own looming disk had obscured the port in the floor, Jake had seen the Fur ship flash and *there had been no collision.* They'd missed.

The human ship was still accelerating in a straight line away from Greentrees. Could it get away fast enough to avoid the Fur ship's weapons? No, that didn't make sense, weapons range had to be longer than that or a warship would be useless in a war . . . Jake closed his eyes and got ready to die.

Nothing happened.

Karim choked out, "They haven't fired on us . . . at least, I don't know what their weapons fire looks like, but . . ."

Jake said, "But if they fired, they couldn't have missed at this range? Could they?"

"I don't know!"

Gail said, "Go back before they shoot at Mira City!"

Jack felt sense returning, all at once, as if it were gravity. It steadied him. "Karim, decelerate. Try for a real-time visual through the port." He didn't trust the alien displays. They were too alien.

Karim brought the ship back for a flyby of the other craft, which remained motionless. As nothing continued to happen, Jake, emboldened, said, "Get closer."

They flew by the ship slowly and at a great distance, then again much closer. Again Jake felt that peculiar sickening sensation in his guts. Fear . . .

"Oh, my God," George said. "Did you feel that?"

"Yes! What is it?" Ingrid cried.

Karim said, "It's the gravity tug of the other high-density disk. We're getting a lateral gravity tug for a few seconds of, let me think, maybe forty percent of gee."

Jake said, "Their ship isn't damaged. At least it doesn't *look* damaged."

"Oh, my God," George said again. "I get it!"

Jake didn't get it. Irritated through his fear, he grabbed George by the arm only because he didn't dare grab Karim. "What? What happened?"

"We didn't miss their ship by much. Ow, Jake, let go! We didn't miss their ship by much, and although we were at maximum acceleration, we'd only been accelerating a few seconds. Our velocity wasn't actually that high then. We went by their life quarters while it was at maximum extension from *their* high-density disk, but much, much closer to *ours.* Gravity isn't a directed beam; it's a spherical phenomenon. The Furs in the other were yanked toward our disk at maybe eighty or ninety gees. Only for a second, but I guess that was enough. They were slammed against the side of their life quarters like . . ."

"They haven't fired at us," Karim broke in. "I think they're all dead."

It was a few more hours before anyone boarded. Then it was Jake, Ingrid, and, oddly enough, Dr. Shipley. Shipley said that if there were survivors, he might be useful. Jake's private opinion was that Shipley had developed some sort of death wish.

They bumped airlocks and once again Jake prepared to die, suspecting some sort of trick. But what? His reason told him how unlikely that was; his gut didn't listen.

Fortunately the two airlocks, once within a certain distance of each other, automatically gravitated together, sealed, and opened. Karim was sure he could figure out everything else on the ship, given time. Cocky after his victory, he'd developed an eagerness not unlike Shipley's in expression, however different its motive.

"All right," Jake said meaninglessly. "Let's go." He stepped out onto the temporary common ground. He had a brief vision of what the hardware would look like from space: two joined balls in the middle of an immensely long stick, each end of the stick bearing a black disk. A double bead inexplicably strung between two saucers.

The other ship was the exact duplicate of theirs. Evidently the Furs went in for neither updated designs nor individualizing touches. Jake followed the corridor to the central room that was the bridge on a Fur ship, much expanded terrarium on a Vine-modified one.

The command console, pilot chair, and ports were the same. Out of one port Jake saw the ship's disk, at maximum distance from the life quarters. The opposite port was smeared with fur and a thick, brownish fluid. The bodies themselves lay piled on the floor. After their brief but deadly slam against the hull, gravity had once again dropped them after Karim's ship flew on.

Shipley at once set out looking for any Fur who had survived having its internal organs, whatever they were, ruptured. Jake couldn't watch. Instead he explored each of the other short corridors. They all led to the same structures he'd seen before. Quee room, shuttle bay, the chamber where the humans had been imprisoned, and some other small rooms whose function he couldn't guess. Although the Furs had to sleep somewhere, didn't they?

Maybe they didn't even sleep. For all Jake knew.

"There are no survivors," Dr. Shipley said when Jake returned. Shipley, Ingrid, and George looked at Jake expectantly. They were waiting, he realized, for his next orders.

"Now we smash the quee on this ship," he said. "So that we can fly it elsewhere without any Furs out in space tracking us. Then we destroy the quee in orbit."

He saw Ingrid open her mouth to say something, think better of it, stay quiet.

"Then," Jake finished, "we figure out how to launch and fly these shuttles. After that, we go home."

It was a lot more complicated than that, of course.

When Jake returned to his own ship, leaving the two craft locked together, Karim had already begun trying to figure out how the shuttles operated. Jake found him in the shuttle bay.

"Vine showed me the bare minimum," Karim said, "but there

wasn't time for some crucial details. Like, for instance, getting the shuttle bay doors open. And if I get into Greentrees' gravity well without knowing exactly what I'm doing . . ."

"You'll end up looking worse than the dead Furs next door," Jake said. "Go slow, Karim. In fact, I want you to stop for a while. You look tauter than space-elevator cable."

"But I—"

"That's an order," Jake said, still mildly surprised to find himself issuing military-style orders, or anyone else listening to them.

"Okay," Karim said. "Jake, I want to name this ship, if that's all right with you."

"Name it? Well, okay. You've certainly earned the right. What do you want to call it, the *Karim S. Mahjoub*?"

"No. The *Franz Mueller.*"

Jake felt as if he'd been punched. Karim said hurriedly, "I know at the end he tried to kill you. But before that, remember, he killed Captain Scherer, just because Franz thought it was the right thing to do. He wasn't responsible for the rebuilt paranoia. Well, okay, maybe he was. But we spent some time together in Mira City, he taught me to fly the skimmer and the shuttle, and I do believe he always thought he was acting in the best human interests."

"All right, Karim," Jake said, hearing the thickness in his own voice. "This ship is the *Franz Mueller.* And the other one is the *Beta Vine.*"

A volunteer team cleaned out the *Beta Vine,* ejecting the Fur bodies into space. By the time this was finished, and Karim announced that he was sure he could fly a shuttle downstairs, Jake had devised a plan. He discussed it first with Karim, on whom it depended.

The young physicist said, "I'm not surprised, Jake. I was thinking the same thing. I don't see any other way to do it."

"If you can get any volunteers to go with you . . . although maybe it's not right to ask anyone else to take the risk."

"I already have a volunteer."

"You do?" Jake said, startled. "Who?"

"Lucy." Karim flushed. "She . . . we . . . she wants to go with me."

Jake stood still, wondering what he felt. The regulation regret, no more. Lucy, that idealist and desperate hero-worshiper, would of course have now fastened on Karim. The Man Who Saved Mira City.

"All right, take Lucy," he said. "But first teach me, George, and Ingrid how to fly these ships. Then make one shuttle run down, alone, to be sure you know how to do it. Then ferry all of us down except me."

"That will take time," Karim said. "Do we have enough time before more Furs show up?"

"I have no idea. But we have to do it."

"Why are you staying aboard after everyone else goes down?"

"Because I'm going to train the new soldiers you ferry up here. Karim, think. We're now at war with the entire Fur empire."

"But they're all going to be made passive and happy by the Vines' virus!"

"And how long will that take? Nobody knows. We don't know the size or distance to their home planet, the number of colonies they have, the number of ships in space . . . complete contagion could take generations. Meanwhile, we're at war."

"With Furs?"

Karim was right to be appalled, of course. The Fur technology was so far beyond pathetic human standards, it looked like no contest. All the humans had on their side was time, and with relativistic dilation, time was a slippery and unreliable ally.

Jake said, "You've been too preoccupied with the ship to think about this. Understandable. But, yes, we're at war with the Furs."

Karim stood still for a long moment. Then he said, "Get Ingrid and George. I'm not really that tired. We'll start the lessons now."

Jake nodded. " *'Si vis pacem, para bellum.'* "

Karim looked blank. Jake wasn't surprised. Nobody learned more than a few isolated phrases of Latin anymore, especially not as a hobby. The only person Jake had ever met who might have been able to translate that sentence was Dr. Shipley—who most certainly would not have agreed with it.

He said, "It means, 'If you wish for peace, prepare for war.' So show me how to fly this ship."

Together they left the shuttle bay for the bridge, and whatever might wait beyond it.

# EPILOGUE: THREE MONTHS OR ELEVEN YEARS LATER

In the pearly dawn light, Jake stood beside Gail and Faisal bin Saud at the edge of Mira Park. The park, itself at the edge of Mira City, was a luxuriant mix of native groundcover and wide swathes of Terran grass. Genemod flowers bloomed in carefully placed beds. There were groves of the tall, narrow native "trees," their shade supplemented by graceful open-sided pavilions. Benches, paths, a playground for children. A lot can be built in eleven years.

How had it happened, Jake thought, that none of them, not even Karim, had considered the time dilation as it applied to their own situation? To the nine kidnapped humans, their terrifying odyssey had lasted a few months. On Greentrees, eleven years had passed. Jake had no idea how far into space the Vines and then the Furs had taken him, but it must have been farther than he'd dreamed of imagining.

"Do you see them yet?" Gail asked, shading her eyes with her hand.

"No, I don't," Faisal said. He was governor of Mira City now, and had been since Jake and Gail had vanished with the Vines. That's how it had appeared to Mira City: its leaders had disappeared for good. Faisal had been elected, although Jake suspected that the "election" had contained more elements than one adult, one vote.

Jake's and Gail's stock in Mira Corporation had been passed to their respective heirs, and getting it reassigned to them after their resurrection had caused some very strained incidents. Gail's stock had been dispersed among her contentious family. Jake's had gone to form a charitable foundation.

Jake had his stock and voting privileges back, but not as CEO. Mira City was no longer a corporation. It had become a city-state.

He didn't really mind. There were more important considerations now, and Jake bore a different title.

"Wait . . . there they are!" Gail said. "On the horizon!"

Jake squinted. Yes, there were dots on the horizon. Slowly the dots turned into a caravan of people and animals. Larry Smith and his Cheyenne, come to hear formally how, and why, humans were now at war with an alien race unknown light-years away, and Cheyenne braves had unknowingly been the first casualties all those months—years ago. Almost three months ago a Mira City delegate had driven a rover to the Cheyenne subcontinent with this information, but Smith had refused to ride back with her to Mira City. The Cheyenne, he'd told the delegate, would send its tribal representatives in its own time and its own way.

"What are those animals pulling the travois?" Gail said.

Faisal said, "They're called 'elephants' by the Cheyenne, something else by our naturalists. They're very slow but not dangerous. Unfortunately, they smell."

"And the Cheyenne don't mind?"

"It seems not," Faisal said, smiling. He looked eleven years older, but his beautiful manners had not changed, for which Jake had been grateful during the last difficult months. Greentrees' colonists had chosen to leave Earth in order to find, each in its own way, a more peaceful life. It had not been easy to mobilize them for war.

He watched the "elephants" approach, pulling travois loaded with teepees and various gear. The animals didn't really look much like elephants, except in a certain lumbering gait. Long, thin, and low-slung, they had small heads and sharp dorsal spines. A shift in the wind brought their scent to Jake. He put his hand over his nose.

Fortunately, the Cheyenne left the elephants, along with most of their people, several hundred yards from Mira Park. Youths began unloading the travois and setting up camp. A delegation of Cheyenne approached the Mira City welcoming committee.

Four men and two women, they were dressed so fantastically

that Jake blinked. Trousers and boots of some animal hide, short tunics of what looked like woven purple groundcover. Yes, it was groundcover, the fibers treated somehow to look both soft and tough. The tunics were trimmed with bright beads, feathers, and shells. Necklaces and hair ornaments of the same materials glinted in the sunlight. Each Cheyenne wore a tattoo on his or her left cheek. Jake couldn't tell if the tattoos were permanent or applied with temporary vegetable dye. They depicted suns, stars, moons, flowers.

"Welcome to Mira City," Faisal said formally. "I am Governor Faisal bin Saud, and these are my advisors, Gail Cutler and Jake Holman."

"I know you," a young man said. "I am Singing Mountain."

Gail blurted out, "Where's Larry Smith? Uh, Blue Waters?"

Singing Mountain said, "My father passed into the spirit world two months ago. We sang his death song then."

Death song. Jake was startled into sharp memory of Beta and Vine. The alien death flowers were stored cryogenically in Mira City, possibly forever.

Faisal said, "I am sorry. Your father was a fascinating man."

"Thank you," Singing Mountain said, while Jake tried to remember Larry Smith's son's English name. He failed. "But don't be sorry. My father has rejoined the earth, whose splendor and gifts sustain life."

Well, not exactly. "The earth" was surely a misnomer on Greentrees, although Jake supposed that "rejoined the dirt" wouldn't have the same majestic feel.

Faisal said, "We have much to tell you, Singing Mountain. Events have occurred in Mira City that may affect the Cheyenne as well."

"So we have been told. If it is true, cooperation will be needed between our peoples."

"I am glad to find you so willing to cooperate."

"We share the abundance and power of this planet," the young man said mildly. "We would defend it if necessary."

With spears and bows? Those were the only weapons Jake saw on the Cheyenne. Although he wasn't going to be too quick to judge. The Cheyenne, judging from this brief initial impression, had done exactly what Larry Smith had said they were going to do: find a way to live in harmony with, and appreciation of, Greentrees, without modern technology to come between them and the mysterious fullness from which all species had sprung. It might be that self-sufficiency would be needed in the years ahead.

The problem was, of course, that nobody knew what might be needed. The Furs might never attack. They might consider that humans were too insignificant to bother with. Although Jake didn't really believe that; the Furs, fellow DNA inheritors, knew a dangerous species when they saw one, even if that species was still young.

Or the Furs might never attack because the Vine infection had rendered them all happy and passive, dreaming in the sun, finding their greatest joy in sharing silence. Even now Karim and Lucy, for whom only days had passed since infecting the first Furs, were speeding in the *Franz Mueller* across the galaxy toward a spot near the Vine colony planet. They would set the infected Furs out in space in the shuttle with the small quee, once programmed by humans and since reprogrammed by Furs, to clearly advertise their location to their fellows. Other Furs would surely pick them up and in turn become infected. With time dilation, that event would occur years or even decades from now in Greentrees' time scale. Years more to prepare for a war that might or might not come.

And humans were preparing. Physicists, engineers, and newly created soldiers had figured out the weapons on the *Beta Vine*, and now could use them. The ship was in high orbit around Greentrees, fully manned. Robot sensors orbited even farther out, ready to detect anything approaching. On the ground, civilians underwent periodic evacuation drills. If Mira City were vaporized from the air, few humans would be in it. Scatter, hide, travel. An enemy in a single ship, no matter how advanced, couldn't eliminate an entire planetful of small groups.

Could they?

Yes, if they used bio-weapons. But it was the Vines, not the Furs, who had those. The Furs only had hardware, deadly enough but unable to kill completely. The proof of this was the wild Furs left over from the Vine experiments on Greentrees. Several had been sighted over the years. The space Furs had not been able to eliminate them all, and they hadn't died out. The creatures still considered themselves at war with the Cheyenne.

So much war. All communication with Earth had ceased, so Jake didn't know if the promised expedition of scientists had ever been launched toward Greentrees. It wouldn't arrive for decades yet, in any case. Jake was occasionally bothered by how little thought he gave to Earth. Even his private nightmares of Mrs. Dalton's library had ceased. And yet . . . Earth was not a factor you could count out completely. Even if she had had some devastating war or die-off, humans on the home world might reinvent themselves as completely as had dead Larry Smith's very living Cheyenne.

Faisal said to Singing Mountain and his delegation, "Please come with me. We have a tent set up in the park, with food and drink. We can talk there." The tent had been Gail's idea. No one had known what to expect from the Cheyenne, despite the delegate's report; he hadn't stayed that long among them. A tent seemed more prudent than a reception in the heart of Mira City.

Jake said in a low voice to Gail, "Is Nan here?"

"No. Out searching for Furs."

Jake was relieved. Nan was still an unpredictable force, a lieutenant in the new army but "detached for special duty." When she was in the city she stayed with Gail, who seemed to have accepted this situation. Nan never saw her father. Which reminded Jake of his conversation that morning.

"Gail," he said in a low voice as they trailed Faisal and the Cheyenne delegation through the park, "Dr. Shipley came to see me this morning with a formal request."

"What?" She was gazing in fascination at the beading on a Cheyenne tunic a few yards ahead of her.

"He wants to go out as a missionary among the first group of aliens, Vines or Furs, that ever shows up on Greentrees."

She stopped dead on the flower-bordered path. " 'Vines or Furs'?"

"That's what he said."

She shook her head. "I always knew that old man was crazy."

But Jake wasn't so sure anymore. The Cheyenne merging with the natural without despoiling its beauty and benefaction, the peaceful Vines "dreaming in the sun," the New Quaker emphasis on simplicity and truth and peace—were the three really all that different? And were they really worse than the place to which "advanced" technology had led Mira City—or Earth?

Jake didn't know the answer to that. And it wasn't really his question anyway. His question was how best to keep the humans on Greentrees alive. He had a new title now. From lawyer to murderer to space entrepreneur to CEO to Commander, Greentrees Provisional Army. He had been reinvented as often as gunpowder.

And maybe, in the long run, it was that protean ability to adapt that might save humanity. From whatever was out there.

"Come on, Jake, we're falling behind," Gail said. "I need to make sure this meeting is supplied with everything it might need." Gail Cutler, Quartermaster General, Greentrees Provisional Army.

She hurried ahead. Jake lingered a moment longer. Above the narrow, purplish trees, the sky was clear and bright, empty of clouds, not even a moon on the morning horizon. Nothing to see. He gazed up anyway, eyes straining against the light, wondering what would come roaring next from the dark space beyond the benevolent sky.

*Si vis pacem, para bellum.*

Greentrees would be as ready as he could make it.